ANNA: WOMAN OF MIRACLES

Anna: Woman of Miracles

The Story of the Grandmother of Jesus

By
Vivian Van Vick
and
Carol Haenni

ARE
PRESS

**ASSOCIATION FOR
RESEARCH AND
ENLIGHTENMENT**

A.R.E. Press • Virginia Beach • Virginia

A.R.E. Press
215 67th Street
Virginia Beach, VA 23451-2061

Haenni, Carol.
   Anna: woman of miracles : the story of the grandmother of Jesus / Vivian Van Vick and Carol Haenni.
       p.   cm.
   ISBN 0-87604-444-5
   1. Anne (Mother of the Virgin Mary), Saint—Fiction. 2. Bible. N.T.—History of Biblical events—fiction. 3. Christian women saints—Fiction. I. Haenni, Carol, 1932- II. Title.
PS3622.A62 A55   2002
813'.6—dc21

                                             2001008085

Cover design by Richard Boyle

Cover art: Detail from *The Saint Anne Altarpiece: Saint Anne with the Virgin and Child* (middle panel) by Bruges (Gerard David), from the Widener Collection, National Gallery of Art. Used with permission. Photograph © Board of Trustees, National Gallery of Art, Washington, D.C.

Acknowledgments

The publication of this work owes much to the support and perseverance of Robert Baker, a close friend of Joseph Tomes and Vivian Van Vick, husband and wife. Their niece, Judith Naumann, has provided helpful information. Joseph Dunn, former Publisher of A.R.E. Press, supported the novel from the first reading. His editors, Jon Robertson and Ken Skidmore, also gave early votes for publication. Then thanks to Brenda English, the present Managing Editor, for her enthusiastic and continuing approval, the novel is successfully published. Additional thanks go to Kate Garrick for her rigorous editing, and Michelle Springer, Library of Congress. The encouragement and assistance of family members, husband Paul Haenni, son Rodney Haenni, daughter Suzanne Crismore, and my cousin Nancy Post and her husband Richard are very much appreciated.

INTRODUCTION

Anna: Woman of Miracles is the story of Saint Anne, mother of Mary and grandmother of Jesus. Though hundreds of thousands of worshippers celebrate her feast day at Beaupre' in Quebec and at d'Auray in Brittany, few know anything of her remarkable story—of her three husbands; her three daughters, all named Mary; her healing abilities; her own religious training; and her lifelong relationship with a Roman legate.

The late Vivian Van Vick was a scholar in French, German, and art at the University of California at Berkeley, and, subsequently a teacher, a World War II air traffic controller, a radio talk show host, a columnist, and an author. She spent five years researching Saint Anne's life in German, French, and Latin documents, and in translations from the Aramaic. She originally planned to write a biography, but quickly learned that Saint Anne's story is mostly legendary, and even contradictory at points, though much of the legend is also supported by renowned religious paintings in Europe. Instead, she used the information gathered during her exhaustive research to tell Anne's story in a framework of historical fiction that has permanent value and contains a great deal of suspense, a story that entertains as it informs, a story that holds interest for all readers—Jewish, Christian, mystic, metaphysician—and for students of religious history.

In my own case, I have been a student of the material in the psychic "readings" of the Christian mystic, Edgar Cayce, for more than twenty-five years. I knew the story of Anne—or Anna, as the readings called her—as told by the source that spoke through Cayce in his altered, trancelike state. When I was given the opportunity to become the coauthor of this story, I did additional research and then wove the Cayce readings' story of Anna, Mary, Jesus, and the Essenes, as well as my gleanings from other sources, into the novel. The inspiring scene of Mary's selection to be the mother of the Messiah comes from the readings, while the dramatic story of Mary's own conception draws on the visions of Ann Emmerich, a German nun who died in 1824.

Even Edgar Cayce spoke of the merit of merging fact and fiction into a story of real value and importance. In reading 1135-1, when asked whether the questioner should spend time writing fiction, Cayce responded, "If this is based upon the *findings* in the mental and spiritual, [it would be] well—for *these* would make for an awakening to the many." In reading 1703-3, he told an author-to-be that the book in question should be "both of fact *and* fiction, fact told in a fictional manner, truth clothed in the message that may arouse that which is innately sought within the inner self."

Carol H. Haenni

PART I

43 B.C.

CHAPTER 1

At early dawn a barefoot woman teacher clad in a white wool robe ran down smooth stone steps to the underground rooms of Solomon's Temple in Jerusalem. The vast substructure housed not only armed guards, priests, Levites, musicians and women teachers, but also the twelve virgins from royal families.

Inside in one of the many cubicles, rested Anna, age fifteen, the oldest of a group dedicated to the temple service of Yahweh. Her close temple friends expected to remain in service to the temple for life, but Anna was experiencing reticence about her future. These feelings disturbingly drew her away from the safety and cloister of temple life. As she had done every morning for some time, she began her prayers by asking for guidance. A soft rap came on her door. Opening it, she faced her agitated teacher, Susanna.

"Anna," the teacher whispered quietly. "Your father,

Stolan, is here to take you home to Nazareth."

The news stunned Anna. "But I was not to leave for at least two weeks yet. I haven't completed my full ten years of service. Why am I leaving early?"

"A Parthian army is moving South across Samaria," an excited Susanna warned. "It's said they've poisoned our ruler, Antipater, and intend to murder his sons, Herod and Phasael. A puppet king will rule our Judaea. This pagan army kills and rapes as they go. Jerusalem is in terrible danger, so hurry and pack your belongings. Your father is waiting."

Knowing how strict and impatient her father could be, Anna quickly gathered her modest personal effects. Turning to Susanna she said "I'm ready now, but I do wish I had a chance to say good-bye to everyone. Please say farewell for me. I'll just carry this warm cloak."

As she hurriedly wrapped a scarf over luxuriant auburn hair, Anna followed Susanna up the steps to the open court where her father, Stolan, and several priests were waiting. Stolan was well known among the temple Pharisees, as he was a former member of the powerful Sanhedrin tribunal. Four years earlier, he had rebelled against the Temple's strict control of its priests and the constant petty power-struggling wars. Along with Anna's mother, Emerentiana, and her two sisters, Sobe and Esmeria, he had moved north to a less threatening life in Galilee.

Anna had never seen this new home. She had been born in Bethlehem and entered into temple service at the age of five. Her relationship with her father had always been a little tenuous because he rarely visited her.

Today, Anna approached him with mixed emotions. She was a little fearful but very respectful of this pale, bald man with the vast forehead and a striking salt-and-pepper beard. Anna regretted that she didn't know him better. She was much closer to Stolan's best friend, Ezra, a gentle man who generously took time to accompany Emerentiana to Jerusalem during her regular monthly visits to Anna.

Anna embraced her father dutifully, then said, "I have few things of value to take with me father, so I am ready now."

Stolan was startled by his daughter's radiant beauty, and felt he was seeing her for the first time. He studied her wide-set topaz eyes and almost-perfect nose, set in a heart-shaped face with a dimpled chin.

"I truly had forgotten how you've grown," he said with an appreciative look. "You have your mother's loveliness. But come we must hurry, Anna. The road to Jericho may become impassable soon with pilgrims coming to the Passover. I have rented fresh donkeys for us. They're at the north gate."

Because of the milling and excited crowd, the quickest choice for father and daughter was to thread their way over the temple grounds, through the Court of Gentiles. A deafening din of voices prevented further conversation. Already, thousands of worshippers pressed toward the booths of eager money-changers, to replace pagan currency for ritually clean shekels. Laymen clustered around solemn priests to argue application laws of holy scriptures. Crowd-jostled rich men on lavish litters screamed ahead to clear the way for their bearers, while sellers of sacrificial animals busily hawked their helpless merchandise.

Anna shuddered. She knew that the lowing and bleating of these terrified creatures would soon be replaced by the smell of disemboweled animals and the stench of burning fat, and that no matter how much onyx, glabanum, and storax were afterward burned on the incense altar, the fragrance could never overcome the smell of the animal holocaust.

This was one reason Anna was not unhappy to be leaving the temple at this time. She had privately wondered why the truculent Yahweh wouldn't accept flour cakes, oil, or even scented offerings as expiatory sacrifices. She had learned from Susanna and gentle Ezra that these kinds of offerings were a custom with the Essene sect, a group of devout Jews.

Father and daughter made slow progress down Mount Moriah over the narrow, cobbled streets. They were going against a human tide, as well as competing with sheep and cattle being herded to the markets. At times, Stolan tried what appeared to be less-crowded alleys, but they often had to retrace their steps when the alley ended in closed courtyards.

Finally, they reached the Fish Gate, one of twelve fortified entrances into the temple area. Here, they met even more confusion head-on, as thousands of tired worshippers funneled through the city gates from various routes. There were travelers from Persia, with elegant silver-and-gold-embroidered cloaks; pilgrims from the plateaus of Asia Minor, in homespun goat's hair garb; somber priests in flowing black robes from Babylon; and Phoenicians in many-colored, striped tunics.

Anna and Stolan found it almost impossible to cross this milling human river to get to their waiting donkeys. They stood, immobilized by the crowds, until a pair of horse-mounted Numidian auxiliaries in crested helmets, leather cuirasses, and short red capes spotted their plight. As hirelings of Rome, the African auxiliaries' job was to control the rowdy Passover crowds. Anna's distressed young face brought them into action. Forcefully, they cleared a path for the two and were quickly rewarded with a radiant smile from one and a grateful nod from the other.

Outside the wall, activities were substantially less hectic. Guards were stationed at intervals of a hundred cubits—less than a spear's throw—to control recent arrivals into the city. Since the weather in the spring month of Nissan was mild, many of these newly-arrived visitors had set up tents in adjacent fields, commonly claiming pieces of ground by merely marking them with loose branches.

Anna sighed in relief as they reached the waiting animals. A young stalwart, whom Stolan had paid well, guarded them. The lead pack-donkey bore panniers of large wicker baskets filled with blankets, dried fruits, nuts, flat cakes of bread, and skins of balsam water. Stolan had planned carefully to make the pair's journey comfortable, even outfitting Anna's animal with a footrest.

As they quickly mounted the animals and cleared the crowds, Anna turned to her father and asked, "Will we reach Jericho tonight?"

Stolan shook his head slowly. "Not with the crowds on this caravan route. We have to be watchful, as we undoubtedly will encounter a motley mix of travelers. There could be dangerous runaway slaves or brigands intent on robbing some of these rich Persian traders of their silks. Most likely, the inns on the road will be full. But don't fear, I've arranged for us to camp. Tomorrow we'll follow the Jordan valley north through Samaria into Galilee, where we should be safe."

"Before we left Jerusalem, my teacher, Susanna, said that the Parthians plan to install a puppet king in Judea. Do you think Rome will agree to this?"

"Probably not," Stolan answered thoughtfully. "The oppressive Romans have fought too many wars with the Parthians over control of the Red Sea. I'm afraid a tempest is about to break over Jerusalem, and when it does Rome will move fast. That's why I felt I had to get you out early, my child."

As her donkey plodded along, Anna wondered about her new life and home. She had been away from the family many years and knew only her mother intimately. Her older sister, Sobe, rarely came to Jerusalem to visit, and when she did, their conversations ended in sibling arguments. Sobe, Anna thought, considered herself an authority on all subjects. Her middle sister, Esmeria, had married and now lived in a village west of Jerusalem. Anna wondered about her sister's safety. She had not had to worry about safety in the past. Her own safety in the temple had been guaranteed for the last ten years.

Stolan interrupted Anna's thoughts. "I've been thinking on a matter, Anna. I had earlier thought you would be the one to stay in temple life, but with the growing turmoil in the countryside, I believe in a year or two it would be better to find a good husband for you. In the meantime I'll instruct Sobe to teach you how to be a good housewife and mother of many grandchildren for your mother and me. I know your studies have taught you Greek and Hebrew, but Sobe can also help you polish up your Aramaic." He smiled comfortably, satisfied with his plans for his daughter's future.

Anna frowned, then burst out, "Please, *Abba*, I cannot do what you suggest. I don't want to marry—ever. Each day for the last ten years, I've heard the agonizing cries of the dying, the lepers, the crippled, and the starving poor who huddle around the temple gates. I have been tortured by their pain and misery. I feel I need to heal rather than marry, father. I have made a promise to God to devote my life to healing. Let Sobe and Esmeria bear you the grandchildren you want."

Stolan's cheeks paled, and his eyebrows arched at the

shock of Anna's heresy. He thundered, "Only Jehovah is a healer! Who are you to play at being God? Who do you think you would heal?"

In a low but steady voice, Anna replied, "Everyone who needs my help."

An exasperated Stolan fumed, "Everyone? Would you heal even pagans or Romans? Remember," he continued, "It was not long ago that the savage Governor Herod of Faille killed thousands of our people during a revolt. Could you possibly succor those who would destroy us?"

Anna fought back burning tears. Although she knew he loved her, she also knew her father to be an inflexible man, intent on preventing any deviation from what he considered the Law of their religion. He could force her to marry anyone he chose. She needed to take away the force of his anger and managed to answer quietly, "How can it be wrong to relieve suffering?"

A mollified Stolan, surprised by her continued resistance, changed his tactic. His voice grew less harsh. "Have your years in Judea made you forget your family's position among the elite circles in Nazareth? Your mother is descended from the royal line of David, through King Solomon, and I come from nobility, through the princely line of Judah. Great responsibilities are a part of our daily life. They are also a part of our family honor and pride. You must remember, daughter, that every act of yours reflects on our entire family. I expect you to be a model of the Law." Stolan waited silently for Anna's reply.

As he dismounted from his donkey he came to her side. Taking one of her hands he pressed it tenderly to his cheek. In a quavering voice Anna said, "I'm proud of my lineage, father, and I'll always be your devoted daughter. I do feel, however, that I have a power within that comes from a God of love, and not from a vengeful Yahweh."

Stolan stepped back frowning. "There is only one God! You cannot call him either loving or vengeful." With a sweeping motion Stolan removed his hat and ran his hand over his bald pate in helpless frustration. "Where did you get these independent notions, my child?"

Anna took advantage of the moment to say quietly, "*Abba*, I've thought on this a great deal. My temple teachers taught that if someone destroys one life, it in effect destroys a portion of the whole world."

Stolan raised an eyebrow questioningly. "So?"

"Then wouldn't the opposite be equally true?" Anna asked. "If it is possible for me to save a life, wouldn't it be as if I had saved a part of the whole world?"

The renowned expert on the Torah was stunned by his beautiful, strong-willed daughter's reasoning. She had turned the Law's words to her advantage. Among equals, Stolan was considered famous for his skill in settling disagreements, but his hesitation in answering told Anna he was hard-pressed to refute her logic.

Stroking his thin beard, Stolan made a final argument. "Remember, daughter, evil in any form delays the coming of our Messiah. Our people have waited thousands of years for him. By healing a Roman, Phoenician, or any pagan for that matter, you may make it possible for them to do further evil. This could postpone the Promised One's appearance. Do you want to be responsible for that?" Anna made no reply. It was enough for right now that Stolan would think about the thoughts she had expressed.

She signaled her donkey to move on through the rugged, uninhabited country. Its hills and valleys challenged even the most sturdy wayfarers. As they plodded along they passed many weary pilgrims calling out to each other the traditional greeting, "*Shalom alekh hem!* Peace be with you."

The pair made camp for the night at a wayside shelter that had ample water and grass for the animals. Due to Stolan's planning, they ate well from the food in the panniers and slept undisturbed all night. At the first light of dawn, they mounted their animals and were again on their way to Jericho.

Traveling through woods in full leaf and flower was a wondrous experience for Anna. It was especially pleasurable since she had been confined within the temple walls for most of her young life. She eagerly enjoyed the mountain streams that strained their banks. With the morning, Stolan was in better humor and called Anna's attention to the spring migration of birds and the patterns they formed in the clear sky. Occasionally they would see young gazelle fawns learning to walk close to their mothers. Hares and conies leapt through sweeps of orchids.

Determined to get along better with her serious father, Anna said to him,. "I look forward to being home again. How is mother?"

"She waits impatiently for your return," he replied. "I probably should not tell you this, but you're her favorite child, you know."

Before Anna could reply, Stolan exclaimed, "Look, Anna! We're coming into Jericho—the revered city that was visited by the great prophet, Elijah."

Anna smiled. Her erudite father found it difficult to make small talk. An unchanging man, he viewed each area and village they passed in terms of biblical history. She stubbornly returned to conversation.

"I've heard it said our Roman rulers are encouraging us to live without hatred toward foreigners and Gentiles," she said provocatively. "How do you feel about that?"

Stolan stopped his donkey to make a thoughtful reply.

"My work as a scribe required me to insist on the strict observance of Hebrew law. The Romans are suspicious of us. They'd like to penetrate our rituals and ferret out a means of destroying our faith in Yahweh. That is why I'm against helping them any more than necessary and why I hope you will forget about healing such people. I did not provide them years of money keeping you in temple training to turn you into a healing sorceress."

Anna smiled. "But what if it's not me but love that can perform miraculous healing? Would that be permissible?"

Stolan looked at Anna resignedly. "No more of those kinds of arguments for awhile, daughter. I believe it was well to have you removed from temple life so that some of this type of learning will be forgotten. You need other things in your life. Soon you'll see how attractive young men are. I'm sure then your notions of being a healer will leave your pretty head."

Anna realized it was now her turn to change the subject. "*Abba*, I have heard our people referred to as Hebrews, Israelites and Jews. Which are we?"

Stolan smiled. "The truth of the matter, daughter, is that all three names are correct. Of Noah's three sons— Shem, Ham and Japheth—our people trace our descendants through Shem. Shem's great-grandson was named Heber, and from him the tribal name of Hebrew developed.

"Then what about the names Jews and Israelites?" asked Anna.

Stolan adjusted his weight on the donkey before continuing. "Before our captivity by the Assyrians, the term Jew was mostly applied to those in the southern kingdom of Judah who worshipped Yahweh in Jerusalem. The ten tribes of the northern kingdom called themselves Israelites. Following the revolt of King Rehoboam against the Assyrians, most of the northern Israelites were taken into captivity and forced to go to Damascus. Later, Jews from the southern kingdom were also taken into captivity. When members of the twelve tribes were free to return home, they were referred to as Jews."

Anna enjoyed listening to her father as much as he enjoyed instructing her. Looking at the countryside through which they passed, she begged, "Tell me, *Abba,* about the history of this area."

Beaming with pleasure, Stolan spoke. "This was King David's country. Our great prophet, Elijah, traveled these same twisting roads to the Jordan River. We could very well be gazing down on the spot where the prophet parted the waters and he and Elisha walked across on dry ground."

Then with a dramatic upthrust of his arms, "Just visualize Elijah's going to heaven in a chariot of fire and leaving his holy spirit to Elisha. Keep faith in our great prophets, Anna. I often call on them for help when making important decisions. If ever you are in a dilemma, remember to call on Elijah."

Seeing tears of emotion growing in her father's eyes, Anna felt the holiness of the surroundings. The pair continued into the valley below.

As they moved ahead, Anna realized that she had gotten off to a bad start with her father. Her devout mother, Emerentiana, would probably understand her deep yearnings. It was certain that her sister, Sobe, would not. Sobe had two sides. One minute she could be a caring and loving person; the next, tyrannical and jealous. Anna needed someone in whom to confide, but it couldn't be Sobe or her father.

Suddenly Anna thought of Ezra. He, like Stolan, had moved from Judea to Galilee to escape the tyrannical dictates of the temple. Instead of becoming a scribe, however, he laid aside the tallith and phylacteries of temple life to put on the white garment of an Essene. Despite this, he and Stolan remained blood brothers, each following the precepts of the Torah in their individual ways. While Stolan busily solved the spiritual problems of the community, Ezra listened patiently to the everyday problems in Emerentiana's life. He would be the logical one to support Anna in her healing mission goal.

Her preoccupation with the future allowed her donkey and pack animal to slow their walk. She realized suddenly that her father had disappeared ahead. She dismounted, hoping that, on foot, she could hurry the animals along and catch up to him. They had passed no travelers at this early hours, so she was shocked to hear a harsh voice demand, "Give me that pack animal, or I'll put a knife in you!"

Anna whirled to face an unkempt brigand brandishing a vicious looking dagger. He was visibly surprised to see he was facing a lovely girl instead of an old woman. "Well, what luck," he cried showing a mouth of missing teeth.

Anna froze in terror. Her father was out of sight. She tried to scream for his help, but no sound came from her throat. As the bandit advanced menacingly she ran to the opposite side of her donkey, using the animal as a shield. The bandit leapt forward. She eluded his grasp and ducked between the two animals. Back and forth between them, she led the chase. Irritated by her ability to avoid his reach, the attacker skirted the rear of the pack animal too close, and the wild-eyed, panicky animal struck out with a vicious kick.

Sprawled on the ground, the thief jumped up in a daze, shouting an angry oath. Anna thought of mounting her donkey and trying to escape without the pack animal, but her attacker was too agile and would quickly overtake the slow-jogging creature.

Both donkeys, confused by the racing and yelling, began to bray and spin. It seemed there was no way she could elude this bandit for long.

Suddenly Anna remembered the recent advice of her father. If in need of help, call on Elijah. This could be the hallowed ground where Elijah's spirit had gone to heaven. Would he hear her cry for help? Shouting toward the sky, she begged, "Great prophet, Elijah, save me! Save me!"

The highwayman looked startled then laughed loudly at her plea. He confidently advanced toward her with outstretched arms. Unexpectedly, he found himself being flung back as if he had struck an invisible wall. Upon regaining his feet, he stood confused for several moments. Shaking the cobwebs from his head, he again came at Anna, who eluded him by jumping behind one of the donkeys. "Don't try any more tricks on me!" he yelled, rushing toward her.

But as before, he hit an unseen barricade and went sprawling. Furious at his failures, he rolled upright off the ground, debating his next move. By now, Anna realized she had an invincible ally. "Don't kill him, Elijah," she yelled confidently, pointing with an outstretched arm. "Let him live!"

A look of absolute terror crossed the brigand's face. He turned, then ran down the road and disappeared in a nearby ravine.

Anna threw her arms around her donkey's head, sobbing with relief as she steadied herself. As her breathing returned to normal she said, "Oh, Elijah, thank you, thank you, thank you for saving me."

Quickly gathering the two animals, she continued down the trail. She would not tell her father of this dangerous encounter because he would blame himself for not being more protective. At a later time, she would tell her understanding mother of the supernatural intervention by the prophet. Her father had said that Elijah neither died nor was buried and still moved about the earth, unrecognized and ethereal, helping those who believed in his loving power. Could the dramatic rescue mean there was a special purpose planned for her life? She felt strongly guided toward helping others and now believed even more that nothing would stop her from her healing goal. She had made contact with the Unseen World.

Chapter 2

By the time Stolan and Anna descended into Nazareth through the green maquis of shrubby plants and multi-colored carpet of wild flowers, she had learned a great deal about life in Galilee. Her father was enthusiastic about this Roman province—so different from sun-baked Judea.

"Judaism is simpler here," he explained. "It lacks the intellectual battle that constantly goes on in Jerusalem, splitting Judeans into rival sects. You'll find that even pagans who settle here tend to adopt our customs. It makes it more comfortable for them to live with us. We are hard-working, but at times an intolerant people." Stolan laughed. "You have come home at a good time of the year. In this two-season land, the days of rain are past, and the days of sun have begun. Winter has suddenly become summer."

Anna made no reply. Her attention focused on the

swarms of nectar-seeking butterflies in the warm, peaceful air. The quiet charm of the area disappeared as they entered the town's common orchard where pear, apricot, and olive trees were carefully tended. Further along came narrow, dusty streets, then dwellings; a haphazard succession of white-washed, box-like structures, with outer stairways that led to flat roofs. Each house boasted a small vegetable garden; most had a corral of donkeys; and some even had an ox.

Stolan related, "You'll discover the people here are more kindly and optimistic than in gloomy, tormented Judea. That's because we're a trading center. Everyone wants to exchange goods for the products of our rich soil and the temperate air. We produce a veritable feast of olives, figs, grapes, wheat, barley and walnuts."

He would have gone on had not a pack of wild dogs, half jackal or wolf, darted past them in pursuit of scurrying rats. Anna found herself amid chaos as she and her father came to the center of town. It seethed and boiled in a babble of innumerable mysterious tongues. Sweating, swarthy men jostled freely with noisy, white traders. Great merchant caravans from the Mediterranean coast rumbled past on their way to Decapolis on the eastern border. Fortunately, the pale-gray Muscat donkeys Anna and Stolan rode were skillful at maneuvering through the crowds.

Anna spoke, "Thank heaven it's forbidden to sacrifice one of our long-eared servants of Palestine." Her father nodded in agreement, well aware by now of Anna's aversion to the temple ritual.

They reached the family home in time for the noonday meal. An anxious, enthusiastic Emerentiana and a sober-faced Sobe greeted them. The emotional and devout Emerentiana wept openly as she embraced Anna. As usual, Sobe was not demonstrative, but did manage a light sisterly kiss on Anna's cheeks. She then devoted her full attention to her father.

This is understandable, thought Anna. Sobe is tall and a little raw-boned like him. She has his stride and air of authority. Sobe's straight hair, sullen eyes, and down-turned mouth were a contrast to the luxuriant waves of Anna's hair, her large topaz eyes, and engaging smile. Sobe pleased only her father.

"Each time I see you, I'm amazed at how you are more beautiful than the last," Emerentiana said to Anna, her eyes reflecting great pride in her youngest daughter. "You've never seen this home have you? Wash up and change quickly into fresh clothes. Our maid-servant, Isabel, will prepare a fine meal for us. Your return has made me feel whole again."

Anna was conducted into a large, rectangular house where a central hall ran back to the hearth and kitchen. On both sides of the hallway were several rooms, formed by movable, light wickerwork screens. They were topped by open trellis-work that reached only part of the way to the ceiling. Anna could see that one had to whisper not to be heard in adjacent rooms.

"I'm glad to be home," Anna said shortly. She adored her mother, a woman of elegant manners and mystical yearnings. There had always been a strong bond be-tween the two. Still beautiful with widely-set eyes and deep auburn hair, Emerentiana devoutly spent much of her time in mediation and prayer. Her exception to this practice was on the day before the Sabbath, when she visited the poor in the city. As did other women in the area, she secretly wished to have a son, one who might even be the long-awaited Messiah. If having all daugh-ters disappointed her, she never spoke of it. She dutifully accepted it as God's will.

Her middle daughter, Esmeria, was married and lived

in Ain Karim, a village west of Jerusalem. A buxom, jolly mother of three daughters, Esmeria had never shown spiritual leanings. Because of this, she had rarely visited Anna at the temple. Emerentiana never passed judgment on Esmeria's life, or for that matter any of the grandchildren. Her three daughters were definitely different from each other, and as a devoted mother, she was the one member of the family who understood Anna best.

When alone, Anna told her mother about her terrifying encounter with the brigand. Emerentiana's eyebrows arched as Anna continued telling of the invisible shield thrown around her when she called on Elijah. Anna realized that this would stretch most people's imagination, but she still blurted out all that had happened.

"Do you believe me, *Emi*?" Anna asked anxiously.

Emerentiana searched Anna's anxious face. Was this a young girl's fantasy? Anna always seemed levelheaded in everything she said and did. If it was true, why hadn't Stolan said something? If it had happened as she said, he would proudly relate how, once again, Elijah had come to his family's rescue. After all, he truly believed that Elijah had helped him through dangerous times in the past. But Anna's face seemed so sincere. No, this was not her imagination. Emerentiana had always felt that Anna was special, but maybe that was just a mother's opinion. If Anna spoke truthfully, it could only mean that Elijah had helped for a special purpose. Emerentiana took several minutes to think the matter through. As she looked in Anna's face, she became increasingly convinced that this was a matter needing further study by persons more familiar with revelations.

"I believe you daughter," Emerentiana said, taking Anna's hands in her own. "This marvelous experience needs to be studied deeper. I believe it appropriate for the holy monks on Mount Carmel. Let's see what we can learn from them about your future. After the meal, I will talk to your father and suggest a trip for us soon to Mount Carmel. I'll ask that our man-servant, Gideon, accompany us."

The family gathered for the noon meal, and after the blessing of the bread, Isabel served great bowls of lentils and freshly-fried mullets.

Back from talking with others in the town, a grave faced Stolan began, "I wonder if Jerusalem is not already lost," he began. "I fear that our hatred of the Romans will force some of our people to aid rather than fight the Parthian invaders. These people foolishly haven't reckoned with Mark Antony and Cleopatra. I think it will be Rome's legionnaires who will finally decide who rules Judea. This could mean that Jews will be once again pitted against Jews."

Sobe asked, "Do you think that Antony will reject this puppet, Antigonus the Idumean? If so, whom then do you think they'd name as King of Judea?"

"Our ambitious Governor of Galilee, Herod" he replied flatly. "After all, he is the son of Antipater, who has just been poisoned."

Emerentiana raised her eyes and spoke to everyone in an uncustomary voice. "God forbid that an Arab should rule our Holy City! We know what they did to the farmers around here who refused to pay Rome's excessive taxes. Crucifixion for all! Herod is a wily opportunist."

Looking directly at Stolan, she continued, "It's imperative that I consult about family matters with the prophets at Mount Carmel. I know you haven't time to leave town with this crisis arising, but Anna and Gideon could go with me. Don't you agree the advice of the monks would be helpful to all of our people at this time?"

"I approve of your taking Anna," Stolan began, "but

not Gideon. He must help me warn the people of Galilee about these dangerous events in Palestine. No, take Ezra with you. I would feel more confident with him along."

Sobe, miffed at being excluded, spoke in a lightly bitter tone of voice. "Well, I can leave my work here," she began. "Isabel can take over my duties. I have never been to the sacred mount and would like to go."

Stolan smiled lovingly at her. "No, dear Sobe, your work here is more important. Your practical wisdom and knowledge of astrology can help us too. We need you here."

Sobe was content with Stolan's remark, much to Anna's relief. She had always wanted to visit Mount Carmel's monastery where devout Essene men and prophets trained lay people in divine inspiration. It was commonly said that it was where Elijah had worked so many wonders and miracles that he had to found a school of prophets.

"Oh *Emi*," cried Anna silently, "thank you for understanding my needs now. And dear *Abba* thank you for not sending Sobe with us."

Anna was so deep in thought that Stolan had to repeat his request twice before she realized he was speaking to her. "Anna, Anna, go to Ezra today and ask him to take my place on this trip to Carmel. You and your mother will go in eight days, as soon as Passover ends. Tomorrow we eat the matsah, just as our ancestors did when they fled Egypt. I will order a yearling lamb to be sacrificed on the fourteenth day of Nissan." Stolan stroked his beard and continued, "God rewards the faithful and punishes their enemies. Tomorrow will be the Night of Watching, when all of us eat of the paschal sacrifice as God holds vigil over Israel."

Anna smiled. Her father was in his glory when expounding on the history of the Hebrews. Every year, he explained the history of Passover as if his family knew nothing of this most important festival.

"May I go to Ezra now, *Abba*?" Anna asked when the family had finished the meal.

"Of course," Stolan replied. "I must get to the House of Prayer also." Turning to Emerentiana he said, "I will need to work there tonight, too."

Anna understood why her father had little time to spend with his family. His days and much of his evenings were spent copying the sacred scriptures, studying the Torah and making decisions for the local worshippers. He was a driven man, spending every spare moment translating holy writings into Aramaic. Scribes were singled out by Yahweh, the Almighty, to explain the complex Torah.

Stolan left at once. Emerentiana shook her head sadly. "I see so little of him, Anna. He is inundated with people who need his approval. His life is not his own: 'Is it permissible to eat an egg laid on the Sabbath?' 'Should one ever sleep on his stomach?' 'Might a woman comb her hair on the Holy Day?' Your father is sent scurrying to find answers within the body of the Law. You can understand why rearing our daughters has been my sole province."

Whenever her mother had visited Anna at the temple, she proudly emphasized Stolan's position in the community. He was learned in all three divisions of the Torah; he lectured on them, taught the Law to school-age boys, and debated it constantly with his peers. Since his interpretations were seldom disputed, what he claimed was constantly quoted as oral tradition and considered almost as valid as the written Law. It was an awesome responsibility. How then, Anna asked herself, could she disobey his plans for her life and follow her own feelings on becoming a healer?

She realized that between her father and Ezra's counsel, she preferred Ezra's outlook, which dealt with meditation, healing, and making contact with her own soul.
He frequently discussed these subjects with her when
visiting the temple. He was a surrogate father, and she
loved him dearly. She especially liked his deep intellect
and probing philosophical nature. A widower in his fif-
ties, Ezra made his home in Nazareth, a way station of
sorts for other Essenes traveling between their settle-
ments at Qumran on the Dead Sea and those on the Sea
of Galilee. The Essenes, besides obeying the precepts of
the Torah, had other beliefs. They ate no meat, wore only
white garments, bathed several times a day in cold water, never kept servants or slaves, and had profound
knowledge of the art of healing. She felt more and more
drawn to their philosophy.

Sobe's sharp inquiring voice pulled Anna away from
her reverie. She stared at Anna intently. "I had a strong
premonition of disaster about you concerning your trip
home from Jerusalem. Both the planets and the numbers told me you were in danger. Did something happen?"

"I'm sorry Sobe, but life doesn't always please the
whim of stars." said Anna carefully. "Perhaps you heard
about the attacks of the Parthians. Luckily, Father and I
got home safely."

Sobe was not put off easily. "You are in a period of danger, Anna. I don't think you should go to Mount Carmel.
I'll speak to *Abba*. After all you've just had a long journey
home," she continued in a persuasive tone.

"That's all right," Anna answered calmly. "I'll be rested
by the time we're ready to leave." She loved her chameleon-like sister, but suspected there was a reason for
Sobe's jealousy. Each had been born in Bethlehem, but
only Anna, of the three daughters, had been sent for

temple training. Their parents had known that Sobe would rebel against the rigorous spiritual training there, and had decided to find her a rich husband when she was thirteen. Sobe was eager to marry, openly thinking that she might have the opportunity to possibly bear the long-awaited Messiah. Her intended, Nathan ben Simon, a widower, age forty-five also had hope of fathering the promised deliverer of the Jews. He had had one happy marriage, so was prone to overlook Sobe's short comings and plain features. At the time of their marriage, Anna had hoped life would be happy for both of them and the rivalry between them would deminish.

Unfortunately, a disaster occurred. A month after their marriage, Nathan and his two brothers went fishing on the Sea of Galilee. An unexpected, violent storm swept down from the surrounding mountains and capsized their small boat. All were drowned.

The tragic event changed Sobe. She became caustic and irritable. Being childless, she would have married her deceased husband's oldest brother under the law of levirate marriage. But in this case, there was no man left in the family.

After Nathan's unexpected death, Sobe moved into the family home to help with her mother's duties. She quickly became expert at hiring and firing serving maids. She was well-known for her promptness in delivering food each week to the hungry. If allowed, Anna suspected, Sobe would thoroughly enjoy following her father's directives and become a relentless and driving teacher in many areas. This wouldn't be all bad. Anna knew she was weak in Hebrew, the holy tongue used only when speaking to God, and felt she expected to do a lot of talking with him in pleading for healing power.

Anna decided to take the initiative with Sobe to improve their relationship. Stolan had left for the House of

Prayer; Emerentiana was in the garden meditating. She faced her sister. "Will you join me at the altar to give thanks for our protection on the way home?" Anna had the help of Elijah in mind and was pleased that Sobe nodded readily in agreement.

The sisters moved to an area near the kitchen, hidden behind two dark blue curtains. Anna was surprised that the house was so functional. It could be changed at will into as many bedrooms as needed. With a small change in the placement of the partitions, a huge dining area or a social room for celebrations could be made.

Sobe lit a candle, and the two sisters dropped to their knees on a cushioned stool before the altar. Sobe removed a small carved chest from a niche in the wall. Inside, she explained to Anna, was a bit of hair once belonging to Sara, the wife of Abraham and mother of Isaac. Anna lovingly touched the venerated relic. Next to it was a bone supposed to have belonged to Joseph, the first son of Rachel and Jacob. Stolan, who had inherited both items from his parents, claimed Moses had brought them from Egypt.

"Sobe, what is this white goblet?" Anna asked.

"Abraham, founder of our faith, drank from this very cup," she replied reverently. "Being the oldest child, I expect to inherit these priceless treasures."

"I hope you'll let me look at them from time to time," Anna replied simply. "Now, let us pray silently. Maybe we will receive a sign."

Anna prayed for two things: for God to delay any possible marriage for her and for the Great Ones—like Elijah—in the heaven world to teach her the secrets of curing disease and healing the mentally ill.

After a little while, Sobe spoke. "No answer of approval or condemnation has come from these holy objects. I wonder who blocked the signs from God? The same thing happened when our sister Esmeria saw her recently."

Anna smiled, saying, "We may never know, Sobe." She suddenly realized why Stolan had never been able to find Sobe a second husband. Stolan had thought he had done so, but the prospective bridegroom preferred the middle sister, Esmeria, creating a rift between the two sisters that still remained.

Anna arose and said to Sobe, "Father said I am to go to Ezra today." It was excuse enough for seeing Ezra, so she went to her room to get a head scarf and another pair of sandals. She was eager to relate to Ezra the events of her earlier life-saving experience while on the road to Jericho.

Emerentiana reentered the home with Isabel. Thinking that only the two were alone in the house, Isabel spoke. "My lady, I know your husband is searching for a husband for Sobe, but don't you think it's time he also found a husband for Anna. It shouldn't be hard. She so takes after you—the same beautiful face and warm, hazel eyes. That abundant hair reaches almost to her waist. Men go crazy over long, shining hair."

Emerentiana replied to Isabel simply. "Anna is my favorite. But not because of the loveliness you mentioned. She is the spiritual one."

The two women were startled as Sobe stepped unexpectedly into the hall. With eyes blazing, she obviously had overheard their conversation. She walked past Emerentiana and Isabel without a glance. Both feared the overheard words would fester in Sobe's mind and, at some inopportune moment, explode.

*   *   *

A short distance from Stolan's was Ezra's house, a duplicate of others in Nazareth. He kept his ground immaculate with well-tended bushes and trees. Anna was happy to be able to visit him alone, since she wanted to converse with him about divine protection, healing and making contact with one's soul. She was so engrossed in thinking about what she would say that she was startled to suddenly have her way blocked by an imposing Roman official.

The man, dressed in a short white toga edged with wide gold braid, asked curtly, "Who are you? Where are you going?"

Anna was momentarily speechless. She looked into two brilliant green eyes that seemed to cut slits in a square-jawed, clean-shaven face. Short, blond curls covered the official's head. With voice trembling, she managed to answer, "I am Anna bat Stolan. My father is the sopher in the House of Prayer. I am on an errand to a family friend."

"And this friend's name?" His voice pierced her.

"Ezra ben Samuel."

"Oh him," the stranger frowned distastefully. "I spoke with him recently. The man is in his dotage. He wasn't much help."

Anna noticed the round, golden emblem on the man's left shoulder. It was an eagle encircled by a laurel wreath—the badge of an official from Rome. His full, sensuous lips parted with amusement. It was obvious he was enjoying her discomfort. His stern eyes traveled from her gentle, flushed face, across her high bosom, and back again. He began speaking in Greek, and when she frowned, shifted to Aramaic.

"I am the data gatherer, Julian—newly appointed by Mark Antony," he began expansively.

Anna looked at the official cautiously. She had been told that, each year, the inhabitants of Palestine registered with the data gatherer so their tax assessments could be calculated. As Roman contempt for the Jews increased, so did their taxes. Those who couldn't pay the exorbitant fees had land confiscated, and families were sometimes forced into slavery. She quietly warned herself not to antagonize this man.

She remained silent, uncertain of what to say in the face of this authority. Young girls were forbidden to visit on the street with any man, let alone an appointee of all-powerful Rome. As she started to move around him, Julian again blocked her path. She stopped, not daring to make him angry.

Julian spoke in a more conciliatory tone. "You appear to be a spirited young woman, and, I suspect, highly intelligent. You can be of service in helping me understand this part of the Empire."

Anna's lowered eyes fastened on his tanned, muscular legs, then dropped to his ironclad sandals. She dared not look at his face. The air about him was electric with power. She felt the full might of his forceful animal magnetism. He took a step toward her, and for a moment, she feared he might put his hands on her. Scowling, she stepped back from him, only to be met with an amused expression from his haughty eyes.

Julian folded his massive arms on his chest, then continued ingratiatingly. "Don't fear me, daughter of Stolan. I need information on an important subject. When I was in Gaul recently, I met many travelers from Asia. They forecast an imminent event of earth-shaking proportions to take place in this part of the world. Our Roman priesthood has been studying the oracles, and some members have received confirmation of these rumors. It is my duty to Rome to learn what the people of Nazareth know of this happening."

Anna realized he was speaking of the coming Messiah, but she was not about to be trapped into talking with this heathen. It struck her that Ezra must have been asked the same question and had pretended ignorance. She recalled a recent remark by her father that would serve her now.

She answered, "Your great Cicero was an avowed enemy of superstition. Yet, in his 'Treaty of Divination,' he wrote about just such a foreboding. Is superstition what you mean?"

If Julian was struck by her sharp answer, he concealed it by airily dismissing her words. "Cicero has just been murdered, so what he said probably won't be held important any longer." The Roman became almost affable now. "With a sopher for a father, you must know what he's teaching and how he interprets these mounting rumors."

"Why then, sir, don't you ask my father?"

"It's more pleasant to get information from a beautiful woman," he said silkily. Turning to one side, he continued, "I recently talked with a colony of trading Jews in Rome. They actually believe a new king is about to appear in Palestine. He will conquer the world and reunite all nations in a Golden Age. I suppose your father thinks this monarch has already been born?"

Anna fell into the Roman's sly trap. "No," she replied emphatically. "He is not yet born." Realizing her error in the outburst she ducked to one side and continued on towards Ezra's house.

Jubilant in getting an unexpected admission, the Roman walked alongside and continued pressing for information. "It's strange that our Roman oracles are silent on telling what sign will announce the coming of this sovereign. What do your Davids and Isaiahs forecast?"

Anna was surprised that an answer to his question formed in her mind as she parried his question. "Rome must be full of astrologers and soothsayers from all parts of the world. Wouldn't that be the logical place to search for the answers you seek?"

"Unfortunately, no," he answered, amused by her challenge. "But I have my own opinion, of course," Julian laughed smugly, as his steely-green eyes looked at Anna, "that this demigod you are expecting has already been born! I'll even tell you his name. It's Octavianus of Rome!"

"But your Octavian wasn't born in Judea as our prophets have promised," Anna blurted out, then bit her lip, regretting the impulsive statement. This Roman was a definite challenge, but she suddenly realized she was intensely curious about other nationalities' thoughts, especially Romans.

"You're wrong," Julian continued emphatically. "We would have no problem in claiming that Octavian was born in Judea, for is this province not now a vassal of Rome?"

Anna flushed with embarrassment at his cleverness. Again, she lowered her head subserviently, seeing only the widespread legs of her inquisitor.

Julian shifted his voice to a softer tone as he caressed each word. "I intend to know your people well. It's my duty, of course. We will meet often, lovely daughter of Stolan, for I intend to make you my teacher here." He smiled for the first time, then stepped aside.

Anna hurried on, shaken by the encounter and anxious to report this meeting to Ezra. As she reached his door, she touched the sacred mezuzah, kissed her fingers, then looked back. Julian still remained where she had left him, watching her.

There was no answer to her knock on the door. She called Ezra's name. No response. The urgency of her visit and the fact the Roman had just spoken with him impelled Anna to carefully push open the door. There on the floor lay the motionless figure of Ezra.

Dropping beside him, she felt for a pulse in his neck. There was no sign of life. Anna ran from the house, beckoning wildly to Julian.

CHAPTER 3

"Come quickly, please help me!" Anna cried to the Roman. "Ezra is like a dead man!"

Julian pushed open the gate and hurried inside, his eyes on the figure on the floor. "How can this be? He was eating when I talked with him just a short time ago."

Brushing past Anna, he carefully lifted Ezra's limp body onto a nearby workbench. He pressed his ear against the old man's chest, listening for a heart beat. Turning his head slowly toward Anna, he said in a flat tone, "He's dead."

"No! No!" she shouted defiantly. "He mustn't die. I need him. Help me revive him."

"Great Jupiter, maiden," Julian cried incredulously. "How do you expect us to do that? The man is dead!"

Anna hesitated a moment. Dare she experiment in front of this Roman official? She wanted to try out some esoteric principles Ezra had told her about, but to do so with the Roman could be dangerous. There was no alternative. She had to risk it.

"Take one of his hands," she ordered Julian, "and I'll do the same. Join your other hand with mine. We will make a circle of life force flow through his body." Her small, soft hand grasped Julian's hard, large fingers with a bravado she did not feel. Closing her eyes, she directed her thoughts, softly saying, "Imagine a stream of white, sparkling light circulating through us into him. It flows like a swift river of energy, bringing him back to consciousness. Visualize it with me. See. The white river is gaining power and coursing through his veins."

With one hand in Anna's and the other grasping Ezra, Julian stared in disbelief. Her words sounded like gibberish to his Roman ears. Suddenly, he was startled to feel a current pulsing through his hands. He looked from Ezra to Anna. Her face showed no change. With closed eyes, she moved her lips silently in prayer. A strange, enchanting perfume emanated from her virginal body. Incredulously, animal thoughts pushed their way into his mind as he held her hand. What a lovely concubine this young girl would make to show Mark Antony and Octavianus.

Concentrating on Ezra again, more strange things developed before his eyes. Rays of light formed around Anna's bowed head. Slowly, they engulfed her shoulders, then her entire body. She was wrapped in a rotating cocoon of scintillating light. It swirled round and round her like a vortex, thickening with each turn. He couldn't take his eyes off the dazzling light. What was happening to his vision? Was this a trick of his mind? Surely it was an illusion, but how did she do it?

Julian looked at his hand, which was still being tightly held in hers. A force issuing from her fingers seemed to flow through him, making his flesh tingle as an unexplained weakness overcame him. His hand now burned with a pulsating heat. He cursed himself silently. "These damned virgins! They always send quivers through me and around my ready fires."

Instantly, the cloud of white light was gone. It must have been an illusion. Turning his face toward Ezra's ashen face, he was startled to see the old man's hand move slightly and his eyelids begin to quiver.

"It's working," Anna whispered excitedly. "He's trying to come back to us." Her delicate face radiated with joy. "Together now, help me send more strength into him," she demanded, gripping Julian's hand while keeping her eyes closed tightly.

As a babbling Ezra began stirring, Julian found himself chuckling uncomfortably as he turned a searching glance toward Anna. She looked so innocent that it was hard to believe she had put him under a spell. Was it possible she was demonstrating a new kind of magic known only to her people? Of course not. Her loveliness must have rattled his thinking. He stared at her pale auburn hair that rippled in silken strands over lithesome, sloping shoulders. She was what he wanted in a woman. Some day soon, he vowed silently, he would run his fingers through that hair.

A tottering Ezra sat up as blood slowly returned to his face. Tears of joy flowed down Anna's cheeks as she embraced him. For a short time, the two seemed unaware of Julian's presence.

"Anna, it was your love that brought me back," Ezra said weakly. He sat up and saw Julian, which brought a frown to his face. "What's this Roman doing here?" he asked hoarsely.

"He helped me bring you out of your faint."

Julian interrupted their conversation brusquely. "If you are all right, old man, I'll be leaving." Turning to

Anna, he added softly, "We will meet again under less unusual circumstances."

Julian reluctantly left the glow of Anna's presence. He felt a great need, a deep longing to be with her, but a strong cultural barrier separated the Jewish beauty from him. When he recalled how she fussed over the old Essene, ignoring him, a Roman of authority and consequence, he smarted with a sense of indignation.

By Venus! He intended to notify Rome that he had discovered sorcery among the Galilean women. That certainly would shake up Mark Antony. This great general had personally told him this province was populated with only shepherds and workmen—humble, unlettered peasants who could be easily tricked. This was why he was totally unprepared for his encounter with this regal young woman. She walked in a perfume of flowers, distracting him, a son of Jupiter, by her magical healing power. Looking back, Julian thought about her sharp answers to his questions. Was it possible she possessed supernatural powers? That old man, Ezra, had been dead. He was positive of this. There was no heart beat when he had listened.

On second thought, Julian reconsidered. He had better wait a while before telling Rome of sorcery. If he could find a way to know Anna better, perhaps she would lead him to other sorcerers among her people. Also, there was something unsettling about the old Essene. Ezra parted his hair in the middle, a style not followed by either the aristocratic Saducee priests or the scholarly Pharisees. This could mean that, besides being unconventional, he was not the harmless old ascetic and scribe Julian had thought him to be.

* * *

Julian shook off his bewilderment as he walked

through the outskirts of town, before arriving at the central hub. It was going to be pleasant to visit Nazareth often, since his headquarters would be in nearby Sepphoris, the capital of Galilee. He had not yet reported to Herod's governor's administrative office there and frankly, wasn't anxious to do so. What he had been told about this younger son of the recently-poisoned Antipater shocked even him, a man bred for war.

It was secretly assumed that certain Sadducees, members of a well-to-do class of landowners and priests, had cunningly put poison in Cicero's cup. This group hoped to restore the Maccabees to power in Jerusalem and bypass Herod. But Herod was crafty, as usual. While the Jewish sects battled among themselves and against the Parthian Antigonus for kingship of Judea, Herod curried favors in Rome.

From what Mark Antony had earlier told him, the Jews of Galilee were strongly individualistic, and it would be well to handle them with care. Why couldn't these stiff-necked people get used to servitude? Their religion must undoubtedly be to blame. It dominated their lives and made their history tragic. In spite of this, Galilee was certainly less chaotic than Judea.

Marcus Lepidu, a member of Rome's second triumvirate, had earlier stressed to Julian the significance of his upcoming work in Judea: "You are neither a spy nor a soldier. You will be an analyst of the Semites, Arabs, Greeks, Aramaeans, and Phoenicians living in that Jewish-dominated place of foment. Find out about their relationships to each other and if there is any patriotism toward Rome. Determine how each family or group can contribute to the advancement of the empire. Think not only of their commodities, but also of their services. In addition, examine the religious thought of these people and, if possible, infiltrate their political activities. You will, naturally, find it advantageous to report those men who neglect or refuse to pay tribute."

In looking back, Julian liked his new political position, which was multifaceted and challenging. It made him a man of power, with an authority greater than the local government.

He also liked this time of year. It was April—the month sacred to Venus. Buds burst and the ground promised fertility. No wonder the mating instinct and the desire for a woman were so strong in him. He admitted to himself that he was more physically impressive than handsome, and that his nose, like his character, was just a little crooked. But he had a vital and healthy body, and the harlots in Rome frequently found it beautiful.

Julian continued slowly through the uneven streets into the heart of activity. Rickety, narrow shops with open fronts lined each side, and competition for sales was fierce. Stepping sideways as the donkeys and camels crowded him, Julian observed the scope and industry of many skilled artisans. There were makers of religious ivory and metal objects, glass blowers, sandal experts, first-class carpenters, and masons.

It was no wonder that his early information of the area had been wrong. These half-breeds weren't as ignorant as he had been told. Galilee was a natural corridor to the Transjordan. People here were in frequent contact with travelers from other lands and were surprisingly in touch with distant events.

Julian's white toga drew suspicious attention as he strode among the long-haired, bearded, and unwashed vendors. Uneasy stares examined his clean-shaven face, topped with blond ringlets. His elegant attire contrasted sharply with the somber dark brown or gray belted tunics of the tradesmen. Let them stare. His toga was easily identifiable and a practical garment. His right arm was free for action, while the folds at the breast served as useful pockets.

The loud chatter of several women attracted his attention to a fountain, where a group had gathered. They melted away quickly as they saw him approach. Several wore make-up; antimony for the eyelashes and sikra for the lips and cheeks. From the lingering air his crinkled nose could tell they also wore heavy scents of nard, cassia and balm.

Women made his thoughts return to Anna. She wore no makeup and no perfume. In spite of this, there was a delightful fresh scent about her, not unlike that of roses or jasmine.

"Slow down, Julian," he admonished himself. "Quit thinking about her. You weren't sent to this free-wheeling part of the empire to hold hands in a ritual of sorcery. That soft, young woman with the beautiful face and engulfing eyes is making a fool of you. Watch her carefully. You can keep in contact with her, Roman, but under no circumstances, fall under her spell."

Chapter 4

Anna, under Sobe's direction, was busy cleaning the house following the eight days of Passover. But her thoughts were on Ezra's recovery. Had she actually brought Ezra back to life? Perhaps he wasn't dead, only unconscious. He might have revived without anyone there.

Another thought disturbed her. Was it wrong for her to have turned to a stranger to help revive the old Essene? She had held the Roman's hand tightly as one would a friend's. Who had dictated her actions? If it was the God of Love and not the vengeful Yahweh, then she was encouraged. She felt a curious kind of wonder at her boldness. Yet she had followed one method of Ezra's teachings, and the results were perfect. Had the Lord God given her a sign to pursue this difficult course?

Naturally, she didn't expect to be as great at healing as the holy monks on Mount Carmel, or at creating invisible walls as Elijah, the great prophet, had done. An oc-

casional success would fulfill her deep yearning to relieve suffering. Often, at night, she would awaken, thinking she had heard the entreaties of beggars at the temple
gates. Or she would hear the cry of the lepers: *AmÉ, AmÉ.*
Unclean, unclean. Half-starved, forced to go bare-
headed, with rags unable to cover missing limbs, these
human wrecks tortured her sleep. If the fierce Yahweh
worked through his wicked angels to punish these poor
souls, then she'd work through the loving angels to heal
sickness.

Anna had just finished arranging lupins in a bowl for
the dining table when Sobe came to check on her.

She asked irritably, "Haven't you made the beds yet?
You know Abba has asked Ezra to come for the noonday
meal."

Anna hurried to the bedrooms to roll up the blankets
and place them behind low wickerwork screens against
the wall. It was difficult taking directions from Sobe, who
put Anna on the defensive. Now she feared Ezra might
tell the family of his fainting spell and how Anna and a
Roman official had come to his aid.

She must turn to the angels for this crisis. Hadn't Ezra
told her many times that, "Angels are God's army, which
allows His perfection and power to flow into our lives"?
She dropped to her knees, knowing that angels don't
come into the world of men unbidden. She had to ask
them for help through prayer and invocation.

Halfway through her supplication, Sobe's voice brought
her to her feet. "The men are here. We pray at the family
altar, Anna, and not in the middle of this room!"

Ezra looked extremely well and happy. He gave Anna a
warm wink and she answered him with a nervous smile.
Sobe greeted Stolan by complaining, "I spend so much
time teaching Anna, I've had to curtail my visits to the
poor. I'm neglecting them."

He replied, "Let's eat that wonderful-smelling soup. We're all hungry, and no one should quarrel while eating. Food is holy, Sobe, and eating is a form of worship." Sobe shrugged her shoulders and sat down beside her mother at the table. Stolan quickly spoke the benediction, "Blessed are thou, O Lord our God, King of the Universe, who brings forth bread from the earth."

Ezra promptly allayed Anna's fears by announcing, "I hear there's a new Roman data gatherer in Galilee. Have you met him, Stolan?"

"No, not yet. The Empire keeps growing like a fungus, while our people are trapped in a mold of our own making—the belief that a Messiah will appear and solve our problems. Galilee could become a pawn, like Judea, in the power struggle between Parthia and Rome. The Judeans scorn us here as ignorant peasants. But they are the slaves—slaves of the Law."

Ezra said, "It's the temple that Parthia wants. We have nothing of value here but our crops."

Stolan shook his head in denial. "We have beautiful women, Ezra. The Parthians will agree to anything if they receive money and women."

The two men finished their meal and went into the garden to talk. Ezra began, "You've asked me to accompany your wife and Anna to Mount Carmel. I wonder how wise that visit will be."

"I'm hoping the monks will reveal information on our future here."

"I'm concerned that Anna's future may be altered by what these monks forecast. Remember, your wife is an impulsive woman, obsessed with courting the future. Ever since she was eighteen years of age, she has gone to Carmel and asked the recluses the same questions: When will the Messiah come? Will he be one of my descendants? Dear friend, Emerentiana is never content with their answers, since they speak only of girl descendants. The trip is risky, but I'll go nevertheless."

Stolan looked fondly at his friend. "The prophets won't change my insistence that Anna marry and not become a celibate healer. My method of choosing the right husband for her is more accurate than the interpretation of the monks' visions."

"You mean by the ritual of the acacia branches?" Ezra referred to the method by which suitors presented a cut branch to the father of the girl. These staffs were not for walking, but used only as a prod in herding animals. If a branch burst with green buds, its owner would be divinely selected as the groom.

"Yes, it's the only way I can be certain she'll marry the right man and bear me many grandchildren."

"I have no faith in that method, Stolan."

"We won't argue the matter. Time will prove me right."

In parting, Ezra turned the conversation to politics, "Rulers of Palestine have joined the Romans in distrusting Messianic speculation. I learned that Mark Antony has warned the aristocracy to be alert to the dangers of this disturbing illusion. Threatening clouds of change are gathering over paradisal Galilee." He restrained himself from adding that Emerentiana's unfounded expectations for Anna could put the family under great scrutiny and stress.

*   *   *

The first pink rays of dawn touched the expectant sky as Anna, Emerentiana, and Ezra mounted their donkeys and headed west toward the Mediterranean. They passed many hardworking farmers, already turning the rich soil for planting.

Close to the road in a large meadow, the travelers noticed a young girl tending oxen. She was no older than twelve, skinny and shabbily dressed. A look of shame came over her thin face when she saw radiant Anna. She turned in embarrassment and limped away. One leg appeared to be considerably shorter than the other.

Ezra said, "She's a slave—a Samaritan. These non-Israelites must serve six years of indenture—that is, unless someone buys their servitude and sets them free. But, who would buy a cripple, especially with the enmity between Samaritans and our people?"

Anna's gentle face lit up with determination. "How much money would it take to free her?"

"Hmm. That depends on how many years she has yet to serve. If she's been sold into slavery by others, then she can go free on the seventh year. If she sold herself to her master, she must wait until the year of the Jubilee—another thirty years to go."

"I don't care about that, Ezra. How much would her freedom cost now?"

"Perhaps four sesterces a year or the equivalent of ten donkeys."

"I knew that we are forbidden to keep slaves of our own people, but I didn't know we could enslave conquered Semitic inhabitants." Anna was upset by the discovery.

Ezra said dryly, "Only we Essenes have outlawed slavery. Under Rome's juggernaut, the traditional social morality of our people continues to deteriorate."

Anna wasn't listening. She asked, "What happens if the girl runs away?"

"The finder should not return her to her master. That would be too cruel. There's no shame in having been a slave. None of us is created superior to another."

Anna persisted. "How can this girl be persuaded to run away?"

Emerentiana interrupted then. "You mean run away to you?"

Anna smiled. "I'll need a servant-maid of my own, won't I?"

"Your father will find you a capable one, so forget about this cripple."

But Anna made a mental note of the location of the farm.

The early part of the twenty-mile journey was easy. Then the trail narrowed, forcing them to lead their donkeys and walk in tandem. Midmorning, they stopped at a running stream to rest. Beneath a hedge of balsam shrubs, they found stone basins left by other travelers to catch the dripping balsam. They added water to make a refreshing drink, ate bread and cheese, and enjoyed the mild air and beauty of their surroundings. Anna was never happier.

On their way again, the path rose steeply, and in the clear spring air, they could see the distant monastery outlined on a high promontory overlooking the Mediterranean. No one spoke, awed by the towering structure ahead. A mystical air hung over the mount. They knew the monastery had been laboriously cut out of the red sandstone by years of patient work and many hands. And here, in the School of Prophets, Elijah, Elisha, and, later, Samuel created giants out of ordinary men.

Emerentiana said in a hushed voice, "You can feel the high spiritual force here."

Anna was deeply moved at the thought of entering the holy sanctuary. She felt caught up in a living stream of energy that carried her toward a strange destiny of unknown dimensions. She walked to her donkey and began stroking it to break the hypnotic spell.

Curious seagulls joined them and watched hungrily as Ezra tethered their beasts and divided the packages brought for the monks. There were dried fruits, skinfuls of olive oil, cheese and handwoven wool for garments.

Coming closer to the monastery, they saw large and small apertures on each level to provide light and air for the interior. Wooden panels, fitted to each opening, permitted closure in inclement weather. Giant steps invited them up the steep slope to the broad terrace above. There was a persistent legend that this holy sanctuary gave forth an aura of sparkling white light whenever the recluses were in meditation.

As if by appointment, three smiling men in long, gray robes waited for them on the terrace. How did they know there would be visitors, Anna wondered. Archos, the venerable hermit in charge, came forward and embraced each one of them. He was an imposing man with penetrating, deep-set eyes, a resonant voice and a forceful manner.

Out of breath by the final climb, the women sank onto stools and watched the flocks of doves circling above them.

"You honor us," Archos said humbly. "Thank you for your gifts of love. These are my holy brothers, Baruch and Tobiah." They were shy men with pensive and gentle faces.

Then, addressing only Emerentiana, Archos added, "I am sure you have an important request, else you would not have brought your daughter to us."

She nodded. "The struggle for control of Judea threatens all of Palestine. My husband, Stolan, begs advice on who the next King of Judea will be, so our people may take measures for survival. Equally important, I must know the Lord's will regarding my daughter Anna's future. She is ready for marriage. God revealed years ago that my descendants were destined for greatness. We need the Messiah now more than ever. Will he come from my offspring?"

Archos answered patiently, "After you have rested, we

will pray together for a sign from God. I cannot determine your future, but He may reveal His wishes to us
because you are a truly good and devout woman."

He directed Baruch and Tobiah to bring refreshments
to them. There were golden combs of honey, pitchers of
cold, cream-topped milk, and flat, sprouted-wheat cakes
baked to crispness in the sun.

When they had finished eating, Tobiah showed the
travelers to their cell-like rooms. He said, "You will hear
a bell when it is time for meditation. Try to sleep."

Anna had not spoken since their arrival. The vibrant
atmosphere engulfed her and held her spellbound.
These holy men knew the mysteries of life and death! In
their presence she felt closer to God than she had ever
been before. If she were a man, she could come here to
be trained as a prophet.

Emerentiana whispered to her, "Do you think the her-
mits will hear Jehovah speak today?"

"If they don't, you must be satisfied, dearest *Emi*. They
aren't magicians, but channels for truth."

"Did you notice the deep recesses covered with
grillwork in the corridor walls? They protect the bones of
prophets who once lived here. These sacred relics are
wrapped in cotton and silk. Look at them when we pass
later and ask for their blessings."

Anna sat frozen in suspense. How could anyone expect her to sleep?

Emerentiana was unusually talkative. "Your father is
fearful of harm coming to you, so he wants you to marry
soon. I think you'll like being married." She sat down on
the narrow, hard cot. "For years I prayed that I would
bear the Anointed One. Instead, I am the mother of three
girls. Your sister, Esmeria, likewise has borne only girls.
Sobe remained barren during her short marriage and
isn't interested in remarrying." She grew increasingly

agitated as she spoke. "Don't you realize what your marriage could mean to me?"

Anna sat beside her and kissed her. "Please don't put your hope in me. I'm far from perfect and not as devout or deserving as you. I can't fast for days as you can, nor sit in endless meditation. I'm interested in all kinds of people. I don't understand myself. I can't hate other races. I'm not worthy of an honor such as you envision. Besides, I want to be a healer more than anything else."

"Surely not more than being the mother of the Messiah! You have a searching, curious mind, Anna. I know you don't feel bound to Stolan's attitudes now, yet you follow the laws of Moses devotedly. In the years ahead, I'm certain you'll be like me."

"I pray I won't disappoint you, for I love you so dearly, *Emi*."

They lay down, fully dressed, on their cots, unable to sleep in anticipation of the fateful experience ahead. It was four o'clock when Archos rang the bell for them to assemble in the prayer room. They placed scarves over their heads and walked slowly along the corridor, pausing in silent prayer before each grilled recess. Before entering the prayer room, they stopped at a metal basin to wash their hands.

The three monks waited for them, heads covered. Archos prayed briefly in the manner of the Essenes. "Heavenly Father and Earthly Mother, send your loving angels to teach us to serve in Thy name. We pray that these angels will write the commandments of God in our heads, in our hearts, and in our hands so that we may carry out God's commandments. May peace be with us." He paused, then turned to Tobiah. "Bring in the prophet band."

It was an unusual prayer which Anna had never heard before. She suspected her mother was disappointed that

Archos had not posed, directly to God, the burning question: Would one of her tribe bear the Savior?

Anna's thoughts were interrupted by the appearance of four musicians in long, white robes. The first one carried a psaltery; another, a timbrel; the third, a pipe; and the last man, a harp.

Anna knew, from her life in the temple, that these bands often produced magical power. Music was closely linked with prophecy; hence, was always a part of the school for prophets. Music helped bring the monks into a state of ecstasy before foretelling the future. As the spirit of God came down, monks often experienced a divine seizure, and evil spirits could be drawn away by the sound of such instruments.

Following the musical introduction, the group sat in motionless contemplation for two hours. It was difficult for Anna, but she managed not to fidget.

Finally, Archos stirred and spoke in a trembling voice. "God has heard our prayers. But he has answered in such a strange way—not through a still, small voice as before, but through an astonishing vision."

Archos looked directly over the head of Emerentiana as he spoke. "I see above you a luxuriant but unusual plant. Its magnificent stem reaches into the sky. I can't see its top, which is lost in the distant clouds. On a sturdy branch grows a luscious, ripe fruit, unlike anything we have in Palestine. Farther along it, there blossoms an exquisite, pure-white flower. Its lovely fragrance envelops me."

"I smell it too," Tobiah whispered. "It's intoxicating!"

Nathan agreed. "There is a definite perfume, but I heard no voice.'

"There was no voice," said Archos, puzzled.

Ezra cleared his throat and said, "The plant must represent Emerentiana. From her, there springs a child—the

branch, which could be any one of her daughters. Do
you agree, Archos?"

"Yes. And this particular daughter will give birth to a
special child."

Emerentiana interrupted, exclaiming, "The Promised
One!"

"No, no. This child will precede the Messiah."

Tobiah frowned and asked, "Wouldn't the flower precede the fruit?"

"It should," Archos agreed. He thought for a few moments. "Yet the stem, in any case, could be symbolic of
one of the daughters. From her will come the fruitful
mother who will give birth to the Anointed One. He is
represented by a pure and stainless, white flower. That's
why the fruit precedes the flower." His tone, however, did
not express total conviction in his interpretation.

Emerentiana was severely disappointed. She asked in
a tremulous voice, "You don't think the Messiah will
come from one of my children?"

"At best, from a grandchild. I'm sorry. Let God's will be
done."

The others repeated his words and left the mother and
daughter. Emerentiana sat in depressed silence. Finally
she said, "Both you and Sobe must marry at once."

Anna protested. "I don't plan on marrying. Esmeria is
your best hope."

"Your father will make the decision, Anna."

                              *   *   *

Archos had said nothing of Stolan's request for information until the trio was about to leave on the return
journey. Then he said, "Tell your husband that a brilliant
Arab of evil mind will soon rule our people. Do not
speak to anyone of the vision. If I have erred in its
interpretation, there would be false hopes and serious

repercussions by boasting of it."

Emerentiana nodded. Yet she intended to put her hopes in Anna. Never had her youngest child appeared so beautiful. Her eager face glowed with wonder and excitement. Her name meant "gracious one," and her straight, refined nose, sensitive mouth, and tiny feet marked Anna as high-born. But a sobering thought drove out Emerentiana's exultant thoughts. Sadly, she realized that the Deliverer would not come in her lifetime. She would never know the Promised One.

Anna struggled inwardly with thoughts of marriage being thrust upon her and what would happen to her dream of being a healer. She also marveled as she envisioned the pure, white flower Archos saw in his vision.

* * *

Stolan, persuaded by his wife that one of their descendants would bear the Messiah, sent word through Galilee, Samaria, and Judea that Anna bat Stolan of the House of David was ready for marriage. Applicants of royal blood were to present themselves to her father in Nazareth. Each must bring a straight, freshly-cut acacia branch.

Within the week, six suitors from noble families came to leave their staffs and discuss their qualifications with the town's brilliant scribe. Their rods lay side by side on a table in a room near the kitchen. The days passed, but none showed any sign of greening.

Anna, not convinced that his method was infallible, asked her father, "What will we do now?"

"It means that your future husband hasn't appeared. I'll make another announcement on the Sabbath."

"There aren't that many of royal ancestry near the proper age."

"Then we must think of someone older—a widower, perhaps."

"Oh, no! I couldn't make an old man happy!"
"You would make any man happy, Anna. Be patient,
I'll find you a worthy husband."

*   *   *

After two weeks of anxiety on the family's part, a
broad-shouldered young stranger arrived with his staff.
This time, the parents allowed Anna to be present.

The new suitor introduced himself with an air of humility. "I am Joachim of the race of David and the tribe of
Levi. I hope I'm not too late. I have been busy with my
flocks in the mountains—so many lambs to care for
now."

His attention shifted to Anna. He flashed her a bright
smile, and she smiled back. He was shorter than her father, but was the first suitor not intimidated by the celebrated sopher. Joachim's soft voice and friendly, dark
eyes impressed Anna. His face and arms were tough and
brown from exposure to the sun, but, most important of
all, he was immaculate in dress and person, and his un-
trimmed beard was framed by curled side-locks.

Stolan appeared interested. "You have double nobility, Joachim, from both the royal and priestly lines.
Where do your parents live?"

"Both died in the recent revolution in Jerusalem."

"That is tragic news. Are there other family members
here?"

"I have two brothers living in Jericho."

"Have you a house for your bride?"

"I have four. One is in Nazareth, another in Jerusalem
not far from the temple, and a country place near
Sepphoris were we might live one day. It's only an hour's
walk from here. Also, I have a simple shepherd's hut in
the mountains where my extensive flocks graze."

"All of this at your—what is your age?"

"Twenty. I began raising sheep when I was fifteen. They have increased rapidly, and I inherited considerable property. I hope the house in the Holy City hasn't been destroyed in the revolt there. It has been a convenient place to stay when bringing the sacrificial lambs to the temple."

Anna saw that her father was favorably impressed.

He boasted, "My daughter, Anna, is highly intelligent and desirable. She was educated in the temple. I believe she is destined for a remarkable future. You can understand why I'm careful in making a decision without verification of God's approval by your staff. Follow me to check on the other rods."

They could all see that the six rods had dried up.

Stolan continued, "If you are the lucky suitor, Joachim, your branch will burst with green buds. I will let you know if that happens."

"I understand." Joachim paused a moment before adding, "There is something your daughter must know. I give one-third of my earnings each month to the temple, the second third goes to orphans, the poor and the crippled. I won't keep more than one-third for my wife and myself. That must be agreed upon."

"I like you, Joachim. You are a remarkable young man," stated Stolan.

Joachim looked at Anna, his eyes twinkling with humor. Then he spoke humbly, "I pray my staff will green, since I'll be greatly honored to marry your lovely daughter."

Stolan nodded. "We will all wait impatiently for God to reveal his decision. See me at the House of Prayer in a week."

After Joachim left, Anna said, "Since you are determined that I marry, I could care for such a man, Abba. Let me touch his staff before you place it with the others."

She ran her slender fingers lightly over it as if she were caressing it, all the time visualizing it covered with young buds.

The next six days were disappointing. But on the seventh day, after the morning prayers and breakfast, Stolan called everyone to join him in the room where the rods lay. He pointed excitedly to Joachim's. Its entire length was dotted with breaking, green leaf buds.

Stolan's usually stern face showed great emotion, and tears filled his eyes. "Anna, I can now announce your wedding. Everyone will hear how God works through nature to help us make important decisions. After Joachim and I come to an agreement on the dowry, I'll set the earliest possible wedding date. You will be happier when married and bearing children."

She would be a wife to please her father, but she would be a healer to please herself. Since the prophet Archos hadn't indicated that she would bear the Promised One, she intended to pursue her own yearnings to make whole the crippled and the diseased who asked for help.

CHAPTER 5

The wedding of Anna and Joachim was set for the first day of the summer month of Tammuz. Stolan was impatient at the delay, but marriages were forbidden during the seven weeks between Passover and Shebuoth.

Both young people were pleased, however, since Anna had to prepare her wedding garments, housekeeping accessories and linens: Joachim needed time to dig out the old vineyard at his Nazareth home, set out new vines and ready the place indoors for his bride.

Emerentiana curtailed her long hours of prayer and meditation to plan the important event. The betrothal ceremonies had gone beautifully. They ended with Joachim's breaking a plate to ward off any evil spirits lurking around. He and Anna were now bound to each other as if married. Only a divorce could break the agreement. Emerentiana decided that the couple should spend a day alone together before the nuptials. She even

selected the location of their first private meeting.
"The weather is ideal for a secluded spot on the road
to Mount Tabor," she announced. "There are great terebinth trees among the maquis of oak, and a small stream
where you can enjoy a lunch that Sobe will prepare."

Anna's heart beat fast at the thought of being alone
with her betrothed. It was incredible how this gentle
young shepherd had driven all thoughts of a celibate life
from her mind. Did Joachim think her pretty or just av-
erage in looks? What should they talk about? Must she
remain shy or could she speak frankly with him? When
he kissed her, should she kiss back with equal fervor or
be passive? These were important questions for which
no one had provided the answers.

When Joachim arrived for their day together,
Emerentiana answered the knock. He surprised her by
handing her a beautiful piece of purple silk, enough for
a dress. After he and Emerentiana embraced, he turned
eagerly to Anna, waiting breathless a few steps away.

There he was, the man she would marry in a few
days—so clean and fresh, so eager and sure of himself. "I
hope I'm not too early," he said.

Anna shook her head, smiled shyly, and said in her
dulcet voice, "Here is our lunch. I am ready."

Joachim took the basket of food and wine, but at the
same time, he grasped her other hand and kissed it. It
was as if lightning had struck her. For a moment she
couldn't think or move. He had changed, it seemed to
her. His tanned face rose from a strong neck like that of a
young god. His generous mouth broke through a delightful, short, curly beard. He radiated such joy and caring.

He held her hand as they walked along the little-used
path into the hill country. They made only small talk,
being content just to be together. The place Emerentiana
had suggested was easy to find. Joachim chose a spot un-

der a spreading terebinth tree and set the basket in its branches.

Then he turned to Anna and held his arms wide for her to come to him. She moved as if in a trance, a force beyond her control drawing her into his embrace. At first, he held her so tightly she could scarcely breathe, and then his lips found hers in a long, fervent kiss. Her heartbeats became drum beats in her ears, and she clung to him with a delight she had never before known. He lifted her up in his arms and carried her to a grassy spot away from the trail. Kneeling with her still in his arms, he kissed her again and again, as if he could never get enough. Finally, he moved away to look at her as if he couldn't believe his good fortune.

He laughed then, a joyous, wonderful burst of happiness, as he pulled a bottle of wine from the basket and Anna held out the glasses. They sipped the rosy beverage in quiet harmony, each occupied with thoughts.

Finally Joachim spoke in a serious tone. "Only two more days until you are fully mine. I can't believe my good fortune. You are sweeter and softer and more beautiful than any woman I ever imagined. I'm so lucky. I thank God for you." His voice choked, and he paused a moment before continuing. "You will never regret becoming my wife, no matter what the future brings. I will always adore you and protect you with my life. Tell me now what I can do to make you even happier than you are at this moment."

Anna remained silent for some time, weighing the risk of her proposal being refused.

"I'll grant it, Anna, no matter what you ask for."

"There's nothing really I need, Joachim. But recently I saw a crippled young girl—a Samaritan slave—painfully working on a farm on the outskirts of town. There was such despair and hopelessness in her face. Ezra said to redeem her might cost as much as four sesterces. I'll gladly go without many things if you would buy her freedom. She could become my maidservant."

Joachim showed surprise at her request, but replied promptly, "You are more noble than I had imagined. You'll have your wish. The crop of lambs has been unusually large this spring, so I can afford it. You realize we may be scorned by many for this charity."

"But we won't be scorned by God, dear Joachim, since we are all his creations. I suspect my life will be anything but ordinary. Will you risk it with me?"

He nodded with a broad smile. "I never thought I would find a woman so right for me. You are the greatest blessing I will ever have. For three years, I searched for you, and now all is magic! You bring sunlight and moonlight and starlight into my dull life. I grow finer every moment by just thinking of you." He paused, almost embarrassed by his outburst. Yet, seeing her radiant face with tears in her eyes, he found the courage to continue. "A delicate fragrance surrounds you—like wild hyacinths or roses. You are sweeter than life to me, Anna. I simply adore you."

She embraced him then in deep humility. She could think of nothing to say after his extravagant speech. She covered her emotions by spreading their lunch out before them.

Joachim shifted his mood now to a teasing manner. "Do you want to know what my wedding gifts are to you?"

"Yes, of course, Tell me."

"You must first promise to look surprised when you open them."

She laughed with delight as he named them—a prayer book, a veil, a sash, and hair combs. Then she confessed, "I worked late last night to finish your gifts. I embroidered your initials on a velvet bag in which you can keep the linen prayer shawl I'm giving you. I also decorated this tallith with religious motifs, and Sobe added the necessary fringes in its corner as a reminder of your deep responsibilities to God."

"I will wear it proudly, Anna."

"Also, I will give you a book of the Passover Haggadah."

"Thank you. But the greatest gift is you, Anna."

Joachim was so right for her, she thought. With him, she would be able to pursue her goal of becoming a healer. Of course, she would also give him many children, perhaps even a very special son.

They embraced tenderly. Then Anna, feeling the need to break the tension of their deep emotion, cried, "Race me to the top of the hill!"

They ran like youngsters, full of wonder and joy at their newfound love.

* * *

On the Sabbath prior to the wedding ceremony, Joachim had the honor of reading from the Torah in the House of Prayer. Then, the day before the nuptials, the young couple fasted, as required by tradition, to atone for past sins. That evening, Anna immersed herself in the ritual bath of purification and washed her long hair in perfumed soap.

Esmeria, her husband Ephraim, and their three young daughters arrived from Jericho the same evening, accompanied by Isaac ben Arach, the priest who would conduct the marriage ritual. Esmeria was needed to help prepare the large, festive meals for the many celebrants.

Although buxom and broadhipped, Esmeria had lost none of her rosy-cheeked girlishness. She was eager to help, not having Sobe's abrasive, jealous nature. She was the first one up in the morning to direct her husband and

Stolan in setting up the chuppah, or wedding canopy, outdoors in the spacious yard. Ephraim was a miller by trade and so capable that the work went swiftly.

The four poles of the square canopy were branches from a pine tree planted in Bethlehem at the time of Anna's birth there. Her marriage required their use. Esmeria was skillful at decorating the poles with ribbons and flowers, then draping a satin ceiling over them. When finished, she went indoors to take charge of Anna's hair arrangement and wedding garment.

She braided Anna's long, auburn hair with strands of pearls and blue, silk ribbons, and draped it over her shapely shoulders. Next came an elaborately embroidered neck covering, and over this the delicate, blue, diaphanous wedding gown. It lay smoothly over Anna's high breasts and tapered to the slender waist, where a blue, satin girdle embraced her. The full sleeves were held by matching ribbons above and below the elbows, causing puffs at the shoulders and wrists. The floor-length robe ended in fringes and tassels and rustled over dainty, gold-brushed sandals as Anna walked.

Esmeria then slipped a white veil, reaching only to the elbows, over Anna's head. She stood back to look at the dazzling radiance of her sister. Anna's face was luminous, as if glowing with an inner light. Her shapely brows framed dark topaz eyes, intense with emotion. She was caught up in a world of her own.

Sobe entered the room, saying with a touch of irritation, "Come, it's time to begin. I've made sure all the men wear a skull cap."

First, Stolan escorted Joachim to the canopy, where the priest waited beside a small table on which stood two goblets and a decanter of wine. Next came Anna, flanked by Emerentiana, Sobe, and Esmeria. She floated past the audience, head high, with the commanding grace of a queen.

When she reached Joachim, standing straight and confident in a long, full coat, she gave him a shy smile, then lowered her eyes to walk seven times around him so he could identify her as his bride. This custom had been included in the ceremony from the time of Jacob, father of the twelve patriarchs, who was deceived into marrying Leah instead of Rachel due to a heavy veil.

The priest, Isaac, gave a prayer of welcome, then the traditional prayer for Joachim's dead parents. After the reading and signing of the marriage contract, he raised a glass of wine and chanted the seven nuptial blessings. Sobe stepped forward and raised Anna's short veil. The glass was passed to the bride, then to Joachim. Sharing the wine sealed their pact to drink together from the cup of life.

Joachim held up the wide wedding ring, and Anna offered the forefinger of her right hand to him as he spoke the words, "Behold, thou art consecrated unto me by this ring, according to the Law of Moses and of Israel."

Isaac pronounced them man and wife, then followed with a blessing: "May the Lord bless thee and keep thee." Sobe stepped forward again and removed Anna's veil. Again, Anna sipped from the second glass of wine, this time wrapped in a thin cloth, and passed the glass to Joachim. He drank from it, then broke it underfoot. It was believed that the noise of the crash was sure to drive away any evil spirits hovering about.

The gathering cried, "*Mazel tov*—good luck!" Now Esmeria and Sobe moved forward, holding a dish covered with a square of silk. The priest and Joachim each took a corner of this napkin, pulled it off, and placed it on Anna's head. Then they gently tossed the contents of the dish—raisins and almonds—over her. These were tokens of fertility.

Promptly the klezmorim band struck up a lively folk

tune and the guests swarmed into the house for the nuptial feast. It was then that Anna turned and saw Julian leaving the house. What was he doing inside? Why had he come uninvited? He was elegantly dressed in a white toga over a gold tunic. He stopped to make sure she saw him. When their eyes met, he inclined his head of tight golden curls in greeting and smiled smugly as if sharing a secret with her. Even from that distance, Julian's enormous power radiated from his demanding nature. Anna saw brutality and arrogance in his face, and also a quizzical expression that confused her. It was as if he were searching for a solution from her—something that both challenged and confused him. Why had he come to her to find the answer? His presence rattled her considerably, and she turned to locate Joachim, hoping no one would notice the flash of recognition that had passed between her and Julian. The Roman strode past the remaining guests, to a waiting black stallion, indifferent to their startled, hostile frowns.

Joachim came to her side and said something to her. He had to repeat it to make her understand. "Your father decided there will be only three days of celebration instead of the customary seven, due to the troubled news from Judea."

Anna nodded her approval and moved inside as the guests crowded to a water pitcher and basin for washing their hands before sampling the aged wine, stored for Anna's marriage from the time of her birth. Sobe and Esmeria directed the women into one room for the feast and the men into another.

Great platters of young lamb, roasted with herbs, large braided hallahs and other breads prepared in special ways, hard-boiled eggs, chopped fish with onions, fruits, and honey cakes waited on long tables for the revelers.

Anna and Joachim stopped at the red-and-white-cov-

ered table where their gifts were placed. Anna was eager
to look at Ezra's gift. He had told her a week ago that it
was his most priceless possession. It was a piece of a garment that Moses had worn. Moses had given it to his
brother, Aaron, and it had been handed down through
many generations.

Ezra told Anna, "You restored me to life, so I want you
to have it. I will bring it to your wedding wrapped in a
yellow piece of silk."

Today Anna looked hurriedly through the piles of gifts
for this treasure. There were dishes, cooking utensils,
bedding, a menorah, Chanukah candles, a Kiddush cup
for Joachim, dried fruits, honey combs, and a variety of
wrapped items, but no yellow package. Then Anna noticed an unusual box covered with red satin. Embroidered on its top were the Greek words, "True love only
grows."

"Open it and see who brought it," Joachim said.

Anna's fingers trembled as she lifted the cover. Who
but Julian would use Greek? Inside the box was an exquisite bracelet. Filigreed gold captured glittering blue
stones in swirls of superb craftsmanship.

"There is no name on it, Joachim," Anna said.

He insisted, "Put it on so the light will catch the gems!"

When she hesitated, he picked up the bracelet and
slipped it onto her wrist. Several people were near them,
so Anna didn't want to protest further.

She would try to return the gift to Julian, but his boldness upset her. Why were her life and that of a Roman
data gatherer strangely entwined? She remembered his
confident words on their first meeting: "You will be my
teacher." Even more annoying was the fact her pulse
quickened with a strange excitement when their eyes
met. Was it fear? Or were they pitted against each other
in a strange battle of good against evil? She suspected he

had deliberately moved into her life and would remain an entangling part of it, in spite of her marriage today.

Ezra now approached Anna, expecting to get her delighted reaction to his gift.

Anna was distraught. "I can't find the sacred cloth, Ezra! Did you put it on the table?"

The Essene nodded and looked perplexed. Then he tried to console her. "Don't be so upset. Whoever took it will surely return it. No one else knows of the consecrated cloth's significance or historical value. It must come back to the person for whom it was intended, and that one is you, Anna." He paused a moment in deep thought, then added, "But not before it has blessed the one who took it."

Joachim spoke now. "It must be here somewhere. We'll find it, so don't let its disappearance ruin our wedding day."

Anna figured Julian could have taken it when he placed the bracelet on the table. Of course, some other guest, uninvited, might have taken the package, since it would be small and easy to conceal. Perhaps she was accusing the wrong person.

She looked at Joachim with gratitude. He had the restrained religious fervor that matched her father's. She must not spoil this special day by having a tantrum over the missing Moses cloth. The celebrants were dancing now in circles in the yard to the music of the folk band. Later they would escort the bridal pair to their new home, and once Joachim and she were alone, they would pray for return of the stolen gift.

Anna slipped the wedding band off her right hand onto the ring finger of her left hand. It was then she saw she was still wearing the stunning bracelet. Was it from Julian?

CHAPTER 6

Immensely pleased with himself, Julian returned to his quarters in nearby Sepphoris. He was doing well in his position as data gatherer. Mark Antony and Lepidus had sent him the beautiful black stallion in appreciation of his comprehensive report on Galilee. What he hoped to do now was to impress these peasants with his thoroughness, weaken their suspicions of Rome, and unravel the mystery of Anna's healing technique.

Her ten years in the temple, doing menial work without adornment or the attention of young passionate males, would make her vulnerable now to his attentions. Of course, she would be delighted with the gold bracelet. Women were weak-minded when expensive jewelry was involved.

Julian drew out the yellow-silk package secreted in the folds of his toga. It had been simple to remove it from the table when everyone's attention was on the rituals.

There was something in Ezra's manner when he slipped the package surreptitiously under the other items that piqued his curiosity. Did it contain something of great value? He tore off the silken covering and was dismayed to find only a strip of yellowed, linen cloth inside. What in the name of Jupiter was the significance of this old rag? He ran his heavily-ringed fingers across it several times. There was a curious warmth emanating from it. Could it be a charm of great power? If so, then he would keep it, not only as evidence of Anna's use of magic, but, even better, as a means of seducing this royal beauty. Of course, she could get it back, for a price—her submission to his constant physical craving for her.

He prided himself on being a opportunist, yet he admitted he hadn't worked fast enough with Anna. Taking a virgin was always exciting, and now she was married. He wondered, though, why was he so obsessed with pursuing an Israelite when dozens of harlots waited eagerly for his sperm? He needed considerable evidence of her sorcery before taking her as a prisoner to Rome.

There occurred to him then a brilliant way in which to monitor her every action. He must figure how to put a spy right in her household! Then he would also know whenever Joachim was in the mountains and Anna in need of servicing. She had the fire to match his, he was certain. No woman had rejected him for long.

* * *

Anna loved the walled garden in front of her new home. Every morning, before breakfast, she spent a half hour in meditation there. Today, as she concluded her prayers, she longed greatly for Joachim. He had gone to the mountains to select sheep for sale so he could redeem the slave girl.

Emerentiana had provided her with Judith, a fine

maidservant, well trained in the dietary laws and the use of separate dishes for meat and dairy products. Married life was good and simple. Anna's hope was that next month, in the month of Ab, she could tell Joachim she was pregnant.

Her musing was interrupted by a man calling her name. The gate opened, and Julian entered the garden, his wicked eyes enjoying her look of surprise. He came confidently to her, his stocky legs spread wide, hands on hips, spiked sandals scuffing the ground.

He began, "I came to see if all went well at your wedding. It's my duty to observe local customs. I hope you didn't mind. I'm learning slowly." His voice was as smooth as butter.

He sat down on a nearby bench, obviously in no hurry to leave.

Anna thought of the lovely gold bracelet left on the wedding table. She said in a breathless voice, "I assume it was you who left me the bracelet. I can't accept it. I'll go get it for you."

"No, no." Julian rose and stepped in front of her. "It is small enough payment for teaching me your healing methods. Let's consider it a gift from the goddess Venus, who sees the great beauty in you." His coarse face broke into a confident smile.

Anna hesitated, then said, "I have no powers of my own. I am skilled only in praying to my God. He does the healing."

"Yes, yes, of course. Is there anything else regarding the wedding you'd like to discuss with an eager pupil?"

Anna flushed, but decided not to respond. This was a good time to mention the missing Moses cloth. He must not think it had any great value, else Joachim would be heavily taxed for it.

She said in a casual tone, "There is something else I'm

concerned about. A special gift disappeared from the table on my wedding day. I saw you leave the house and wondered if you noticed anyone removing a small package wrapped in yellow silk."

"No, I don't remember that. If it's valuable, I'll try to find the thief, and, if possible, return the item to you."

Anna replied evasively, "It probably is of value only to an Israelite. We often cherish things others would discard."

"Is it a powerful herb, often used by sorcerers to promote fertility? Would you use it to heal a leper? Or might it be a kind of charm that would draw a reluctant woman to a man who wants her."

Anna countered, "Since I didn't see the gift, I have no idea what it is or how I would use it. All I know is that it was enclosed in yellow silk."

Julian frowned. "That's not much information, but I'll try to retrieve it for you"

He inclined his head slightly, and left, appearing piqued.

Anna was distraught. Her overwhelming desire to help unconscious Ezra had put her in the clutches of a godless Roman. He would come to her anytime it pleased him. If she knew where Joachim was in the mountains, she would go to him. Now all she could do was wait for his return.

*   *   *

Joachim arrived home two days later, bringing with him the Samaritan, Zandra. He was able to sell enough sheep to meet the demands of her owner.

Anna heard him come into the house and rushed from the kitchen to face a frightened young girl with short red hair and freckles. Anna surveyed her a moment, then went to her and took both trembling hands in hers.

"You are welcome in this house of peace and love," she said, flashing a warm smile. "Meet Judith who will offer you a bath and refreshments and then explain the workings of this household."

When they were out of sight, Joachim took Anna into his arms and kissed her passionately. "I've missed you terribly, my lovely bride. Let me wash up, and I'll be back to hear everything you've done while I've been away."

"Thank you for Zandra. You have made me very happy. I intend to try to straighten her body in the near future." Yet Anna wondered if she had made a serious mistake in taking in a cripple. She had intended to try less difficult problems.

"Anna, for Heaven's sake, don't expect to heal everyone!"

"I know I can't, Joachim, but I'm driven to try at least. Understand this overwhelming need in me. I try to follow what Ezra has taught me, since I have no greater purpose in life."

"Yes, you do!" he shouted. "You are my wife, and your purpose is to bear me children! Who knows, perhaps even the Messiah."

Anna began to weep bitterly. "No, I'm not worthy of that honor," she managed.

Joachim took her into his arms, ashamed of his anger. "Dry your tears. I'm a hungry grouch, who has been yelling at sheep for so long, I forget myself. Forgive me."

CHAPTER 7

The New Year, which began with the celebration of Rosh Hashanah, was no sooner past than early rains blessed the earth. Overnight, the hills were blanketed with orange sterngergia flowers. They forecast the arrival of winter birds from the north who came to feed on the abundant wild fruit of the area.

Joachim remained in Nazareth with his bride throughout the summer months and into the change of seasons, praying that Anna would become with child. He left the care of his flocks to his shepherds while he spent his days building a small structure on the back of his property for the use of the two maidservants and his manservant, Aksel.

He had grown up in this house; his brothers and he had built the dense wall that surrounded the outer courtyard. Interwoven with branches, its high stakes and rods provided total privacy from the narrow street outside. Now, determined to produce a child, he wanted even more privacy in his home.

It had been six months since their marriage, yet Anna had not conceived. Today, as she surveyed the main living area, her heart was leaden. This lovely room, so large it could be made into several ordinary ones, was used less and less with each passing month. Her friends, in abandoning her, claimed that barrenness was evidence of God's wrath. Also, during the Sabbath service, conducted by her father, Stolan, the other women treated her like a leper. It was customary for them to stand behind a curtain, removed from the men of the congregation. But, one by one, these devout women refused to stand next to her for fear she would contaminate them, and keep them, too, from bearing children.

Of course, they knew why God was punishing Anna. How could she act pious when the servant gossip claimed she had been visited by a Roman official—all pagan Romans being unclean? Invitations to social gatherings ceased. Old friends found excuses for not visiting her. And only yesterday, when she went into the market area, they crossed the street so as not to pass her. They were all trying to destroy her.

"Oh, God of Israel, why is it sinful to love those with different skins and speech and customs? Give me a sign that You have not forsaken me!"

No sign came, so she occupied her days teaching Zandra the rigid regime of the household. Since eating and drinking were held to be religions rites, Anna required the three servants to say the benediction before meals and grace afterwards, even though they ate separately from her and Joachim. When they shopped for food, they dared not buy bread, wine, cheese, or milk from a Gentile, since these foods would not have been prepared in conformity with the dietary laws of her people.

Of course, the day before the Sabbath was a busy time for them. There were meat, vegetables, and bread pudding to prepare for the next day, when no cooking was allowed. Week in and week out, Judith directed the making of the braided challah, stuffed fish, noodles in chicken broth, and fruit tzimmes. Zandra asked for more lamb but Anna was determined that a vegetarian regime would be gradually introduced. She dreaded the thought of killing animals, and since her return home from the temple, she had eaten only fish. Ezra had told her that eating flesh would lessen her healing powers. Even fish disappeared from her diet.

Anna was grateful for one thing. Joachim suffered less than she over their ostracism. He was accustomed to a solitary life in the mountains and could bear rejection easier. He did his best to make her happy and constantly showed his love. On each Sabbath eve, he faithfully sang to her the ancient hymn, "A Good Woman," which extolled her role as a wife and mother.

"I am not a mother, Joachim, so why do you persist in this ritual?" she asked.

He replied adamantly, "Your love and care of this home fills the requirement of motherhood. Even if you never bear my child, I will always sing it to you and adore you."

"Thank you for your love, but I am depressed beyond belief. I must do something to earn God's grace. You know it has been some time since I practiced healing anyone. Tomorrow I will seek to free Zandra of her affliction. Do you think it possible to straighten her crooked body?"

Joachim appeared unsure, but he said with forced confidence, "It's worth trying. I will pray with you."

The next morning Anna told Judith of her plans. "First you must promise not to tell anyone about this healing attempt. If it does take place, it won't last if you talk to an unbeliever about it."

Judith nodded her agreement. "I want Zandra whole the same as you."

"Very well. Now take one of the donkeys and ride to the end of the valley, where there is a special herb growing in the moist dells. It is the chickweed plant. You'll recognize it by its pale blue flowers, whose petals form a star. Gather as much of it as you can find—leaves, flowers, stems. Hurry now."

Judith was reliable and returned three hours later with two large sacks of chickweed.

"I have spread a linen sheet on the floor of my bedroom" Anna told her. "Empty the leaves on it and sprinkle them lightly with water." Then she removed flowers from the plants and squeezed their juice into a goblet. To it she added a bit of warm water.

Then she called for Zandra. "You must drink this nectar before I begin. It will taste like diluted perfume, but it has been used from the time of Moses, with good results, to cure deaf people and those crippled by rheumatism." As soon as Zandra had drunk it, Anna gave her a white cotton robe to put on.

Both women were nervous. Anna really didn't know how to begin the healing process. "First show me where you hurt when you walk," she said.

Zandra indicated the troublesome hip, and Anna pressed the wet flowers on it, saying, "Relax completely, since this may take some time. You have nothing to do but close your eyes and rest."

Joachim passed the open door and was puzzled by the unusual sight of a servant lying on a bed of leaves and flowers. "What are you doing, and can I be of help?"

"I need mostly your prayers. Dear husband, come kneel beside me and hold my hand." Then she remembered the prayer of Archos, the Essene monk, on her visit to Mount Carmel. She began it as he had, "Heavenly Father and Earthly Mother, send your angels of mercy, those unseen messengers of love, to this suffering girl. Straighten her young spine, straighten her young legs, let Zandra walk free of pain and limping for the rest of her life. Amen."

Then they waited. There was no vision, no voice, only silence. Anna was disheartened. A half hour passed, and then the air in the room started to flow as if a light breeze had entered. With it came the unmistakable fragrance of frankincense. Anna and Joachim exchanged meaningful glances, and she motioned for him to leave.

From time to time during the afternoon, she laid her hands lightly on Zandra's crooked legs and prayed; she pictured her with a strong, healthy body, running and dancing with no limp. Yet there was no change.

"What more can I do? I have given her the relaxing juice of the chickweed flower. I have had her lie on the moist herb most of the day. I have prayed. Why do I fail?"

She had to try something else. She pulled gently on the shortened leg, commanding it to obey her. "Short leg, lengthen and straighten yourself! Be useful as God intended you to be!" Over and over again she spoke aloud the decree, each time tugging on the leg.

Finally she stopped, seeing no change whatsoever. She had failed. She dropped the leg, but immediately it began to twitch and move as if in a spasm. In small jerks, it stretched itself ever longer until the two legs were the same length.

Anna watched its movement as if hypnotized. At least she could believe her eyes. "Almighty God of Israel! You are sublime!" She crouched beside Zandra, fearful the change would not hold when the girl stood up. Finally, she dared pull her to her feet. She repeated firmly the words which the Lord spoke to Abram, "Walk before me, and be thou perfect."

Zandra took a few hesitant steps, then danced back and forth before Anna. "I don't limp any more! I feel no pain! Tell me what happened."

Anna answered with tears flowing down her cheeks, "The chickweed is a miracle plant. All it did was relax your tight muscles and let your leg assume its normal position." Anna didn't believe this was the healing, but Zandra would never understand the mysteries of prayer and angels and decrees and fiats and supplications, let alone the picturing of wholeness. However, Anna knew she must insist on one thing from her.

"Don't describe what happened here today to anyone, or you may find yourself a cripple again. Will you promise me that?"

"Yes," Zandra agreed. "I'm filled with joy. I'm a new person. I feel such love for everyone! I won't spoil my healing by talking about it, I swear to you."

"God love you. You deserve a holiday tomorrow to enjoy your new freedom. I will give you a few shekels to spend on yourself in the markets. Do what pleases you all day."

Zandra ran to tell Judith the exciting news of her healing. Anna walked to her favorite bench in the courtyard to meditate and give thanks for the blessing.

Joachim joined her there, bursting with pride at the successful results. "I admit I was skeptical that anyone could change Zandra's twisted frame. I know now that you possess a mysterious power. Perhaps that is why God doesn't want you to bear children. You have another purpose in life—to heal."

"Faith comes at a high price, dearest love. God surely knows I also want children. I want to please you first of all, and I yearn for the love and respect of our neighbors and former friends. I am being destroyed by their scorn and vilification."

Joachim put his arms around her. "Anna, they won't be able to destroy you because I'll never forsake you. One day, when they are suffering greatly, they will come to you and plead for a cure. What will you do then to get even?":

Anna said, "You know perfectly well that I'll do all I can to help them"

They both laughed.

CHAPTER 8

Julian moved restlessly about his living quarters in Sepphoris. He held the stolen piece of linen in his hand, wishing he could return it to Anna. He would say he had found it on a thief and hoped it was the lost wedding gift. There was certainly significance in this old scrap of cloth, but what? Why did it cause his hand to burn when he held it too long? It could be his imagination and an obsessive fear that it held some sort of spell for the owner. He had seen Joachim in Nazareth, so he had to stay away from Anna. Curse the cruel gods! He must wait impatiently to bring her the cloth.

Meanwhile, his need for a woman became unbearable. He decided to ride to Nazareth and find a better looking harlot than he had bedded down in Sepphoris. It was only an hour's ride south on his stallion, and the weather was perfect. The first drops of rain had produced unending carpets of green, and waves of delicate flowers nodded to him as he passed. Thousands of coots, starlings, and ducks flew overhead in vast formations heading for every pond and lake in the area. It was a beautiful day for mating. His needs had never been greater.

Julian reviewed his last message from Rome. Mark Antony informed him that his superior legions had vanquished the Parthians in Judea, but there would be an uneasy period of adjustment while a new procurator took over its rule. Herod's uncanny ability to put down a rebellion in Galilee a few years earlier had so impressed the Triumvirate that they made him Governor of Judea, and bestowed upon him the honor of *res socius*, ally of Rome.

Mark Antony also asked a curious question: Would Julian give his impression of this obviously talented Herod? Indeed he would. There was something about the man that irritated him whenever he thought of him. He was a crafty administrator and had confided to Julian that prosperous Palestine could expect a new fiscal policy in the future to support his extensive building plans. To Julian, his demands to make his aims come true amounted to nothing short of extortion.

In his reply to Antony, he also claimed, "Your tax collectors, while required to pay a fixed amount of denarii annually to the Empire, have become incredibly enterprising. They tax more than you ask and keep the loot for themselves. My salary is far less than theirs. Therefore I request humbly that alterations in my income be made.

"You also ask, sire, for me to comment on what the Judeans think of Herod. If he foolishly asks for an oath of allegiance from them, as he did in Galilee, all Israelites will refuse, and we'll have another bloody revolt. They claim their allegiance is to the one God, the unseen Yahweh, whose name they dare not utter aloud. Herod calls himself an Israelite, when we know he is an Idumean—nothing more than an unwilling convert. He can restore peace, since he is not only shrewd and deceptive, but brutal.

"I am in the serious process of investigating well-founded rumors of sorcery among the women here, but I need more time to get necessary evidence. These women are so devious."

It would be interesting, Julian thought, to see how Herod would cope with the intricacies of Israelite Law. Its followers took offense for the most frivolous of reasons. Palestine was prosperous, but how long would it accept Herod's tyrannical control? To himeslf, he admitted he was jealous of Herod for his power. He also feared what Herod's directives would entail for him.

He must remain in Galilee to be around Anna. She had become an obsession with him, haunting him during the day, disturbing his sleep at night. There was a mystery about her; she had the inner strength of a Hercules, the femininity of a Venus, and, damnation, a husband who kept Julian away from her. If he could dispose of this sturdy shepherd, he could win her trust. There were times, like today, when he would do anything she asked—everything except undergoing that ungodly rite of circumcision.

He suspected that she leaned toward the beliefs of the Essene sect, due to her affection for the old man, Ezra. Surely she knew that married Essenes believed in a minimum of cohabitation, and then only to beget children—never for sensual pleasure. Anna must not undergo such hardships, if he could prevent it.

Julian turned his attention to the fields on both sides of the road. Farmers were now harvesting olives and pressing them for oil. Olives were the reason Roman conquerors came to Palestine, of course. This fruit supplied not only food but also fuel and medicine. Other farmers worked the fields with crude plows, not giving a glance at him, an official of the Roman Empire, who rode an expensive black stallion. These indifferent people!

Yet, Galilee was his favorite assignment. Surrounded by pagan and colonial townships, it displayed the greatest influence of Greek life.

He entered the village, scattering goats and wayward chickens. Here everyone lived in modest, one-story houses of mud bricks. Skirting the marketplace were the shabby shops of potters, weavers, shoemakers, and carpenters. What a hubbub of different tongues they made! Even the numerous dialects of Aramaic could drive one crazy.

In the center of town were bronze-faced camel drivers, beggars, merchants hawking their wares from carts and just ordinary folk buying their daily food. In order to make any progress through them, he was forced to dismount and lead his animal.

A group of young boys, heading for their daily lessons in the House of Prayer, passed him. That was where Anna's father, Stolan, taught them Hebrew. Why didn't they learn a more noble tongue like Greek? Here and there in the square, old men had gathered to examine their faith and interpret Yahweh's wishes. Simpleminded people! What did they know of the world—peasants who never traveled more than a day's journey from their homes? He watched briefly two wrestlers and won a few shekels by picking the winner.

He moved on, searching the crowd for a harlot. Then he caught sight of Zandra, turning into a side street. What had happened to her? She no longer dragged one foot in that repulsive way, but skipped along like a young child. He had met her one day with Judith, and the sudden change in her was certainly real evidence that sorcery had taken place. He would investigate this remarkable transformation.

Julian pursued her, thinking that here was his opportunity to relieve his physical needs without paying a shekel for it. Zandra appeared quite attractive today.

"Zandra," he called. "What happened to your limp?"

"I don't understand it myself," she replied, not looking directly at him.

Julian ran a ringed hand over her cheek, touching briefly her full lips. She liked the unaccustomed attention, he could tell, and was obviously in a receptive mood for it.

"Would you like to ride on my stallion? Few in Palestine have the opportunity to actually ride a horse. You'll be safe on him, since I will lead him. We can go into the hills where it is cool."

Zandra hesitated for only a moment. "All right. I'm free for the entire day—a holiday my mistress gave me."

Julian knew she couldn't resist the new experience of being in the company of an official from Rome. He hoped she didn't read the glint of passion in his eyes. He headed for a secluded vale close to town, since he had trouble controlling his desires. When they reached a little-used, sheltered spot, he lifted Zandra off the animal but did not release her. He knew how to get compliance and induce new emotions in virgin girls. He laid her on the grass and ran his fingers lightly up and down her thighs until she moved closer and closer to him. She was getting the electric shocks he intended. He removed her outer garment without any resistance on her part, then eased himself onto her prone body.

"You never thought you would experience the wonder of a passionate man," he whispered. "Now you will know what others have enjoyed all the time. After the first shock of penetration, you won't get enough of me.

I'm a master at this, so relax."

It was an easy conquest, but Zandra proved a surprising match for him. It took a long time before he could completely satisfy her. Julian kept his eyes closed much of the time, trying to imagine that this was Anna beneath him. But the vision never came.

Finally, he pulled Zandra to her feet. "Don't tell your mistress that you have seen me today, or about the fun you have had. She would punish you severely. Tell me, what or who changed you from being a cripple?"

Zandra shook her head, put on her robe, and walked to the stallion for her ride back to town. Julian told himself he could wait for a repeat performance with her, when she would surely give him specific information on Anna's healing tricks.

CHAPTER 9

Whenever Anna visited her mother, Emerentiana, she faced a hostile sister. Today, Sobe opened the door only a few inches.

"*My* mother is confined to her bed," Sobe whined. "I think she's dying."

Anna said quietly, "You mean *our* mother, don't you?"

"How can you claim relationship, when your behavior is so outrageous? Still childless after all these married years, you have shattered her dream of being a grandmother. Her intense disappointment has made her health deteriorate rapidly. You defy the holy Torah by treating pagans the same as us. I'm so ashamed of you, I could commit suicide." Sobe pushed her straight hair from her eyes and did her best to look abused.

"Don't be so dramatic. I can't despise people who were born in another place or of another race. If I'm to be punished for my shortcomings, let God do it. Now, open the door and let me speak alone with Emi."

Sobe's voice was rough as a file. "Make your visit short!"

As Anna turned to her mother's bedroom, she thought of the countless times Sobe had belittled her. Oh, why are you so jealous of me? You can be so loving when you wish. You don't elevate yourself by humiliating me. I can't count the number of nights I've cried myself to sleep because of your deep resentment of me.

Sobe let her pass, but her narrow, sullen eyes were pinched together in suppressed anger.

Anna found Emerentiana extremely weak and pale, yet there was much love and joy in her tired eyes when she saw Anna.

During their embrace, Emerentiana whispered to her, "I have only a short time left, dearest daughter. Don't try to delay my passing. I meditated a long time yesterday, and an angel spoke to me. He told me not to grieve over your barren state, since you are God's beloved child. He said you will eventually become a mother, and one daughter will bring great joy to heaven. Isn't that wonderful? I have told no one else this. You have been my greatest blessing, Anna, and I know how deep your love for me is. When I am gone, remember me in your daily prayers, for I will always be close to comfort you and to watch over you." Her voice was so faint Anna had to put her ear close to her lips.

Anna kissed her mother's fragile hands and held them against her heart. She would not dispute Emerentiana's wishful thinking.

Sobe entered the room now, bringing small goblets of sweet wine and ginger cakes. "You've had enough time to share your little secrets. Emi must not talk so much—it takes her strength."

Emerentiana took a few sips of the wine and quickly

fell asleep. Sobe munched one cake after another in a ravenous fashion, at times talking with her mouth full. Anna took nothing.

Sobe asked suddenly, "Are you prepared to see your father? He will be home shortly. You drove a sword into his heart when you allowed a Roman to attend your sacred wedding and make away with Ezra's holy gift."

"Julian came without an invitation, Sobe."

"Sure. Sure." Her voice rose with sarcasm.

Anna wanted to leave then, but decided not to give Sobe the satisfaction of being frightened away. Now Stolan entered the house quietly. When he saw Anna in the bedroom, he stopped in the doorway. The expression on his face was unfriendly.

He asked, "Have you brought good news to your mother?"

Anna's reply was scarcely above a whisper. "I am not with child, if that's what you ask."

"Then you should not come here to torment her."

"I came, as always, to bring her my undying love." Anna dared not look at his unrelenting face.

"Your neighbors tell me a Roman—that data gatherer—has visited you. Since you cavort with the 'unclean,' I no longer consider you my flesh and blood."

The accusation was so grave that Anna fought back. Her voice was quiet but firm. "Then your God and mine are not the same one. I worship a God of love and not one of vengeance. Whether you deny me or not, I want your love, Abba."

Partially mollified, Stolan said, "I know that Joachim has gone with sacrificial sheep to Jerusalem. Once again the priests will refuse them, since he has produced no offspring. He will have to sell them to the heathen Gentiles." His anger returned. "You know he can divorce you when ten years of your barren marriage have passed.

Then you'll realize what defiance of our Law means!"
His loud voice awakened Emerentiana. She moaned.
Anna rushed to her bedside. "I am in such pain," her
mother whispered. "Is there nothing that can help me?"
"When I leave today, I will go to Ezra. He will know of a
narcotic herb."

Stolan, hearing mention of his old friend, interrupted
their conversation. "Another thing, Anna. Essenes like
Ezra never keep servants. Yet, you have two, one a despised Samaritan, so it's obvious you don't follow their
teachings any more than you do mine."

Anna remained calm. "Perhaps you are right, Abba,
but I agree with Ezra that nothing happens without
God's will."

"So—you take what you like from each doctrine, is
that it?"

Anna cut off the argument by changing the subject.
"Do you have any garments you no longer wear? Ezra is
in need of men's clothes for travelers who stop at his
house en route to the Qumran and Dead Sea settle-
ments."

Sobe, who had stood aside with obvious delight over
the quarrel, was not in good humor. "There are several
discarded garments in the next room, Anna. I'll bundle
them up for you to take to your mentor."

As soon as she left, Anna rushed to Ezra. The white-
haired Essene fastened his deep-set, gentle eyes on her,
asking, "What's the matter?"

"My mother is in excruciating pain. Is there a narcotic
that will stop her suffering?"

He nodded. "Get the mandrake root, and either
squeeze the juice from it or make a brew. It grows beyond the common orchard, in that deep wadi. The plant
has large leaves and will have already flowered. The fruit,
called the love apple in the book of Genesis, may be ripe

enough to pick now. It's too late for you to locate it today, but in the morning you'll find it wherever there is a trickle of moisture. Take a tool with you to dig out the roots." He paused, then added gently, "You might profit also from the juice of its ripe yellow fruit. It has a sickly taste, but some claim it promotes conception."

"I'll remember, dear Ezra. Only you and that conniving Roman, Julian, treat me with consideration. Why haven't you turned against me?"

Ezra laughed softly and stroked his flowing, white beard. "What a foolish question. You are the dearest woman in the world to me—a cherished daughter. You must carry on my life's healing work in your own special way. You will fail at times. You may save the life of strangers, but not those you love the most. That is one of life's mysteries. Your father doesn't know how cruel he is to you. He is totally consumed by the rigid precepts of the Pharisees. Patience and fortitude are but some of the lessons we all must learn." He took her hands in his. "In my meditations, I often see you, much older, walking with a beautiful child of your own. Like Sara, wife of Abraham, you will emerge from this trial a venerated mother. She was very old, remember, when she bore Isaac. You must break away from old traditions and find your own path. Turn to the angels for help. They don't come into the world of men unbidden. One must invite them, through prayer and invocation, to help us when in trouble." He stopped and smiled. "You've had your sermon for today, so go home now, and be happy."

Being with Ezra always buoyed Anna's spirits, but they fell again when she neared home. Tethered at the gate was Julian's stallion. What should she do? Go back to Ezra? It was better to face Julian, much as he upset her. She feared him, yet was fascinated by the beardless face and tight golden curls hugging an arrogant head. He was an exciting man, a challenge to her deep need to understand people of all races—especially the conquerors. Julian was so sure of himself, so accustomed to getting his own way with women. He challenged her every moment.

When she opened the gate, she was surprised to see Zandra fleeing into the house. She had apparently been talking with Julian, but why would she run when Anna came home?

Julian rose easily from her meditation bench and waited for her to reach him. He held out a package wrapped in yellow silk to her. "Could this be your lost wedding gift—the one the old Essene gave you?"

Anna opened it eagerly. Yes, the Moses cloth was still inside.

"Where . . . ?" she began.

"A thief in Sepphoris tried to sell it to me, but wouldn't say where he had gotten it. Is it what you expected?"

Anna was so grateful, she explained, "It's a piece of a garment worn by an ancestral leader—we Israelites prize such things for sentimental reasons. It has no monetary value."

Julian shrugged his shoulder, saying, "It is a curious cloth, though. Worn and obviously very old. It grows warm in one's hand. Has it special properties? I mean, would it be a love charm? Would it bring help from the gods to win over a reluctant woman?"

Anna knew what he meant. Unruffled, she replied, "It is a holy cloth, Julian. It would help a person only to love God more."

He made a grimace and changed the subject. "Do you go often to Jerusalem?"

"Joachim owns a home in the city, but it has been too dangerous for me to go there. I haven't been back since my spiritual training in the temple ended."

Why was she telling him all this? Was it because she no longer had women friends to gossip with? Julian was so interested in her, while everyone else avoided her like the plague. What difference did it make if she conversed with the genial data gatherer?

Julian continued quietly, "Our Governor of Galilee, Herod, has been made procurator of Judea, so I expect to be transferred to Jerusalem. He will make it safe for you to go there." He paused, then, after eyeing her carefully, asked, "You are not yet with child?"

Anna shook her head. Why wasn't she shocked at such an intimate question? What difference did it make to him?

"Then I have something else for you." He handed her a sack bulging with something moist. "This is moss that grows in the cracks of your temple walls. I heard that if a woman makes a tea from it, fertility may result. Would you like to experiment?"

Anna was visibly moved by his desire to help her. "You are very kind. I hadn't known about this."

He took her arm and pulled her down onto the bench with him. "I blame Joachim for your sterility. It couldn't happen, otherwise, to anyone as lovely as you."

This was a crazy subject to be discussing with an appointee from Rome. Yet, Anna found herself explaining to him, "No one is to blame. If I have no children, it is God's wish, not his punishment. I get pleasure in healing people."

Julian moved closer to Anna. His voice dropped to a whisper. "You are an unusual woman. You fascinate me beyond measure, and I think of you constantly."

Anna rose from the bench and said firmly, "Julian, do not delude yourself with useless imaginings. I am deeply in love with my husband, and will always obey the laws of my God. But I am a lonely person, unable to be what everyone else thinks I must be."

Julian's face registered no change. He replied with his customary confidence. "Remember, when Joachim dies, I will still be a willing captive of yours."

Anna laughed, pretending it was only flattery. Julian was about to say more when Judith returned home from a shopping trip. She ignored Julian, but asked Anna, "How is your mother today?"

"She suffers greatly. In the morning, I must find some mandrake and make a tea for her. Ezra claims it grows in the wadi up that mountain." She pointed in its direction.

"Yes, I know the place."

She hurried into the house with her foodstuffs, then turned to say good-bye to Julian, and was surprised to see him smiling, as if immensely pleased by something. But he wasn't looking at Judith. His cool green eyes were fastened on her.

CHAPTER 10

It was a gray morning in the rainy month of Tevet when Anna rode her donkey into the hills above Nazareth. The sky was close to the earth and there was an uneasy stillness in the oppressive air. Nothing stirred in the woodland. What was nature waiting for? Ancient oaks stood like statues, and a herd of roe deer huddled under motionless sycamores. Why didn't the animals flee at her approach?

She felt unwelcome today in her fertile homeland. In Galilee, wheat and barley and vines and fig trees and pomegranates grew in abundance. Only she was unproductive. She thought of the moss Julian had brought her from the temple walls. She would make tea from it upon her return today. His thoughtfulness, when almost everyone else criticized and avoided her, softened her mixed feelings of him. Yet she suspected he had ulterior motives, and she was uncertain how to deal with the wiles of a Roman official under powerful Herod.

If only Joachim were here. His love for her never wavered. She should have gone to Jerusalem with him, but the journey was always so tiring when he took sheep to the temple for sacrifice.

As her donkey carried her through dense honeysuckle creepers, Anna noticed that neither insect nor bird life was moving in the woods. Also, there should be at least some wild sheep and goats grazing in the open area. Could there be a leopard or bear nearby? She spotted only a clutch of conies hiding in the thick undergrowth. All nature sounds were muffled or silent, and distant Mount Tabor appeared withdrawn in a mournful shroud of gray.

Anna continued up a wadi lined with wild pear trees. She knew it led to the freshwater spring she sought. There, she found growing large numbers of the narcotic mandrake. She slid off her animal and hurriedly began to dig out the plants. In no time, she had filled her sack, set it on the back of the donkey, and prepared to mount for the ride home.

At that instant, the mountain sprang to life. It rolled and buckled and rolled again in long waves. Anna was pitched to the ground. Hundreds of birds shot into the sky, their flapping and screeching adding to the panic of small animals in the brush who attacked each other in fright. Anna's terrified donkey took off down the mountain.

As if attempting to destroy every living thing, the tormented earth ripped and crushed and ground itself in agony. Anna lay still and waited for the earthquake to stop.

There was a brief respite, then again a violent tremor hit. To Anna's horror, it split wide open the banks of the wadi near her, shooting out, through an enormous break, the terrified inhabitants of a den of vipers. Rocks, earth, and poisonous snakes were catapulted directly at her. Uncertain as to the nature of their enemy, the vipers fanned out in all directions with mouths wide open and heads drawn back for the deadly strike. Barely out of their range, Anna leapt up and was about to run into a clearing when another sharp jolt, followed by a rolling movement, struck. She tried to regain her balance, but either tripped or stepped into a hole. Losing her footing, she was pitched against a boulder. All went black.

* * *

She heard her name being called from a great distance. She tried to open her eyes but they refused to respond. Someone spoke softly to her, "My darling Anna, you are safe in my arms and far away from the vipers."

Thank you, God of Israel, for bringing Joachim from Judea to my rescue. Her terror left in his comforting embrace, but her head throbbed with excruciating pain and she just wanted to lie still and feel secure. Too faint to answer her rescuer, she clung to him in relief. She turned her head so he could kiss her lips over and over again. Then he kissed her eyes and cheeks and hair with a passion he hadn't shown in a long time.

When she finally had the strength to open her eyes, she was shocked to see the head of Julian's black stallion in front of her. It was Julian who had rescued her! She was aboard his mount and his hard-muscled arms held her limp body in a tight embrace. Her head scarf was gone, and her long hair fell over his arms. She began to tremble when his beardless face pressed boldly against her cheek. This was an outrageous predicament! She was too dumbfounded to say anything yet.

Julian spoke again in a cheerful voice. "You have a

bloody head, Anna, but you'll live. I didn't find any broken bones. I reached you just in time to snatch you from a mass of mean snakes. Your four-legged transportation passed me in a hurry, headed for home. Now since you are in no condition to walk back to Nazareth, I'm sure you won't mind riding tandem, will you?"

"Put me down," Anna said weakly. "I can walk."

Julian promptly took his arms from around her. Her world spun and she would have toppled to the ground if he had not caught her.

"You see," he said, sounding immensely pleased, "You're still wobbly, even though I've brought your pulse beats up considerably. You aren't a piece of ice, thank heaven. If it will relieve your mind, I'll do the walking when we get into town. Though I can't see what difference it would make with people who already scorn you. Meanwhile, let's enjoy this romantic ride."

Anna had never been on a horse before, and she seemed to be so far above the ground and helpless. On a donkey, one's feet nearly touched the earth. She concluded she had no choice but to accept this embarrassing situation, and hold Julian's ardor in check.

She asked, "How did you know I was here?"

"Yesterday I heard you tell Judith where you were going for mandrake roots. I wanted to be alone with you, so I followed you here. Lucky, wasn't it?"

"Yes, you saved my life. I will always be grateful for that." Anna kept her embarrassed face turned away from him.

"Adorable one, enjoy me while you have this marvelous opportunity." Julian gave a hollow laugh, then abruptly stopped his mount. "Great Jupiter! Look below. There's terrible devastation from the earthquake. I wonder how many are still alive?"

Anna's concern over Julian now shifted to her family

and servants. Would she find them buried in the ruins? And where was Joachim today? Had the earthquake struck neighboring Samaria and as far south as Judea? Julian interrupted her thoughts, speaking with unusual emotion. "I must take advantage of this chance to tell you how I feel. You are a magnet, drawing me constantly to you. You have become an obsession with me. My nights are tormented by thoughts of possessing you. You have been badly treated by everyone in Nazareth these many months. Your shepherd husband has kept you sterile. He is the one to blame, not you. He will divorce you one of these days, as your Law allows. Then I will take you to Rome to live. You can have a large family of children there."

"As your concubine?" she asked lightly.

He made no reply to that, but tightened his arms around her. She felt his hard kisses on her neck and hair. Then he abruptly swung himself to the ground, and began leading the stallion.

Anna feared his passions now, but she must control her words so as to get safely home. Somehow, in the days ahead, she would put an end to his romantic notions. Now he was a threat to her beloved Joachim.

She spoke seriously. "We are worlds apart in every breath we take. You know that, Julian. I try to understand your Roman desire for conquest, but we Israelites are a different breed. I can never forget that I am a descendant of King David and part of a thousand years of Hebrew history and suffering. You and I need not be enemies, but we can never be lovers." Anna was surprised how calmly she had spoken.

"You are too frank." He scowled and his reply was harsh. "You have an unnatural control over me now. But when you prove to my satisfaction that you use evil spirits in your supernatural healings, those thousand years of history won't do you any good!"

Anna had antagonized him more than she intended. She ignored the threat saying, "Please take me to my parent's home. My mother is extremely ill and I wanted the medicinal roots to relieve her pain. Oh, I forgot! I've lost the mandrake!"

"I picked up your sack. See—it is tied behind you."

"Again I am indebted to you. Thank you for today's rescue."

"You are too headstrong." He sounded more friendly now. "Someone has to look after you." The tension between them left.

They entered the destroyed village, scarcely believing the extent of the devastation. Houses had become rubble; stunned and injured people ran crazily about, many weeping and screaming for help. Angry shop owners pursued thieves looting the ravaged business district. Children moaned over parents lying silent in the ruins of their home. Fires went unchecked in many quarters, their dense smoke causing further misery. Terrified camels and donkeys milled through the debris-filled streets, adding to the chaos everywhere. No one was in charge.

When desperate people screamed for Julian to help them, he called back, "I'll return shortly and do what I can."

Reaching her parent's home, Anna was shocked to see its total destruction. She was sure no one would be alive in it. Julian went ahead, clearing a path for her through and over the shattered mud bricks and broken furniture.

"Emi! Sobe! Are you alive?" Anna called.

She heard a moan and found Sobe helplessly pinned under a collapsed outer wall. Julian pulled her out and carried her to the front yard while Anna continued to search for her mother. Finally she saw a foot sticking partially out of a heap of ruins. Emerentiana must have been crushed in her bed. Anna frantically dragged away chunks of shattered ceiling and wickerwork screens and uncovered the lifeless body of the gentle woman.

Anna debated whether she should try the same reviving technique she had used on Ezra. Julian could help her again as he had done then. No! No! It was too risky after his expressed suspicious of her being a enchantress. Then she recalled her mother's whispered words at their last meeting: Don't try to delay my death.

She held the dead woman in her arms and sat in the rubble rocking and silently talking to her. Precious Emi, I have loved you devotedly all my life and am saddened that I have given you no grandchildren. Ezra has taught me much about healing with herbs and prayers and even commands. And he claims the Moses cloth will attract to me more curative power, and perhaps even a child.

Julian returned and interrupted her thoughts by saying callously, "She looks very dead to me."

"Wait. I need a moment more alone with her."

Then into her mind the words tumbled as clearly as if she had heard them spoken out loud. "Let me go, beloved daughter. Let me be free. Don't have sad thoughts. Stolan needs you. Cry later. Pray later for me. Tend to the injured Sobe now. Be guided by God's love for you. And remember my vision—one of your daughters will bring great joy to heaven."

The thoughts stopped. The message was over. Oh, Emi, how I love you.

"Take her gently," Anna directed Julian. He carried Emerentiana to where Sobe lay semiconscious and bleeding from the mouth.

Julian turned to Anna. "I must leave now to help others. First, I'll go to your home to make sure everyone there is safe."

"If you hear any news of Judea, will you return and tell

me? I'm frantic with worry over Joachim."

Julian nodded, but his green eyes showed disappointment, and his face hardened.

Anna found her father's manservant, Gideon, crouched in terror near the animal pens. "It's all over, so get control of yourself," she told him. "Help me build a fire out here. I need hot water. Where is Isabel?" She was sure her mother's maidservant was not in the ruins of the house.

"She left for the market before the earthquake struck," the slightly built, nervous Gideon replied.

"Search for her later. As soon as you can, go and see if Ezra is safe. If possible, bring him here."

Anna cleaned and chopped mandrake root for brewing while Gideon started a fire. There would be many besides Sobe whose pain it could ease. By the time Anna returned to her sister, Stolan arrived home.

He looked with despair, first at Sobe, then at the lifeless body of his wife. Anna went to him, but he rejected her embrace.

"She is with the angels, but I'm certain she didn't suffer," she told him.

Stolan's reaction was one of anger. "Why have I been allowed to live and she taken from me?" He stared in disbelief at what had been his home. "I have neither wife nor home. But I have a daughter who plays at being Jehovah and brings down his wrath on me for her actions!"

Scalding tears filled Anna's eyes. She left him to get a cup of mandrake tea for Sobe. Her father would never understand her motives. To him, life was either black or white. There could be no deviation from the Law. "God of Abraham, Isaac and Jacob, am I responsible for the earthquake? Do I cause everything bad that happens to my family? Did I, unintentionally cause my blessed mother's death by being with an official from heathen Rome? If I am a part of you, oh God of Love, then I cannot hate those who are different in skin and ignorant of you. Please soften Abba's heart toward me. Help him understand my motives, and show me how to earn back his love."

When Anna returned with the narcotic brew for Sobe, she took the initiative by saying to Stolan, "You two must live with me until this house can be rebuilt. Joachim finished the servants' small house before he left for Jerusalem, so there is plenty of . . . " She stopped short, realizing that her own home might also be in ruins.

Stolan responded bitterly, "Neither of us will set foot in your unclean dwelling. We'll sleep in the street first!"

"I'm sorry you don't understand the life God has decreed for me. I obviously inherit my stubbornness from you, Abba."

Stolan's reply was prevented by the arrival of calm and capable Ezra, dressed as always in white linen. He quickly examined Sobe's injuries, then said, "There's a break in one arm. The rest are severe cuts and bruises, which I'll treat with this ointment. Anna, see if you can find some strips of cloth and some wickers. That's mandrake she's drinking?"

Anna nodded and began searching the ruins for the items. Ezra turned to Stolan. "I suspect you've blamed Anna for Emerentiana's death, since she doesn't fit your rigid laws of behavior. Yet she is so like her mother. Anger will only consume you, because Anna follows her destiny, regardless what you or anyone else may think. I wish she were my daughter. And I wish you'd come to your senses, dear friend."

Anna knew her father respected Ezra's opinion more than anyone else's. However, when he spoke it pertained to his wife.

"I'll send Gideon to get able-bodied neighbors. We must move Emerentiana to the House of Prayer. Thank

God, it is still standing. There I will try to revive her."

Ezra nodded, then turned to Sobe, who, by now, was adequately drugged to endure the pain of setting her arm. He gave it a skillful twist, bound it up, and Sobe fell into a deep sleep. Isabel had returned home in the meantime, unhurt, so Anna put her sister in the servant's care. "My father needs me now more than Sobe," she said.

When she entered the House of Prayer, Stolan had just begun chanting the 119th Psalm. Anna knew he believed it was possible to restore a newly-dead person to life through the magical intervention of this psalm when it was spoken in a special manner. During Stolan's recitation of its twenty-two sections, each corresponding to a different letter of the Hebrew alphabet, Stolan skillfully shuffled the sequence of the sections so that the matching Hebrew letters spelled her mother's name.

When Stolan finished the recitation, he waited hopefully for some reaction from his wife's lifeless body. Finally, when nothing changed, he said to Anna, "I must try something else. Bring me the Pentateuch."

He riffled through the first five books of the Holy Testament until he spotted the name of one of the matriarchs. It was Rachel, so he began calling his wife by that name in his prayers. According to an age-old belief, this act might deceive the Angel of Death so that the original decree would be changed to one of life.

Meanwhile, Anna located two candles, lit them, and placed them at her mother's head. Ezra joined them now, and Stolan told him sadly, "I've done everything I know, but she doesn't respond. We must say the sacred Shema."

Together the three of them repeated seven times, "Hear, O Israel, The Lord our God, the Lord is one."

Gideon arrived with potsherds to place over Emerentiana's eyes and mouth. This custom, they all believed, would prevent evil spirits, who circle about the body of the dead, from penetrating it and causing harm. Then Stolan turned to Anna. "It's time to wash your mother. She must be ready for burial as soon as possible."

Anna worked quickly to prepare the body as best she could outside of a home. She anointed it with fragrant essences of aloe and myrrh, and Ezra brought white linen cloth to use as a shroud. Together they reverently sewed her into it, making sure her fingers were not closed. None of them actually knew why this was important.

By law, the dead were buried the same day, but the shattered town had so many corpses that grave diggers were unable to keep up with the demand. Emerentiana's funeral would have to take place the next morning. A few friends joined Anna, Stolan, and Ezra for a vigil at her side through the night. Isabel would care for Sobe at a neighbor's house.

After the burial the following day, Ezra suggested to Stolan, "Why don't you and Sobe stay with me until your home can be rebuilt?"

Stolan's reply pleased Anna. "I appreciate that. The new home, however, will be for Sobe. I intend to move to Sepphoris and retire."

With Ezra present, Anna took a chance to ask her father, "Must you continue to hate me, Abba?"

Stolan was taken aback by her question. Stroking his short salt and pepper beard, he thought carefully a few moments before answering.

"Anna, I shall never be separated from the holy Law, not even in death. Throughout my life, I have loved the Torah more than my own flesh and blood. Yet, at this moment, I'm not so sure I have been right in interpreting it."

Anna's face became radiant. This difficult concession amounted to his forgiveness of her. She made the first move to embrace him, and for some time they wept together in an unspoken reconciliation. Anna thought how ironic it was that it took a shattering earthquake to soften her father's heart.

Not until after Emerentiana's burial did Anna have time to think of the great devastation and loss of life in Judea. Was Joachim among the thousands reported killed in Palestine? All she could do was continue to wait and pray for his return. She recalled, with mixed feelings, Julian's romantic overtures. He both attracted and repelled her. He accepted her, a childless, married woman, for what she was. It was painful to be isolated from young women her age and lack the religious support of her people. Without Joachim, her life would be exceedingly lonely.

The next time she encountered Julian, she would explain what sorcery was and what healing was not. Sorcery used evil entities to do one's work; healing used the infinite power of God to alter the unwanted condition. Surely he would understand this difference and stop threatening her. Could it be that he was unconsciously in search of a spiritual anchor, and in her, he hoped to find it? If not, then the time would come when they would square off against each other in a life-and-death struggle.

She needed Joachim desperately to comfort her empty life. He accepted her excursions into the mystical world of healing with no criticism. In spite of the torment of her barrenness, he never failed to tell her often, "We share our failings and our bounty. I will never divorce you, because it would be like cutting out my heart. I can bear the scorn and ridicule if you stay in love with me."

Anna remembered her reply. "I will always love you and cherish my marriage." Yet the sparkle she once had in her life was gone.

Rumors of the great devastation from the earthquake in Judea rode the winds of Galilee. It was claimed thirty thousand people lost their lives in Jerusalem alone. Herod had called in armies from Rome to start its rebuilding. Julian had been ordered to the Holy City to direct disaster relief.

Where could Joachim be? Their home in Nazareth had been miraculously spared from damage. She must wait and occupy herself with weaving and sewing.

Zandra came to her one day and announced boldly, "I will give birth to a baby before you do."

Anna was dumbfounded. "Do you know who the father is?"

"Of course—the only man I've bedded down with. Julian."

"Oh no!" Anna was outraged that he had taken advantage of this unsophisticated girl. Had he hoped to prove his manliness to her by impregnating her servant? So this was how he decided to punish her for rejecting his advances. What a fox he was!

Trying to remain calm, she said, "Would you like to return to your parents after the baby comes? I understand they have completed their term of indenture." She didn't want her home to become a nursery for Julian's child. How cleverly he managed to have a pliant spy in her house. Julian knew everything she did and said!

Yet, she didn't blame Zandra for submitting to him. Despised as a cripple for so many years, it was understandable that she would revel in her new straight body. A man of lesser persuasion and power would have been equally successful in seducing her. Julian's animal magnetism was not easy to ignore. If he returned to Nazareth,

Anna would suggest he give some compensation to the Samaritan. After all, the girl hadn't sold her services and was not a whore.

With the whereabouts of Joachim still a mystery, Anna tried to visit Sobe often during her recovery from a broken arm and grief over their mother's passing. Their relationship remained strained, but when Anna found it necessary to reveal Zandra's predicament, Sobe was contemptuous.

"Joachim should divorce you! Your bleeding heart attracts scum to you, so the Lord God continues to express his displeasure of your life style. Joachim was a promising young man when you married him. Now you have dragged him down to your sinful level!"

"I don't expect you to love me, Sobe, but at least try to understand me. I worship a God of mercy, whose plan for my life is still unknown to me. I refuse to think he is punishing me. I only know that I'm under his divine direction. Of course, I'm not content with myself. I rail constantly against my shortcomings, but Emi gave me hope before she died."

"What did she say?"

Anna shook her head, determined to let Sobe's curiosity bedevil her.

* * *

A bedraggled, exhausted Joachim finally came home. He took Anna in his arms, tears of gratitude flowing down his sunburned cheeks. "I feared I would never see you again." He flooded her with kisses, but she asked him no questions until she had bathed his feet and given him a drink of balsam water.

"What kept you?" Anna asked finally.

"You've no idea of the chaos in Jerusalem. The Roman Legionnaires wouldn't allow anyone to leave, since we all were forced to help bury the dead, rebuild streets and dwellings, and repair King Hezekiah's tunnel. You remember that it supplies water for the city from the Spring of Bihon to a reservoir inside the walls. The earthquake ripped it apart, making the situation life-threatening. Cisterns that stored water for emergencies were split open."

Anna's first thought was to give him a good meal. While he ate, she told him of Zandra's condition, but not who the father was.

"She'll go home to her parents after the child is born," Anna said. "I couldn't bear to watch grow an infant not our own." Then she changed the subject.

"Was our home in Jerusalem destroyed?" she asked.

"Since it is dug partially into a limestone hill, the walls held and there was little damage to repair. The incredible destruction and death were caused, not so much by earth movement, but by falling mud bricks and hysteria. Incidentally, I saw that Roman, Julian, there assigning work. Herod has promoted him to a position of considerable power. I'm accustomed to being treated with scorn, but when we passed each other, I saw deep hatred in his eyes. I wonder why."

"What happened to the donkey you rode from here? Why did you have to walk home?"

"The night I finally made my escape, a band of robbers beat me into unconsciousness and took my money and food, plus the animal. Being home again with you has made me whole."

"Joachim, let's spend a month or two at your sheep camp—no Romans, no servants, no one to revile us. Judith can run this place, and she gets along well with Zandra."

Anna paused, then in answer to Joachim's surprised look, she explained, "I'd like to be away from people, where we can renew our love. Close to nature, the Moses cloth might work its magic for us. It pains me unbearably to see Zandra's burgeoning body."

"Agreed. But how long before she gives birth?"

"Less than two months. We'll return in time for the delivery. I've already engaged a midwife."

It was the delightful month of Tyar when Joachim and Anna rode their donkeys to the slopes of Mount Tabor. Two other animals carried provisions for them to the comfortable hut Joachim had built there. The shepherds' shelter was some distance away.

The woods were in leaf, and the mountain streams raced with joy. Vast banks of orchids lined the water, and buttercups dotted the hillsides. The spring migration northward had begun, bringing great flocks of storks overhead. Ground birds were feverishly making their nests in the earth along the singing waters. It was the time when many animals bore their young—hares and conies, wild boar, and ibex.

Joachim said with envy, "See how nature is intent on multiplying."

"Take heart in the words of my dying mother," Anna said. "She promised us a child, remember."

In the stillness of the mountain, where the stars hung just out of reach, they made love with total abandon. Joachim didn't wait for darkness now, but undressed Anna in the afternoon and carried her to their bed. His gentle touch sent her ready fires flaming.

Between kisses on her soft breasts and firm thighs, Joachim whispered, "In the panic in Jerusalem, I tried to recall your every feature—your heart-shaped face; the perfect nose; the eager, full lips; your cascading, sweet-smelling hair; topaz eyes beneath a brow that never frowns—but it was too painful." His hands slid over her shoulders and down her arms, deliberately tantalizing

her, forcing her to want him with every fiber of her being, letting the tension build between them, allowing her
banked fires to anticipate the fulfillment of their desires.
She whispered, "I love you beyond life itself, Joachim."
He could hold back his passions no longer, and his
burning body possessed her in a rapturous embrace.
With no one to disturb them, their passions resulted
in a deeper, more satisfying love, but not the hoped-for
pregnancy. The time came for them to return to Nazareth.
Zandra's baby was due to arrive.

A tragedy waited for them. The child was stillborn.
Anna was both angry and sad. She must keep Zandra
now, since the confused girl needed understanding and
emotional support.

Anna and Joachim sat in the garden discussing ways
they might prove to a sacred and majestic God that they
deserved to be "fruitful, increase and fill the earth."

Joachim said, "Nothing seems to help. The priests say
only, 'When your wife is with child, we will accept your
sacrifice. Not before.'"

Anna spoke with determination. "Nevertheless, let's
go to Jerusalem. I want to see the extravagant new
temple that Herod has built. Perhaps the priests will remember me from my ten years of study there. Let us begin with gifts of doves. If they are rejected, then we will
try flour and oil, as the very poor people do."

Joachim studied her suggestion for a moment, then
said, "I spoke briefly with your father today. He told me
that the Zealots—those fanatics who use a short Roman
dagger called a sica—are now on a marauding spree in
Galilee. They are out to waylay not just Romans, but also
those of our people—Romanophiles, they call them—
who cooperate with our detested conquerors. Do many
people know that Julian has visited you?"

Anna's face blanched. "The whole neighborhood

watches everything at this place. Wouldn't we be safer now in Jerusalem?"

"Yes and no. Stolan also told me that Julian has been elevated to the position of legate, or emissary of Herod the Great. His son, Herod Antipas, is now Galilee's new governor. We can expect Julian to come here on business, but will he continue his sexual relationship with Zandra?"

"Not if I can stop it, but he is a determined man." Anna flushed, remembering Julian's passionate kisses and electric physical domination when he saved her life during the earthquake.

She suggested, "Another reason for going to the Holy City now is that we'll be less of a target among the hundred thousand other residents there. The servants aren't likely to be harmed by the Zealots."

Joachim agreed to the journey at once, but, on second thought, Anna wondered if they were exchanging one fearful situation for another.

CHAPTER 11

Julian shaved carefully, washed his yellow curls while he bathed, and added a bit of perfume to his chest. A summons to hurry to Herod had arrived an hour earlier, and Julian had laid out his best tunic and a new linen toga for meeting this ruthless vassal of Rome's new emperor—Octavianus, who had named himself Augustus. Now, Herod aimed at turning Jerusalem into a Greek center. People spoke of him as the Augustus of Judea. Greek scholars arrived with each ship to encourage literature and art. New ideas and Grecian styles of clothing became evident in public gatherings.

Julian suspected why Herod had selected him as a confidant and adviser. He had been educated in Greek ideals, and, at their previous meetings, Julian had advised him on building a theater and amphitheater where Greek athletic events now took place. Later, at his prodding, Herod promised there would be gladiatorial contests, with naked wrestling for entertainment.

Yet, as Julian approached the sumptuous gardens leading to Herod's Greek palace, he wondered if the benefits Herod had brought to Palestine balanced the injustices he imposed on its people. He was a brilliant dictator, all right. He could outtalk and outscheme you at the very moment you thought he was taking your advice. As his vassal, Julian must be wary of him. What did the powerful procurator want of him today?

A hardened cavalry soldier escorted Julian to an elegantly furnished room where Herod sat, drinking a heavy red wine. A second goblet, filled to the brim, waited for Julian.

"I have important news for you, Legate!" Herod called loudly. "Augustus has noted from your reports that the Israelites are increasing too fast for us Romans. The Emperor has decreed that male Romans in this far-flung Empire who are under the age of sixty must marry and start producing more Roman babies. You have less than a month in which to find yourself a wife."

Julian gulped the wine hastily, thinking this was ridiculous.

"Does it make any difference what nationality she is?" he asked hopefully. He would marry no one but fascinating Anna bat Stolan.

"Marry a whore if you wish, so long as you procreate for the Empire." Herod rose to his feet, an erect, proud hulk of a man. His great nose separated a pair of tormented eyes, and deep lines furrowed his face. Today, he looked ugly to Julian. Several wens cursed his cheeks, and the wine brought out beads of sweat on his swarthy, broad face. There was something of a beast about this man.

Herod paced before him with irritable movements. "Sit down—I think better when I walk. I need your advice, Julian. I am surrounded by nothing but spies, and worn out by the nightly demands of my nine young wives. I think they are trying to kill me through sexual excess. Now, tell me, why do these Palestinian Jews hate my guts? They scheme night and day to be free of my authority. Be frank with me, since I'm up to my navel in fawning, prostrate advisers. They say only what they think I want to hear."

"Very well, brilliant sire," Julian began in a soft voice. "I see you as generous in many ways to your subjects, but you have no morals. You show enormous skills of leadership—a ruler beyond compare, but you have no scruples. You brought an uneasy prosperity to the country following the earthquake, through your extravagant rebuilding program, but you tax the workers exorbitantly—far beyond their ability to pay. So they despise you thoroughly."

Herod dropped onto a chair, stunned by Julian's penetrating frankness. "I don't think I'm entirely to blame for their passions. There's something else stirring them to revolt. Palestine is gripped in Messianic convulsions. The Jews—I refuse to call them Israelites—keep asking me unanswerable questions: When will the Messiah appear? Is he alive now in our midst, hiding out until the invisible God tells him to appear? How will we recognize this new king, when there are dozens of self-proclaimed messiahs running among us? How then will we be able to distinguish the real Messiah from the impostors? Will there be signs in the heavens warning us of his imminent coming? I am a Jew, too, yet I get no help from the Sanhedrin in the temple. What have you heard?"

"Only the rumor that he is not yet born," Julian repeated Anna's words.

"But I am told that, when the magic moment comes, we'll see him sitting at our main gate among the poor and wretched. There he will suffer as a leper, waiting for the Almighty's command to reveal his true self. First, though, they tell me the people must undergo suffering beyond all imagination.

"The earthquake and its resultant great loss of life might have been a sign of that. It could have been the great tribulation that prophets say precedes the Messiah's coming."

"The earthquake wasn't punishment enough. The oracles of Rome claim that blood will ooze from the trees, rocks and streams will cry out in agony, and the heavens will resound with the clashes of fighting warriors. I don't know what to believe. Do these rumors come from the vivid imaginations of hysterical people?"

"Sire, I'm convinced that the great Augustus in Rome is the Messiah the Israelites have cried for over countless centuries. In time, they will recognize him as the Anointed One."

Herod clapped his hands in approval. "You give me more support than any one of my officials. You have considerably relieved my worries. Ask me for a favor in return for this valuable interpretation of the 'Messiah madness.'"

Julian drew a heavily-ringed hand over his eyes to conceal the surprised glee he felt. He weighed the offer for a few moments, then said craftily, "Since Imperial Rome orders me to marry, there is an Israelite woman I desire to own. She lives in Nazareth, but unfortunately has a husband. I request your permission to get rid of him—an unlettered shepherd of no importance."

Herod laughed loudly. "So you fell in love with one of our women! Half of my wives are Jews, and I can guarantee they are marvelous in bed. Passion runs in their veins. This woman has no children?"

"She has been childless for years."

"The priests here disdain Galileans. They are too simple, not orthodox enough for Judeans. Fishermen and farmers, aren't they? I can recommend a priest who has no sympathy for anyone from that province—name is Uziel. Don't worry. I have the priesthood under my thumb. You would be amazed at the intrigues and outright murders committed by the High Priest himself. He rules over some twenty thousand priests and Levites now—half of them rogues." Then, as if realizing the wine had loosened his tongue, he asked, "Does the husband come to Jerusalem with sacrificial gifts for the temple?"

Julian nodded.

"If sufficient silver drops into the hand of the priest I mentioned, he will put your Galilean in chains for you. His act is justified, since YHVH—I dare not pronounce the secret name of God—despises those who have failed to multiply."

Julian knew that this scheming procurator would kill his own children if he could profit from it. He felt uneasy being Herod's confidant. Herod was reputed to devise the cruelest of punishments for those who crossed him. Julian guessed why he, himself, had progressed up the well-graduated hierarchy to his present position close to the procurator: He spoke Greek and Aramaic fluently. While the peasants spoke only Aramaic, Herod insisted on Greek being used in both government and literature. He was intent on making this a Graeco-Roman city.

Even though more and more people hated Herod, the ruler maintained order in the five provinces he controlled—Judea, Idumea, Samaria, Galilee, and Perea. Julian suspected that Herod wanted to be more than the King of Judea. He intended to be worshipped by the Greek world for having embellished Jerusalem beyond anyone's imagination. His unbounded dreams encouraged Julian to do likewise.

He would have Anna—the remote beauty, the mysterious magician, the woman he desired more than power or wealth. He relived a thousand times the ecstasy of holding her unconscious body in his arms during the earthquake and kissing her soft lips, her fragrant hair and face. He had never considered marrying. But now, with a command from his idol, Caesar Augustus, the idea appealed to him. If he must, he would give up the thirty thousand Roman Gods for one invisible. But would he have to undergo circumcision? He refused to think of that horror now.

Walking back to his living quarters, Julian paused to admire the towering Corinthian columns and extensive porticoes of the Temple of Solomon. To balance their dramatic effect, Herod had placed high at its entrance, a great golden eagle, symbol of powerful Rome. Julian smiled. Israelites entering to worship had to pass this graven image—forbidden by their Torah. No wonder the Judeans constantly plotted against Herod.

Getting closer to the temple entrance, he was surprised to be confronted by a stone block inscribed in Greek. It read, "No alien (that meant no non-Jew) may enter within the balustrade and the enclosure around the sanctuary. Whoever is caught will have only himself to blame for his death."

Julian was dismayed. How could he speak with a priest, when he couldn't even enter the place? He stood, highly irritated and uncertain what to do, when a priest noticed him and came down to speak with him.

"Can I be of help?" he asked in a rasping voice. "I am Uziel."

Julian noticed the shifty eyes of this huge man whose black beard reached to his waist. He'd have to go through with the plan.

"I am Julian, confidant and emissary of Herod to Galilee. Herod told me that if a childless married man enters the temple with unwanted gifts of sacrifice, you are empowered to arrest him. Is that true?"

"Yes, but only if someone specifically asks that this be done. Otherwise, we simply refuse the gift and turn him away."

"The man I want seized is Joachim ben Gideon. He has been childless for many years."

"Yes, I know the man—a wealthy shepherd. We have refused his gifts several times." Uziel's hand was extended as he spoke.

Julian dropped a handful of sesterces in his palm.

"Your request is granted. I'll notify you when I have Joachim in chains."

They parted, Julian walked for a few steps, then paused in the summer shade of a spreading bay tree to listen to the high wailing of the eunuch priests that drifted through the still air. Two young men stood nearby, discussing marriage. Julian overheard one say, "The sopher told me that if I die without fathering a son, I'll have no eternal life."

That reminded Julian of the Roman belief that if a man left no son to tend his gravesite, his spirit would be punished forever. It would be well, then, to marry. His son by Anna would be especially handsome, inheriting her topaz eyes and refined features. Why did he insist on marrying Anna when he had only to ask any of a hundred women to be his wife? In Jerusalem alone, there were innumerable beauties worthy of his name, but they held none of her mystery.

Anna not only understood Greek, but her Aramaic was melodious. She would be a sensation in Rome. He could imagine her walking with him about the Forum shops, visiting the many temples Augustus had built, strolling under the colonnades that moderated the summer sun,

and attending performances in the theater named for
Marcellus, son-in-law of the powerful Emperor. Surely
Anna would want to visit this sophisticated capital, ruled
by a god.

Augustus had surprised everyone recently by declar-
ing that severe penalties would be imposed on celibates,
spinsters, and childless wives. Marriage had suddenly
become obligatory throughout the Empire, not only for
males less than sixty years of age but for women less than
fifty. Augustus was determined not to permit Roman
blood to be diluted with that of aliens. Yet, since Palestine was a part of the Empire, there should be no problem with Julian's marriage to Anna, descendant of King
David.

CHAPTER 12

Anna and Joachim's house in the Holy City was close
by the spring and pool of Siloam. The rear had been built
in the hollowed-out rocky hillside, and a masonry wall
surrounded the front section. This gave the house a privacy they both wanted.

It was a far simpler dwelling than the one in Nazareth.
A fireplace occupied its center, with a smoke opening in
the roof. Screens formed by suspended rugs separated
the cooking and eating areas from the sleeping quarters.
Near the entry was a prayer alcove. There Anna kept the
venerated objects from her parents' sacred chest. After
Emerentiana's death, Stolan gave it to Anna as a gesture
of reconciliation. However, this created added friction
with Sobe. Each day, Anna and Joachim prayed over
Sara's lock of hair, Joseph's bone, and Abraham's goblet.
Joachim's prayer was always the same: Let us bear a
child. Anna's was: Let me be a healer of those who suffer.

They continued to give one-third of their earnings to the temple, even though Joachim's offerings were rejected. Ezra advised Anna to discontinue drinking milk, following the admonition of the Essenes. She promptly substituted water flavored with a few drops of terebinth sap.

"Today I will accompany you to the temple when you bring doves," Anna told her husband. "Perhaps I am the one who has displeased God by staying away these many years."

They passed the fortress, the Antonia, impregnable with its four towers protected by steep inclines lined with slick stones. From this part of the city, they got a glimpse of Herod's imposing palace and its magnificent gardens graced with bronze statues. Not far away was the tremendous complex of the renovated temple. While retaining the ground plan and interior arrangement of the original temple of Solomon, Herod had set the building higher, with three stories, and adorned their facades in extravagant Graeco-Roman style.

Anna felt uneasy at the embellishments. The royal portico boasted towering Corinthian columns which lured one to public gardens and pools. The first wide flight of steps took them to the Court of Women. From there, they proceeded through gates of silver and gold, up another wide flight of stairs to the Court of the Priests. There in the open air rose the great altar where the priests offered burnt sacrifices to Yahweh.

Joachim whispered to Anna, "Herod has increased the number of priests greatly. There are twenty-four orders now, each with its own special duties. Our religion used to be simple. Now it's complicated beyond belief."

"Yes," Anna agreed. "The priests decide every aspect of our lives, from food, wearing apparel, and behavior to ritual matters. It has a suffocating effect."

Joachim smiled, unused to hearing complaints from her. "I wonder if Moses realized what a theocracy of total rule he created."

"When I was in training here, I took care of priestly garments and washed their sacred vessels. But young as I was, I saw that the High Priest was often motivated by politics and not love."

"Is that why you never came back here until today?"

Anna shook her head. "I never understood the need for sacrificing thousands upon thousands of animals to flatter the Deity. Why aren't the first fruits and vegetables, or wine, oil, and grains used in the sacrificial rites?"

"Your father said that, by offering Yahweh a gift of domestic animals, which man needs for life, we gladly deprive ourselves to give to him."

"So God needs the gift of dead animals?" Anna prodded him.

"Remember, the offering is wholly or partially burned. It can't be taken back, and it goes into the world of the invisible, where God resides. It takes on a spiritual form by rising in smoke. That brings Yahweh closer to us."

"Flour and oil would accomplish the same thing."

Joachim shook his head. "No, blood, as the lifegiving part of us, is necessary in the sacrifice."

"I intend to follow the teachings of the Essenes, who believe this practice is abominable," Anna said stubbornly.

"Dear Heart, we're quarreling over something that doesn't really affect our love for each other."

By now, they had entered the interior courts where carved figures of cherubim, palm trees, and flowers were all overlaid with gold. Priests and Levites hurried past and disappeared into storage rooms. There, Anna remembered, were kept the temple treasures, the ceremonial vestments, the two menorot, the sacrificial knives, and the musical instruments used for the services. She smelled the familiar aroma of freshly-baked shewbread. It made her recall how the select maidens prepared the ritual bath of purification for the priests and checked the woodshed to make sure there were sufficient logs for the sacrificial fires. That was a long time ago. She was now twenty-three years of age and had been married for seven years.

She turned to Joachim. "Go deliver the doves now. I'll continue into the temple to pray for your success."

Halfway up the broad stairs, Anna stopped to look back. She was surprised to catch a glimpse of Julian in the street in front of the entrance. She thought he would be in Galilee carrying out his new functions. She also saw Joachim as he approached the animal-holding pens with his doves. She waited to see what would transpire. To her shock, after a brief conversation, a priest tossed aside the birds in rejection, then beckoned to two guards to seize Joachim. They hurried him away from the steps into the street.

Anna rushed down the two flights of stairs, but by the time she reached Joachim, the guards had put him in chains. They forced him off the temple grounds and were about to take him elsewhere. Anna raced up to the men screaming, "What are you doing?"

From the surprised look on their faces, they hadn't expected to encounter her here. One spoke gruffly, "You should be glad to get rid of a husband who is despised by God. Leave us at once, or I shall put you in chains, too!"

Anna didn't flinch, her eyes blazed with fury. She feared they intended to crucify Joachim as they did all critics of Rome. "Oh, God of Abraham, Isaac, and Jacob, save Joachim from harm! He is my whole life!"

She told herself, "I've practiced for years, under Ezra's guidance, to become a master of the cosmic laws of creation. He taught me the technique of imaging clearly a blueprint of the condition to be changed. With all my power, I now reach for those higher octaves and get from the God of Israel my beloved's life. Release him!"

As she stepped closer to them, Joachim tried to stop her. "Don't come any closer! Go home! God will save me!"

Julian approached her just as Anna surrounded herself with a rotating column of sparking white light. "Remember our experience with Ezra! Free my husband!" she cried.

Julian hesitated briefly, stunned by seeing the swirling column of light envelop her. "Guards, remove the chains!" he ordered. With a clatter, they dropped from Joachim's limbs.

Immediately, convulsions began to rack Julian's body. He fell to the ground, unconscious, mouth open, writhing and helpless. The strange, gurgling sounds of an epileptic seizure came from his lips.

Joachim rushed toward his wife.

"Stay back a moment, Joachim," she cried. "Don't touch me yet!"

He stopped and watched the cloud of light dissipate, like mist in the sun. Then Anna held out her arms to him for a loving embrace. Before them, Julian lay motionless on his back in a deep sleep. Rattling snores came from his gaping mouth.

"Come, let us go home," Anna said in a trembling voice. "He won't try this again."

In a tone of amazement, Joachim said, "Blessed wife, you saved me from heaven knows what fate. I won't ask you how you did it because I know it's a special gift."

"It may not always work." She frowned. "I had no knowledge of Julian's affliction. When the time is right, I must try to heal him of his epilepsy."

"It's inconceivable—you have no hatred of him? You

must be an angel in disguise, walking the earth. I'm the luckiest person alive."

"No, Joachim. I'm the lucky one to have such an understanding husband." She put her arm around him, and they headed for home without a backward glance at the sleeping Roman official.

* * *

The next day a messenger delivered to Anna a beautiful chaplet of wild celery leaves. The attached note, written in Greek, read, "From the Vanquished."

Anna understood the message. Victors of contests in both Greece and Rome were crowned with garlands of wild celery. By this unexpected act of defeat, Julian acknowledged the superior power of her invisible God over his thirty thousand Roman divinities. Yet, she felt no exultation for what she had done. She had greater problems than Julian's interest in her.

She worried a great deal over Joachim, since they lived in a sterile world, without friends. Her barrenness ostracized them from the mainstream of life. What more could she do to become with child? She had tried the bitter moss tea from the temple walls and the insipid-tasting fruit of the mandrake bush, with no results. Ezra, her wise and trusted mentor, had moved to the Essene settlement at Qumran. Her sister, Sobe, avoided them; sister Esmeria never came to visit; Stolan withdrew to a near-solitary life in Sepphoris. It was depressing to envision the future without friends or family.

She again used the Essene salutation to prayer: "Oh, Heavenly Father and Earthly Mother, I can weep no more. My soul is dry of tears. But soften the heart of Julian, who must one day know God."

Why did her pulse quicken at the sight of him? Was it his boldness that challenged her own inner strength? For some intangible reason, she sensed their destinies were bound together in a strange relationship. What would that be as each aimed to bend the other to his will?

PART II

CHAPTER 1

Anna and Joachim, on their nineteenth wedding anniversary, returned to Galilee, hoping the climate there would be better for him. Joachim had aged considerably and had grown withdrawn and uncommunicative. The temple priests still refused to accept his sacrificial lambs, and the worshippers in the House of Prayer turned him away from Sabbath services. His youthful vigor lessened with each passing year, and he became suspicious of everyone except Anna. He stubbornly held to the opinion that God was not unjust in denying them children, but that his own people were bigoted beyond redemption.

In desperation, Anna sent an urgent message to Joachim's two brothers and a sister in Shiloh to visit them. His health was declining fast.

She told him repeatedly, "I love you with every fiber of my being. I couldn't love you more if we had a dozen children. You are my life, never forget that."

His reply was stubborn and bitter. "I won't stop asking God the reason for his denial of my deepest wish. With my dying breath I will demand to know why? Why?"

His depression spilled over into Anna's moods, and she found herself becoming more negative in her thoughts. This worried her and she fought daily the impulse to feel sorry for herself. She was now thirty-six years of age and feeling old. It was up to younger women to bear Israelites.

Joachim's two brothers arrived within the week, accompanied by his young sister, Hermana. It turned out to be a joyous occasion for Anna, since they waited on her as if she were a queen, anticipated her every wish, complimented her when she did the slightest thing out of the ordinary, and were effusive with praise over the meals, the house, even the weather. Anna suspected it was a conspiracy to bolster the morale of both her and Joachim. She loved them for it, since she was starved for approval by her own people.

Joachim, too, blossomed under the jovial and caring attention of his relatives.

Anna's favorite among them was Cleophas, a handsome, square-shouldered giant with a body of unleashed energy. He had honest blue eyes, that softened whenever he looked at Anna, and a stunning head of rich auburn hair. He was a caring person, with four adult children and an invalid wife. Yet, he never criticized anyone or complained that life wasn't fair. Anna liked him very much.

Then there was Salamo—lank, tall, and red-haired, with the sensitivity of an artist. He took pride in creating fine bronze and copper jewelry and vases that commanded high prices in the best shops in Jerusalem. He rarely agreed or disagreed with his brothers, keeping his opinions to himself. But when he and Anna were alone, he became talkative and eager to tell of his children's activities and his concern for his wife's health. Anna suspected he was a complicated man who assumed most people wouldn't understand him and so withdrew into a remote reserve.

On one occasion when the two of them were alone, he said without preliminary, "I admire you beyond belief. You bring out the best in all of us. Whenever I look at you, I think of the angels the psalmist sings about. But why are you so unhappy? Joachim has steadfastly refused to divorce you, insisting that he is the one cursed by sterility. As I sit here now, talking quietly with you, a radiance has formed about you that I have never seen around any priest or holy man. Can you explain that?"

Anna smiled to cover her embarrassment at his compliments. She answered seriously, "Everything is in the eyes of the beholder. It is you, Salamo, who sees the beauty in our world due to your own high spiritual thrust. I am a mirror for you."

He studied her intently for several minutes. Then tears filled his eyes, and he left her to take a walk.

In the family circle was also fifteen-year-old Hermana, who insisted upon filling Zandra's role until she, herself, married. The Samaritan had found a husband during Anna's long stay in Jerusalem. Hermana was easy to be around. She smiled and sang a lot and showed great initiative in helping with the housework. To Anna, she was a foster child to be loved as her own.

One thing Anna did not mention to anyone when Zandra departed: Julian had boldly bought the house next to hers—an obvious scheme to be able to spy on her when in Nazareth, since his source of information was gone. He had grown in power in Herod's inner circle of confidential advisers. He was now an envoy to Samaria, as well as Galilee, for the powerful procurator. The black stallion was long gone, but Julian now rode a high-stepping, gray gelding. She had been mistaken to believe the move back to Galilee would rid her of him. He was now closer than ever. She wondered if he continued to have seizures. She must remember to ask him. Deep within her was the haunting fear that, when it was most important, her power to heal would be denied her.

Often she tried to analyze her feelings toward Julian. She was not in love with him, yet they were bound together in some unfathomable way. In spite of his many liaisons, he had never married, yet had pursued her relentlessly throughout their twenty years' acquaintance. What was there about this intolerable man that held such fascination for her?

One day, when Joachim left for the mountains, she knew that Julian would come to see her. She dreaded and yet looked forward to the encounter, wondering what he would say regarding his scheme to have Joachim imprisoned—or worse. That was a long time ago, but the episode was still vivid in her mind.

There must be a resolution made of their uncomfortable relationship. She would never forget the experience of being seated on the saddle cloth in front of Julian on his black stallion. She remembered her feelings of great love when she thought he was Joachim, embracing and kissing her.

She couldn't help but be indebted to him for having saved her life. He was thoughtful—he had brought her temple moss to help her conceive. Or was he a schemer, toying with her needs? She couldn't be sure. She dreaded, yet anticipated with an inner trembling, their next encounter. He would wait patiently for the right moment when no one else was around.

They would meet alone as sure as the sun rises. Was she strong enough to withstand his magnetic force? She didn't know. She must remember to ask for the protection of the angels and not to be caught unawares, else Julian could crash through her emotional barrier. She feared him—that was it. Yet, in a strange way, she was fascinated by his arrogance, his unabashed need for her. Their relationship was not just mental but had physical overtones that bothered her immensely. She had to take a definite stand with Julian to break the link that bound them. She must put an end to her contradictory feelings. But did she really want to sever their mutual attraction? She couldn't answer that.

Joachim appeared to be in a better frame of mind by the time his brothers left for home. They persuaded him to make one final attempt to have his sacrificial sheep accepted in the temple. New priests were now in charge of the offerings to Yahweh.

So, against Anna's advice, Joachim set out for his mountain camp to obtain the needed animals. From there, he would follow the same route south to Jerusalem that Anna and her father had traveled when she left the temple service. Joachim promised to return to Anna within two weeks.

During his absence, Judith and Hermana did all the shopping so that Anna was able to stay safely ensconced in her high-walled garden. She spent much of her time in prayer and meditation, since she feared Joachim would die of grief if the priests again refused his gift.

*   *   *

It was a beautiful fall day in Elul, the month for gathering the grapes. The first flocks of storks had made their appearance, and Nazareth was teeming with caravans and visitors from other provinces.

Anna had to escape from her self-imposed confinement. She hadn't seen her neighbor, Julian, around for some time, so she decided to risk going to the mountains where Joachim and she had spent their first thrilling hours following their betrothal. There she would renew her loving devotion to this patient man and recall the joy of marrying him.

She informed Judith of her plans, mounted a trusty donkey, and took a route that did not pass Julian's house. She sang to the animal as she rode sidesaddle, while keeping control of her lunch and skin of terebinth water.

She was happier this moment than she had been in many years. Cleophas, Salomo, and Hermana had made her feel so worthwhile and dear to each of them. Their visit helped both Joachim and her.

She located the great terebinth tree that loomed in the maquis of oak where she had first kissed Joachim. There was enough water in the small stream for dipping her head scarf and cooling her face. She picked a few late flowers and stuck them in her heavy hair, feeling young again for the first time in nearly twenty years. She dropped to the earth, loving its pungent smell. She lay full-length on the drying grasses and breathed deeply of their fragrance. She stretched her arms high, reaching toward the cloudless sky. "I embrace you, God, with all my heart and soul," she said aloud.

A voice answered her, "And I embrace you with all my heart." It was a man's voice and it didn't come from the sky.

She spun about on the ground and looked into the triumphant, smiling face of Julian. His golden curls were now silvered at the temples and his former icy-green eyes held a warmth she had never seen before. He had obviously followed her, tied his horse some distance away and approached her quietly on foot.

Anna sat up, quickly pulling her long robe over her exposed legs. Then she remembered she had removed her scarf and that exposure of a woman's hair to anyone but family was held to be a form of nudity and an open invitation to sin.

Julian read her mind, snatched up the drying scarf and thrust it under the belt of his tunic. He spoke in a serious tone, "We need to discuss several things, Anna, all of them dealing with you and me."

When Anna remained silent, he continued in a voice that sounded as if he had memorized his speech and spoken it a thousand times. "You are a special kind of sorceress, I know, because you have me bewitched. I can't be happy far from you. I am like the sand on a beach where the high tide is in. You are that tide, always tugging at my emotions. What am I to do?"

Anna didn't know how to reply.

He continued, "You sent me into an seizure in Jerusalem—though, I admit, I have had them many times before. But you left me in the street like a wounded dog." His voice had become harsh and accusing.

Anna did not wince. Her reply was controlled, although within she was shaken. "I could set you free of this ailment, Julian, if you changed your thinking. So long as there is hatred and revenge in your heart, I can do nothing to prevent further attacks."

Julian dropped to the ground close beside her. He spoke quietly as if to himself, "I would give anything to be free of this humiliation, but no one has been able to help me. If I change to the person you want me to be, would you cure me?"

She felt his sensual magnetism and fought for control of her voice. "Not I, but my God can. Of course, your attitude and emotions must be right."

"What do you mean by that?"

She had to be straightforward. "You cannot covet a married woman. You definitely cannot covet me."

"I don't understand what you mean by coveting. I

want you for my wife. I must take you to Rome to meet
Caesar Augustus—the true Messiah for whom your
people have waited."

"What has changed you? I thought you wanted to take
me to Rome as your concubine." She felt happy and was
unable to keep the humor from her voice. What if he took
her into his arms? She was vulnerable.

Instead, Julian said soberly, "That was a long time ago.
I am no longer the passionate youth you first met. I'm
wiser and more in love with you than ever."

Anna regretted her lighthearted speech. She said seriously, "That is a delusion. You know I will be true to
Joachim till the day I die."

"Till the day he dies, you mean." Julian waved his arm
as if thrusting the idea far away. "You need a child. I could
give you one or many."

"Julian, we are migrating birds who pass in flight—
nothing more. If we are kind to each other, our wings will
grow stronger."

"I would change for you. I would love you alone."

"Only hypocrites and saints cause a person's morals
to change."

"Then there is hope for me—since you are a saint,
Anna. I realize that now. I beg you to heal me of epilepsy.
I have a deathly fear of having an attack before King
Herod, and again before you, whom I love passionately."

"If you became free of this disease, how would you
change inwardly? No outer manifestation without an inner change of heart and soul will last. You can't believe in
countless divinities and be an object of my healing work.
There is only one heavenly Father. Until you accept that
idea, and believe it, I can do nothing for you, Julian. I do
not heal. God works through me as his instrument and
makes a cure manifest."

Julian sat as if stricken, his sharp mind apparently

weighing her demands. Finally, he said in a subdued voice, "Anna, I wouldn't know how to pray to an unknown God."

Anna said softly, "I will help you."

She looked at the virile man beside her. He was a potent mixture of earthiness and passion and cunning. Why did she even consider the possibility of curing his epilepsy? Joachim would be shocked by such an act, yet she was driven to prove her ability to stop this ailment, which plagued so many people. She couldn't resist her great desire to make Julian whole.

The Roman finally raised his tormented eyes to her and said, "Could my search for something outside of myself be that I'm looking for your invisible God? Introduce me to him, Anna."

She rose to her knees on the grass. "Kneel with me, Julian, while I pray. Take my hand in yours. I'm not sure if I'm using the right method, but God will know and respond in the way he chooses. I will make myself only a channel for him to show his mercy on you. I may not be able to help you, but I'll try."

She grasped one of Julian's large hands in both of hers, annoyed at noticing the soft hairs on its back. She was surprised to feel no gaudy rings today on it. Why did she notice unimportant things like that at this critical time? She needed a few moments more in which to concentrate her forces.

"Close your eyes, Julian." Then she surrounded herself with an ever-widening globe of brilliant light, visualizing it encompassing not just the two of them but extending over the surrounding woods. Today, she was surprised to see, in her inner vision, sparkling diamonds in the light. Like crystals they danced while reflecting the colors of the rainbow.

Now she spoke aloud. "God of the Universe, change

the heart of this Roman, who needs to believe in Thee as
the one God, the one Creator of us all. If this be done, let
his disease vanish, make his life productive and a blessing to everyone. And may he always be my true friend.
Thank Thee, Lord God."

Julian knelt as if transfixed. Anna couldn't tell what
went on in his mind, but his face had softened. She felt
the ecstasy that always followed a healing. She said quietly, "Julian you are free of epilepsy, but only so long as
you harm no one. You can become more useful to society and eventually a great blessing to everyone."

She saw that he was still skeptical. No matter, she had
built a large fire in him, a thirst for the deity he had always scorned. It was not enough that his body was
healed. God must also heal his soul. It might take time
for that transformation.

Julian stood up and lifted Anna to her feet. He was
trembling as he held her at arm's length.

"I need time, Anna. The change is too great for me to
grasp in a few minutes. Caesar Augustus has decreed
that all unmarried men in Palestine must take a wife. You
Israelites are multiplying too fast for us. I am waiting
until you are a widow."

When Anna started to protest, he added, "I have a constant need for you. You are never out of my mind."

Anna stepped away from him, weighing her words
carefully. "Time will overcome this illusion. I ask only
one thing of you—several times a day, and at night before retiring, repeat aloud these words: "'I have a guardian angel assigned to me by Divine Decree. Through this
angel's love, I commune with the heart of God.'" She
paused briefly, then said, "Repeat it now after me."

Obediently he spoke the words twice to make sure he
had memorized them. Then he laughed softly. "You are
my guardian angel, Anna."

"No, no. I am not. I am showing you a new path to happiness."

"But you are that path, Anna. With you, I would be fulfilled."

"We have a mutual attraction, I admit, but it is the magnetic force of the souls. I don't understand it myself. We could never be man and wife. I can marry only from the blood line of King David. That is the law of Moses. You are a well man now, free of the humiliating fits. See to it you don't need any further chastisement from the healing God of the Universe."

Julian brought her two hands to his lips and kissed them. "You promise me help if I need it?"

"I promise." He left her then.

Anna couldn't see him go because tears of relief flooded her eyes.

CHAPTER 2

Four months passed, yet Joachim did not return home. Anna grew increasingly worried, since his shepherds claimed he had not come for sacrificial sheep to drive to the temple. Where had he gone? Was he still alive? Why had he promised, not only her, but his brothers that he would make a final attempt to persuade the priests to accept his offering? It was mystifying, since Anna's countless inquiries in both Nazareth and Sepphoris brought forth no inkling of the cause of his disappearance.

She finally sent an urgent inquiry to his brothers in Shiloh. Within a week, the oldest brother, Cleophas, came to her. He said that no one in his area had seen Joachim either. He immediately set out to question everyone he met in Galilee—farmers, shopkeepers, herdsmen, housewives. He combed the surrounding hills and went as far as Mount Carmel to query the monks there, yet there was no trace of the missing man anywhere. Cleophas was in no hurry to return to Shiloh since his invalid wife had recently died. Sharing their mutual grief supported both of them. At times they sat together in the courtyard, hoping that Joachim would suddenly put in his appearance.

The evening before Cleophas was to return home, Anna pointed to the sky. "Have you noticed how brilliant in color the sunsets have become? Autumn clouds are making their appearance too. That means the rains are not far off. Just as my lovely flowers have gone to seed, I, too, am withering a little more each day. I'm tormented by the thought that Joachim lies dead in a remote place where people never go."

Cleophas spoke gently. "I share with you the agony of uncertainty, but you will destroy yourself if you continue to despair. You must think of your future. God has special plans for you—in his wise timing. Now that you have been denied children, what do you seek from life?"

"The pleasure of healing people, of relieving pain. I draw such strength from you, Cleophas. You are very special. You are the only person who has been able to take away my feeling of guilt and unworthiness. Your coming has brought me great comfort."

Cleophas' deep blue eyes looked lovingly at her. He took her hands in his and kissed them. "You've replaced my pain with understanding. Along my route home tomorrow, I'll inquire in every house of prayer in Galilee and Samaria and Judea. If Joachim does not return soon, I will be back. You have never been weak, Anna. The Lord God will sustain you, and, I hope, me. We must continue to believe Joachim is alive, somewhere."

* * *

The night following Cleophas' departure, Anna was

awakened by the sound of celestial music. It was so exquisite, she was sure it came from a heavenly choir. She
sat up in her bed, the music faded away, and on the wall
next to her a large golden letter, M, appeared. What did it
mean? She slipped into a robe and went to her shrine.
There she removed the small casket given her by her father, Stolan, so long ago. She fingered lightly its holy objects, then prayed silently over them for some time. The
fresh night air invited her into her garden. She felt a high
elation now. She was happier than she had been in years.

She sat down on her customary meditation bench.
Why was she filled with this strange, all-encompassing
joy? Was Joachim on his way home? The high vibration
in her body and mind caused her to wait expectantly for
something to happen. Yet nothing stirred in the silent
yard. Nature slept.

Then a curious thing took place. A soft breeze came
out of the night and swirled around her with a sighing
sound. It enveloped her with the perfume of roses—delicate, intoxicating. The garden itself was dark, but she
found herself engulfed in a blue light. It was like pale
moonlight, but there was no moon visible. Unexpectedly, a red rose, fresh with dew, fell into her lap. How
could that be? Roses were not blooming at this time of
year. Yet this was a real flower of extraordinary size and
beauty. Its sweet fragrance enveloped her. She laughed
softly. Who had manifested this symbol of love? She
pressed the flower to her breast and waited, scarcely daring to breathe. The air became electric. She no longer felt
sorry for herself or abused by the world. She felt instead
a wondrous elation and gratitude.

At that moment the figure of a vibrant being of light,
with great silver wings, formed before her. She must be
dreaming or else hallucinating. She should return to the
house.

Before she could rise from the bench, the being spoke. "I am the Archangel, Gabriel, Messenger of the Lord God. Beloved Anna, you are like a grain of wheat that has waited these many years to be planted. Now, you will be set into the rich earth and the magic seed will sprout. With your unwavering faith in God's goodness, you have maintained an unbounded feeling of responsibility toward your fellow human beings and an unselfish stewardship of your material possessions. You have healed others without thought of reward or aggrandizement. You have learned compassion for others. God's bounty is now yours. You no longer need to waste your energies in worry and despair. God chooses only the strong for his special missions, but, I warn you, there are still many steps for you to climb. Rejoice in the knowledge that you will be a channel for His life substance that will benefit all mankind for countless ages to come. You have made yourself a chalice of love. The bruises of your life are now healed because you have forgiven the heartlessness of others, not once but seventy times seven."

The words came to Anna like cosmic thunder. The Archangel Gabriel paused, but Anna was so stunned she could not speak. In the silence of that sacred moment, she could only ask herself what the archangel wanted her to do.

He continued gently, as if reading her mind. "Make immaculate your thoughts, for tomorrow you will leave for Jerusalem to meet your devoted husband at the golden gate of the temple. I have already informed Joachim to join you there. Yes, he is very much alive and well. He has prayed and fasted these many months in a secret cave at Mount Horeb, and God has answered his prayers. You both have been put through a cleansing fire, so that God's crown of love would fit your humble heads. Your life has always been one with the will of God. Now, divine creative energy will be given to you."

He waited for Anna to speak, but the moment was too sacred for her to express words.

He continued, "Remember the Psalm of David: 'For the Lord God is a sun and a shield: the Lord will give grace and glory; no good thing will be withheld from them that walk uprightly.' You, Anna, a descendant of King David, have walked uprightly, and I rejoice with you in the blessings to come within the year. Selah!"

The archangel vanished in a gust of wind that sprang up out of the quiet night. It kissed Anna's flushed cheeks, and its tinkling note was like a happy sigh of content.

She sat motionless, as if in a spell. The archangel had said Joachim was alive! "Thank Thee, all merciful Father!" She would soon be reunited with her husband in the Holy City. But, more than that, she sensed that some wondrous event was to take place, else why did she feel an ecstasy beyond description? Then she realized what Gabriel had told her, not in ordinary words but in metaphor: She would bear a child. What would it feel like to be treated again like a desirable member of society? When their baby came, Joachim's suffering and shame would also end. His sacrificial offerings to God would now be accepted by the temple priests. It was late in life for her to be starting a family, but no matter. The archangel said she had walked uprightly! How bountiful was her God of Love!

She spoke to the night sky with its flickering stars, "O Lord my God, I cried unto Thee and Thou has healed me. Thou hast put off my sackcloth, and girded me with gladness; to the end that my glory may sing praise to Thee and not be silent. O Lord my God, I will give thanks unto Thee forever."

She did not go to bed that momentous night. She laughed and wept and danced alone with overwhelming joy. Her mind leapt and soared to unknown heights of ecstasy and wonder as she walked, trancelike, about her garden. The flowers and shrubs gave forth an exquisite perfume in celebration of the wondrous news. God had sent his mighty messenger, Gabriel, to shower her with stardust. Her beloved Joachim would meet her at the golden gate of the temple, he said. And, after twenty years of longing, a child would be born to them.

Anna threw kisses to the sky, telling the clouds to soar to the invisible God who loved her. The impact of coming face to face with the Great and Luminous One had changed the very fabric of her being. She would never again doubt God's goodness and mercy. "O Holy Father, my soul is yours; my life is yours."

* * *

When the sun's first rays entered her garden, Anna awakened Judith and Hermana, directing them to prepare for their journey to Judea. She was unable to eat, so great was her emotion, but Judith prepared for her a drink of balsam.

"I will never be the same," she told the servants. "In the twinkling of an eye, God made me a whole woman."

Then she remembered that someone must care for the animals in the enclosure during their absence. She had no friends here but perhaps Julian was in town. She would be forced to ask help from him, so was relieved to see his mount feeding in the adjacent pen.

He answered her knock in a quiet voice. "You are unbelievably radiant today—like the young woman I met so long ago. What happened to cause this transformation from a downcast, aging beauty?'

She ignored the question, saying, "My two servants and I must go to Jerusalem to meet Joachim. I need someone to care for our livestock."

He let her wait for several moments before replying, and again she felt the strong physical pull of this intense man. He had changed somewhat, though. The coarseness of his features had vanished. His once-cold, green eyes now sparkled with genuine warmth.

"Of course, Anna. How long will you be gone?"

"Perhaps as much as ten days."

"I'll be in Sepphoris much of the time, but will make sure the animals have water and feed."

He followed her into the street, continuing, "I'm glad you came. I wanted to tell you I haven't had an attack of epilepsy since I began repeating the prayer you taught me."

"You no longer have those devastating attacks?"

"You frightened them out of me." He laughed. "I'm grateful, of course." He took her hand. "Anna, I have a great need to be near you, to know always what you are doing. Day by day, you are gaining control of my thoughts, my actions. I told Herod of your beauty, but not your power. He wants to meet this 'Jewess' who has changed many of my attitudes—not without extreme measures, I might add. Will you let me take you to him one day?"

Anna shook her head vehemently. "I fear him more than the poisonous vipers of the mountains. You would have to rescue me again." She laughed, saying in jest, "You wouldn't want me to create that magic cloud and put him into a deep sleep on the palace floor, would you?"

"No, no! Have you no respect for the King of Judea?"

"I deplore his taxing us beyond all reason just to build a luxurious palace at Caesarea."

"But we finally have a seaport on the Mediterranean—a blessing to Palestine." Then he changed the subject abruptly. "Wait here a moment. I have something for you from Rome."

He returned and handed her a large, elegantly designed porcelain vial, encrusted with rubies. Then he left her.

When Anna reached her house, she opened the vial and found it contained the essence of roses. He had selected her favorite scent. She would take it with her to Jerusalem and apply some before her reunion with Joachim.

While making travel preparations, Anna found that Julian remained in her thoughts. They had become more than adversaries, she decided. They were intent combatants on an emotional level of consciousness that she had experienced with no one else. This awareness of each other had a life of its own, yet it was separate and removed from her enduring love of Joachim. Perhaps Julian yearned for something in her to satisfy a deep soul-longing for the one God. His attitude toward her always masked a veiled, unspoken threat. She thought of it now as a challenge to her own stubborn, one-directional nature. Obviously, they had a curious need for each other. Perhaps one day, she could sort out her feelings toward him and understand them.

She occupied her mind with packing. Live doves in wicker cages, along with food and clothing, must ride on the small donkeys. She wondered why the Archangel Gabriel had not directed Joachim to come home instead of meeting her at the golden Gate in Jerusalem. And why had her husband gone to Mount Horeb instead of nearby Mount Carmel?

Anna's desire to reach Joachim as quickly as possible decided her to take the shorter north-south route through Samaria. It was considered the more dangerous road due to a long-standing enmity between the Israelites and the Samaritans, but she had to risk lessening the travel by a full day.

They were careful not to draw attention to themselves, and slept in the fields. One night Judith asked her, "Why does Julian scheme constantly to find an excuse to see you?"

Anna considered her words well before answering. "I imagine all relationships are based on need. We gravitate toward those who balance our lives to make them whole. You help balance my life."

They traveled as fast as possible, taking to dirt trails when near villages. By late afternoon of the second day, they came within sight of the temple complex. Herod had extended it out over surrounding valleys. Its massive walls of native stone blocks were a triumph of Roman ingenuity. While the women rested above the Kidron Valley, Anna pointed out the high temple building, set in a series of courts enhanced by gardens and pools on the highest hill, Mount Moriah.

Herod had embellished it considerably since Anna was trained there. Its three stories rose higher than before, and the new Graeco-Roman facade of polished granite and dark marble, made it, in Herod's words, "the most beautiful building in the world."

The travelers descended quickly into the valley. Judith and Hermana continued with the donkeys to Joachim's house near the Pool of Siloam, while Anna raced with her basket of doves toward the golden gate.

Chapter 3

Joachim had arrived ahead of Anna. An angel accompanied him to the temple and the Tabernacle of Solomon, and they proceeded, unchallenged, until they paused briefly before the high priest. Though astonished, the priest acknowledged the angel, bowed, and swept his hand, showing his permission for the angel-led Joachim to enter the Holy of Holies. As the angel's arms opened to salute the Ark of the Covenant, Joachim saw about the ark a circle of light filled with two intersecting, pulsing segments of white light. Joachim fell to his knees before the Ark. The angel dipped one hand into the circular light symbol and motioned Joachim to rise. He saw a shining spark in the angel's hand and watched as the angel placed the glowing flame on his breast, just over his bare heart. Joachim again sank to his knees, feeling numb with ecstasy. The angel disappeared, and very soon the high priest entered to find Joachim absolutely radiant with a surrounding golden light and a look of joy unlike anything the priest had ever seen. He helped Joachim to his feet and out of the holy place. Other priests ministered to him with smelling salts and a rosewater drink. Joachim recalled the angel's instruction to proceed to the subterranean passage that would take him to the golden gate to meet Anna. The priests led him to the doorway to the passage and then stepped back, as the presence of angels signaled to them that Joachim was to be accompanied by the angels.

This procession of the worldly Joachim and the otherworldly beings continued along the pillared pathway to a pillar shaped like a palm tree covered with leaves and fruit. There was Anna and an entourage of angels coming toward Joachim. As the devoted couple met under the pillar-palm they were enveloped in heavenly light issuing from the angels. With radiant and holy joy, the husband clasped his ecstatic wife to his breast. The holy, glowing seed from Joachim's heart momentarily sank into the receptive heart of Anna. Both of them felt such an intense influx of unconditional love that they remained speechless and breathless while the angelic host filled the passage with brilliant light and heavenly music. At last, their earnest prayers for this long awaited conception had been fulfilled. Gradually the music faded, and one angel, still aglow, led them along the passageway, until it led upward to an exit that opened into a little chapel. The aura of a miraculous event surrounded them. The priests saw the angel depart and came to minister to the still-glowing, joyful couple.

Finally, servants of the priests accompanied the couple to their house near the Pool of Siloam, where Judith and Hermana had patiently awaited and prepared for Joachim and Anna's arrival. They were awed by the radiant joy emanating from the couple and, although they did not understand the extent of this joy, they themselves felt quite joyous to see the couple reunited and so very happy.

While they all ate of the prepared food, Anna and Joachim briefly explained some of what had occurred at the temple. Then Joachim suggested, "Let us return soon to Nazareth, by way of the Essene settlement at Qumran, to tell Ezra our good news."

Anna happily agreed. She wanted to tell Ezra of the wonderful event. Also, she had many questions to ask him regarding healing methods. He was her only teacher.

At last all were settled for the night's rest. Joachim and Anna dreamed many beautiful dreams associated with the marvelous events of the day and the subsequent events that would unfold in the days to come.

In the morning, while Joachim slept, Anna decided to take Hermana to the Pool of Siloam, where the diseased and crippled huddled, waiting for the angels to move the waters. No one knew when this would occur, but it was believed that the first person into the pool when the waters boiled would be healed of his affliction. It would be a dramatic experience for Hermana, who was deeply interested in becoming an Essene.

* * *

They joined the miserable crowd of perhaps a hundred people—suffering from every conceivable ailment. Anna spotted a frail young boy about eight years of age, whose crippled mother tried in vain to maneuver him closer to the pool.

Hermana was a strong and agile young woman. "I'll try to get that boy into the moving waters first, if you'll help me."

They made their way with difficulty to the anxious woman.

"What is your son's ailment?" Anna asked.

"He's blind. He had a bad fall when he was very young."

"Let this girl help get him to the pool for you."

The mother hesitated when Anna pointed to Hermana, but Anna's loving look persuaded her, and she turned the child over to the athletic, bronzed girl.

"I want you to learn how to heal," Anna told Hermana. "I won't interfere."

They sat impatiently for an hour or more, waiting for the waters to churn. A wailing began as the children and adults in pain could stand the suspense no longer. Then Anna felt her own body begin to shake. She motioned to Hermana to race with the boy into the pool. She submerged the stunned youngster into the turbulent waters and then brought him out sputtering. It took several minutes for them to work their way back to the mother through the screaming crowd.

No one knew if any one had been healed until the boy looked at his waiting mother and cried, "I see you now! I see you!"

While they were embracing, Anna whispered to Hermana, "Let's go quickly. The miracles of God must not be discussed." Then she turned to the parent, saying, "Go at once to your home and express your thanks there. Be silent until then."

There was such authority in her voice that the woman took her son's hand and they fled the crowd.

As Anna and Hermana walked back to the house, Hermana said in an awed tone, "I have never moved so fast. And the boy became as light as a feather. This makes me more determined than ever to study the Essene beliefs, since they put emphasis on the work of the angels."

"And the archangels," Anna added. Her garment today had small bells attached to the hem. They tinkled when she walked.

Hermana, ever curious, asked, "Why did you sew those bells on your robe? Are you superstitious?"

"Perhaps. But the bells are to attract the angels."

"Should I, too, believe in such entities?"

"Definitely. Angels are the personification of God's presence.'

"Do they have names?"

"Yes, the Archangel Michael is the guardian angel of the Hebrews. He carries out God's decrees. Gabriel is the leader of the celestial hierarchy—the divine messenger, an Angel of the Presence."

"How can you be sure Michael and Gabriel aren't demons? I've been taught to fear demons."

"You can't see demons, Hermana. I have seen Gabriel. Although the demons have wings like the angels, they eat and drink and die like we do." Encouraged by an eager listener, Anna further explained, "Angels have three human and three angelic attributes, according to Ezra."

"Then they can appear in human form and speak for God?"

"That is what happened to me. Archangel Gabriel spoke for the Lord."

By now they had reached the small house where Joachim still slept. In a few more hours, he awakened and appeared to have regained much of his strength.

Anna asked him, "Do you feel able to visit Ezra now?"

He nodded. "He's my dearest friend, and we must share our newfound hopes with him. The shortest route to Khirbet Qumran on the Dead Sea is by way of Bethlehem. Since I'm not sure how difficult the route is, let's plan on staying the first night there. We must be prepared to encounter some of the radical Zealots who prey on that caravan route to Jerusalem. They are called Sicariis and they carry daggers and are dedicated to kill not only the Romans, but also any Israelite who harbors them. Just speaking to a Roman in a friendly way puts one in danger. Your father is a Pharisee, Anna, and they have a murderous hatred of Pharisees."

"Why is that?" Anna asked with growing apprehension.

"Long ago, Arabs and Edomites were forcibly converted to Judaism and circumcised. Since the merchants of Judea collaborate increasingly with the Romans, these assassins have grown more fanatical. Thank heavens they haven't spread as far north as our Galilean valley yet. They exist in small robber bands here."

Anna was stunned. "Then I could endanger all of our lives by going near their area?"

"Let's risk it, Anna. We both must share our good fortune with Ezra."

Their route took them through the beautiful hill country of Judea, where villages were less than twenty minutes apart. The terraced and heavily fertilized slopes boasted choice plantings of fruit, olives, and vegetables. Herod called this area his "Jewish Garden." It was the envy of Rome.

They found comfortable rooms in an inn in Bethlehem that first night without arousing any interest. Anna slept little, concerned over the possibility of encountering the Sicarii. She had been so sure, after Gabriel's miraculous appearance, that her life would be beautiful and free of worry. Now a new threat had appeared on the horizon.

* * *

By noon of the next day, the fertile farms had disappeared. Before them lay a tangle of endless, furrowed hills of rock. They were now in the wilderness of Judah, and beyond were the barrens of Qumran.

Joachim, alert to possible danger, saw two fierce-looking men approaching them. He motioned for the women to stop their donkeys off the trail. Anna occupied the two women in conversation, their backs to the road.

The men moved on, then suddenly one of them returned to question Joachim. Visible beneath the stranger's girdle, he saw the Sicariis' weapon of terror—the deadly *sica.*

Joachim pretended to be emptying his sandals of dirt when the stranger approached him.

"Have you passed any Romans today on this road?" he demanded.

"I am a shepherd from Galilee. I don't associate with my enemies," Joachim answered in a humble tone.

"Where are you going?"

"We have an old friend at Qumran to visit."

The ruffian appeared unsure Joachim spoke the truth. He studied him for a few moments, glanced at the three women huddled together, then turned and abruptly left.

"You were so brave!" Anna told Joachim. "Thank God they didn't challenge you."

They continued, with the heat and motionless air near suffocating over the sun-baked sandstone. A thick, blue haze hung over the Dead Sea before them. Fed by the Jordan River, it had no outlet, and its eastern shore was flanked by the stark and sterile Moab cliffs. Joachim pointed to their destination—the caves of Qumran on the northwest coast of the lake.

They followed a dry wadi leading to a high tower in the Essene settlement. Beckoning them across the lifeless, ochre slopes were the green vegetable gardens planted inside low walls to prevent erosion. They were the pantry of this strictly vegetarian sect.

A man in a long, white garment emerged from a cavern and spotted them. He waved, and they hurried to meet him.

The Elder spoke first. "Shalom! I am Brother Thaddeus."

Joachim returned the greeting and introduced everyone.

"Our Order welcomes you," Thaddeus said sincerely.
"You must be thirsty and in need of rest. Please follow
me."

They entered a large cavern in the hillside, which
proved to be surprisingly cool. Low, wooden stools
formed a semicircle at one end, and Thaddeus motioned
for them to be seated. He left them, to return with a
pitcher of refreshing rain water.

He said then, "We are preparing the evening meal now,
so I will offer you food later."

Joachim said, "We wish to stay here only overnight,
and will leave early for Jericho. On our donkeys we have
several rolls of linen cloth and sandals for your people.
May we be granted your hospitality?"

"Of course. Please tell me why you came to this remote
place."

Joachim motioned for Anna to explain their visit. "We
are both dear friends of Ezra ben Samuel. We came to
tell him some wondrous news. May we speak with Ezra
now?"

The Elder turned to Joachim to answer. "We receive
guests only on the Sabbath. Why have you come today?"

Joachim replied in a proud tone, "We had a revelation
from the Archangel Gabriel and came to share it with
Ezra. He is like a blood brother to me and a father to my
wife."

Thaddeus spoke with less hostility now. He turned and
directed a young novitiate to locate Ezra, then said, "We
get so little news here. You say you are from Galilee. Who
is the new legate to your province under Herod?"

"The Roman, Julian, a favorite of Augustus Caesar."

The Elder looked stunned by the revelation. "We know
Julian here, only too well. As a data gatherer, he was a

cruel, demanding man. He came here to try to force us to pay taxes to Rome—something we have never done, since we neither buy nor sell anything. He reviled our most devout priests. Be wary of contact with him, else the Sicarri will make you all targets of their uncontrolled hatred."

Anna and Joachim exchanged startled glances, but neither made any comment about Julian.

Chapter 4

While waiting for Ezra, Anna and Joachim walked about the grounds. They counted eleven caves in which Essenes lived and worked. A communal kitchen had numerous fireplaces and adjacent eating rooms. Beyond were a cemetery, a mill where men were grinding corn, and an intricate system of reservoirs that held their precious water.

An Essene working at a potter's kiln told them, "We abandoned this settlement for many years, following the earthquake. Now we are making it a stronghold against the Romans."

Joachim asked, "Do you go to Jerusalem for the Holy Days?"

"No. We take no part in temple worship since we don't believe in animal sacrifice."

Ezra waved to them from the community center, eager to see them again.

"Forgive me for this delay in meeting you," he called. "No one wanted to interrupt my meditation." He embraced each of them warmly. "Let's go to the dining area. Our meal waits."

The visitors were surprised when young women served them a thick vegetable soup.

Ezra explained, "We believe in perfect equality of the sexes. We have several women here and many married couples. Since a woman bore all of us, how can one consider her less than a man?" He stopped short, adding apologetically, "Forgive me. I know you came here to tell me something important."

"Yes, old friend. Anna and I were both visited by Archangel Gabriel and promised a child within the year. We are beside ourselves with joy and had to share the news with you." Briefly they told Ezra of their ecstatic reunion in the temple.

Ezra clapped his hands. "I've told Anna many times that what is impossible with men, is possible with God and his angels. I'll come to Nazareth when that child is born."

"You are happy here?" Anna asked.

"I love my life now. We eat as Methuselah did—the grains and grasses of the field, the honey of bees, and the milk of animals. The result is little disease. So lifespan is great. One hundred to a hundred and twenty years are normal here."

Hermana, who had been silent up to this time, took advantage of a pause in the dialogue to ask, "If I were accepted here as a novitiate, how long before I would be initiated into the order?"

Everyone was stunned by her question. Joachim asked her, "When did you develop an interest in the Essenes?"

"Anna has told me many of their beliefs, and I approve of them."

Immensely pleased, Ezra asked, "Beliefs such as what?"

Hermana replied confidently. "I know you get rid of what is bad by strengthening what is good; you become free of disease by increasing the vitality of your body; and, let's see—our body is what we eat, and our spirit is what we think."

They all laughed, delighted at her wisdom.

She continued, "Don't plan on my coming here for at least four years, though. I intend to be near Anna until her infant is placed in the service of the temple."

Joachim explained, "That will be when the child is three years old, Ezra."

"So young? No one has ever been dedicated to the service of God at that age."

"We made that promise to Him long ago, if He'd give us a child."

Ezra shook his head in amazement, then motioned for them to follow him. "It's time to show you your sleeping quarters. The women will share one cave, and Joachim and I will use the adjacent one. We two have much to discuss. It has been many years since we've had a good argument."

*   *   *

Thaddeus awakened everyone before sunup. They quickly ate a breakfast of wheat cakes and cheese, and headed north. Everyone was happy to leave the burnished, lifeless furrows of rocks for the delta of the Jordan River. Here, it had relentlessly gnawed its way from the Sea of Galilee to its graveyard in the Sea of Salt. The temperature was comfortable as they crossed the expanse of marl and salt and followed the river bank, with its heavy growth of reeds, willows, and tamarisks.

In addition to the ever-changing lights and shadows of the distant mountains, flocks of white herons and sparrows provided interest for the slow-moving group. They reached Jericho at nightfall and went to Esmeria's home. She and her husband were happy to see them, since their daughters had all married and left home. Esmeria missed the activity of cooking and sewing for active girls and teaching them the skills required of a future wife. Anna found no change in her nature. She was still the full-breasted, plump, and dynamic woman of her youth, a contrast always to the lanky, sullen Sobe. What Anna liked best about her was her lack of jealousy. She never felt in competition with anyone and was proud of her husband's trade as a fine miller.

Anna had warned Joachim, "Let me be the one to broach the subject of my conception. I want Esmeria's reaction first."

When the two sisters were alone, Anna said without introduction, "I'm going to have a child."

"You have stopped your menses?"

"Oh, I don't know yet. In two weeks, I can be certain."

"You probably haven't conceived. What gave you such an idea after all these barren years?"

Anna was reluctant to tell her of the visitation of Gabriel and the experience in the temple. Esmeria had no interest or knowledge of metaphysical or esoteric practices. She hedged by saying, "I feel so happy now. I'm bursting with energy and life for the first time in years."

"That's no indication, Anna. We all have our swings in moods. What does Joachim think? Has he suddenly become virile enough to procreate?"

"Esmeria, don't blame him for my barrenness these nineteen years. The fault is mine."

"Humph! It's your husband's return from his wanderings—goodness know where—that has given you this curious elation. Dear sister, I don't want you to be disappointed again. Return to Nazareth and heal the sick. Forget these unnatural flights of desire."

Anna was crushed. She had to convince Esmeria. She burst out, "The Archangel Gabriel visited me one night recently and promised me a child."

"What did he look like?" There was no curiosity in Esmeria's voice.

"He was a being of radiant light, and I knew he was from the heaven world."

Esmeria shook her head and took a deep breath. "I can believe most everything you tell me, Anna, but not this. You're like our sensitive mother, Emerentiana. She, too, spent a lifetime in fanciful yearnings. Why, she imagined one of her daughters would bear the Messiah! Yet, I have had only girls, Sobe had no children, and neither have you. Forget the admonition to be fruitful and multiply. We've enough Israelites for the time being. Be happy in your healing work. I often wonder how much easier life would have been without being up nights with sick daughters and a petulant husband who yearned only for sons. Face reality. No voices speak to me in the night. No winged beings, created of dazzling diamond-light, speak to me in prophetic tones. You're a dreamer, Anna. You believe what you want to see. Tell me, did you actually touch Gabriel?"

"On, no! I wouldn't dare touch a celestial being."

"I know you to be a deeply religious woman on the earthly plane. That I can believe in. But until I see you large with child, I won't consider this fanciful story."

The foursome stayed only one night in Jericho. By following the old caravan route north in the Jordan Valley, then west along the Valley of Jesreel, and finally north at Afula, they arrived home in three days.

A week later, Joachim left for Mount Tabor to check on his flocks and shepherds. He and Anna agreed not to tell anyone else of their extraordinary promise from Archangel Gabriel until she showed obvious signs of her conception.

*   *   *

Sobe was the first person to visit Anna. Her tepid greeting was followed, without preliminary, by the bold statement, "I've been thinking, Anna, how different we are. You're materialistic. I'm spiritual. Look at you—with a large house, special quarters for two maidservants, attractive clothes, and good food. I'm committed to a devout, simple life—every moment spent with the sick and needy. You travel to the Holy City, where I haven't been in years. I've seen you wear an expensive bracelet of filigreed gold with dazzling blue stone. Joachim has thoroughly spoiled you."

Anna gestured to a chair, and the two sisters sat down facing each other. Anna was stunned by Sobe's unwarranted accusations. She had hoped to share with her the joyous message from Archangel Gabriel, but she realized now that Sobe would only ridicule it as Esmeria had. Yet, she felt sorry for Sobe. She lived alone in the home of their parents. Stolan, their father, had died a few years back, making Sobe's life more empty than before. Like him, Sobe had a rigid, unforgiving nature.

Anna wanted desperately her affection, but Sobe's jealous reaction to any opinion Anna expressed, manifested itself in a debasing response. The world of the unseen, which Anna had penetrated, was also outside of Joachim's interest. She needed someone with whom she could share speculation on the Unknowable and the Intangible. That was why Ezra, an advanced Essene, was so important in her life.

He had taught her how to partake of the etheric essence of unseen planes of existence. Walking the cosmic highway toward God was bewildering, and, at times, Anna felt she had an identity beyond her physical body.

Sobe, however, with her caustic remarks, always quickly filled Anna with doubt of her worth and life's purpose. After each encounter with her sister, she suffered from severe depression and wept frequently.

Still a chameleon on this day, Sobe interrupted Anna's thoughts by asking in a silky voice, "Have you baked bread this morning?"

Anna nodded. "I'll send two loaves home with you."

"Another thing I'm interested in—what ever happened to the Moses cloth that disappeared on your wedding day?"

"I had misplaced it. It's in my altar box. Why do you ask?" Anna had no intention of revealing Julian's theft of the cloth or his return of it.

"I'd like to show it to the poor people I visit."

Anna replied testily, "I'll not give it to you or anyone. It was a gift from my dearest teacher, and I hold it sacred."

"It can't be that holy—it hasn't made you capable of conceiving!"

Anna cried out in indignation. "For all you know, I could be carrying a child at this very moment." She was tempted to tell her about Gabriel's promise and that now she knew for certain that God had blessed her womb at the temple experience. But she remembered the lesson she had learned from Esmeria's reaction.

Sobe dismissed the subject with a shrug of her bony shoulders and changed the conversation. "Since you won't lend me the Moses cloth, give me two pillows, a large piece of cheese, almonds and walnuts, and a lot of dried figs, all for a sick family."

"You'll get one pillow, nuts, and an herb that relieves fever." Anna ignored the smirk on Sobe's face and collected the items.

When Anna returned, her sister whirled around the room as if she carried a secret that was bursting to be told. "I'm going to Shiloh, Anna, and need a new dress. You have that lovely lavender robe that I could lengthen. Let me try it on."

Anna was immediately suspicious of Sobe's intentions. "What's so important in Shiloh?"

"I've decided to remarry. I know that shocks you, but I am terribly alone now."

"Is there someone in Shiloh who is interested in you?' Anna's tone was doubtful. Sobe was forty-five years old, lacking both an attractive appearance and personality.

"I intend to marry Joachim's brother, Cleophas. His wife has been dead for some years, and I learned he is wealthy. No one can understand why he hasn't taken a wife by now. I heard he's secretly in love with a married woman."

"What gossip! You're building up false hopes, and I doubt my lavender robe will change his mind." Anna was fond of this quiet man who had come to her during Joachim's disappearance and given her strength. Gentle Cleophas would be miserable with domineering Sobe. Besides, he was an Essene to the same degree she was. Married members of the sect lived under different rules than the single celibates.

"You'll put in a good word for me with him, won't you?"

Anna evaded the question, asking, "Will you be a jealous wife who schemes to get what she wants?"

Sobe danced in awkward steps around the room, coming to a stop in front of her sister. "I'll have as much—no, more than you have. Who knows, maybe I might be the one to bear the Messiah, since both you and Esmeria are out of the running. It's up to me to fulfill our mother's dreams. It's entirely possible at my age. I'm very healthy, you know."

Anna couldn't resist asking, "What do the stars say?"

"That's my secret. Now, what about the robe I want? Where is it? That color will soften my features. I'm sure you don't wear it any more."

Anna smiled at her conniving and got the garment. It was one of her favorites, but she wouldn't be selfish if it meant so much to Sobe. "Take it, Sobe. It's yours."

"I'll sew a strip of purple on it so it will be long enough." She brushed her drab, stringy hair from her angular face and held the robe in front of her. Anna wanted to say that Sobe was too flat-chested for its high-breasted cut, but decided against spoiling her triumph.

"Isn't there a matching scarf, Anna?"

When Anna returned with the scarf, she said sincerely, "I wish you all luck. If not a marriage to Cleophas, then one of his widower friends. You deserve all happiness."

"Good-bye, Anna. You'll be the first to know."

As Anna accompanied her sister to the open front door, she was dismayed to see the confident figure of Julian entering her courtyard.

Sobe let out a gasp of mock horror. "What an untimely visit! Shall I stay to protect you from his ardor?"

"Your sick family needs you, remember? I don't!"

Sobe turned around with a flourish, arms loaded with her gifts, and hurried out of the house by the rear door.

Julian flashed Anna a confident smile as she joined him in the garden. He had aged, she thought. The face was more florid, the curls now gray, but he stood erect and authoritative in a stunning white toga with the eagle emblem prominent on his shoulder. That meant he was in Galilee on official business.

He spoke without greeting her. "I am ready to retire, Anna. Herod has gone mad in his ambition to make this a Hellenistic state. Temple priests have no longer any power, although they continue to secretly conspire against Herod. His uncontrolled suspicions have already meant death for his lovely wife, Mariamne, and two sons. His mother-in-law is now marked for death, I'm positive. I fear his anger and ruthlessness."

Anna was surprised at Julian's frankness. "Come sit with me here." She indicated her favorite bench.

The obviously upset Julian continued as if talking to himself. "Herod just completed a theater and amphitheater in Jerusalem. My job is to encourage Greek dress, art and literature in every province. I am to set up gladiatorial combats, wrestling contest and musical performances." He buried his face in his massive hands. "I'm being crowded by Herod—and by you. I'm in your debt for curing my epilepsy, and that upsets me."

"You owe me nothing, Julian. We both search for a more satisfying life. The God of Israel sends messengers to prepare the way for others to follow. Perhaps I'm a messenger of sorts, since I yearn for your heart to beat in rhythm with God's forgiving heart."

He stared at her in disbelief. "But I like myself as I am. I lead a lusty, fast-paced, dangerous life. I don't want it to change."

"Nevertheless, I'll pray that divine light will enter your life, so this existence won't be wasted." She knew she spoke in riddles to him, but no matter.

Julian sprang to his feet, obviously agitated. He confessed, "I consulted the oracles on my last assignment to Rome. They said Joachim will have a short life. So the next time you soar into those divine octaves of something or other, ask your angels how soon you'll marry me. It's inevitable, Anna!"

Anna could not face his burning looks, but she managed to say firmly, "We are strange friends, I admit, but we can never be anything more—I've told you that many times."

"Damn you! I both hate and love you. The day will come when one of those emotions will triumph." He rose and hurried out the gate.

How she wished she could have told both Sobe and Julian that she carried a child in her. She cared not whether it was a girl or a boy. Either was a holy gift at her age—thirty-seven. Joachim was now forty-one. He must be the first to learn that Gabriel's promise was fulfilled. It made no difference when the conception took place. She regretted that Sobe would be unable to relay the information to Cleophas. She liked him immensely.

There was almost no one with whom Anna could share the surprising news. Her years of sterility had stripped her of all friends except Ezra, Judith, and Hermana, and, yes, Julian. She wished Sobe wouldn't constantly try to make her feel inferior. They were not in competition. Yet, this lifelong jealousy on Sobe's part drove her now to seek a marriage with Cleophas. Being richer than Joachim, Cleophas would certainly soften her jealousy. Yet, Anna had to admit Cleophas was much too good for Sobe.

She went inside to pray at her altar before the evening meal. From the small, carved chest, Anna removed the precious lock of Sara's hair. She venerated Abraham's wife, and having this relic to touch made her feel closer to God. She held it to her heart and spoke aloud, "I trusted your wisdom, O Lord my God, and thou sustained me. Now, my mourning has become ecstasy. My soul rejoices in thy boundless mercy. I love thee; my unborn child loves thee. We give thanks unto thee forever."

Tears flooded her face as she heard footsteps behind her. Then two strong arms lifted her from the floor and Joachim kissed her over and over again,

"I overheard you. So now we have proof, my angel wife. Life has become wonderful and good again."

CHAPTER 5

Julian let his stallion take his time as he rode through the winding, crowded streets of Jerusalem. Herod had summoned him to the palace unexpectedly. What would the erratic ruler's mood be today? Julian hoped he wouldn't be drunk as he was at their last meeting.

The "King of the Jews"—a title Herod had selected himself—needed persuasive emissaries such as Julian to further his grandiose plans. Already he had refurbished, at great expense, the fortresses of Hyrcania, Alexandrium, and Masada. A recent tax increase made it possible to fortify Sebate and build there a Corinthian temple, dominated by a towering statue of Augustus. Herod's plans for Julian in the months ahead were to accelerate the construction of the seaport of Caesarea. Then, the olives and fruit and grain of the provinces would move swiftly to Mother Rome.

Recently, though, Julian wanted nothing more than to

retire in Galilee—close to the woman who bedeviled his thoughts. Early in their acquaintance, Anna had cut short his ardor by telling him that she could only marry a descendant of the House of David. Not satisfied with that excuse, Julian enlisted the help of Hillel, president of the powerful Sanhedrin, in researching the early Hebrew patriarchs. To his delight, he learned that Abraham, the "first Jew," had an Egyptian wife; the patriarch Moses, married the daughter of Jethro, a Midianite priest and idolater; King David married the former wife of Uriah, the Hittite; and Solomon was the most intermarried of the lot. So there was no reason why a widowed Anna couldn't marry a Roman. Of course, he'd have to pretend to accept her beliefs, and even undergo the required circumcision to have her.

Approaching Herod's storied palace, he turned his attention to the blending of styles that made it rich and brilliant. The use of marble and color, of arches and slender Doric columns expressed the procurator's love of luxury and splendor. There was a porter's lodge to the right, and a stable filled with magnificent hunting horses to the left. Herod was unexcelled with the bow and arrow. Julian turned his animal over to a waiting groom.

Guards then admitted him into a huge atrium set in the midst of several small rooms. These, he knew, were assigned to Herod's slaves and unmarried sons. He followed a guard up the sweeping stairs to an inner peristyle open to the sky. Around its decorated colonnades were the rooms of Herod's wives, their slaves, and his unmarried daughters.

They turned into a separate wing, where the walls were adorned with sculptured stucco work and pilasters, crossed an expanse of brilliant-colored tiles, then entered a sumptuous room where Herod sat, trying, Julian told himself, to look like a Greek god. His silk toga was elegantly draped to reveal a naked right shoulder and breast. One foot tapped impatiently on the marble floor.

Herod studied Julian through narrowed eyes for a moment. Then, without a greeting, he said, "You grow more handsome with each passing year. Your face is less harsh, and has a more youthful appearance in spite of your graying hair."

Julian said, "Thank you, sire." He knew that flattery was one of Herod's many weapons. What scheme was stirring at this moment in his fertile brain? Julian was tired of playing a servile, fawning subject.

Herod rose, belched a couple of times, then said with candor, "This Judean wine gives me no rest. I'll return in a moment with a surprise for you." He clapped his hands for a guard. "Send Hillel here at once."

Julian was not fond of this Rabbinical sage whose philosophy placed emphasis on religious and ethical truths. As a Pharisee and the president of the authoritative Sanhedrin, Hillel had attracted a large following of gifted disciples. He was controversial, though, and engaged in so much dispute with his opponent, Sahmmai, that Judeans claimed they now had two Torahs. He preached, "Be of the disciples of Aaron: love peace and pursue peace; love your fellow man and draw them closer to the Torah." This fanatic insisted that one should love every human being, since "what is hateful to you, do not do to your fellow man." Why had cruel Herod called Hillel for consultation with a Roman?

Julian knew that priests were under Herod's thumb, but the summons here to meet Hillel was extraordinary. Ruthless, dictatorial, articulate, persuasive, and without any morals, Herod was totally in command of Palestine. Everyone jumped when he crooked his little finger.

Julian tried to concentrate on the naked bronze statues encircling the room. He rose from the marble bench and examined the array of gold vases. Finally, Hillel stepped into the room.

He spoke in a low voice. "You know that I must carry out Herod's orders, even though I heed the highest ecclesiastical and secular tribunal of my people. What is about to transpire was not my idea. Unfortunately, I can't tell you."

Julian remained silent, eyeing him with suspicion. He saw before him a balding man in his mid-forties with a skimpy salt-and-pepper beard, but large, eloquent eyes. His garb was the usual tasseled, black prayer shawl and phylacteries (those ridiculous little boxes said to hold scriptural passages) bound to his left arm and forehead with wide leather straps. No matter, Julian knew him to be the most potent and dangerous teacher in Palestine.

Herod returned in a more jovial manner. He addressed only Julian. "You may have heard that I have fourteen children—no, twelve now. Among these is a daughter whom I intend to bestow on you. Augustus directed you many months ago to take a wife. All Romans—men or women living in the colonies—must marry to increase Roman influence among the prolific Jews. You have contented yourself with harlots instead. Caesar will be pleased to learn that I have arranged for your marriage today, in accordance with his orders."

"What farce is this, sire? I am capable of finding my own wife!"

"You haven't, so your devotion to my Greek ideals has earned you the hand of my daughter, Salina. Her name means 'salty' and I admit she has been an unbearable aggravation to me."

Julian was stunned by the trap he had walked into. Salina was said to be an imbecile, unable to speak due to an uncontrollable stammer. She was known as the scourge of the palace.

Hillel protested mildly, "Sire, this action could be unreasonable. Isn't there an alternative?"

Herod laughed contemptuously. "I follow the dictates of the Empire. Julian is still in my employ." Then turning to Julian he added, "You surely have the ability to service one wife, considering that I have the capacity to meet the needs of four wives and several of my daughters."

Julian faced him with fury. "I told you I love a Jewess in Galilee, who, according to the oracles, will soon be a widow. I refuse your madness without first consulting me!"

Herod thrust his great sunburned nose forward and growled, "Then your blood will soil these lovely tiles." He snapped his fingers, and four guards rushed in with unsheathed broadswords. "Have Salina brought in!"

A dark-skinned slave woman accompanied a slender girl whose headscarf covered much of her face. Julian saw only a pair of terrified eyes.

Herod introduced her with much flourish to both men. She tried to respond, but her head flew back as she struggled to force sounds from her throat.

"You will speak the words for her," Herod ordered Hillel. "Be brief!"

Julian heard none of the rituals. The blood pounded in his temples, and his tongue was so dry he could only mumble.

When the short ceremony was done, Herod said, "Salina's clothes are packed. There is a horse waiting for her in the stables. She is now your property, legate. You will report to me in three weeks—sufficient time to install Salina in your Galilean household. She understands Greek. You will enjoy her, since I have made sure she is not a virgin." He laughed smugly.

Julian managed, "You forget I know Augustus well. He will be informed of this outrage!"

Herod countered, "If Caesar rebukes me, I will order withheld the next grain shipment for hungry Rome. He will think twice before being so rash."

Hillel looked embarrassed by his part in the sordid affair. He took Salina's trembling hands in his, saying, "You'll be happier in Galilee, away from your painful life here. May God go with you."

Julian grasped Salina's arm and turned with loathing from both men. One thing he decided as they rode away from the palace—he would produce no grandchildren for the rabid King of the Jews. His future was uncertain now, for wily Herod would conceive other wicked ways of dominating him. He had no one to turn to but Anna. She alone was an oasis in this bedeviled land.

*   *   *

Julian brought his bride to Anna immediately upon their arrival in Nazareth. After relating his encounter with Herod, he asked, "Am I to spend the rest of my life with an idiot who can't even talk to me?"

Anna looked at the dark-skinned young woman. She had lovely black hair and intelligent eyes. Once the terror could be wiped from her expression, she might be fairly attractive.

"The situation is far from impossible, Julian. It may take patience on both our parts."

"Then prove how great you are with your witchery."

"Go home, Julian. She needs to be away from you. I will give her the kindness she has never had."

"Remember, this is Herod's daughter, so you had better not make her any crazier than she already is!"

Anna cringed as Salina winced and tears began to flow. "Leave us, Julian. I have never faced a situation like this, so I'm not certain how I can help."

Julian's harsh tone shifted to one of pleading. "Help

me, help me! Use that damned white light of yours on her."

"No, that is reserved for extreme physical needs. Salina suffers emotionally from enormous stress. She is a lovely young woman, and we will become good friends."

Anna took her to the rear garden. "Salina, no harm will come to you now. Sit here while I prepare a refreshing herb drink. While I'm gone, toss this bowl of grain to the birds. Call them to you as you scatter the feed. Encourage them to come closer each time, and talk to them as if they were your friends."

Anna purposely stayed away from Salina for some time. But she stood near the open door to hear any sounds from her. At first there were only grunts as the birds moved closer for the feed. Then, as they twittered in delight around her, she spoke clearly, "Beautiful creatures." There was no stutter.

Anna brought out two mugs of tea and sat down next to her on the bench. She ventured, 'Tell me if you like this drink. It is my favorite."

Salina opened her mouth to speak, but at once her head flew violently backwards and the words were locked in her throat. The young woman was still fearful of trying to speak, so Anna decided to see if the animals in the corral could be useful.

"Come help me water the donkeys," she said, moving ahead of Salina. "This frisky one is called Phineas— which means a mouth of brass. You should hear him bray!" Anna laughed, and in response, a slight smile crossed Salina's face. "Now this near-white fellow is Laban. Can you say his name? Laban."

Salina tried again, but once again the words were blocked. Anna had to think of a different method. If she could relax Salina's extreme tension, she might be able to help her.

She decided to have her sigh—a long sigh. Anna demonstrated what Salina should do. In the midst of the sigh she should try to say "Anna." It took a half dozen attempts, and then the word came clearly without a stutter.

Anna embraced her, exclaiming, "Wonderful! Wonderful!"

"Now let us try another word—Julian. Take a deep breath, let it out slowly, but in the midst of the exhalation say 'Julian.'"

It didn't work. The thoughts of her husband produced too much stress. But Anna felt she had now the key to the stammer. "Tomorrow we will try again, and you'll be successful," she told Salina gently.

Then Anna spent the afternoon talking to Salina about herself. She told Salina that she would soon give birth to a wondrous child and that Salina could help her make swaddling clothes and little garments. She thought it would be a girl, but she wasn't sure. As Salina listened, she became more relaxed and her terrified expression disappeared.

Herod's daughter proved to be skilled in embroidery, and she worked diligently on each item given her. She had other skills too. She knew how to cook and helped Judith in the kitchen when Anna was otherwise occupied.

Again, Anna tried experimenting with Salina's breath. She was convinced it was the first syllable in each sentence that provided the blockage. "Anna" was easier to say than "Julian" so she had her practice on words beginning with sounds other than j, t, b, d, g and p. It was grueling trying to stop the stammers at first, but after a week, Anna felt she had found the secret of preventing it. Once Salina realized it had to do with how she began to speak each sentence, her fears lessened.

"You must start your speech very slowly and softly, especially the first syllable which rides out of your mouth on a gentle breeze."

At first, Salina developed a breathy voice. "No, push lightly on your breath just before you say the first syllable. Try now to say 'Julian.'"

Salina was highly intelligent. She could follow instructions accurately. She did as told and was shocked to hear herself say "Julian" without a blockage. Then she wept with relief and clung to Anna with gratitude.

"I want you with me for a few more days, Salina. There'll be no more facial struggles, no more gasps. You will speak as well as I do. Here in Galilee, you will be free of the degrading treatment you received in Jerusalem. You no longer have anything to worry about. I need you to help me prepare for my child's birth. Will you do that?"

Salina was overcome by the kindness of this strange woman. "My fear of stuttering is gone since you became my loving protector."

"You are such a bright young person. Shall I invite Julian to visit with us today while Joachim is with his new-found friends?"

Anna sent Judith to bring Julian. He came, expecting the worst.

"Salina is free of her stuttering," Anna said. "But if there is a relapse, I want her to come back to me until it is again overcome. She is to have no stress or verbal abuse of any kind. Salina, have you lost your fear of Julian?"

The girl responded clearly but in a soft voice, "Yes, I am no longer afraid of him"

Julian was speechless. Finally he said, "You have performed another miracle, Anna. Again I'm in your debt. But if Herod should learn of this, all of us will be punished. Let him think he has pulled off a great prank on me. He need never see Salina again. I plan on eventually taking her to Rome, where she wants to live. She must be far away from the reach of her father."

"Go home and celebrate Salina's happiness. Judith, give them some of the warm honey cakes and that aged cheese."

Julian made no move to follow his wife. Perplexed, he asked, "How did you do it, Anna? You have so many tricks. I'm deeply grateful of course, but I want you to know I do not intend to consummate this forced marriage. You know the reason."

"If you want to keep her from stammering again, you must be gentle—no stress of any kind."

"Of course. By the way, Anna, I heard that Joachim has been admitted again to the House of Prayer. Why would he accept these people after being mistreated for all of your married life?"

Anna hesitated before answering. It was none of his affair. Yet, she wanted to shout to the world that their God had seen fit to end their suffering—in his time, rather than when they wished it. She wanted Julian to care about her child's birth. Why, she couldn't explain.

"I am to become a mother. Our joy is so great, we forgive everyone for their failings. I have forgiven you, Julian, many times." Her voice broke.

Julian ran his great hand through his gray curls. "You dangle me like a fish on a long string. Why don't you forbid me from ever coming near you? Why do you save me from myself? Are you still scheming to convert me to your God?"

Anna laughed to break the tension building between them. "No, it would take a Messiah to do that! However, I admit I would like to see that happen in my lifetime."

He appeared loathe to leave her and continued the conversation. "You want a boy baby?"

"It makes no difference. We will dedicate our first-born to the service of God, even if it is a girl."

"I wouldn't do that."

"There is much to learn. Remember, I spent ten years studying in the temple."

"What did you learn there?"

"Humility and how to invoke the might of the angels in time of crisis. One person can become as powerful as an army if the need is great enough."

Julian smiled. "I see no difference between your angels and my hundreds of gods, do you?"

"My angels are daily companions, for one thing." Anna was about to say more but Joachim returned unexpectedly.

He stopped and demanded angrily of Julian, "Why are you here?"

"I came to congratulate both of you on your wife's fertility. She had a long wait."

"It's none of your business!"

Julian bowed to Anna and went home.

Joachim said, "I don't like the way that Roman devil looks at you. Why do you tolerate his coming here? Now that people are starting to accept us, you must stop speaking to him. I've also great doubts about your meddling with Herod's daughter. Have you forgotten that the Sicarii have started raids in Samaria? They'll be in Galilee next."

"You knew when you married me I showed great interest and curiosity in other races. If only I could be a bridge . . . " She didn't expect orthodox Joachim to understand such notions.

"There's plenty for you to do with building bridges among our own people—Pharisees, Sadducees, Essenes, Zealots, Levites—you take your pick. None of them agree on many things. You contaminate yourself by associating with those lacking spirituality."

"Dearest Joachim," Anna began firmly, "for nearly twenty years our people scorned us. I turned to anyone who didn't despise me. Now my heart aches for Salina. She has been severely abused. She needs love and help as much as we did in the past. God has blessed us now. Can't we be forgiving?"

His voice rose to a shout. "But don't you see how Julian lusts for you? Yet you show no animosity toward him. Why? What is his subtle attraction?"

Anna did not retreat. "If the Messiah were here today, I believe Julian would follow him. What he seeks is not me, dear one, but a yearning to know God. He's hungry for what you and I always have known.

"Ridiculous! He's cruel, calculating, despicable! Men understand other men better than women do. Julian will strike back at me through you the first chance he gets. Keep away from him!"

Anna had never seen Joachim so upset or harsh with her. She flushed, but defended herself. "I needed friends. I was terribly lonely when all our friends deserted us. I didn't care if a Roman or Chaldean or Egyptian showed me attention. Julian made me feel worthwhile."

Joachim swallowed his pride. "I'm sorry for my brusqueness. The kingdom of the Messiah must be close now. That's why the hosts of Satan are especially active among us. There are more demons than angels around us. Julian resents your spiritual power. Can't you believe me?"

Anna shook her head and skillfully changed the subject. Her face softened and became radiant. "A girl moved in me, Joachim. I'm sure of that. I often see a golden letter, M, on the wall by our bed during the night. What can that mean?"

"Perhaps the first letter of the child's name. Micah, Matthew or Mordecai."

Anna shook her head. "None of them seems right. There's Muriel, Morla, Martha and Mary. I like Mary, don't you?"

"If it's a girl, then we'll call her Mary." Forgive me for having been so jealous and possessive of you. I've been on the defensive for so long, I overreact now."

"You are my great and devoted love, Joachim. Our argument is forgotten."

They kissed with great tenderness. The unborn child had woven its magic.

*   *   *

The summer heat waned as fall made its uncertain appearance. Winter birds arrived to replace the migratory flocks heading south. Anna's confinement had arrived, and anticipation of the long-awaited event made Anna love everyone. She had not seen Sobe since her sister's departure for Shiloh and the pursuit of Cleophas. Obviously, nothing had come of it. Nevertheless, Anna sent word to both Sobe and Esmeria to be here to assist her. If needed, Esmeria was capable and experienced in child-birth. She had delivered several babies besides bearing three daughters in Jericho. Anna refused to call in any of the local midwives. She asked herself, "Why should they have the honor of delivering my precious infant, when they despised me for countless years?"

Two days before the anticipated birth, a well-dressed Roman woman arrived at the house. "I am Aldora," she said. "The legate, Julian, sent me to you since I am a midwife of renown in the Empire. I have already been paid for my services, so you will owe me nothing."

Anna looked sharply at the large-built woman in her sixties before her. The animated, intense blue eyes and confident manner made Anna consider her offer.

Aldora continued, "I have a letter here from Rome,

certifying my great competency." She handed Anna the parchment sealed with the familiar medallion of Caesar Augustus. Written in Greek, it recommended her without reservation as an experienced professional. She had delivered some five hundred infants, both in Rome and in Palestine, among families of wealth and position.

Anna was impressed and, at the same time, relieved. No ordinary child was to be delivered here. An expert, instead of a sister, was certainly preferred for its birth. She thought of Julian's motive. His kind interference meant he wished her well.

"You are most welcome, Aldora. I put my trust in your capable hands." Then she called Joachim to come and meet Aldora.

He became upset and highly irritated. "With experienced midwives in Nazareth, why accept a hated Roman?"

"Dearest, you know I don't hate anyone. And neither do you when the greatest event of our lives is about to take place. I have confidence in this woman."

Joachim agreed reluctantly. "As soon as the child is born, I must send servants to the temple with my finest sheep."

"That will be your sacrificial offering, dear husband, but mine will be a perfume. Among the priestly texts of my father, I found a recipe for a special fragrance in the book of Exodus."

"What on earth does it contain?"

"It's a simple formula—one you can have made for me in Jerusalem. It contains equal parts of onyx from a special kind of shellfish; galbanum, a gum resin from a certain plant; and storax from a tree, plus incense. The temple priests know how to make such an offering on the altar of perfumes in front of the Holy of Holies. When I was a virgin there, I often watched them."

Joachim shook his head. "You never fail to amaze me, Anna."

Aldora was a gray-haired tower of efficiency. She asked Anna a number of questions and made some suggestions regarding the birth position. Then she stated, "Only I will be at your bedside until your time has come, so you may be able to sleep. Husbands are too nervous to have in the room."

Sobe arrived the next day and assumed undisputed authority in running the household. When she learned of the change in midwives, she ranted, "So Julian paid Aldora to come here—from Heaven knows where—so Rome and Herod can be immediately informed if the newborn infant is a boy and if he might be the Messiah! Julian is plotting something. Let me throw Aldora out of the house."

Anna showed no concern. She replied quietly, "You and Esmeria will be of great help to her. She is not a spy for Augustus. I'm impressed by her advanced method of delivery and have total confidence in her. Now, let us all go into the garden and pray on the spot where . . . " She stopped herself from saying, "Archangel Gabriel," then lamely added, "where I often meditate."

They sang several hymns there, and Joachim joined them for a final prayer. Joachim, seeing a suffused, rosy light form around Anna, motioned for the others to go into the house. He embraced her saying, "Call me if you need me tonight."

Anna was too filled with joy and wonder to sleep. This was the night for which her soul had prepared her these many years. She heard the celestial music of the most high saints and the rustle of angels' wings. God had begotten her for this wondrous experience, so she was unafraid. The time was close now, for she smelled the fragrance of roses around her. "Oh, blessed angels, I love the Lord my God with all my being."

* * *

Hazel-eyed, golden-haired Mary was born on the eighth day of the month of Tishri, shortly after the New Year's celebration of Rosh Hashanah. Anna, in a state of ecstasy, remembered little of the birthing. Aldora was a marvel of efficiency. She allowed no one in the room until she placed the infant in Anna's arms. When Sobe and Esmeria were invited to see Mary, Aldora said, "A perfect child—more beautiful than any I have ever delivered!"

Then Joachim entered, and after viewing the baby, dropped to his knees in thanksgiving. Soon Sobe swept everyone except Aldora out of the room, saying, "There's work to do for the christening in the morning."

They cleared the front rooms of the wickerwork screens to make a spacious area. There were special dishes to prepare, priests to notify, swaddling clothes to ready, an improvised altar to set up, and a suitable stand to locate, on which the infant cradle would be placed.

The next morning, five priests, imposing in prayer shawls with long ritual fringes, made their appearance. The room was already filled with excited well wishers. Anna did not appear, but she chose Sobe to carry the infant to Joachim. Mary lay serenely in red swaddling clothes covered with embroidered white gauze.

The priests began by leading the group in chanting the ages-old creedal affirmation, the Shema. All arms were extended as the priest, Caleb, spoke a prayer. Then he took Mary from Joachim and laid her in the wickerwork cradle set on the stand. The other priests took turns reading from scrolls while Caleb cut off three small tufts of the infant's golden curls. These he burned in a metal dish on the improvised altar.

Next, chanting blessings, he anointed Mary's ears, eyes, mouth, nose, and breast with holy oil, then asked Joachim, "What name shall we give this child?"

"Mary. Mary bat Joachim." The words rang with uncontrolled pride.

Caleb wrote the name on a sheet of parchment and laid it on her. While hymns were sung by the group, Sobe returned Mary to her mother. At that moment, everyone was startled to hear the loud warbling of song birds in the front yard. Hundreds had gathered in trees and bushes, vying with each other for beauty of expression.

Caleb said, "Listen to the birds rejoicing. When I came here today, I saw a great halo of light over this house. It hung there briefly like a sparkling, golden crown. I believe it was Elohim, the Lord God, showering his blessings on this newborn child."

Sobe entered then with a basin of water and towels, so all could wash their hands before breaking bread. A long table at the end of the room bore platters of freshly-baked breads and great bowls of nuts and fruit. Joachim proudly filled glasses with wines from Judea's prized vineyards.

Anna remained in her bedroom until the last guest had gone. When Mary fell asleep in Esmeria's arms, Sobe insisted that Anna come into the room to enjoy some of the food. She appeared in a flowing blue robe, and her light auburn hair, piled on top of her head, gave her a queenly look.

Joachim surprised her by saying, "To show our gratitude for this birth, Sobe and I have planned a celebration for the poor and crippled of Nazareth on the fourth day after the Sabbath. This afternoon, Sobe will shop for food and clothing to be given away. She knows who the needy are and what they would like. There must be sandals and tunics and robes for young and old."

"That's a wonderful idea, Joachim. And give each of them a few shekels too."

Joachim continued, "Esmeria has offered to shop for the food to give them. She loves to visit our markets. Today, the farm produce will be brought to town, so we decided to do the shopping today. Judith will be with you until we return."

"No need to hurry, Joachim. I feel wonderful," Anna answered.

Once the shoppers had left, Anna said to Judith, "There's so much good food left on the table. Go next door and invite Salina and Julian to see Mary while everyone is away."

Anna knew that no Israelite ever broke bread with another nationality, but no one ever said Romans couldn't eat by themselves in her house.

They came, eagerly bearing gifts for the new-born. In presenting infant garments to Anna, Salina said, with no trace of stuttering, "I embroidered them with much love."

Julian handed Anna a gift wrapped in white silk. He spoke softly. "It's for your daughter, but you are to wear it until she is grown."

It was a stunning pearl and topaz necklace. "Oh, Julian, this is so extravagant!" Anna said.

"But suitable for this remarkable occasion." He followed Salina and Judith to the room where Mary lay sleeping. While the two women looked at the numerous gifts there, Julian returned to Anna. She told him, "In a few days, our front yard will be crowded with the destitute and needy people of the area. Joachim will set up tables laden with wearing apparel, fruit, grain, honey, and cheese. My sister, Sobe, will take charge of the affair, so I won't need to go out of the house."

Julian frowned but did not immediately comment on it. After mulling it around in his mind, he said with surprising intensity, "If there's trouble with any uninvited beggars or greedy sots, send Judith for me at once. I will delay my return to Jerusalem until the affair is over." His voice dropped to a whisper, "I love you, Anna, beyond anything else in the world. One day your God must give you to me."

"Julian, what you see in me is only the light of my beloved Lord. If you renounce your old ways and accept him, the ascended beings will help you."

"I've changed, haven't I? By the time the oracle's message comes to pass—Joachim's death—you will find me pleasing."

"We are strange friends, I admit, but we will never be lovers. There's a silver cord that connects you and me to God. You can be a master of life, Julian, for the golden age of Israel is within each of us. I deeply care what happens to you." Tears flooded Anna's cheeks.

Julian dropped to his knees before her, and she felt weak and vulnerable. He whispered, "Give me hope, Anna dearest. You mean more to me than Venus or Vesta."

She shook her head. "The angels have power over my life. When you accept the One God of Israel, they'll shower you with blessings. Speak to them as I instructed you. The path of my life has been predestined. I follow a celestial music others may not hear. I can't change it."

Judith and Salina returned then, so Julian moved to the table for a goblet of wine.

Salina had said little during the visit. Noticing this, Anna spoke kindly to her. "You wear such a happy face today, young lady. Herod will be pleased to see your lovely transformation."

Salina answered heatedly, "I won't ever go back to

Jerusalem! I never want to see my cruel father again! Let him believe I'm still his imbecilic daughter who can't speak a word.'

"Do you think that wise?"

Julian answered for her. "Yes, we both do. Let Herod have the impression he's punishing me severely. If he saw how bright and attractive Salina has become, it would upset him terribly to have failed to gore me. She must never go back to him. When I travel to distant places in my work, she'll have you, Anna, for good company."

"Of course," Anna replied. "I'm happy to have her living next to me. We've become good friends." She beamed a warm smile to Salina, wondering if she and Julian had cohabited by now.

When it was time for the Roman couple to leave, Julian told Salina to go ahead, since he had something personal to say to Anna. Again he warned her, "Be extremely cautious of those you let enter the yard during your celebration of Mary's birth. There could be intoxicated visitors or just curious onlookers. I wish it were possible for me to be here in your yard to make sure no harm comes to anyone. But of course, there would be great animosity over my presence. Have Judith be on the alert and come for me at the first sign of anything unusual, any disorderly conduct. Promise?"

Anna was stunned by his insistent attitude that there was need for concern. "I expect Ezra and perhaps a fellow Essene to be here by then. They can help Joachim handle any unwanted behavior."

Julian fairly shouted, "Not Ezra! He is too old and is a holy man! This morning I heard the clatter of crows! That's a serious omen!"

Anna signed deeply. "I intend to remain indoors. Sobe and Joachim will be with the crowd."

"Promise me you'll not go into the yard for any reason. I must ride to Sepphoris in the morning, but intend to return before your affair is over."

"Very well, Julian. I appreciate your concern." She frowned, puzzled by his belief in such a ridiculous superstition.

CHAPTER 6

J ulian paced back and forth in his bedchamber, his square-jawed face lined with worry. He was concerned over the forthcoming festivities for the poor to be held next door to him. Yet Anna and Joachim deemed it necessary to show their gratitude to an unseen, unknowable God for the gift of a child.

In his hand Julian held an official communication from Herod warning him that the hard core of the Zealot sect—the Sicarii, had penetrated peaceful Galilee for their planned slaughter of Romans and those who traded with them.

Julian knew how this infamous group of Jews came into being. Exorbitant taxes actually lay at the root of it. Yet, Herod persisted in increasing them to fund his extravagant building craze. This caused the Sicarii to roam farther and farther north to enlist cooperation for their cause with other hard-pressed taxpayers. Wearing a deadly sica or dagger, they were often given food and lodging by sympathetic Zealots and Sadducees who told where Jews friendly to the Romans lived. Anna was in danger, but how could he protect her?

The unusual birth of a first child to a couple married for twenty years, had attracted considerable speculation throughout Palestine. With increased attention on Nazareth, would the murderous Sicarii learn of Anna's kindness to Salina and him?

He had advised Herod some months ago to cut back on building so many amphitheaters, coliseums, fortresses, and gardens with elaborate fountains and bronze statuary. Wasn't the enormous cost of the port city of Caesarea enough for the hardworking peasants to finance for the time being? Herod's answer was, "He who has power is justified in all things." This attitude obviously fueled the extremists into action.

Julian's life was now frequently threatened by angry farmers who were forced to sell their families into slavery in order to pay off back taxes. That's why he carried with him always a long sword. A few of the early victims of this abuse managed to escape and hide out in the marl heaps and badlands below the Dead Sea. Their numbers were augmented by Arabs and Edomites (like Herod) who, living in that area, were forced to convert to Judaism years ago. Actually, the father of Herod, Antipater, belonged to this group.

Its children inherited a murderous hatred of the wealthy Pharisaic Jews who had become traders, owners of fertile land, ships, caravans, and large synagogues which were replacing the small houses of prayer. One day, the Sicarii swore, they would destroy all the wheat and barley in Palestine and let the Pharisees starve. They believed they acted under God's orders.

Joachim was no protection for Anna. He was a shepherd, albeit of royal lineage, unskilled in fighting with fist or sword. All Julian could do was hope to be available if any trouble developed. He certainly couldn't warn Anna of peril at the moment of her greatest joy. He dared not tell her that, last week, two families in the towns of Hippus and Gadara, situated to the east and southeast of the Sea of Galilee, had been murdered because they traded with a Roman caravan.

In his own way, Julian tried to ward off danger to Anna. It would not be enough to appeal to the household protectors—the benevolent *penates* and *lares*, for such a potentially dangerous situation. He must pray to the three most powerful Gods of the Empire: Jupiter, the celestial ruler of all Romans and Master of the Thunderbolt; Mars, protector of warriors like himself; and Quirinius, who ruled over crowds.

Julian was not adept at prayers, he realized, but shortly after saying them, he observed a great flock of birds blanketing a part of the sky. That meant that Jupiter was active. Good! He would surely protect Anna from harm.

On the morning of the charitable affair, Sobe came early to take charge of the display tables. She had carefully selected the sandals, scarves, yarmulkes, and tunics for the needy.

Judith and Hermana prepared baskets of fruits and vegetables, freshly baked loaves of dark bread and hard-boiled eggs to be taken home by the celebrants.

Their work was finished just in time, for many arrived ahead of the appointed hour, fearful of not getting their share of the food and clothing. Sobe knew most of the guests and kept them moving along to the table where small cakes and cups of balsam drink waited. Joachim stood at the gate to welcome each arrival, and when a guest departed, he gave him a few shekels.

Anna remained indoors, but occasionally looked out hoping that Ezra would arrive from Qumran as promised. She saw Joachim suddenly drop his basket of shekels and slump to the group. She rushed out to him, asking, "What is the matter, Joachim?"

"I'm dizzy. There's a great weight on my chest. I can't get my breath."

Just then Ezra came through the gate. Joachim said to him, "Stay here with Anna. I'm going indoors to lie down. I've been standing here for hours. Don't worry. I'll be all right." Hermana, who was helping Sobe, came quickly and took him into the house.

Anna remarked to Ezra, "Life has a strange way of reversing itself. These people today came so eagerly to get something for nothing. Yet, it was less than a year ago they spat at me when I passed them on the street. They'd cry, 'You are an evil woman, cursed by God. Leave Nazareth!'" She sighed deeply. "I admit there are deep scars left. On the other hand, I've gotten only friendship from Julian and now his young wife, Salina. I've missed your teachings, Ezra." She looked with great love at this devout man whose flowing beard and snow-white hair reminded her of Moses.

They were so engrossed in each other that neither noticed a fierce-looking, unkempt stranger enter the yard. He glared at Anna as he approached and appeared to be heading for the tables. Then, when within a few feet of her, he pulled out a sica. Ezra, immediately aware of the man's intent, jumped in front of her as the man lunged to kill her.

Ezra was tough for a man over sixty-five years of age. He grabbed the attacker's raised arm and maneuvered him into the street. However, Ezra's long garment gave him less mobility than his opponent, who wore a short tunic. Anna stood helpless, but Sobe screamed for Judith to get Julian. There was no use in calling Joachim for this dangerous business.

Julian had just arrived home from Sepphoris, and, alert to any possible problem next door, he had left his horse bridled outside and his broad sword ready. Sobe's screams sent him racing to Anna's garden, and it was then he saw the struggle between the fanatic and Ezra. Before he could reach them, the Zealot leapt wildly at the old man and plunged his sica into Ezra's abdomen. Ezra fell to the ground as a torrent of blood gushed over his white tunic. The unknown assailant paused a moment to smile horribly at Anna, then fled down the street, darting behind houses and across gardens.

Julian ran back and leapt on his horse to track the assassin from his superior vantage point. Now and then, he caught a glimpse of him, or householders would point out the direction of his flight. It was not long before Julian had him cornered in an animal pen.

Expert with weapons of all kinds and trained as a wrestler, the Roman now leapt from his mount, at his enemy, with terrible intent. The short, bloody sica was no match for Julian's heavy sword. He swung it with full force at the fanatical Sicarii, and in one powerful sweep, knocked the dagger from the killer's hand. Without hesitation, Julian drove his sword entirely through the man's body.

"You vile bastard! You tried to kill a holy woman!" he screamed at the fallen man. He pulled his sword free and debated whether to plunge it again into him. On the ground, the stranger's body quivered, a gurgling sound burst from his throat, and then he lay still.

Julian, his face livid with rage, galloped back to Anna who held the dying Ezra in her arms. She was covered with his blood, and sobs racked her shaking body. Joachim, hearing the commotion, came from the house and burst into tears. He took Ezra's lifeless hand and prayed aloud, "Holy Elohim, gather your angels around this devout brother of mine and embrace him in your loving care." His voice broke, and he couldn't continue.

Julian shouted in a voice hoarse with fury, "There'll be no more cowardly Zealots in Galilee. I swear by all-powerful Mars I'll make them the hunted prey."

Anna whispered to him, "Oh, Julian, I had no way of saving Ezra. Why couldn't I have done something?"

"He had a good life. But you, Anna, are irreplaceable." He lifted the lifeless man from her embrace. "Where shall I put him?"

"Sobe, show him," Anna said to her sister.

Joachim's manservant came to help carry Ezra indoors. Julian returned to Anna, who sat dazed on the ground in abject despair. He pulled her bloody hands from her face and drew her to her feet. He said gently, "Many others will give their lives for what they believe is right, Anna, before the world of love you want comes to pass. Yet, I believe you move that day always closer."

She raised her face with its expression of anguish and gratitude to this strange Roman. "Is Joachim all right?"

He nodded. Sobe now joined them. "You are no longer needed here, Julian. I'll take care of my sister."

Julian said to Anna, "I'll be close if you need me."

When he was out of earshot, Sobe said in an unfeeling tone, "You brought this tragedy on yourself, Anna. No matter how much you desire it, you and I will never see the time when Pharisees, Zealots, and Romans will look upon each other as brothers. Your zeal to heal doesn't always work, does it? It's a dangerous enthusiasm, an imagined hope. Where were your angels today when demons invaded your home? Your presence gave Ezra no protection from those who continue to stab openly in our streets. Your devotion to Essenism, instead of the

Pharisaic belief, has made you weak. You are under foreign influence, I believe. I call it Hellenistic Judaism."

"Please Sobe, no lecture now."

Sobe stood over her, determined to vent her long-
standing jealousy of her sister.

"What can you, a descendant of the second king of Israel, have in common with the Essenes who lead a communal or monastic life? You reject the sacrifice of
animals, you refuse to eat meat, you attach great importance to the healing properties of plants, you talk with
the angels—even archangels! All rot! Anna, you flee from
reality. The Qumran community never should have accepted Ezra as a monk. It would be a blessing if Essenes
were swept away by the desert winds!"

Sobe stood like a vulture over its carrion. She sensed
her power over her sister, now weakened in this moment
of grief and horror. A lifetime of stored resentment and
hidden jealousies within Sobe dared now come to the
surface. Anna was so stunned by the attack at this time,
she remained silent, and allowed Sobe to continue to
batter her.

"Another thing I've not mentioned to you was my visit
to Joachim's widower brother, Cleophas. I made no
headway in getting him to propose marriage. He talked
of no one but you—not even his deceased wife. He told
of the time when Joachim disappeared in the wilderness
for five months and you thought him dead. You wrote
for Cleophas to come here to search the Mount Carmel
and Tabor areas. How he comforted you, a childless
widow! His face always took on a special glow when he
spoke of you. It's a disgrace how you deliberately attract
other men. You are responsible for my being denied marriage to Cleophas! You deserve the bloody mess you're in
now!"

Anna began to shiver, although the day was warm. In

a state of shock from Ezra's murder, followed by this vicious attack, she made no attempt to defend herself. The pain of realizing that Sobe actually despised her tore Anna's defenses to shreds A wave of despair hit her. She went into a state of shock. She began to sob softly, yet Sobe continued her scathing abuse.

"What a bloody mess you are, Anna! You were the favored one, the pretty one, the spiritual one sent to study for ten years in the temple. Did you know our parents paid considerable money to get you in and keep you there? I never had that chance because they thought me ugly and ungainly. Then when you returned home, holier than anyone, of course, but so ignorant of housework and dietary rules, I had to teach you everything. Abba insisted I instruct you in Hebrew and Greek and polish your Aramaic. It's time you realize how much I've suffered because of you!"

"Oh, Sobe. I never knew you hated me. I never meant to bring you pain."

Sobe never heard her words, because she turned and ran to the house. Then Anna felt strong arms envelop her and lift her high against a pounding heart. She knew she was being taken , not to her own dwelling, but to Julian's.

He spoke to her now in the soothing tone her father used when she was very young and hurt herself. This was followed by kisses on her hair, just as Stolan did when she cried.

Salina opened the door to them. Julian directed her, "Get water and wash Anna's face and hands. Then brew a soothing tea. She has been attacked, not once today, but twice." He placed pillows beneath her head and straightened her long auburn braids which had lost their scarf. He held one of her trembling hands against his heart. He whispered, "Draw strength from this hardened Roman, who, like Ezra, would give his life for you. But avoid, like a leper, that she-wolf who would gnaw on your vitals."

Salina reappeared with a cup of steaming tea. "This will relax you, Anna, and stop your shivering. Can I bring you a blanket?"

"No, Julian. Don't blame yourself. No one could have anticipated today's events. The hardest thing I have to live with now is Sobe's hateful denunciation of me. I thank you deeply, Julian. Now I must go home."

He helped her to her feet, saying, "We both love you, remember."

She walked slowly home, asking herself how she could have prevented Sobe's attitude toward her. They had shared many good years together. Yet the latent jealousy, stemming from Anna's entry into the temple at age five, was no fault of anyone's. All these years the sore had festered. "Why have I been so blind to her emotional needs?"

She was grateful for Julian's intervention. Joachim, with physical problems of his own, was in a state of shock over Ezra's murder. Julian was the strong one to turn to now. It wasn't romantic love she felt for him, she kept telling herself. Yet, it was an attraction that defied analysis. He challenged her; he constantly tested her emotional control. But he was also a source of great comfort—perhaps the brother she had always wanted.

Today, she was sure Julian exaggerated his feelings toward her. It was a game he played with all women. He was fascinated by her independent opinions of right and wrong; that was it. Of course, he knew that she loved Joachim above anyone else. When you weep and despair with someone for twenty scalding years, an indestructible bond is forged between you. Any other husband would have divorced her, and she would have become an outcast. Joachim's love had been unwavering, as solid as the high mountains on which his sheep grazed. They both knew their cosmic purpose. With the surprising birth of Mary, they could now identify with the will of God.

Yet, why did she have a curious need for Julian's friendship? Where did he fit in her life? She wanted desperately for him to accept her God of Love, since it was a prelude to something important that would occur later in their lives. This riddle probably wouldn't be solved until the Messiah revealed himself. And that was countless years away.

* * *

Anna and Joachim finished their evening meal of parched grain and chick peas and left the table at once, since Hermana and Judith needed the space to prepare food for the next day. There were eggs to boil, a leg of lamb to roast, bread to bake, and vegetables to prepare, since no cooking was allowed on the Sabbath.

Ezra had been buried, and both Anna and Joachim were in a sad and quiet mood.

Anna spoke first. "Let us say goodnight to Mary. Then I have something important to discuss with you."

As they bent over the contented child in her crib, Joachim whispered, "Mary, your hair is spun gold, your eyes are shining copper coins, your cheeks are the petals of a pink rose. How I love you, little cherub!" He kissed her, then turned to Anna. "I know she understands everything I say."

Anna smiled, and they went back to the sitting room. Joachim continued speaking. "Have I told you how much younger you look since Mary came? I love you beyond life itself, Anna. Will you always remember that?"

Anna nodded, and her eyes grew moist. "At this moment, dear Joachim, you have made yourself very vulnerable, and I shall take advantage of you. Forewarned of my intentions, I want to express first my gratitude for your being so tolerant of my mystical nature, of my Essene beliefs and love for Ezra's teachings, of my deep feelings that can't be expressed in words, and of my daring steps into the realm of healing. I hope, once again, you will be understanding of the reason I ask another favor of you."

Joachim looked mystified but said, "Yes, yes, Try me."

"I want us to move to Sepphoris, into the lovely home you inherited from your parents. We can afford to keep this place. It's for Mary's use when she has finished her temple training and returns here to marry."

Joachim's face became grave. "You aren't happy here?"

"No longer. There are too many traumatic memories in the yard. You know how deeply I loved Ezra. He taught me everything I know about healing. That other house sits on the heights above the Zabulon Valley. We could make a new beginning there. Please?"

Joachim sat in stubborn silence for a long moment. Then his face flushed and he spoke louder than he intended. "That house is close to where Julian has his headquarters!"

"He won't be there. Herod has sent him on business to Rome, Greece, and Phoenicia. He has taken Salina with him, and they may be away for years."

Joachim ignored her remarks. He ran his fingers through his graying hair, then pressed his hand to his mouth as if to stop what he intended to say. Finally, he spoke in a strained voice. "I hate that man! His eyes grow soft when he looks at you. His voice drops almost to a whisper when he speaks to you. He's a deadly chameleon, changing colors to impress you! When I die, will you marry him?"

Anna rose quickly from her chair and dropped to the

floor at his feet. "You can't be serious. I'll love you forever as no one else." She pressed her head against his thigh and clung to him. Joachim kissed her hair, but said nothing. She continued, "You are justified in feeling hurt. I've neglected you since Mary's birth. Forgive me for being so totally devoted to her. I haven't forgotten how you stood by me during all those years of our disgrace—never wavering, never listening to those who told you to divorce me. Do you think that I would ever stop loving such a dedicated husband?"

"It's just that Julian is a reviled Roman—a legate of despicable Herod. He's no abstract situation in need of understanding. He's a virile man, tough, self-centered, lying in wait like a jaguar for you, hoping I'll die so he can have you!"

Joachim stood up, his stocky body rigid with righteous authority. "You have a child now, so get on with your life as a mother. Forget your desire to heal people."

Anna had a disconcerting habit of lowering her voice to almost a whisper when she was upset. Joachim was forced to bend over her to hear her reply.

"Remember, angry husband, our Mary will not be with us for long. We promised God to place our firstborn in his service at the age of three. She will live with no earthly mother or father for at least ten years. I remember how I longed for my mother, Emerentiana, when I was a virgin in the temple. Nothing can replace a mother's love. I wonder if I can be strong enough to bear her loss . . . " Her voice broke.

Joachim said contritely, "We'll visit her often."

Anna shook her head. "Not often enough. Your flocks need you, and what's worse, the priests allow only a short visit each time. I'll never know her precious growing years. Mary will share her childhood fears and hopes and questions with Naomi as her teacher. How little time there is for me to instruct her before she leaves us! When she returns to Nazareth, she will be a young woman ready for marriage."

Moved to tears by her words, Joachim dropped to the floor beside Anna, and took her in his arms. "I have been unbearable. Will you forgive me for everything I've said?"

Anna nodded, too emotional to speak. Joachim returned the conversation to their move to Sepphoris. "Will you miss the many friends you have made since Mary's birth?"

"I wonder how sincere these newfound friends are."

"Come, come, Anna. Haven't you forgiven everyone by now?"

"Superficially, I suppose. Deep down, there must be scars. Perhaps, that's why I can look upon Romans, Egyptians, Samaritans, and other peoples in Palestine without hate. They didn't revile us for twenty years. But the Israelites, our own people, did. Your steadfast love for me cannot be compared to any other emotion in my life. What is driving me away from this house is actually a combination of Ezra's shocking death—he saved my life by taking the blow intended for me—and Sobe's heartless denunciation of me in my moment of agony. I never imagined she hated me so much. I thought it was sibling rivalry, nothing more. I will never get over it."

Joachim rose and paced the floor, speaking in a conciliatory tone. "That house in Sepphoris is large—it can accommodate the servants well, and it does have a wonderful view of the Zabulon Valley. Besides, it's only an hour-and-a-half walk—less, on the donkeys—for me to attend Sabbath services here and be with old friends regularly. Perhaps, a totally new environment would be good for both of us."

Anna knew he was doing his best to convince himself of the wisdom of such a move. Finally, he sighed in resignation. "It's settled. We'll start packing at once for our new home."

Anna leapt to her feet, hugged him, and danced around the room with joy. She looked forward to devoting her entire time to preparing Mary for admittance into the Essene Community as one of the twelve select virgins. A committee of Essene rabbis would conduct a verbal test of the child before recommending her to be one of the twelve. Her answers to their probing questions must convince them of her spiritual knowledge and proper attitudes, since it would be an exception for her to be selected at the tender age of three.

Were they wrong in giving her to spiritual training so early? That had been their promise so long ago, when they prayed desperately for a child. Now, they must keep their word to God.

Anna had, at first, thought she would send Mary to the temple, where Anna had been sent by her parents. Ezra had talked with her at length about how the Essenes were preparing to teach a class of very carefully chosen young virgins, in hopes that one of them would become the proper channel for the Messiah to enter. Her deep respect for Ezra, her strong influence from her mother and Emerentiana's desire to bring forth this special son through her blood line, and Anna's firm conviction that Mary was conceived in deep spiritual love instead of a physical union, spurred her to the decision of sending Mary to the Essenes. She could transfer to the temple when she was older and, thus, have the advantages of the spiritual training and knowledge of both places.

CHAPTER 7

The move to Sepphoris pleased everyone. The house was spacious and secluded. It was fronted by a charming courtyard enclosed by a wall of stones and a high wattle hedge. In its center was a fountain that supplied their water needs. Weeping fig trees dipped their branches to the ground to take new roots and shoot forth eager young saplings. In their arbors, Mary played, while her mother sat close by. Anna ignored all other duties in order to share these last months with her child.

Once Mary was weaned and learned to walk, Anna began daily lessons in Aramaic, prayers in Hebrew, and short readings from the Holy Scriptures. It was a joyous time for both of them.

One morning before breakfast, Mary surprised Joachim by telling him it was time to say the first prayer of the day. At the end of the meal, he asked her in jest what the first commandment was in the Scriptures. She answered with a giggle, "Be fruitful and multiply." He was delighted.

"How long, Anna, have you drilled her to give this answer?"

"Obviously long enough to please you, Joachim. Ask her questions about the angels, and hear what she remembers."

"Very well. Mary, who is the guardian angel of Israel?"

"Michael," Mary answered without hesitation.

"Then who is Gabriel?"

Mary thought for a moment, then remembered, "The one who brings messages."

"That's right. He's the leader of the archangels." Joachim's face grew grave and he cleared his voice. "One day, Gabriel will appear before you with a beautiful message. Will you remember that?"

Mary nodded dutifully. Then, to show off her wisdom, she said, "I learned today that you don't plow with an ox and a donkey together. And you don't graft an apple twig on a pear tree." She paraded back and forth before Joachim, a happy smile on her childish face.

"Now here's a question for you. Would you weave silk and cotton together in the same garment?"

Mary stopped short. She weighed the question as if her future depended on it. Then she answered, "Not if you don't plow with a donkey and an ox together."

Joachim lifted her high in the air before smothering her with kisses. When he put her down, he said to Anna, "You are doing more than making her a parrot for the examining committee. She already knows how to reason. I'm proud of both of you."

"There's still so much for her to learn."

Mary spoke up immediately. "Don't worry, Abba. I'll just call on that angel who carries messages."

"Yes, call on Gabriel if you don't know the answer."

Both parents grew silent, remembering their own encounter with the divine emissary of God. Anna whispered to Joachim, "Will he bring Mary the wondrous message we've waited for all our lives?"

"Of course. No one in heaven would have the heart to disappoint you two." They both laughed.

*   *   *

It was a warm spring day with trees bursting into bloom when Joachim's mountain pastures called for his return. Anna occupied herself with bathing Mary and washing her fine golden hair. She permitted neither Judith nor Hermana to perform these chores.

An unexpected knock on the front door brought Hermana to answer it. Before her stood a distraught woman, holding a baby covered with round patches of a fungus infection. Scaling skin and small blisters kept the infant crying.

The stranger spoke in a pleading voice, "My baby is dying from a skin ailment. He has had no sleep for days. Will Anna of Nazareth help me?"

"Come inside and wait," Hermana said. "I will ask her to look at him."

In a few minutes, Anna finished bathing Mary, dried her and turned her over to Hermana to dress. Then she went to the suffering child and took him in her arms.

"How did you happen to come to me for help?" Anna asked. "I have just moved here."

"A Roman official passed me on the street and saw how desperate I was."

Anna thought, "So Julian is testing my healing ability. I know I can't cure everyone's ailments, since the decision rests with God. All I can do is pray with all my might, with all my love."

Then, as the stranger waited, an idea occurred to

Anna. "I will set your son in my infant's bath water. He's so feverish it might help him. Please wait here."

She placed the suffering boy in the unemptied receptacle used for Mary's bath and splashed the water over his inflamed body for several minutes. As she did this, she formed a clear mental image of unblemished skin covering the child. Then she dried him, wrapped him in one of Mary's blankets, and returned him to his mother.

She told her, "Keep this blanket over him for an hour. By then the round patches will be gone and he will be free of all pain."

After the woman left , Hermana asked Anna, "Do you really believe you cured him? I think he was so exhausted, he just went to sleep from feeling the cool water."

"Perhaps," Anna replied, well aware of Hermana's skepticism regarding unusual healing attempts.

However, the next day, the overjoyed mother returned with her son. "Aaron's skin is free of blemish! There's no rash, no pain, no scars! He slept peacefully all night. How can I thank you enough?"

Anna took the child in her arms and kissed him. "God loves you, little stranger," she said to him. Then turning to the mother, she added, "I am grateful that you let me know he is well again. That is enough thanks."

After they left, Anna mused out loud, "So Mary's bath water has healing power. Can it be that she will become the mother of the greatest healer of all?"

Hermana asked, "Mother of whom?"

"Of a great son of her own," Anna finished lamely, realizing she had almost said, "The Messiah." She dared not reveal more to Joachim's sister, since she was inclined to gossip, brag and exaggerate.

*   *   *

Anna had never been so busy. She spent all of her time drilling Mary on possible questions the rabbis might ask her before recommending her as one of the twelve. Anna's own experience at the temple was invaluable in guessing what subjects they would cover.

Mary must learn the rigid dietary laws of her people: no meat and milk products to be eaten together; separate utensils, dishes and silver for each; a lapse of one hour's time after eating meat before consuming dairy foods, one-half hour after eating dairy foods before one could eat meat, etc. But Mary was especially interested in the world of angels.

She asked her mother, "Will I ever see an angel?"

"Yes, one day Gabriel will come to you in human form. He will have wondrous wings of silver and carry a message that will change your life."

"What if he gets old and dies before I see him?"

"Mary, angels never die."

"When he comes to me, do I say, 'Shalom, Archangel! What is your message?'"

Anna laughed. "My darling, you won't be able to speak!"

*   *   *

The day after the celebration of Mary's third birthday, the Essene examining committee was due.

Anna wished that Joachim were here, but he had left earlier to distribute the weekly donations of food to the poor. This ritual had always been carried out by Sobe, but after Ezra's death and their move to Sepphoris, Sobe had not communicated with them. This depressed Anna immensely, but, for the moment, she had more important things to do than pursue a jealous sister.

The examiners were dressed like triplets. Each wore

an unbleached wool tunic gathered at the waist by an embroidered girdle. Tasseled prayer shawls covered their heads, and, on their left hands and foreheads, leather thongs held firm their *tefillin*—those small leather cases containing passages from Exodus and Deuteronomy, inscribed on parchment. Their sandals of camelhide were the same as everyone's. Anna was pleased that no special clothing was worn to impress her three-year-old with the seriousness of the occasion.

Now Anna called Mary and met her at the door. She took Mary's hand and brought her before each rabbi for an introduction. A surprised murmur went through the group at the sight of the beautiful child. Mary did not smile, but acknowledged each with a deep bow.

Seth, the leader of the gang, promptly cleared his throat and said, "We promise to be brief. Mary, be seated and look upon us as friends who have come here only to get acquainted with you. Your ancestry is pure—a direct line from King David, so there is no question as to your eligibility. Let me begin by asking you what the most important food of all is."

Mary jumped from her chair and stood straight. "Bread," she answered softly.

"That's right. I see a table beyond this room, obviously in the cooking area. Is that where you eat?"

"Yes."

"Should we consider the table just a piece of furniture or something greater?"

"No, it is a symbolic altar of God."

Anna breathed a sigh of relief, since she had drilled Mary long on the word "symbolic."

Uriah continued the questioning. "You have beautiful long curls. Why doesn't your mother cut your hair?"

Mary thought a moment before answering. "That would show someone had died."

"Correct. It is a sign of mourning.

He asked, "If we pray to God for help, does he come in person?"

Mary looked startled by the question. She thought it over then said, "He never has."

"Then you've prayed to Him for help?"

"Yes, but I ask Him to send an angel, since I know He's so busy."

"In order to speak to this angel, what is most important that you feel?"

"Feel? Why, only a love of God."

The men exchanged delighted smiles, and Uriah indicated that it was Lemuel's turn to interrogate her.

"Mary, do you believe that one day you will meet God face to face?"

"No, we can't see Him."

"If you can't see Him, where is God?"

She gave him a mischievous smile. "He hides in my heart."

"That's the best answer I've ever heard. He lies within our own selves. A final question, Mary. What is the greatest gift God can give us when we go to the heaven-world?"

"You mean when we die?"

Seth nodded. She thought a long time and looked to her mother for help. Anna smiled her encouragement.

"Oh, I know what you mean. It's the gift of forever-and-ever life."

"That's correct—eternal life." He turned to the other rabbis. "This child is so extraordinary, there's no need to question her further."

The other men nodded in agreement. Each in turn rose and embraced Mary. Seth spoke for all. "Congratulations to both of you. Anna, you have taught her well. She may begin her life in the Essene community at once."

Anna waited until the men were gone before she let her emotions show. Then she burst into tears. Her pride in Mary's answers could not overcome her sadness. Once Mary left for Mount Carmel, she might never return to her parents. Preparations must be made at once for the family's journey to the Essene community and Mary's formal presentation. These activities would, Anna hoped, lessen the pain of her departure.

In the weeks that followed, Anna was besieged with mothers whose children were ailing. They begged her to place their offspring in Mary's bath water, each waiting her turn with a crying infant. She regretted having begun this ritual. Finally, she was forced to stop bathing the strangers in order to prepare Mary for her presentation.

Hermana, who had married one of Joachim's shepherds but spent much of her time with Anna, was a fine seamstress and agreed to create three sets of garments for Mary. Each one consisted of an undergarment, a bodice and a robe in different colors to signify special meanings, according to ecclesiastical ritual.

The day for the family's departure for Mount Carmel came too soon for both parents, but they successfully hid their grief from their daughter. Mary seemed aglow with anticipation, but at the same time, she sensed her parents' sadness.

* * *

Obadiah, Joachim's manservant, led the donkey on which Mary rode. He had devised a comfortable seat with footrests for her. Although each person had an animal to ride, walking often was more satisfactory. Hermana and Judith took charge of the pack animals, laden with clothing and food. Joachim appeared unstable on his feet at times and used a rod to support himself.

There were hills to climb and streams to cross before reaching their first night's lodging at Endor. Frequent stops were made where balsam shrubs grew. The dripping sap, when caught in stone basins, was diluted with water and quickly revived the weary travelers. Also, the servants found ripe berries, and with flat cakes of dark bread and aged cheese, no one went hungry.

Mary never complained of fatigue, although the others frequently did. She appeared to be mentally preparing for her presentation to the Essene community and said nothing. Only when Anna washed her flushed face did she smile her appreciation.

On the second evening, the party camped at Bethhoron. It was a Levite town where they had agreed to join Esmeria and her husband, Ephraim. Late in the evening, Cleophas and his two daughters also arrived there. Joachim's youngest brother, Salamo, sent word that he and his wife would find the party in the city. Anna had dispatched an invitation to Sobe to meet the others here, but she had heard nothing from her.

During the last half of the journey, Cleophas supported unsteady Joachim often and kept a close watch on him at all times. He had little opportunity to speak to Anna, but she sensed his desire to do so.

The travelers crossed several stone bridges that spanned valleys within the city and made their way to the ceremonial inn, which Joachim had rented for this occasion. There was a large room for cooking on the hearth and serving meals. A private courtyard opened onto comfortable, adjacent sleeping rooms.

Obadiah unloaded the pack animals, and the men carried bags of clothing and food into the central structure. The men and women broke into two groups for washing their feet, then came together at the large basin of water set out for washing hands and face.

At this time, Mary's cousin, Elizabeth, and Elizabeth's husband, Zacharias, arrived from Joppa, and the party took on a festive air. They all hurriedly changed clothes and joined each other in the courtyard to walk to the community room, farther up the hill, for the initial ceremony.

Mary was enchanted by the bewildering events and, especially, by her new clothes. She was dressed in a pale orange undergarment with white bodice and burnt-orange robe. On her head sat a white silk wreath, decorated with orange roses, and a short veil that tickled her nose.

"Do I really look pretty?" she asked, pirouetting before Anna.

"Yes. Don't you hear the angels clapping their hands? Now, I must show you how to lift your veil before you eat. It must be done in one gesture, using both hands. Make it look as if you were accustomed to wearing a veil every day."

Mary laughed, anticipating eagerly each part of the elaborate ritual. "Do it slowly, Emi."

Anna went through the motions twice, then said, "Now, it's your turn."

Mary tossed the sheer fabric back onto her head with a determined sweep of her hands.

Anna laughed. "No more practice. A rabbi waits for us in the dining hall."

When the family gathered around him, he announced, "I am Axel, and beside me is Naomi, the widow who will be in charge of our new virgin. You women will eat over there to my right, and the men to my left. Mary is to sit next to me, since I have a few questions to ask her."

Naomi, who appeared to be kind and understanding, came and sat next to Anna. She hoped this teacher would be gentle with her sensitive daughter and protect her from difficult work as she grew older.

She noticed that Mary ate little, taking care to select only those foods she ate at home. Anna had warned her that the rabbis would test her on unacceptable combinations. She must avoid milk, and, if she took meat, then she mustn't eat fish. It was a lot to remember.

Mary had responded, "I'll eat neither, and make the rabbis guess what I'll do."

Now, by the pleased look on Axel's face, Anna knew Mary had passed this first test. He rose and clapped his hands for quiet.

"You'll have the balance of the day for rest and a chance to get acquainted with family members. Have an early breakfast tomorrow, as we begin the ceremonies midmorning."

Everyone left for the inn to visit. Sobe, to everyone's surprise, stood waiting for the party at the inn. Anna greeted her with caution, but Sobe acted as if nothing had occurred between them to strain their relations.

She spoke first and with a touch of arrogance. "I knew someone was needed to cook for this gathering, so I will take charge of the meals."

Anna smiled. "I deeply appreciate your being here, Sobe. Make good use of Judith and Hermana, else they will feel hurt. After the ceremony tomorrow, Mary will leave us, and we will come back here for a banquet. There will be much for all of us to do."

Anna looked around for Mary, and found her with Cleophas on the opposite side of the room. "You must take a nap, darling," she said to the child. Judith spoke then, "Let me go with her, Anna. I have many things I want to say to her."

Anna nodded her approval, then turned to Cleophas. "I thought you'd have married by now. We've missed your visits."

He responded by taking her arm and conducting her

outside, where they sat down on a bench in the court-yard.

"What a sacrifice you've made, Anna," he said. "I believe she will be happy here. She appears more like a child of five or six."

"Thank you for being so supportive. I always wanted a brother, but now I think of you in that way—caring, always ready to help."

Cleophas remained silent, so Anna asked him bluntly, "Why haven't you remarried by now. It has worried Joachim."

"I haven't found the right Essene, Anna, so I will remain single until I do. I've wondered, if Joachim should die in the years ahead, would you remarry?"

Anna felt a strange quickening of her pulse. She chose her words carefully. "I have never thought of such a situation. I'm past forty years of age—certainly not attractive to a man who wants children."

Cleophas placed his hand over hers, and she tried to curb her slight trembling. "You are more beautiful than I have ever seen you, yet you are making a great sacrifice. Other parents would be feeling sorry for themselves. Not you and Joachim. How do you give up a child after waiting for her for half a lifetime?"

"One must keep promises made to God."

Cleophas, seeing that Hermana beckoned to Anna to come indoors, spoke hurriedly, "I'm concerned about Joachim. He appears ill with shock and more. Would you mind if I travel back to Sepphoris with you to make certain he can complete the journey?"

"Oh, would you, Cleophas? How thoughtful of you!" She flashed him a warm smile and joined Hermana.

He left the inn to walk through the residential area, where the thick-walled houses were built on terraced streets.

Cleophas had mixed emotions. He was worried over Joachim's pallor and deep grief over Mary's departure. Cleophas also knew he was in love with Anna, but his feelings toward his brother's wife must remain hidden. Had he been too obvious in what he said to her just now? He was a romantic person with an active imagination; so was Anna. They had grown in the same direction, both adopting the beliefs of the married Essenes. He, too, accepted miracles as everyday, normal occurrences and spoke of angels as if they lived next door to him. This alienated him from his Pharisee relatives.

Deep in thought, he nearly collided with a Roman in white toga on the narrow street. He stepped aside to let the official pass, but the man spoke to him.

"You are a member of the group celebrating the new temple virgin, Mary bat Joachim?" he asked.

"Yes, and who are you?"

"Julian, legate to Galilee. I know the family well, having lived in Nazareth near them. Can you tell me at what time the formalities will take place?'

"Midmorning, I understand." Cleophas guessed that this was the Roman whom Sobe had mentioned to him on her ill-fated visit to Shiloh. He was everything she claimed him to be—conceited and radiating enormous power. The clean-shaven face, the piercing green eyes, the short curly hair, and the rings on many fingers gave him an air of self-importance bordering on majesty. He hesitated as if he wanted to say more, then appeared to think better of it, and went on his way.

Cleophas wondered if he should mention this encounter to Anna, but he felt an unexplained jealousy of the Roman and decided against it.

*   *   *

The following morning, eleven young virgins in pastel

dresses came to the inn to escort Mary to the temple. Each wore a garland of flowers about her neck.

Mary was dressed in her special costume for the presentation ceremony. It was the color of hyacinths, with a silk bodice and deep-purple velvet robe that ended in a short train. A gold, silk crown, embroidered with pearls, held a medium-length veil on her blond head.

Two priests met the girls and took charge of Mary. One of them asked her, "Will you rise each night to pray?"

Mary nodded eagerly.

"Just once a night for now. Later you may be asked to rise three times."

Anna and Joachim, who followed Mary, exchanged angry looks. Were they trying to frighten the child?

Naomi now joined the parents, saying, "I'm sure you will want to see Mary's room."

They descended the stairs into the subterranean section, where the praying cells were located. From there, stairs led to small cubicles built in the thick walls.

"This room is Mary's for as many years as she remains here," Naomi said.

Inside was a roll of carpet which would become Mary's bed, and a small cupboard for her clothes. A lamp, set in a niche in the wall, gave out a feeble light.

Anna placed the bundle of Mary's clothes on a table and debated where to set the jug of terebinth water. Joachim placed a sack of fruit on the floor and walked out. He was too overcome with shock to remain in these crude surroundings. But Mary showed no emotion. Her mother had prepared her well.

The rabbi led the group as they left the outer court to climb a broad flight of stairs to the inner walled area known as the Court of Women. Here the ceremony would take place.

The priests directed the men to stand on one side and

the women on the other. Cleophas and Salamo stood beside Joachim, ready to support him if necessary. Essene women, in long, white robes with wide sleeves and rope girdles, directed the family where to stand, since room had to be allowed for the musicians. They were young boys dressed also in white, carrying either a flute, woodwind, or stringed instrument.

The young virgins sang a psalm, accompanied by the musicians, then a priest led Mary up the fifteen steps to the altar. The steps represented the six orders of the saints and the nine choirs of the angels.

The priest, resplendent in white, entered and moved to the altar. His heavy garment reached to the floor in three cascades. The center overlay was fringed with tassels; the upper garment was embroidered with the jeweled Urim and Thummin—that dazzling breastplate needed for divination. It was said to be used by the priest to determine God's response to questions answerable by "yes" or "no."

Mary's expression was one of total wonder as she looked at his mitered crown of white satin, encircled by a gold plate inscribed with Hebrew letters. He lifted her onto the third step of the altar, where she danced a few steps in delight.

The Priest smiled, "You look upon my headdress with interest. Can you read the inscription?"

Mary said softly, "Holiness to the Lord."

"Excellent! Another question: Should we hate people who are not of our faith?"

Again Mary replied without hesitation, "No, that is a cardinal sin."

The priest appeared to be hard-pressed for an appropriate question to ask such a young child. Then he spoke in an encouraging tone, "Can you recite our most revered prayer, the Shema?"

Mary nodded eagerly and turned to face the audience. In her clear, sweet voice, she began the holy words: "Hear, O Israel, the Lord our God, the Lord is One! And thou shalt love the Lord thy God with all thy heart, and with all thy soul and with all thy might." She hesitated and looked down to her mother. Anna nodded her encouragement. Mary took a deep breath and continued, "And these words which I command this day shall be upon thy heart; and thou shalt teach them diligently unto thy children . . . " She paused to catch her breath. The priest whispered, "and shalt talk of them . . . " Mary continued faster and faster, "when thou sittest in thy house, and when thou walkest by the way, and when thou liest down, and when thou risest up."

The delighted priest turned to the audience, lifting his hands high as all responded loudly, "Hoshahnah!" He embraced Mary, while the choir played triumphant music. The relatives moved toward Mary to congratulate her. Joachim was the first to reach her and lifted her in his arms. His voice broke with emotion as he said, "Remember at night the words of the psalmist which we recited together, 'In thee, O Lord, do I put my trust; for thou art my rock and my fortress.' Oh, blessed daughter, into God's arms I commit you with such love. You will never know—such love I have for you."

Mary said nothing, but she clung to him with eyes closed, as he kissed her cheeks. By now, Anna had reached her, and she fought back threatening tears, saying, "I will come to visit you as soon as it is permissible. If there's anything you need or want, send us a message by Naomi. She will learn to love you as we do. You look so beautiful today, and you were wonderful in remembering everything. We are all so proud of you."

Naomi, dressed in white veil and long, white robe, took Mary's hand and pulled her away from the group.

"We must go now," she said.

Cleophas held Joachim's arm, realizing the strain had been great on him. Anna stood with eyes closed, remembering the anguish of her own parting from her mother when she was left at the temple in Jerusalem. She was five, not three. The other women left her alone and returned to the inn. She returned to the entrance. Here she stood in sober remembrance of her reunion with Joachim, following his long absence in the desert, when she thought she was a widow.

Someone touched her shoulder, and she turned to face the intense gaze of Julian. "At last, we meet again," he said in a quiet voice. "It's been nearly three years, and I've counted the days."

Anna flushed with surprise, but managed to ask, "Is Salina here, too?"

Before answering, Julian indicated they should move away from the steps, to a more quiet spot.

"She stayed in Rome. She wanted to be out of her father's reach. We were divorced, and with the help of Augustus, I found a fine position for her as a nurse in the home of a noble family. They had a child who stammered badly, and she wanted to help them as you had her."

"I'll miss her. I loved her very much."

"I know. She asked to be remembered to you. In fact, she sent you a small gift." He handed Anna a book bound in blue leather. "You read Latin, I know."

Anna saw it was a book of poetry by Virgil.

Julian continued, "They are pastoral sketches, full of love. Everyone, whether fool or philosopher, writes poetry in Rome now." He seemed embarrassed for a moment, then explained, "Augustus has built two public libraries since I was last there. He intends to make the city the rival of Alexandria, and Herod now wants a library in Caesarea. I have drawn up plans for it. I learned a great deal during my work in Sidon and Tyre. Herod was especially interested in the construction of their Greek buildings. He wants to be more than King of the Jews, Anna. By expanding his role into Phoenicia, he aims to become the idol of the Hellenic world—a second Caesar Augustus." He laughed cynically. "I doubt if he'll realize those schemes. Wherever I go I hear of plots against his life."

Julian moved closer to Anna as he continued, "I need to return to Galilee, where there are no marvels of architecture or edifices of white stone. But there are greater marvels to be found there—like you, Anna."

She was prepared for his flattery and answered in a quiet voice, "I include you in my daily prayers, Julian, hoping you'll discover your real purpose in life. I'm certain that, one day, something meaningful, something totally wonderful will happen to you." She turned to leave him, adding, "Thank you for driving all sense of desolation from my thoughts. You, too, can be a magician, when you want to."

They both laughed at her remark. Julian said, "Until we meet in Sepphoris, Anna bat Stolan."

She walked slowly down the path to the inn, stopping once to look again at the lovely book of verse. Had Julian really changed that much, or did he hope to weaken her defenses? He had gotten rid of his wife, yet he didn't appear to be a free man. He was bound to a dream of marrying her one day.

Her thoughts returned to Mary. She was surprised that her daughter had shown no grief at leaving them. This had greatly upset Joachim. Did Mary subconsciously know her mission in life? Was the gift of stoicism given her so that, in decades hence, she could face enormous tests? Or were Anna and Joachim deluding themselves in thinking that God had selected Mary to bring into fruition the dreams of every Israelite?

The answer to these questions, Anna knew, remained shrouded in mystery. She forced herself to be happy today and was especially grateful for Sobe's efficient presence. Esmeria spent her time in gossiping and took no interest in lighting candles or setting food on the table.

Sobe, with chameleon-like ingenuity, played the role of a charming housewife today, obviously for the benefit of Cleophas. She hummed as she worked; she fairly skipped from one chore to another. She directed Anna's two servants with gentleness, and, for once, her hair was tastefully arranged. A new, pink silk robe, with wide girdle, revealed her trim waistline—to the envy of buxom Esmeria and the other aging wives.

If Cleophas was impressed, he didn't show it, so preoccupied was he with taking care of Joachim. But Sobe lost no time in making other plans when she overheard Anna say to him, "Joachim has begun to run a fever. I'm worried about getting him home, but I'm relieved that you'll be with us."

Sobe stepped quickly to Anna. "You and Cleophas won't mind if I travel home with you?"

"You're welcome, but I don't know how fast we can go with Joachim. He's extremely weak."

"No matter, sister. Cleophas and I will lessen your burden." She took him by the arm in a possessive gesture.

His face was a mask as he said, "We'll take good care of both of you, Anna."

CHAPTER 8

Anna stayed indoors before the warm hearth, while the cold rains of the month of Kislev pounded the heights overlooking Sepphoris. She felt consoled by Virgil's romantic book of poetry given her by Julian. Re-reading its pastoral descriptions reminded her of Joachim's tenderness and love. Her devoted husband had been laid to rest a year ago, following their return from Mary's presentation at the temple.

Anna wore sackcloth for a month, following his burial near their home just outside the walls of Jerusalem. Only Cleophas and Salamo accompanied Anna and the body there. It was placed on a bench cut out of the rocky hill-side and covered with aromatic herbs. Then the men set a great round gate, like a millstone, before the tomb's entrance.

"We'll return with you, Anna, to whitewash the stone in Adar, the last month of the liturgical year," Cleophas had promised. "That is according to a Pharisee custom and Joachim's belief."

Anna had left all arrangements to the brothers. They went with her to break the news to Mary and were surprised how well she accepted Joachim's death.

Mary asked only one question. "Is Abba among the angels now?"

"Of course," Anna replied, "but he will always be close to you, protecting you with his deep love."

"Can I talk with him?"

"Yes, but only you will know in your heart what he answers." That seemed to satisfy the child.

Anna was grateful that the virgins were kept so occupied that they had little time for grieving over absent parents. She visited Mary each month, accompanied always by Cleophas.

"I won't allow you to go with only servants to Judea," he said sternly. "Herod has now killed five of his sons. He's so inhuman that even Augustus is reported to have said, 'It's better to be Herod's pig than his son.' He has reigned now for twenty-four years and has made Israel a police state. He thinks he's being persecuted and sends his conspirators everywhere. If he learns of your curing Salina's stuttering, his wrath will fall on you, too."

"There is something bothering you, Anna," Cleophas said. "I know your moods so well. Tell me what it is."

"There is a great deal of pressure on me to remarry. Rumors have sprung up—perhaps from the Carmel prophets—that Mary is destined for greatness. The sopher of the new synagogue in Sepphoris tells me I am duty-bound to produce more children, even at my age. He has seen to it that suitors from all over Palestine have presented their qualifications to me. What do you think I should do?"

"Marry the man who has loved you for years—me. I

adore you, Anna. Will you be my wife?"

There was no hesitation in Anna's reply. She held out her arms to him, and they kissed with deep emotion.

Anna spoke first. "O, Cleophas, now I can laugh again. I warn you, though, I'm ordering another daughter. Can that be a part of our nuptial agreement?" They both laughed.

"I will close my sandal shop in Shiloh," Cleophas said. "I don't need to work, but I would like to continue on a small scale, making only elegant sandals for weddings and special occasions. I'll find a place in the market square here."

"Hermana's husband has taken charge of Joachim's flocks, and has promised to continue giving one-third to the poor and one-third to the temple. Have you any objections to that?'

"We have more than we need from my income, Anna. At our age, there's no reason to delay our marriage."

*   *   *

Upon the couple's return to Sepphoris, Anna found a message waiting for her from Julian. It had been written two months earlier. She remembered that he often called her "a woman meant for more than one husband." She wondered eagerly what he was doing in those far-away, romantic places such as Phoenicia, Greece, and the City of Seven Hills. Time had not severed the invisible bond between the two of them. He had no way of knowing that Joachim was dead and that she had promised to marry his brother. For a brief moment, she wished he were here—to challenge her feelings and make her examine her motives for marrying. Yes, even to forbid her to marry Cleophas or anyone but him.

The message was simple and could have been written by a friend. In part, it read, "Rumors here claim Herod is hated more and more. His enemies went so far as to place human bones in the holy sanctuary before the last religious festival, defiling it so no services could be held. Alarm is growing in Rome over Herod's inability to stop constant revolts. One day, you may need my protection, and I will come. I would give my life for you, Anna." She placed the letter to her lips, then burned it.

Ten months after Anna's marriage to Cleophas, a dark-haired, blue-eyed girl was born to them. Anna insisted they call her, too, "Mary."

She explained to everyone, "My first Mary was a gift from God. Yet I know her destiny doesn't include a life with me. She'll marry as soon as her training is complete. On the other hand, my second Mary is a gift from Cleophas. You know the custom is followed in many families where they lose a favorite child. The newborn Mary will be Mary, the Younger, or Mary bat Cleophas. She won't lack any luster by sharing the name."

However, there was a difference. This child was extremely frail from birth and needed constant care. Anna rarely left her with Judith. But when the wife of Cleophas' brother, Salamo, died, they felt required to go to Shiloh for a brief visit. The maidservant was reliable and loved the child. Now two years old, Mary's health appeared to have improved, and Anna believed she could safely be absent for a few days.

It was the spring month of Nissan, when the weather was erratic, and inclined to sudden changes. During the parents' absence, the burning *khamsin* wind swept into Galilee like a searing fire. It forced the temperature up to 108 degrees and filled the house with a fine sand from burning desert areas. That same night, the temperature plummeted to the freezing point—a phenomenon that Judith hadn't experienced before. This sudden weather change produced devastating inflammation of the child

Mary's lungs. She died soon after, before Anna and Cleophas returned.

Anna was devastated and blamed herself for the tragedy. It was obvious that God didn't intend her to raise a child, she told herself. When people came to her to be healed, she refused to try to help them. She had lost all confidence in her ability. Sensitive Cleophas let her emotions run their course, and she appeared to have become reconciled to her childless state again. She was quieter than usual, though, and Cleophas gave her a great deal of attention and love.

For an entire year, Sobe didn't come near Anna. Then, one day, she appeared, unannounced, as if no time had passed in her visits.

Anna was shocked by her appearance. Her hair was dyed henna, and she wore antimony on her eyelashes and sikra on her cheeks and lips, and had colored her long nails with khanna ashes.

Anna couldn't restrain herself from asking, "Why the unusual adornment, Sobe?"

"Today is the twenty-fifth anniversary of my husband's death. I'm celebrating my failure as a woman." She paraded back and forth before Anna in a bright orange robe.

"You have done a great deal for the poor people. They consider you an important, loving person. So do I."

Cleophas came from his workshop to greet her and didn't recognize her at first. Her heavy scent of nard caused him to sneeze repeatedly so he excused himself and left the two women to spar with each other.

Anna waited for Sobe to explain her excessive use of cosmetics. She looked at Anna with a smirk, then said, "I've decided to go to Magdala where my husband and his brothers were drowned. They never found dear Nathan's body, you know. He's still there, in the Sea of Galilee, waiting for me."

Anna was stunned by such an irrational statement. She couldn't let her sister, now appearing unbalanced, go to Magdala alone. The people there were mainly fishing families, making *muries*, a salted fish renowned throughout the Empire, and she would be safe enough from the inhabitants. But was she safe from her own self?

Anna called in Cleophas, and when he was unsuccessful in dissuading Sobe from the trip, he said, "Sobe, if you'll restrain yourself from using that abominable-smelling nard, Anna and I will go with you. Neither of us has ever been there, and I hear it's an interesting town."

Sobe's mood changed. She smiled, well-pleased now, and they decided on an early departure time the next day.

After Sobe had left, Anna said, "Sobe acts as if she's still married. Is she mentally unstable?"

"She could be punishing us for marrying each other. I feel sorry for her. Going on this 'pilgrimage' with her might be the kindest thing we can do."

Anna embraced him, saying, "You are so loving. I adore you, Cleophas. Every night I pray that I can bear you a son. Then my happiness would be truly complete. You know, I haven't healed anyone for a long time. I fear I have lost that power, along with the loss of two beautiful daughters."

"Only one daughter, Anna. You still have Mary in Mount Carmel. Don't chastise yourself in this way. You have brought me such great happiness. All good things come in threes. You'll have another child, and I don't care if it's a boy or a girl. And you will heal again, gracious one. Remember that I have already had one family of children, so you aren't depriving me of that experience. You are all I want and need."

Anna was silent a moment as she regained control of her voice. Then she said, "I am so lucky in having you,

Cleophas. Now, enough scolding for today. We must go
to sleep at once, so we can leave early for Magdala."

Sobe arrived well before the appointed time and wearing the same heavy makeup of yesterday. Red sikra
flamed on cheeks and lips, eyebrows were wildly arched
with black *pouch*, and her robe was most shocking. It
was the lavender garment she had wheedled from Anna
when Sobe went to win Cleophas years ago. It was anything but a traveling dress, but Anna made no comment
on it.

The first day of the three-day journey over mountains
and along valleys went smoothly for the trio. Sobe was in
unusually high spirits, regaling them with tales of her
short life with Nathan. But the second day, she was the
opposite—despondent, irritable, and crying a great deal
of the time. Her companions were hard-pressed to cope
with her moods. Yet, on the third day, Sobe appeared
more normal, only extremely quiet and uncommunicative. This time, she dressed in a long sackcloth and wore
no makeup. Anna and Cleophas decided she was back
to reality and promised each other they would grant her
every wish that day.

When they reached the village of Magdala, where everyone made a living from the lake's dried fishes, Sobe
insisted on going to the shore. There, the first of two
wooden boats left for its fishing spot with a round throw-
ing-net, with leads attached to its edges. Within a short
time, it returned with a good catch. Sobe was elated.

"Keep your eyes on the next boat, with a seine." she
cried. "That is how Nathan fished."

This boat carried a seine hundreds of feet long, with
floaters and sinkers on it. Men on shore held one of the
long ropes attached to one end of the net, while the boat
played out the other end and lowered the net into the
water. It traveled in a great semicircle before returning

to the shore. Then, the boatmen went over the side into the water and swam with the other end of the rope, to pull the seine to the shore while closing it to trap the catch. It was a dramatic scene.

Anna and Cleophas were so engrossed in watching this skillful operation, they didn't notice that Sobe had left them. She had taken a small, beached boat and was already some distance from the shore. The fishermen were so excited by the exceptional catch that they began dancing about their bounty, yelling and chanting. It took several minutes before anyone would pay attention to Cleophas' questions regarding Sobe's disappearance.

"Has anyone seen the woman in the sackdress who was here with us a short time ago?" Anna asked one man after another. Finally a young boy spoke up, "She's out there in a small boat."

Everyone became alarmed. At this time of day, it was customary for a sudden wind to spring up and race down the surrounding hills onto the lake. This created high waves. Sobe would be incapable of handling a small craft under such conditions.

A group of fishermen with Cleophas jumped into the nearest boat and rowed frantically toward distant Sobe. When she saw the men approaching, she stood up in the boat and waved to them. Then she jumped into the water and disappeared.

Several boatloads of men searched for her until darkness descended. Anna and Cleophas remained five days in Magdala hoping the body would be found. It never was. Like her husband, Sobe had vanished in the beautiful harp-shaped Sea of Galilee.

Anna was distraught. She told Cleophas, "I lost my child and now my sister. Had I been more alert, I might have prevented both deaths. Perhaps if I hadn't married you . . . "

Cleophas put his arms around her. "No, no. Get rid of those guilt feelings. You weren't responsible. The Law of God is both personal and impersonal—since he chastens those he loves most. Remember the words of David." He began the forty-sixth Psalm: "God is our refuge and strength, a very present help in trouble. Therefore will not we fear, though the earth be removed, and though the mountains be carried into the midst of the sea . . . " He hesitated, letting Anna continue, " . . . though the waters thereof roar and be troubled, though the mountains shake with the swelling thereof. Selah."

Cleophas pointed to the lake, now a molten, gold mirror in the late afternoon sun. "Look! Sobe's hidden tomb is ringed with flowering jasmine and mimosa. She has found peace here with her husband. You, too, Anna must find peace with yours."

Anna smiled bravely. "You always say the right thing."

CHAPTER 9

Anna and Cleophas had just finished their noonday meal when a young man came to their door.

"I am Unni," he said. "Servant of the priest Uriah. He's extremely ill and wants Anna to come."

"I have a few important errands, but will hurry to him later," Anna said.

Uriah was one of the rabbis who had tested Mary when she was three. From time to time, he had visited Anna to learn of her daughter's progress, and a warm bond had developed between them.

Cleophas warned her, "Uriah lives a long way from here in the wooded hills. Please don't stay late there. I must go to Cana today to pick up hyena and jackal hides for my shop. I have many pending orders for festival and wedding sandals. People aren't satisfied with camel's footwear for these occasions.

"I understand. I have a lot of salted fish here for the

poor—Sobe's poor. It lessens my deep feelings of guilt to continue her chores."

"You've been doing this for several years, Anna. Missing one day can't be that important. Please take Judith with you to Uriah's."

Anna shook her head. "Today, she has to prepare food for the Sabbath. I'll deliver the fish, then come back for the bread to take with me." She turned to Judith, asking, "How long before it will be ready?"

"By the second hour. You're in luck, since I made several extra loaves this morning."

Cleophas kissed Anna several times, then held her at arm's length and studied her still-youthful face. "How I adore you! You will be careful in the hills?"

Seeing deep concern in his eyes, she promised, "I'll be back long before dark. If I'm late, I'll take the shortcut through the cypress grove on the edge of town. That should save me an hour's walking time. Please don't worry."

While Judith packed the fish in a basket, Anna covered her auburn braids with a large yellow shawl. She always thought of her stern father, Stolan, when she did this. He had warned her repeatedly, at an early age, that "exposure of a woman's hair to the view of strange men is a form of nudity and an open invitation to sin." She was grateful for his strict Pharisee upbringing.

The waiting poor on Anna's rounds took more time than she had planned. They delayed her by long conversations, so it was the fourth hour when she reached the green maquis where Uriah lived.

Bird-nesting was at its busiest, and swarms of nectar-seeking butterflies filled the warm, peaceful air. She regretted not having time to dawdle here.

Unfamiliar with this wooded area, she found herself on a dead-end trail, where a heavy growth of thistles blocked her path. In retracing her steps, rank wild broom snagged her sandals and forced her to stop frequently to remove its thorny spurs.

The basket of bread grew heavier with each step. She stopped to rest a moment and watched a flock of storks gliding overhead. When she rose to continue, throaty snarls behind her made her jump. She spun around to face a threatening pack of wild dogs. Ordinarily a single dog would not attack, but this group looked ravenous. They surely smelled the fragrant bread in her basket.

Anna's first reaction was to feel sorry for them. They looked half-starved, with ribs showing and coats matted with burrs. Their erect ears and long muzzles reminded her of the area's despised jackals.

Suddenly, the huge, scrawny leader moved close, body low, fangs bared. He was ready to leap on her. The rest of the pack, in waiting for his signal, formed a menacing circle around her.

She yelled at them, "Go! Go! Get away from me!" That didn't frighten them, so she looked about for a stone or branch to throw at them. There was nothing near her. She dared not set the basket down. The dogs would jump for it and devour the loaves in a flash.

Now, the animals moved in concert with more courage. They tightened the circle about her. Their horrible mouths dripped with saliva. Their determined eyes slanted in hate. With a snarl, the leader leapt for the bread. Anna jumped back, tripped on a jutting root, and fell over backward. Yet she managed to hold onto the basket. Uncertain of their next move, the dogs hovered over her. Anna screamed. The startled animals retreated, and she scrambled to her feet.

Her uncertainty encouraged the leader to move close once again. Growling, he inched his way toward her, urging the pack to circle her. Anna snatched up a loaf, tore it into chunks and threw them as far as she could. She knew she had to climb a tree for protection. Some twenty feet away was a terebinth with low, outstretched branches. But how could she reach it without being attacked?

She grabbed one loaf after another and threw them high and far from her. Then she fled to the tree and scrambled onto a gnarled limb out of the animals' reach. She was safe for the moment, but would they keep her in the tree all night?

When the dogs had eaten the last of the bread, they departed as silently as they had come. Anna climbed down and made her way to the priest's dwelling, still shaken from the encounter.

Uriah lay pale and weak on his pallet, surrounded by a group of relatives and worshippers.

When he saw Anna, he whispered hoarsely to them, "Leave, please. We must be alone." Anna bent over him, taking one of his limp hands in hers. "First, dearest Anna, do not try to save me. I know you have great healing powers, but in my case it is not to be used. I have little strength left, so listen carefully."

Anna knelt beside him to hear his faint words. He said, "I had a vision, or dream, I don't know which. An archangel stood before Mary and gave her a sacred pronouncement."

"Was it Gabriel?" Anna asked in breathless suspense.

"Yes. You must bring your daughter home and find a worthy husband for her, but one who will promise to remain a celibate for as long as the Lord desires."

"How can one ask that? It is against the law of Moses!"

"But not against the law of God. He desires that she give birth to a wondrous son, whose name shall be holy for eons of time."

"You mean this child will be conceived by immaculate conception?"

He nodded. "Keep this a secret as you have others. I must go to my rest now. Do not fail me, Anna. Find a willing hus—" He collapsed in Anna's arms.

She felt his last painful exhalation and the familiar death rattle in his throat. She rocked him lovingly for several minutes. "I will keep my promise to you, dear Uriah."

She wished she might have tried to extend his life, but not against his will. The deaths of Joachim, of Mary ben Cleophas, and of Sobe under such tragic circumstances had shaken Anna's self-confidence. Would she ever heal anyone again? Would she, in her lifetime, ever achieve the ultimate goal of bringing someone back to life? That was her secret hope.

She called in the other mourners now, saying, "I'm heartbroken. He wanted to go. There was no way I would work against his wishes. God's blessings on all of you."

She left at once and saw with dismay that the sun had set. At this late hour, she must take the shortcut through the cypress grove in order to reach home before total darkness descended. She regretted this choice when she found that the heavy foliage provided little light on the path.

The crowded trees were unfriendly, even hostile—like the faces of the priest's friends she had just left. Their branches reached out to her in a threatening manner. It was cold in the damp shade here. A sudden chill shook her body.

There were strange sounds in the forest, magnified by the heavy dusk. She couldn't identify them as animal, bird, or human. Twigs snapped, followed by heavy sniffing. Then come an ominous silence. A creature must be following her. She began to run.

Instantly, the brush near her exploded. She froze as a

deer sprang past her in wide-eyed terror. Then came snorts from the thicket.

Near exhaustion, Anna slowed her pace and tried to pierce the darkness. Was that the icy glitter of animal eyes stalking her? She couldn't tell. Here the trail narrowed, drawing her into a trap. She whispered over and over again, "God of Abraham, Isaac, and Jacob, get me safely home!" She had gone too far on this path to retrace her steps. In the descending darkness, the longer way home would be equally threatening, since there was no habitation there, either.

Once again, she heard something breathing heavily behind her. Don't panic, she told herself. It could be a wandering donkey or a cow that had strayed. Now, a bird flapped in the branches nearby. Ahead of her, something indefinable crossed the twisted roots of the trees. She couldn't make out anything clearly in the dim light. It was what she heard and felt that made gooseflesh rise on her skin. Her blood started to pound in her ears. She spun round and round, trying to locate her enemy. Terror now engulfed her.

Then, birds screeched in sudden alarm, and their panicky wings sliced the air as they sought to escape. Anna froze. She dropped her basket. Facing her, with confident eyes and bared fangs, was a large leopard, poised to leap on her.

Anna fled, hoping it was a female leopard who would not pursue her far because of young ones to protect nearby. The animal gained quickly on her and, just as she sensed he was about to grab her in his jaws, she shrieked hysterically over and over again.

With no warning, a snarling black comet flashed out of the woods and leapt for the leopard.

Four more wild dogs followed their leader and hurled themselves at her enemy. They attacked it from all sides with determined fury. Panicked by the unexpected on-slaught from so many dogs, the leopard managed to break free and disappeared in the thick undergrowth.

Obviously pleased with their success, the dogs gath-ered expectantly around Anna. She tried to speak to them, but her mouth was so dry, no sound came forth. Then, the black leader came to her and licked her hand. The other animals moved closer, wagging their unkempt tails for approval. Finally Anna managed, "Good dogs! Oh, you are such good dogs!"

Apparently satisfied she was safe, they headed into the brush, leaving Anna alone in near-darkness. She scolded herself for not remembering that leopards, like lions and bears, occasionally appeared in this area.

Before continuing on her way, she dropped to her knees to give thanks for her rescue. These were the dogs she had unwillingly fed. They had apparently followed her into the woods, hoping for more loaves of bread. Yet, when a dangerous enemy threatened to kill her, they bravely defended her. How strange and wondrous were the workings of her God of Love!

Her great depression over not being able to save the priest Uriah diminished now. Her God had not aban-doned her. One day she would heal again—when he de-cided who the recipient would be. She had learned an important lesson: Not everyone could be healed of their ailments if God wanted them with him. She wished Ezra, the Essene, were still here to counsel her.

She wondered about Uriah's message regarding Mary's future. He could have been delirious when he had the vision. Yet it agreed with the Carmel prophet's vision that a descendant of Emerentiana and Stolan would bear the Promised One. How she wished she could discuss Uriah's vision with someone. She would have to tell Cleophas something. She would simply tell him that Uriah assured her that Mary would soon be announced as the chosen channel and felt he had to tell her that before he departed.

CHAPTER 10

The Essene community at Mount Carmel had been Mary's home for nine years. Judy, the leader, was a devoted teacher to the twelve virgins preparing to be the channel for the Messiah. They participated daily in exercises to cleanse the body, mind, and spirit. Various teachers guided their development in intuitive abilities, astrological charting, dreams and vision, meditation, varieties of prayer, unconditional love, purity of heart, the philosophy of rebirth, and other esoteric studies that Anna had not been offered during her years at the temple in Jerusalem. She was satisfied that Mary was being well trained by both men and women teachers, in a disciplined but loving environment. Also, Mary had learned much about the divine within the self, the I AM, whereas the temple teachers focused more on the divine without. Still Anna knew that Mary also needed to learn the service of the temple to be completely prepared for the role she would surely be selected to fulfill. The time for the transfer had no doubt arrived.

"Cleophas, we must visit Mary within the week and discuss taking her to the temple in Jerusalem so that her training may be complete in all possible areas."

"If you think that is necessary, Anna, we can leave in two days."

The familiar journey brought them to the visitor lodging center, where they were warmly greeted by other visiting families. Naomi, to whom Mary had been assigned from her first day, immediately took Anna to see Mary. Cleophas unpacked the food that Judith had prepared for them and readied their sleeping space.

Anna warmly embraced Mary and felt an especial closeness to her serene, gentle daughter. How quickly she had arrived at the brink of womanhood. This glorious gift from God was also Anna's gift to God. There had been some reluctance among a few of the community leaders to accept Mary as one of the selected twelve because they doubted Anna's statement that Mary had been conceived without an earthly father. But Mary's gentleness, mental alertness, and spiritual devotion had long ago won over the objectors, and the eleven other virgins loved her like a sister.

"Mother, I'm so sorry about Aunt Sobe. How sad that she could not make peace with herself and her family. I pray that she will be at rest with God. Perhaps my little sister will find her and give her comfort on the other plane."

"Yes, we can hope that her parents and Joachim will help her spirit find the peace that eluded her here. Let's go have our supper with your Uncle Cleophas and talk about the next phase of your training."

The meal was arranged on the mat, and cool water from the well was in a gourd nearby. Mary greeted her uncle modestly and seated herself between Anna and Cleophas. They were all happy to be together, as much love connected the three of them. After the meal, Mary reported that she was to lead the group of girls at the early morning ritual in the altar service. Her mother and Cleophas could attend if they desired. They eagerly accepted.

Mary told them of her classes and the increased duties assigned to her. She seemed to patiently and willingly accept whatever was required of her. Though the teachers were never given to open praise of any of the girls, it was always obvious that they were more than pleased with Mary's progress and positive attitude.

"We're gratified with your progress, Mary," Anna commented, "and we will be talking to your teachers about the next step in your spiritual training. You have developed your psyche beautifully here and have been taught a living and loving spirituality that I did not find so evident while I lived at the temple in Jerusalem. But there are lessons to be learned there, also, and now it is time for you to study there as soon as arrangements can be made. We will discuss this with your teachers here and then go to the temple school to prepare for your training there."

"I will miss my dear sisters and teachers here, but I trust you, dear Mother, and I will do as you and my teachers advise."

Naomi appeared then and reminded Mary that evening vespers were to begin quite soon. Since this was a private service for the community residents, Mary said goodnight, and Anna and Cleophas prepared for bed so that they would be awake early for the service and their talk with the teachers.

The virgins' chanting provided a serene, melodic background for Anna and Cleophas' meditation time before they retired.

The next morning they awakened before sunrise and moved along quickly to be in plenty of time to see the procession of young girls. The parents of Edithia, Andra, and Sophie were also visiting, and all seated themselves on the benches facing sideways to the altar. That way, they could observe the entrance of their daughters and their procession toward the front of the modest temple and up the steps to the altar. The girls, led by Mary, moved in unison in their simple white robes while their delicate lyrical chanting wafted upward in the still morning air. They seemed to float up the steps to the altar.

Just as Mary set foot on the top step, the sunlight flashed through the arch beside the altar and bathed the virgins in shades of rose and amethyst. Mary's head was radiantly surrounded by oscillating shades of violet and purple, and golden light pulsed from her heart area in front and behind in the upper back area. All breaths were suspended as the angel Gabriel appeared to float in pure white light and take Mary by the hand to lead her to the altar. Lavender incense filled the air as the message sweetly drifted over the temple.

"This is the chosen channel of the Prince of Peace," the archangel said.

All breathed in the ecstasy of the moment of the completed preparation, and the other virgins gathered around Mary and began the ritual of glory and thanksgiving to God.

It was a moment of great joy for Anna as she saw her beloved daughter being chosen, but within her heart she felt a sudden pang of pain as she knew that, with the great honor, came great responsibilities. She knew that, in times of trial and fear, total faith would sustain this handmaiden of the living God, and her heart overflowed with love.

Later in the day, Anna met with Judy, Mathias, and

Chapter 11

Hermana, sister of Cleophas, and her husband, Obadiah, agreed to accompany Anna to the Holy City. Cleophas would remain at home. As the chief shepherd of Joachim's former flocks, Obadiah was accustomed to bringing sacrificial animals to the temple and knew the best route to take each month of the year.

Arriving in Jerusalem too late in the day for Anna to go to the temple, the three travelers went to the house Anna and Joachim had lived in from time to time and which she still owned. Nearby was his tomb, so Anna left Hermana and Obadiah to visit it alone. She was relieved to see that the whitewash on the sepulchre was still good. This was important so passers-by would be warned that it was someone's grave.

Anna approached the tomb with deep sadness. Joachim was her first love, the husband who stood by her through twenty years of shame and rejection, and loved her to the end. She regretted that he had not lived to know the beautiful, young Mary. She knelt for a brief prayer, then started back to the house.

Someone called out, "Anna, Anna—is it really you?"

She turned, and her heart leapt. It was Julian, striding, then running toward her.

He still had a fine physique and stood straight as before. His curly head of hair was now white and reminded Anna of a heron's feathers. His short, loose tunic revealed sturdy, tanned legs, set in the four-banded Calceus sandals only Romans wore. She remembered her first meeting with Julian on her way to Ezra's house and how, together, they had brought the old man back to life. That was a long time ago.

He spoke first. "I passed your house near here, and seeing someone there, inquired about you. I was told you married Joachim's brother during my absence from Palestine."

"Yes. Cleophas."

"Have you children by Cleophas?"

"I had a girl. She died in infancy."

"I'm sorry. That family of men breeds only girls. I could have given you a son." The old arrogance was still there. Julian continued with confidence, "You don't look happy. Why aren't you?"

Anna hesitated a moment, then confessed, "I think I've lost my healing power. A priest recently died in my arms, forbidding me to try to save him. Did he suspect I couldn't?"

"Forget him. He was meant to die."

"But Sobe committed suicide, and my second Mary died when I was away. I might have saved both of them had I been more alert."

"Stop torturing yourself! What can I do to make you happy? That is, what will you allow me to do?' He took her two hands in his and brought them to his lips.

She dared not look at him. "Believe in me, Julian. Be my friend."

He laughed bitterly. "You ask me for friendship when I love you beyond anyone in the world?"

Tears filled Anna's eyes. With lowered head, she pleaded, "You can restore my faith in myself. Am I a healer or am I a hoax?"

He was silent for several moments. Then he said soberly, "You are a woman of miracles. What advice can I offer a magician?"

Anna dared now to look into his intense green eyes. She said softly, "We are antagonists, Julian. Yet I need your concern for me. I don't know why you're a part of my life."

He walked back to her house with her, and they talked of Ezra the Essene, of Salina, and of Anna's plans for Mary in Galilee. Julian knew how to project strength and power into her, and she felt her old confidence returning.

"I brought you, as before, a remembrance from Salina," Julian said, as he removed from his small finger a dazzling ring set with emeralds.

"I can't accept that," Anna said, suspicious of the actual donor.

"Don't argue. Salina would be upset if you refused it." He took her left hand and slipped the ring on a finger. Then he was silent, and his face grew sad.

"Thank you both," Anna said. "You two make me feel very happy. I'm curious. What do you say to Herod when he asks about his daughter?"

"I tell him that Salina is sterile, mean, stammers worse than ever, is a terrible housekeeper, and makes me suffer daily."

Anna laughed. "He believes you?"

"Of course. It's what he wants to hear. I want to retire

in Galilee, where you'll never be far from me. But Herod keeps thinking up new projects for me and won't let me go. I'll find a way though, to be near you in the dangerous revolts ahead."

"God bless you, Julian."

"Good-bye, dear Anna."

The next morning Anna went to the area of the temple where she had studied for ten years. She was well-known there, although nearly all her teachers had left this plane. Susanna was still a temple teacher, and it was to her that Anna turned.

"Susanna, how much you refresh the memories of my years here at the temple."

"And I remember your devout service here and how you wanted your father to leave you here instead of requiring you to marry."

"That is true, but not too surprisingly, I've found God's wisdom far exceeds my limited knowledge. As you know, I married Joachim and we were, after many years, blessed with Mary, a wonderful gift from God."

Susanna smiled, remembering only too well the disappointment and surprise felt at the temple when Mary was taken to the Essenes instead of to the temple in Jerusalem for her training.

Anna continued, "Now Mary has completed her training at Mount Carmel and is ready to receive the training here at the temple. I have come to ask that she be accepted immediately. Are Samuel and the prophetess Anna here so that I may discuss this transfer with them? They both blessed Mary when she was christened and know she came to us with a very special mission."

Susanna led Anna to an inner room to meet with Samuel and the prophetess. They came, talked to Anna, and made arrangements for Mary to move to the temple as quickly as possible. They anticipated two or three years of training for Mary. She would learn the temple service, just as her mother had done. She would also learn the ways of the Pharisees and Levites, areas not stressed by the Essenes.

The following morning, Hermana and Obadiah returned with Mary to the waiting Cleophas. After two days of rest and preparations, the four set out for Mount Carmel.

There was an atmosphere of expectation, sadness, and joy all mixed together. The twelve virgins were like devoted sisters, and they felt sorrow to have Mary leaving their midst. Mary loved them all dearly and did not fully understand this great change taking place in her life. She knew that the message from the Angel Gabriel had great significance, but it would be a few years before she more fully comprehended the ramifications of Gabriel's announcement.

After a special service for Mary, where all wished her God's speed and expressed their love for her as they embraced her, Mary thanked her teachers and the other girls for all the lessons she had learned and announced that she felt certain that their lives would intertwine again in the future. She felt secure in God's love and trusted completely in the transfer to the temple as another part of God's plan for her life. Anna's heart overflowed with love for her devout daughter, who trusted so completely in her heavenly Father.

Mary, her mother, Cleophas, and her aunt and uncle were on their way very early the next morning. They would travel to the home in Sepphoris and stay a few days before taking Mary on to the temple in Jerusalem to continue her training. There was a need for rest and contemplation, and Anna was grateful for an opportunity to spend a little time with this daughter she had dedicated to God.

During the days at home, Anna and Mary talked about numerous topics. Among other things, Anna had an opportunity to tell Mary about family news, her aunt and her families.

Mary was especially interested in her cousin Elisabeth, daughter of Anna's sister, Esmeria. Zacharias, Elisabeth's husband, was a member of the priesthood, and twice a year, he joined others from all over Palestine to officiate for one week in managing the affairs of the temple. In this manner, he hoped to compensate for the fact that he was childless and had no offspring to dedicate to temple services. Anna and Joachim had always been especially empathetic with Elisabeth and Zacharias and could comprehend more than anyone the pain they felt at remaining childless. Mary expressed a desire to see her cousins before she entered the temple school. Cleophas and Obadiah agreed that it would be only slightly out of the way to go by way of Jutta, a village in the hills west of Jerusalem. There, on a small farm, lived Elisabeth and Zacharias.

Judith prepared provisions for the trip to Jerusalem, and like everyone else in the household, was more than happy to do all that she could for Mary. Very soon, it was time to travel.

The travelers reached Jutta in the early afternoon of the third day. Elisabeth was delighted to see her aunt and cousin. Since she was an Essene she had seen Mary a few times at Mount Carmel, but just for brief periods.

"Mary, it is so wonderful to see you here. Have you finished your training at Mount Carmel? I thought you were going to remain there."

"Yes, I thought I was, too, but my mother, teachers, and, most of all, God have other plans for me, and I am going now to train for two or three years at the temple in Jerusalem, where mother took her training."

Zacharias looked pleased. How Anna wanted to tell him of the vision of the priest Uriah, but he had warned her to keep his vision a secret. At least she could tell him about Gabriel's appearance at the service at Mount Carmel, which she did. In spite of their own personal disappointment, Elisabeth and Zacharias felt very happy for Anna and Mary, and the adults talked later, after Mary retired, about the meaning of Gabriel's announcement.

The next morning, Anna and Mary said their good-byes to the relatives. Hermana and Obadiah had the gear on the donkeys and were ready to travel on to the Jerusalem temple.

PART III

CHAPTER 1

The three years Mary trained and served in the Temple of Solomon passed in the twinkling of an eye, it seemed. Now, Mary was going home with her mother, and Anna relished these precious days knowing that Mary's marriage would take place in the near future. Foremost in this process was breaking the news to Mary that she would soon become betrothed. Much preparation was needed.

As they traveled on large, strong Muscat donkeys, the journey home through Samaria went quickly for Anna and Mary. Hermana and Obadiah always traveled ahead of them, allowing mother and daughter to make up for lost years of companionship.

They took the most direct route to Galilee, passing through Shiloh where Cleophas had lived, then Sebaste, the former destroyed city of Samaria, now rebuilt by King Herod. This was the area where the Samaritans lived.

This ethnic group were held by other Jews to be unclean since they did not go to the temple with sacrifices and prayers. But Obadiah had once been helped by kind Samaritans when he dropped beside the road from heat exhaustion, so he felt secure in bringing Anna and Mary through their domain.

Wayside inns eased their travels, and Mary was fascinated by the activities in the fields. It was the month of Tishri, when the crops of wheat and barley were being sown by the "august motion" of the hand—a sight unknown to Mary.

When Anna had told Mary of her cousin Elisabeth's pregnancy, Mary had happily replied, "So there is the 'John' I have seen in my dreams. I must go to her soon."

"First, though, you will marry. Then you will have a wondrous message of your own to tell her." Anna decided not to reveal to her Uriah's forecast, in case the priest was delirious when he thought Gabriel had spoken to him. Yet, the more she looked at the radiant beauty of Mary, with her pale, red-gold hair that rose from a high forehead, the more she believed Uriah's story.

Mary was silent for several moments, then said firmly, "I don't ever want to marry, Emi. My life must be devoted only to God."

Anna laughed. She remembered her identical attitude which her father, Stolan, had had to overcome. "Gabriel will soon change your mind." Anna was reluctant to promise anything more.

By noon of the third day, the party had reached the plains of Dothan and then Jesreel, where the prophet Elijah had his summer palace. Now, they were in gracious and fertile Galilee.

Anna revealed to Mary then that the Nazareth house, in which Joachim and she had lived, would be ready for her following her marriage. "You will enjoy the house where you were born with such great love. Cleophas and I live only a short distance from there, so we will be able to visit each other easily."

"I remember it well," Mary replied, "but I don't see myself living there but a short time."

"No matter. It will always be there for you."

* * *

Both Cleophas and Anna were deeply aware of the difficulty before them until Mary changed her attitude about marriage.

"Shall I tell her she will be the mother of the Messiah to make up her mind?" Anna asked him.

Cleophas was swift in making decisions and shook his head.

"I will go to the monks on Mount Carmel and ask for their advice. Perhaps they will confirm our belief and give me the name of the man she will marry. You know he must be an Essene, since no other sect will accept chastity in marriage."

"I pray that during your absence, Mary will be moved by the Holy Spirit and learn her great destiny. We cannot force her to marry. She is no longer a child, but a special woman who must make up her own mind."

"Meditate with her in the garden during my absence tomorrow. Mother and daughter together in prayer might produce a revelation."

Cleophas always found simple answers to worrisome problems. How lucky she was in having his uncomplicated attitude toward this new crisis. She must not tell Mary her miraculous destiny; the knowledge of her future must come from within herself.

The two devoted women enjoyed each other's company greatly during Cleophas' absence. The fact that

Anna, too, had spent ten years in temple service, made for complete understanding of each other. They took long walks together in the hills; they stayed up late at night to share their experiences. Judith prepared the delicious dishes Mary had never been served during her stay in Jerusalem. Each day was a celebration of their being together, and they looked forward eagerly to their morning meditations together.

One day, Anna overslept and was surprised to find Mary shaking her and crying, "Emi, Emi, awaken! Gabriel appeared to me with a confusing message!

Anna sat up, smiling.

Mary continued, "He said, 'You will marry at once but remain a virgin, since your firstborn must be free of original sin. Your child will be conceived through the Holy Ghost, so that his birth will be a sacred one, a holy one, in order that an incarnate being of perfection might manifest himself.' Now I know what my mission in life is! I'm delirious with joy!" Mary stopped, then frowned. "But, Mother, who would want to marry me if he can't have conjugal rights?"

"That's God's problem, not yours," Anna answered, laughing. "Let me embrace you, mother of the Messiah." They wept together in exquisite happiness, and Anna remembered the prophecy of the monks at Carmel. Their vision showed the lovely fruit preceding the pure-white flower, which represented the Messiah.

Cleophas returned from Mount Carmel's monastery highly elated. The monks had given him a name: Joseph. He confided this only to Anna and immediately set about canvassing the countless Josephs of Galilee. Finally, after weeks of checking families, he narrowed the field to three. One was a water carrier, an important trade since few homes had their own fountain. The second was a fuller, an honest business of doing the laundry for others. The third was a miller of corn.

After talking with the three Josephs, Cleophas told Anna one night in bed, "None of these is the right one, I know. They are all young men with personal ambitions. Mary needs a devout, self-effacing husband. Shall I go to Jerusalem and continue my search?"

Anna snuggled into his arms and was silent for some time. Finally she said, "A young man would not be a good husband for Mary. If we could find an older man who would agree to the unusual conjugal arrangement, that might be the answer. Have you any relative in a far away place who follows the rules of the Essenes?"

"I have it!" Cleophas whispered excitedly. "Joseph, my cousin. But I have no idea where he lives."

"You can inquire of your brother, Salamo. He might know. Would there be any problem of blood relationship?'

Cleophas thought a moment. "None at all. Joachim came from David's line through Hathan, while Joseph came from David's line through Solomon. Someone in Bethlehem would know where he is."

During the week that followed, Anna secretly made plans for Mary's wedding in the temple. Knowing how persuasive and determined Cleophas was, she was certain he would locate the elusive Joseph. It was mandatory that the marriage take place at once to satisfy those who couldn't accept an immaculate conception.

After days of search, the two women found the right material for Mary's robe. They selected a brilliant blue silk embroidered with white flowers. Like Mary, Anna had learned to be an excellent seamstress in the temple. Their days were occupied with designing the garment and sleeveless scapular. There were countless pearls to attach and a fringe to add to the hem. Yet, the dress was ready when Cleophas returned home.

With him was a shy man of gentle face and ready smile. He was old enough to be Mary's father, but no matter. Anna studied his aura. It was gold and blue, and its outer edges flared with white fire. He was definitely the one.

Following introductions, Joseph handed Mary a bouquet of wild iris and tulips. He looked stunned by Mary's beauty and could think of nothing to say.

Anna moved quickly to embrace him, then asked, "Where did Cleophas find you?'

"Near Sebaste, where I've worked as a carpenter for many years." His voice was soft and musical, and his eyes sparkled with happiness.

"Hurry and wash up, both of you," Anna said. "Cleophas, bring out your best wine. This is a night for celebration!"

During the evening, Joseph's shyness left him. He said, "I belong to the outer Essenes. Are you also an Essene, Mary?"

Mary nodded shyly. Anna explained, "She entered the order in her third year. She followed its dietary laws during all her years at Mount Carmel and in the temple at Jerusalem."

"I'm pleased beyond expression," Joseph said with a smile. "I want you to know that I, too, have the 'open sight.' Cleophas has explained to me the need for a celibate husband for you, Mary. I understand. I'm willing to forego cohabitation as long as is necessary."

Then Mary, who had remained silent during the meal, cleared her throat. She said in her sweet voice, "Mother, I can love this man. I'll gladly be espoused to him."

Anna clapped her hands with joy. She spoke excitedly, "We'll prepare at once for your wedding in Jerusalem. Mary's dress is ready, and Cleophas will make all necessary arrangements with the temple priests."

They toasted the future with another glass of wine.

Then practical Cleophas announced, "Tomorrow we'll hold the betrothal ceremony."

A week passed during which Joseph was busy setting up a carpentry shop in Nazareth. Cleophas was in Jerusalem, making the wedding arrangements.

Anna and Mary meditated each morning on comfortable cushions in the yard. On this day, Anna noticed how radiant her daughter's face was. There was a half-smile on her face and stars in her eyes.

Anna exclaimed, "You grow more beautiful each day. I'm surprised how quickly you accepted the idea of marriage."

"Joseph is so special. He's so masculine, so strong. I could have searched forever and not found anyone equal to him." She hesitated a few moments before bursting out, "I have such wonderful news for you! I'm with child! You understand, don't you, Emi? Through the will of God, through the power of the Holy Ghost, this miracle has taken place within me."

Anna was so overcome, she had difficulty replying. Finally, with tears streaming down her cheeks, she said, "It is as prophesied, my darling. Think how thrilled Joseph will be! Since your wedding will take place next week, there's no need to tell anyone your infant is not of Joseph's sperm. We must all keep his divinity a secret. When the time is right, the grown Messiah will announce his own presence. There would be grave danger to you if the Romans and other pagans knew our Deliverer would be born within the year."

"We will tell only Elisabeth and Zacharias," Mary said running her hands lovingly over her abdomen. "Joseph will help me decide on a name for this Holy One now dreaming in my womb."

"He will be a perfect child, just like you," Anna said quietly.

They both sat in silence for a long time, filled with the wonder and enormity of the future event.

Finally Anna pulled Mary to her feet. "We'll begin today making his swaddling clothes. Come, let us go indoors."

The day passed quickly as the two women planned Mary's future. Joseph arrived at the sixth hour, and they ate supper in as calm an atmosphere as the women could manage.

When the meal was over, Anna and Judith excused themselves and went outside. Mary must break the overwhelming news to Joseph alone. He appeared puzzled by their unusual behavior but said nothing about it.

Mary began in a breathless voice, "Dear Joseph, I've a message from God for you."

He looked startled. "From God, you say? What could that be?'

"The Messiah lives within me!"

Joseph, face livid, jumped up from his chair. He pointed an accusing finger at her, shouting, "You tricked me into a betrothal, knowing all the time you were with child!"

"No, no, Joseph. My child was conceived through immaculate conception. I swear I've not deceived you!"

Joseph turned and ran out the front door. He turned and yelled back to her, "There'll be no marriage."

At that moment, he was struck by an invisible hand with such force that he was flung to the ground. There he lay, as a wondrous voice reverberated in his ears. "Joseph, the son of David, fear not to take unto thee Mary thy wife, for that which is conceived in her is of the Holy Ghost. And she shall bring forth a son, and ye shall call his name *Jesus*"

Joseph staggered to his feet. He held his arms wide to the sky crying, "Oh, Lord God, how I have offended thee!

Forgive me. I promise I'll devote my life to Mary and your Holy Son."

Mary came running to him, panicked by what she had seen. "Are you all right?" she cried.

He caught her in his arms, saying, "I've been stupid, arrogant! Forgive me, angel. I'll never doubt you again. I'll love and treasure you forever." Then he began to sob.

Mary said softly as he carried her back to the house, "If God can forgive you, so must I."

CHAPTER 2

Mary's wedding was an elaborate affair. Her exquisite gown, with train and veil, was of silk from the master weavers of Mount Zion. Cleophas had skillfully crafted the white-and-gold sandals for her dainty feet. And Esmeria, Anna's sister and mother of Elisabeth, had created her stunning coiffure. She divided it into plaits and interwove the hair with satin ribbons and pearls.

Joseph was splendidly outfitted also. Anna made him a fine linen shirt and embroidered an elegant girdle that went twice around his waist.

She told him, "I wish it were of gold and silver like the loin cloths of the archangels, but it's the best I could do."

Joseph was immensely pleased, since a splendid girdle was not only a mark of high status, but it held his billowing blue cloak in place.

His only relatives at the wedding were a brother from Dabbesheth and two others from Bethlehem. Their parents had died long ago.

When curious friends asked Anna why Joseph and Mary hadn't observed the customary year of betrothal, she satisfied their curiosity by replying, "God told them to marry at once."

Cleophas was equally supportive of the young couple. He refused to accept Joseph's offer of fifty shekels as a dowry. "You bring much to this marriage besides devotion. Your willingness to forego cohabitation is a great sacrifice."

Joseph replied, "Hard work will be my panacea."

After a week of celebration in Jerusalem, Joseph left for Bethlehem to take care of family affairs. Mary returned with Anna to Sepphoris. However, within a few days, Mary decided to leave for Jutta to be with her cousin, Elisabeth, until after the birth of John.

It was a shattering disappointment for Anna. She was deeply hurt not to share with Mary those months of her pregnancy. Hadn't she already deprived herself of her daughter for many years in the service of God?

When Joseph returned to Galilee, Anna established him in her Nazareth house. It was already furnished, and Judith cared for his clothing and brought him food. Joseph occupied himself with making furniture and wicker screens in his small shop. He took the separation from his wife stoically.

"It's important that Mary be present when Elisabeth's son, John, is born," he claimed. Yet, he couldn't say why. He appeared content to spend each Sabbath with Anna and Cleophas.

Anna, on the other hand, was anything but happy. Each day when Cleophas returned home from his shop, he found her in a depressed and unresponsive mood.

Finally, he could keep silent no longer. "Ever since Mary left, you've felt sorry for yourself. You treat me like a stranger. Why am I not enough now?" His voice became husky with emotion. "You've brought me such happiness. You've always been so stimulating and devoted to me. Why now this withdrawal? Have you forgotten you're my universe—my sun, my moon, my lode star?"

Anna was shocked by his words into a realization of her bad behavior. She put her arms around him and kissed him. "I'm totally ashamed of my self-pity. I've been feeling abandoned and unimportant because my daughter prefers another woman's company. I've neglected a dear, devoted husband. I've been terribly selfish. You know that my marriage to you is a deep and satisfying miracle all by itself. Your love has given me a type of security that doesn't come from material things. I'm deeply sorry."

"A truce then? When you fall, I'll lift you up and carry you until you can put your feet back on the ground." Cleophas then changed the subject. "Your birthday isn't until the month of Elul, but I bought you a gift in Jerusalem. I think you deserve it now. Stay there while I get it."

He returned with a rectangular piece of fine yellow silk. Anna asked with a laugh, "You want me to start sewing again?"

"No, no. You can wear this right now. It's called a *himation*. The shopkeeper said it's the latest rage in Greece. You wind it elegantly around the body, then the rest of it goes over your head for a scarf. Try it."

Anna, at fifty, was still slender. Her hair had not yet grayed, and her face was one of beauty. She skillfully draped the garment around her and paraded before her husband. She had a queenly carriage and a graceful walk.

"You look like a goddess! Hellenic fashions were certainly made for you."

She ran to him and held him in a long embrace. "What

a truly good person you are. You know my moods so well. Your understanding love is my sanctuary."

Cleophas closed his eyes to stop the burning tears.

Their mood was shattered by a loud rap on the door. It was a distraught Joseph.

He said angrily, "Augustus has just decreed that a census will be taken in the colonies. Mary and I have to go to Bethlehem to register. I'll go by way of Jutta to pick up Mary."

Cleophas spoke reassuringly, "We'll pack everything you need—bedding, food, clothing, utensils. Two of our strongest donkeys will speed your journey. All will go well."

Joseph, however, was in a rebellious mood. As they loaded the animals he cried, "Why must we be counted in the district of our birth? Why not where we live?"

Cleophas gave him a cool drink of water. "Don't be so upset. This is how Augustus establishes his authority over us. It's a mark of our subjection to mighty Rome."

Joseph continued to rant. "How much longer will we be ruled by foreigners? And who gave that foul heathen, Herod, the right to tax us to death while building his palaces? We are no more than cattle in the marketplace."

Cleophas remained calm. "There have been benefits, Joseph. The Romans have held the Parthians at bay. We have a fine harbor, better roads, too."

Anna joined them and added fuel to the fire. "Those of us who are less rigid in our religious attitudes get along much better with our conquerors. The wealthy Sadducees and the temple officials are perfectly content with the current regime."

She thought of Julian, a frequent intruder in her thoughts. What would the oracles tell him of the unborn Jesus?

Joseph continued angrily, "I adhere to our tradition.

One part of Palestine after another revolts. Today, it's Jerusalem; tomorrow, Jericho. The massacres, the cruci- fixions of helpless people will soon come to Nazareth. In a few years, our Holy City will be a cemetery with hea- thens ruling it."

"Well, Joseph," Cleophas interrupted him, "We can't settle the problem tonight. How will you let us know when the child is born?"

"My brother, Zadok, is now in Bethlehem. On his re- turn to Galilee, he'll bring you news of the birth."

When Joseph was gone, Anna laughed. "He was so agi- tated, he didn't even notice my beautiful *himation*! Come, let us pray."

They knelt at the altar, and Anna removed the chest holding the holy relics. She touched only the strands of Sara's hair. The beloved wife of Abraham held great meaning for Anna. Sara had been barren until she was eighty. It was then she gave birth to Isaac, and her death was recorded at 127 years.

Surely, Anna thought, a prayer to Sara would bring protection to Mary and Joseph on their difficult trip to Bethlehem.

Within a fortnight, Zadok arrived in Sepphoris to re- port to Anna.

"He is born? she cried expectantly.

With a hearty laugh, he picked her up and whirled her around before answering. Then, with a smug look, he announced, "Never saw such a healthy, perfect child! He's blue-eyed, with Mary's golden hair, and such a good baby."

"And Mary? Is she up now?"

"Oh, yes. Remember, I promised I'd find her a good midwife, and I did. The delivery was an easy one. Unfor- tunately, when they arrived in Bethlehem, the one inn was filled. No one knew the roads would be so crowded with families trying to beat Augustus' deadline. However, they found a grotto where farmers often keep animals. So it was there Mary gave birth."

"Who's taking care of her now?"

"A group of Essene women make things comfortable for her. They continue to act as protectors of the family. They keep the crowds of curious people away and make sure there's water and food in the stable."

"Has Jesus been circumcised?"

"Yes, on the eighth day. When Mary's days of purification are over, they'll take Jesus to the temple to be consecrated to the service of God."

"We'll go there at that time to bring the family back here," Anna said joyfully. "I want Mary to spend all her time with her infant. She will have no cares about housework or shopping. I will take care of everything."

At long last, Anna thought, I can see my daughter and grandson every day.

CHAPTER 3

Along with several hundred others, Julian was invited to a great feast at Herod's palace. The occasion was a celebration of the procurator's thirty-one years of rule over this volatile Roman protectorate.

After talking with a few acquaintances and enjoying some excellent wine, Julian could no longer stand the bedlam of raucous, drunken revelers. He left them for the terraced gardens set high above the street. Here, Herod had recently installed a beautiful swimming pool. Rumors persisted that he had promptly silenced two of his enemies in it.

The night air was pleasant; the stars in the dark sky were jewels. Julian sat down on a marble bench to think of his future. Immediately, someone called out his name. He turned and saw Herod, quite intoxicated, weaving his way toward him.

Herod shouted, "You've avoided me since you arrived, Legate. You know how ill I am. Yet you make no attempt to ingratiate yourself with me. I like that. Only laudanum keeps me going. Certainly not you or my friends. There's a surprise coming, though, for my high officials and the corrupt priests of the temple. At my death, I've ordered that all be killed so that many tears will flow at my funeral." He staggered back and forth before Julian. "I'll be carried on a golden litter, studded with rubies and diamonds. My body will be anointed with nard and lign-aloes from India. Hundreds of slaves will follow me, bearing sweet calamus and other aromatic herbs."

Herod paused, then laughed grotesquely. "Of course, Julian, you aren't that important, so you needn't worry about your neck."

Before Julian could think of an appropriate comment, a soldier hurried to Herod saying, "Sire, you must go below and speak to three travelers from the Orient. They claim to be astrologers who have followed a brilliant star to Judea. They want to know where the newborn King of Israel is."

Herod frowned. "Bring the strangers to the lower street terrace. Don't let the high priests and scribes here know of their presence until I can decide how demented they are. Come with me, Julian."

They descended the ornate stairs and entered a secret passage that took them to the ground level. Before them waited three men of such astounding dress that even Herod was taken aback.

"I am Kaspar from Persia," the eldest stranger said. He wore a green velvet tunic decorated with huge gold buttons. His headdress rose to a peak that ended in a flowing purple scarf.

Then he pointed to the man next to him, a tall, dark-skinned fellow wearing a white silk, full-sleeved tunic. "This is Melchior, king and renowned astrologer from India."

The third man stepped forward for his introduction.

"And this is Balthazar, the youngest of our group, but the greatest diviner of stars in Egypt." His yellow shirt and red cloak paled in comparison to his round hat gleaming with jewels.

Herod was so stunned that he just stared at them. Melchior continued, unabashed by the ruler's silence. "We've traveled for three months, following a brilliant star. We knew it would lead us to the newborn king of the Jews. Where is he? We bring him valuable gifts."

Herod burst out laughing. "You say you followed a star? Come, come. You are richly dressed, so I assume this is a ruse to sell me expensive merchandise from your countries. I've heard of no such king. I've seen no dazzling star in the heavens."

He noticed then that each stranger wore a girdle of silk from which hung stuffed pouches from heavy gold chains.

Balthazar then spoke up in a proud voice, "We are descendants of Job of the land of Uz. God has bestowed upon us the gift of prophecy. Our ancestors have observed the stars for more than 500 years. They saw in them the events leading up to the coming of the Messiah here."

"Step outside on the terrace with me," Herod said condescendingly. "Point out the ball of light that went ahead of you."

Kaspar explained, "The star faded as we entered your city. It had preceded us even in daylight. We followed its long trail all the way to the outskirts of Jerusalem. The shepherds on the hills of Judea reported to us that they, too, have seen this star as it crossed the night sky."

Herod clapped his hand on Kaspar's shoulder. "That was a comet you followed. No one here has seen such a star. Perhaps, you thought it was the moon, since it glows yellow in the daytime."

Julian could see that Herod was deeply disturbed by these men and eager to get rid of them.

He continued in a pompous manner, "I'll provide food and lodging for you and your party tonight. In the morning, my legate here will take a company of my finest soldiers to a village not far distant. Near Bethlehem are fields where shepherds graze their flocks. Perhaps, someone there can be of more help, and you can bring me word of him." He looked pointedly at the three kings' bulging pouches.

Kaspar understood the gesture and removed from one a thin bar of gold. He handed it to Herod, saying, "For disturbing you."

Julian then conducted the strangers to the street.

Melchior said to him with an amused smile, "We'll not accept your king's offer of shelter. Our retinue of servants, camel-drivers, and slaves number a hundred or more. We are camped outside the south gate of the city, and will meet you there in the morning. What time do you suggest?"

"When the trumpets announce the first prayer and you hear the clang of the double Nicanor gate as it opens, then I'll meet you. I'm curious, Melchior. Why would you expect the new king of the Jews to be born in a village with fewer than three hundred people? Why not in their Holy City?"

"Don't you know that the shepherd-king, David, was born in Bethlehem? Of greater importance is that eight hundred years ago, the prophet, Michah, named it as the place of the Lord's birth."

"A good reason," Julian said amiably. "Now what if you find several newborn male infants there? How will you know which one is the new king?"

"By the white aura around him, of course. Only a few of us with inner sight can see it."

"I can believe that," Julian said with a chuckle.

He knew of only one person who skillfully used "white light." That was the enigmatic Anna of Galilee. She had surrounded him with it and healed him of epilepsy. Then wouldn't a child, born with such an aura, be a special healer of enormous power? Here was a mystery to liven up his dull life. He returned to his quarters but couldn't sleep.

*   *   *

At the first light of day, and even before twenty strong men swung open the heavy bronze Nicanor Gate, the three magi had their entourage ready to march. Herod's Idumean cavalrymen, resplendent in gold helmets and red capes, followed Julian. Leading the long line were the three magi on camels, with their drivers. In the chill morning air, they wore long cloaks with embroidered hoods.

Next came their large retinue of family members, servants, and slaves. Bringing up the rear were the great dromedaries, loaded with carpets and boxes of goods, and camels bearing fodder in sacks. Finally, there were donkeys carrying pigeons in cages and cases of flat bread and dried fruits.

Julian noticed that most of the men had scimitars tucked into the folds of their girdles.

When Julian's party reached Bethlehem, he saw it was no different from countless other villages in the hill country. Modest, box-like houses of whitewashed mud bricks clustered around a common well and market place. Helmeted Roman sentries stood at the main gate, checking each arrival. They were accustomed to caravans from far-off lands. When the magi slipped a few coins into the guards' outstretched hands, the procession moved quickly into the town square.

The area around this northern gate was bustling with activity. Smaller caravans with spices and silks had arrived before them and were in competition with farmers and herdsmen trying to sell grain and sheep. Women in colorful headscarves stood in line at the well, with water jars to be filled. Young boys raced in front of Julian's horse to their synagogue to learn Hebrew. Shy girls peered out of deeply-recessed windows, attracted by the noisy entrance of the magi's caravan.

There was one caravansary near the town's market square, and here, raucous merchants hawked their wares. What an unwashed crowd of mendicants, thieves and traders cluttered the place! When Julian raised a jeweled hand to wipe his perspiring face, the stones flared in the sun, and beggars fussed at him with pleading cries. He hadn't thought of this when he put on his costly ruby. He touched his heels to his mount, and the decury of soldiers followed him into a side street.

He told them, "You can conduct your search without me. I'll meet you back here at the fifth hour."

Julian wanted to locate the roads leading out of town. He wasn't sure why this was important. Yet a plan kept rising in his mind to be used if the soldiers actually located this supposed newborn Messiah.

He had only ten men with him. What if the family made an attempt to escape, once they heard of the plot to take the infant to Herod? These people were clever at forming a defiant, unruly crowd at a moment's notice. Yet, daytime was propitious. Many able-bodied men were in the fields, preparing the bleak soil for planting.

A merchant told him the shepherds had driven their flocks to the fields southeast of town, through a long wadi. These, then, would be the men who had witnessed the star described by the magi. As Julian headed south to check on that road out of town, he caught sight of the

Oriental kings examining the limestone grottoes some distance away. These caves were either naturally or artificially hollowed out for the use of domestic animals or burial crypts. The magi had obviously had no luck in their search in town.

The southern gate had only two Galatian guards on duty. Julian approached them, saying, "I am Legate Julian, on a mission from King Herod. Where does this road go?"

One of the men answered, "To the coast, if you want to go that far. Herod comes through here often on his way to his fortification, the Herodium. It's to the east of the main road, if that's what you want to know."

"From Hebron, where does the road go?"

"To Gaza through Canaanite country. Few travel that difficult route. Mostly nomad tribes with their flocks."

Julian found it exhilarating to be plotting an imaginary intercept of a fleeing family. He needed a challenge. Yet, carrying out Herod's orders would be like killing a grasshopper to save the grain fields of Palestine.

Could these men be bribed? Being hired foreign soldiers—Gaulish, Germanic and Galatian—none would have even met Herod. So long as they were fed and paid, they had no allegiance to these Roman provinces who feuded among themselves.

The Roman Empire, to which Julian had devoted his life, was crumbling. The Jews wouldn't fight alongside pagans, so they got complete exemption from military service. Anna told him once that the warrior king, David, claimed no army. Judea needed a new king to replace cruel Herod.

Of course, not a newborn infant, but someone who would do more than dot Palestine with fortifications such as Masada, Hyrcanium, and the Antonia Tower. Why did Herod build hippodromes and amphitheaters in Caesarea, Sebaste, and Tarichaea for the enjoyment of heathens and not the Jews? The revolting spectacles Julian had once enjoyed, the killing of condemned men by lions and gladiators fighting each other to the death now suddenly sickened him.

He recalled that Anna had said to him after he'd ridiculed her belief in angels, "Time will become your angel. You'll change."

He was changing, and he blamed it on her influence. He returned now to the market place to meet the cavalrymen. They reported to him that, with one exception, all newborn infants were girls.

"And that exception?" Julian asked with deep interest.

"There's a boy living with his parents in the limestone caves in the hills. Many people and animals go into these grottoes during the noonday heat. Few shade trees grow in this rocky soil."

"What's the father's trade?"

"A carpenter," the soldier replied. "He wouldn't let us see his wife or child. They have no possessions, so we didn't insist. No king would be born in a stable. Let me point the place out to you—see there, on the hillside."

"You've done well. I'll give your report to Herod as soon as he returns from Caesarea. That should be within a few days. Are all the gates of Bethlehem guarded at night?"

"Only the north one. At the south gate, there are ropes with attached bells strung across the road. Rarely does one travel this route—going or coming, after sundown. So no sentry is stationed there until the morning watch."

Julian was pleased. By the time Herod made his decision, he would have devised his own plan for preventing this heralded newcomer from falling into the ruler's bloody hands. Why a man of Herod's power would fear an infant baffled him. Julian had no idea why he must save this child, but the impulse came to him strongly.

It would be a game of wits against a pitiless executioner. Herod, however, was far from secure in spite of his Gaulish, Thracian, and Germanic guards. These mercenaries were stationed in Syria, requiring time to come to his aid. Julian might get help from the heavily-taxed Jewish farmers. It was stimulating to think about outsmarting this devilish man.

CHAPTER 4

With their servants, Anna and Cleophas set out for Bethlehem as soon as they learned of Jesus' birth. Traveling during the short days of the month of Kislev, they had to make camp in the hills of Judea, a few miles distant from their destination. As darkness descended, they prepared their beds and ate a simple supper.

As they sat there, they heard the rumble of tramping hooves and strange voices. Into their camp stepped three enormous dromedaries. Each was elegantly caparisoned and bore a darkfaced rider seated between rolls of carpets. These men were followed by heavily-loaded camels and donkeys with panniers, guided by a retinue of servants and drivers.

For a few moments, neither Anna nor Cleophas could speak. They had never seen such rich and sumptuous clothing. The strangers' velvet tunics, satin girdles, and unusual headgear must have come from kingdoms far removed from Palestine. And Israelites never rode dromedaries.

Cleophas rose to greet them. "Shalom, travelers! Where is your homeland?"

The fairest and oldest of the three answered, "Blessings on you! We're from three regions—Persia, India, and Egypt. We've followed a wondrous star to Judea. For 500 years our great ancestors promised that a savior would be born in this part of the world. Having seen the newborn child in Bethlehem and recognized him as the fulfillment of this covenant, we are now returning home."

Convinced that these were honorable men, Cleophas pointed to Anna. "This is my wife, who is the child's grandmother. We've come from Galilee to take the holy family back with us."

The three magi bowed deeply to Anna, then shook their heads. "No, no! Don't risk doing that. Hear our experience first."

The three men dismounted from their animals and joined them. "My name is Kaspar from Persia. This is Melchior, Indian magi of renown, and Balthazar, Egyptian diviner. Let them reveal our experience in Judea."

Balthazar said in a strong foreign accent, "The guiding star disappeared from the heavens when we entered Jerusalem. We were lost, but a soldier directed us to Herod's palace to learn where the newborn king could be seen. What shocked us was that no one in that holy city knew what we were talking about. We had expected there would be great rejoicing in the streets."

Melchior cleared his throat and continued the story. "We made the mistake of telling Herod that we brought priceless gifts from distant lands to the infant, Jesus. We sensed Herod's fear and jealousy, yet he tried to cover them by directing a company of ten cavalrymen and one of his legates to take us to Bethlehem. They located a grotto, used at times as a stable, where a male child had recently been born. But when they saw only a poor family there, they suggested we question the family carefully and report back to Herod in a day or two."

Kaspar now took up the narration. "We thought this was an unusual request. So that night as we prayed to God, each of us became aware of Herod's intention— have the newborn child killed if we confirmed the rumor that the long-awaited Messiah had come. Of course, we could not risk that."

"You are fleeing tonight?" Cleophas asked.

"Yes, after an hour's rest. We have lanterns to help us find our way, and shortly the moon will give us enough light. We are no match for Herod's troops. We intend to split up into separate groups and travel along little-used roads."

Balthazar then interrupted, saying, "Our presence with the holy family turned out to be unfortunate for them."

"In what way?" Anna asked.

"The townspeople heard we had brought rare gifts to the poor family in the cavern. Beggars by the hundreds crowded the entrance constantly, demanding alms. One day, Joseph was forced to give them some of the gold we brought in order to keep them out of the cave. You see, our richly ornamented saddles and bridles, our retinue of servants, and our valuable oriental rugs produced only greed among them."

Cleophas spoke in a confident tone. "Surely, the holy family can live securely in one of the northern provinces."

"No! No!" Kaspar interrupted him. "Herod will look for them there. They are not safe anywhere in Palestine. They must flee to Egypt. If we had gone back to Herod, he would have tortured us to reveal all we astrologers know of the future of Jesus. This we could not risk."

Balthazar spoke a final warning. "Do not admit to anyone that you are related to the Messiah or that he is anyone but a poor carpenter's son. If necessary, you must lie to save him. Trust no one."

Anna was deeply agitated by such stern warnings. Melchoir, seeing her concern, quickly brought her two small rugs of great beauty. "We give the grandmother of the holy child these Persian weavings to remember us by." Then he took a stick and traced a crude map on the ground. "This is where you will find your daughter and family. Move with caution. Herod has stationed guards at all the exit gates. It will be extremely dangerous to get the holy family out of Bethlehem, but our prayers go with you."

As Anna and Cleophas approached the cave of the nativity the next morning, two women ran to meet them. One said, "We are Essenes who watch over the holy family. Mary told us you were near. It's no longer safe for them to leave the stable. Continue past the donkeys to the rear cavern, where you'll find the family."

The women remained at the entrance while Anna and Cleophas made their way slowly into the dim cave. Mary called to them, and they could see her seated with Jesus on her lap. The infant was barely visible beneath the sheer white veil covering him.

Anna was so overcome with joy that she couldn't speak. Mary held out the child to her, and, with trembling hands, Anna took him to her heart. For several minutes, she rocked him and wept silently. She knew this would be the only time for years to come that she could hold her grandchild. By touching him now, she felt her own spiritual shadow grow.

She returned him to Mary, saying, "I had dreamt of teaching him many things as a child."

"No, dearest Mother, this Son of Man will learn all he needs to know from his Heavenly Father. It is I who will learn from him." She rose and placed Jesus in a wicker basket behind her. Then she turned to Anna asking, "Do you bring us good news?"

Anna shook her head. "We met the three magi last evening after they had seen you. Herod had told them to report back to him what they learned by their visit here. Being men of spiritual perception, they were warned during a meditation to flee from Judea, else they would be forced to reveal the true identity of your infant."

Cleophas added, "Herod has plans to have Jesus killed, so fearful is he of his kingship in this province. Now, we must think of a way to get you out of Bethlehem."

Joseph came to Mary. "I did not want to tell you this, dearest wife, but I, too, was warned last night in a dream to take flight. But where can we go so Jesus will be safe?"

Mary looked at Cleophas, asking, "Will we be out of Herod's reach if we can escape with you to Galilee?'

"No, little mother, you must head for Alexandria, Egypt. Judea will be a giant trap for you as soon as the Maccabean Dedication Festival is ended in Jerusalem."

With a look of surprise, Joseph said, "So that's why the beggars left us to work the more affluent crowds there." He paused, and shook his head. "Tomorrow is the Sabbath Day. God does not permit us to travel on this sacred day. However, we can make all necessary preparations for leaving the following day." His voice trembled with uncertainty.

Cleophas suddenly raised his hand for them to be quiet. He whispered, "Roman soldiers just passed. They prowl the streets, searching for someone who knows the birthplace of Jesus. Let's go farther back in the cave to make plans for your escape."

They gathered around a simply made altar of cedar.

Joseph lit the seven candles of the menorah set in the wall. "I must take this candelabrum with me on our flight," he said, as if reminding himself. "Let us pray."

When Anna opened her eyes, she saw a globe of brilliant light blotting out the figures of Mary and Jesus. It spread like a moving cloud, until it encompassed the entire grotto. No one dared speak. Gradually it faded away.

Joseph made no mention of the phenomenon and rose from his stool saying, "I must feed the donkeys."

At the entrance, he heard someone clear his throat. He turned around to face a Roman. He froze with a look of great fear on his face when he saw the stranger's white wool toga embroidered with the unmistakable royal eagle on the shoulder. This emblem carried with it the authority of Augustus Caesar.

The official asked in a brusque voice, "Your name and size of family?"

"Joseph, I have a wife and child, named Mary and Yeshua."

"Is there anyone here who will verify this or must I enter this miserable stable?"

"Anna and Cleophas from Galilee are here. I will bring them to you."

Julian's face flushed at the mention of Anna. "I need speak only to the woman." Could this be the Anna who haunted his dreams? What was she doing in a grotto in Bethlehem? She had a daughter, he remembered. Was it possible that Anna's daughter had born the child whispered to be the King of Judea? Was this the reason something indefinable, a power outside of himself, had drawn him back to Bethlehem? He thought it was simply curiosity. Had Anna, with her unfathomable powers, called to him through the ethers, pleading for his help in saving her grandson?

There she was, walking toward him with that grace

that set her apart from other women. Her lovely face wore a frightened look that pained him, since he knew he was the reason for it.

She spoke first. "Why did you come here, hireling of Herod?"

"Anna, Anna, don't fear for your grandchild. Because of my love for you, I'll plan a way of smuggling him through the guarded gates. Remember, I'm a servant of Augustus, not working for an Arab Jew." He paused, then added, "I've never lied to you, Anna."

She nodded. "If you have a workable plan, let Joseph and Cleophas hear it with me." She called to them, and the men approached Julian warily.

Without greeting them, he stated his plan. "I talked with a tribe of nomads outside of town. Day after tomorrow, they plan on moving their flocks south for better pastures. I'll try to bargain with them to let a family of three escape in their midst as they go through the south gate. In that direction lies your only chance to avoid capture. What do you say?"

Joseph and Cleophas were stunned by the clever proposal. Joseph turned to Anna, asking, "Can we trust this Roman who works with a deranged tyrant?"

"I believe he wants to help you. I know he hates Herod."

Joseph sighed deeply. "How many denarii will this cost me?"

"None, even though you are in no position to bargain. I'm saving your lives because of Anna. Now listen. I'll try to arrange your departure with the nomads before the cockcrow watch and change of the guards. Semidarkness will be your ally. The sentries won't be suspicious of this tribe, with their goats and sheep. They pass this way frequently. There'll be a lot of confusion, with the wayward animals bleating and the women and children yelling to the men. It's an ideal way to escape. The problem for me is to persuade the old chieftain to agree to it."

Anna's look of gratitude and relief made Julian soften his irritable attitude. His mind was in a whirl, thinking about this sudden change in his plans. He had come here out of curiosity. To discover that Anna was the grandmother of the hunted infant came as a great shock. Of course, he didn't believe all that nonsense about a newborn king of the Jews. Every year or two, someone claimed he was the Messiah, although this was the first time it was a baby. He wanted to impress Anna more than anything else in the world. Now he had a dangerous opportunity to do so and outwit Herod at the same time. His thoughts were interrupted by a question from Joseph.

"Tell me, after we go south from here, what route do we take to Egypt?"

"You mustn't stop before reaching Hebron. That's where you'll turn west to Beth Gibelin. Go past Eglon, and follow the road leading to Gaza. You'll be in Philistia, birthplace of Herod. Then travel south along the seacoast, and you'll be in Egypt soon enough."

"When will we know for certain if the chieftain accepts your plan?"

"I'll be back to advise you. You and your wife must look like nomads. Your beard hides most of your face, but I assume your wife is fair. Later, I'll bring some *stibium,* which Roman women use to blacken their eyebrows and lashes. She can darken her face with it."

Then Anna, her eyes warm with gratitude, asked Julian, "Will you be with my children when they go through the south gate?"

"Of course—to relieve you of worry." He smiled with more confidence than he felt. He would be risking his life, but it didn't seem to matter. He was full of joy and a sense of purpose, if only for a few hours.

*   *   *

Julian rode immediately to the tribe of nomads camped outside the north gate. He quickly spotted the chieftain and approached him with an air of great authority.

"You are the leader of these people?" Julian asked.

"I am Caleb, patriarch of my tribe. We have disturbed no one here. We stopped earlier because two of our women gave birth—unfortunately, the infants were girls—and could not travel. But the day after the Sabbath, we seek better pastures."

"Would you like to earn, for doing nothing, fifty shekels? Listen carefully, Caleb. There is a husband, wife, and newborn child who must get through the south exit gate that same morning, early. If you will allow them to travel, unnoticed, in your group, until you have all cleared the sentries there, I will give you that reward."

"First, tell me what these people have done to be hunted?"

"The young woman married the man she loved, not the one chosen by the parents. You know how it is with you—children must do as the fathers decide."

"That is bad," Caleb said, shaking his gray head. His wizened eyes, narrowed by the hot sun over a long lifetime, studied Julian carefully. Finally he said, "Not enough."

"Well, then how much?"

"It's up to you."

Julian knew how these men liked to haggle. It was an insult to agree to the first figure given.

"Sixty shekels. That's a good sum for doing nothing, Caleb."

"The sentries won't let my large tribe and animals go

through the town. We have always, before, had to go around it."

Julian doubted this statement. "I'll speak to the sentry at the north gate and tell him you need to enter to make sales of some of your animals to the merchants. But, of course, you won't stop, but will go at once to the market square. There, I'll join you with the family. They'll mingle with your people. Now, will you do this for sixty shekels?"

"Not enough."

"How much, Caleb?"

"It's up to you," he repeated with a shrug.

Irritated, Julian said, "My final offer is seventy-five shekels. Will you shake hands on that?'

With a crafty smile, Caleb held out his hand.

Chapter 5

On his ride back to the grotto the next day, Julian decided his escape plan might not be as easy as first thought. Nomads had a reputation of unreliability. Most of them were actually robbers at heart. If they double-crossed him, he would have to carry out the rescue alone. If all else failed, a good supply of shekels might make for success. He intended to forego his present plain tunic and tomorrow wear a dramatic military dress to impress not only the guards at the gate but also wily Caleb.

Approaching the cave, he was relieved to see Anna sitting outside alone. As he leapt from his mount, she ran to him, crying. "Do you bring good news?"

"Yes, the chief has agreed to our plan. The tribe will pass through the north gate near dawn, and your family can join them in the town square and be a part of the group leaving through the south exit. "

"You said yesterday that Herod has ordered a close check on everyone departing Bethlehem."

"I'm hoping that one or two guards can't block a rushing herd of goats and sheep mixed with determined people."

"I'm worried, Julian. Let me call Mary and Joseph to discuss this further."

"Wait, Anna. I want you to know that the risk I'm taking is entirely for you. If Herod discovers my duplicity, I'll never see you again. Remember, you have brought me the only beauty in life I've ever know. Think well of me if I fail."

Anna flushed deeply. He waited in misery for her quiet reply. "There's no way I can repay . . . " Her voice broke, and she put her hands over her face to hide her tears.

Mary and Joseph came out of the cavern. It was the first time Julian had seen Mary. He was stunned by the sight of her beauty. She floated rather than walked across the intervening space. Her eyes were like her mother's— large, expressive topaz jewels. She had Anna's fine nose and lovely chin. Red-gold ringlets of hair peered from beneath her white head-scarf. He was seeing again the young Anna who had dazzled him in Nazareth a lifetime ago.

Mary was the first to speak. Her musical voice was so soft that Julian had to strain to hear her words. "I'm grateful, Legate, for the risk you are taking to help us."

Julian replied, "I think the plan of escape will work. There will be other women with newborn infants in the tribe. Take your cues from them, and, if challenged, show no fear."

Anna interrupted then. "If you can save only one of the family, it must be the child."

Mary nodded agreement.

Julian turned to her, offering a small package. "I

brought you *stibium*. Use this to blacken your fair lashes and brows, then blend it over your face and hands."

"Now, Joseph," he continued, "if you become separated in the confusion, keep traveling south toward Hebron. I'll see to it you are reunited."

Joseph appeared dubious of the plan. Noticing this, Anna said, "You can trust Julian. Forget your fears."

Julian gave her a grateful look, then spoke again to Joseph. "Dress as scrubby and unwashed as you can. Don't walk anywhere near your wife and child. Herod has issued orders to look for a family of three. I've asked the chieftain to tell the new mothers in his party to likewise walk separate from their husbands. I'll come for you before dawn, so be ready to join the moving nomads once they've passed through the north gate."

"Bless you, Legate," Mary and Joseph said simultaneously. They returned to the grotto to make final preparations.

Anna's face was full of pain. "Julian, you're jeopardizing not only your position but your life. I couldn't bear to have Herod crucify you."

Julian took both her hands in his. "What do you see in my eyes, Anna?'

She studied him for a moment. "Courage, selflessness, a willingness to risk all for total strangers."

"None of these, Anna. You see a passionate love for a woman who torments me. You are my sanity in a universe that has gone mad with killing and greed and taxes."

"We travel separate roads, but, strangely, parallel." She paused and quickly changed the subject. "Do you think my children will be safe as they cross the desert to Gaza?"

"Safe enough. It's in these Judean hills that lurk the threatening packs of beggars, workless shepherds, and escaped slaves. When will you return to Sepphoris?:"

"We leave at the same time as you."

"I will try to keep you informed of any developments here. Herod will expect Mary and her family to go to Galilee—never to Egypt, so their chances of reaching it are good."

"I ask that God go between you and all harm tomorrow." She dared not look into his tormented eyes. She left him then.

Julian did not move for a few minutes. He thought of the oracles' message on his last trip to Rome. "A widow from Galilee will one day change your life into one of exquisite purpose. She, alone, can show you the way— so stay in contact with her." That surely meant that one day Anna would be his wife.

Anna and Mary talked long into the night, knowing that in a few hours, they would be separated for years to come. A solitary candle flickered on the wall. Joseph and Cleophas had gone to sleep in an adjacent alcove.

"Oh, Mary, my heart is breaking," Anna sobbed. "I have had you, my only daughter, with me less than four years of my life. And now because of irrational Herod, I will be stripped of, not only you, but my precious grandchild, until that madman dies. I had foolishly imagined my visiting you every other day in Nazareth and watching my grandson grow each month. Oh, God, my heart is breaking."

Mary quickly rose and brought Jesus to her. "Hold him while I tell you of the gifts the three magi gave Jesus." She returned shortly with a basket. From it, she first lifted out several small bars of gold. "Kaspar said that gold represents the physical body, the material existence. Melchior brought Jesus frankincense, which relates to one's mental body. And Balthazar gave him a plant of myrrh, saying it expressed the ethereal world. Together, these three gifts symbolize mankind's body, mind, and soul. What greater offering could they have given him?"

"None greater," Anna said, gently rocking Jesus in her arms. "Cleophas and I brought you more than food and clothing, too. We give you now our eternal love."

Mary said sadly, "We can take little else with us. The extra articles will be distributed among the shepherds and families by our Essene friends." She took Jesus from her mother and placed him in a wicker basket. "How can a newborn child be such a threat to King Herod?'

"The magi told us that he dared not dismiss as idle gossip their insistence that the Messiah was born here. However, if he seized Jesus immediately, the people would believe that the princes from the East were telling the truth. When rumors about Jesus' birth lessen, then Herod plans to kill him. That's what Kaspar claimed."

"We haven't a day to lose," Mary said in a worried tone.

They were both silent for a few moments, then Mary asked, "When did you first meet Julian, and why is he helping us escape?"

"I met him when I was fifteen, and he was the data gatherer in Nazareth. I healed him of epilepsy."

Mary's eyes widened. "Why don't you practice the healing arts now, mother?"

"I have been haunted by Sobe's drowning—her suicide. I should have been able to prevent it. I consider myself a failure in the healing arts. Through her meanness, Sobe was crying out for help. I didn't hear her. She took something of me with her into the Sea of Galilee." Anna's face was drawn and tormented.

"Hush such foolish talk," Mary said. "Without you, we would not be able to escape tomorrow. Julian would have reported us to Herod. You healed his thoughts. You haven't lost that power."

"I wish I could heal Herod's thoughts. Recently, he or-

dered a lamb of gold to be made and set over the arch-
way to the Court of Sacrifice. One of the temple priests
saw this blasphemy and knocked it down. Of course, it
broke into many pieces. Herod had the man crucified.
So never reveal Julian's help in your escape, or his fate
will be the same."

"No one will ever know, dearest Mother."

"Cleophas insists you take one of our three donkeys."
Anna moved about the cave. "Have you a spare pair of
sandals?"

Mary shook her head.

"Then you will take mine. And each of you must have
a thick cloak, as the nights can be very cold. We have
brought extras for you."

Her worried thoughts continued to race. "Has Joseph
a staff to defend you if necessary?"

"Yes, Mother."

"And what about water?"

"I don't think Joseph has . . . '

"I will fill two skins now and add a bit of vinegar to
them."

Mary smiled. Perhaps one day she would live close to
this caring parent.

Chapter 6

Julian returned from Jerusalem at the close of the Sabbath to spend the night in Bethlehem's caravansary. He slept little and rose before dawn to shave and carefully put on the borrowed uniform of a cavalryman. Over the yellow tunic went a skirt of brass-studded leather. Next came a sword whose scabbard buckled on the right side, then a thick, red wool cloak decorated with brass epaulets and a long-plumed red helmet. He was sure he looked sensational.

He rode at once to the edge of town, where Caleb had promised to meet him at dawn. No one was about. He dismounted and sat down on a tree stump, listening for the sound of approaching animals and the shouts of herdsmen. None came. An hour passed.

Rose-tinged morning clouds appeared on the horizon. Slowly, daylight peered over the hills of Judah. Julian wondered if the tribe had left in another direction. The chieftain was unreliable. He shouldn't have paid him in advance. He had stressed the need of avoiding a daylight departure, since someone might spot the holy family and report it to Herod's sentries.

The sun was now up. Yet, there was no sign of the nomads. Knowing that Anna and her family would be worried, Julian rode to the grotto. Everyone waited nervously outside the stable. Mary sat on the ground, holding Jesus, while Joseph helped the Essene women remove all traces of their occupancy here. Julian noticed that Jesus was still in swaddling clothes—a custom of the Jews who believed straight limbs would be assured by binding long linen strips tightly about the infant. Neither arms nor legs could move.

Anna and Cleophas were about to head north along the Jordan Valley to their home in Sepphoris. Julian told everyone, "The nomads haven't come, so I'm going to their camp. I hope they haven't departed in the night." He turned to Anna. "I will do my best for you. Nomads or not, I'll get your family out of Bethlehem." He wheeled his horse around and galloped off to the tribe's campground.

It was a relief to find the nomads still there, milling around.

"You're long overdue at the marketplace!" he shouted to Caleb. "Why the delay?"

The chieftain ran to him. "Our herd was raided in the night by wolves. They killed some of our sheep. The terrified animals scattered everywhere. We've just rounded them up."

"Can you come now?"

"Yes, we're ready." He shouted to the other herdsmen, and the caravan made its slow way south. The guards at the north gate knew Caleb from previous years, so they waved the nomads through. They continued into town, but before they had reached the market square, Julian brought Mary and Joseph into their company.

He handed Joseph a dried, empty gourd with a rope attached to it. "Here's something you may need in drawing water from any well. It has a stone in it to give it sufficient weight."

Joseph was visibly surprised. "You are very thoughtful, Julian. We will never forget your concern for us."

He walked with the donkey that carried the panniers loaded with their meager possessions, while Mary rode the other animal with Jesus completely hidden in her arms.

Julian noticed how skillfully she had applied the *stibium* to her hands and face. She looked little different than the sunbrowned tribal women.

The slow movement of the flocks and people aggravated Julian. He left them to join Caleb riding a donkey at the head of the procession.

The moment they entered the main street of Bethlehem, chaos struck. The square was seething with crowds of unwashed mendicants and overbearing merchants shouting their bargains for the day. The goats panicked. They burst into open shops, scattering the goods everywhere. The sheep took their cues from the goats and jumped about bleating hysterically. Some turned around and tried to go against the stream. The herdsmen shouted wildly in their attempt to control the animals. Shopkeepers pelted them with sticks. Yet in spite of the turmoil, the women and children managed to continue on their way.

Julian spotted Mary, with her precious bundle, trying to guide her bewildered donkey through the unruly creatures. He forced his horse through them to reach her and took the animal's rope from her hand. He quickly led the confused animal out of the disorderly mass. By now, the troop of nomads had gotten into the outskirts of town.

Behind them, Julian could hear the angry screams of the protesting shop owners, since the panicky animals had littered the streets with their dung.

The six-week-old Jesus, frightened by the hubbub and bleating around him, began to cry. Mary was obviously fearful that attention would be brought on them. She shushed him, and he grew quiet.

Julian, out in front of the melee, was shocked to see not one or two sentries waiting there, but a half dozen. He seethed with anger. If these overly devout Jews had left yesterday, Herod wouldn't have had time to send additional guards here. Joseph had tried in vain to explain the stupid law that forbad its people from traveling on the Sabbath farther than the distance from the Mount of Olives to Jerusalem. Why that was a distance of only six *stadia* or a walk of twenty minutes!

Julian took the offensive. He rode up to the new sentries demanding, "Why are you here? I was asked to escort this tribe through the gate and send them on their way."

"Herod ordered us to examine all the departing infants. We are looking for the new king of the Jews."

"There is no need for that. The babies are all girls. Isn't that true, Caleb?"

The chieftain nodded vigorously, too frightened to speak.

The sentry said determinedly, "We'll check each one, nevertheless."

They spotted the first mother, snatched her infant and tore apart its blanket. Seeing it was a girl, they looked around for another mother and child.

Mary rode along with head lowered, urging her donkey to move faster. Julian forced his horse through the nomads to her.

While the sentries were occupied checking the second

mother's infant, he snatched Jesus from Mary's arms and thrust him under the folds of his generous cloak.

"This is our only chance," he said quickly. "I'll wait for you beyond the gate."

She was stunned by the suddenness of his action. Joseph, seeing the transfer, panicked. He suspected it was a clever scheme on Herod's part to get Jesus. He shouted, "Stop that Roman!" No one paid any attention to him in the confusion.

Seeing that Mary was not carrying a child and the other women had been checked, the head centurion called out, "The one we seek is not here! We return to Jerusalem!'

Julian had now reached the gate where two of the sentries waited. He yelled to them, "I'm not needed here any longer, so I'll be on my way."

The guards nodded and turned their attention to the bleating animals coming through.

After riding a short distance south, Julian brought out from beneath his cloak the half-suffocated Jesus. The infant was awake, his brow frowning at the sight of a stranger. He didn't cry, but focused his expressive blue eyes on Julian's red-plumed helmet. Looking back, Julian saw the legionnaires head north, so he stopped beside the road. In a short time, frantic Mary and Joseph reached him.

Mary wept when he handed Jesus to her, and Joseph stood shamefaced before him. "Forgive me for suspecting the worst," he said humbly. "We'll thank God every day for your bravery."

Julian replied with impatience, "You must travel as fast as possible today. I'll try to turn suspicion of your escape to Samaria or Galilee. Good luck on your way to Gaza." He took a long look at Jesus, wheeled his mount around, and headed north.

It was curious, he thought, how his arms and hands tingled. He would never forget the beautiful eyes of the infant he had pressed against his heart. Anna's grand-child was special. He had not screamed, as so many children did. It would be interesting to see him when he was grown. Would he look like exquisite Mary or plain Joseph?

Julian had learned at the last moment that a group of Essenes had left ahead of the holy family, and another group was to follow them, by way of protection, all the way to Gaza.

He breathed a sigh of relief. It had been an exhilarating day! Anna would be enormously impressed by his actions. And he could go back to Herod, knowing he had triumphed over him. To outwit this insane ruler had become a new and exciting goal for Julian. Yet, he felt a vague fear for the missing infant and family. The procurator, with vast armies at his command, would continue the search relentlessly.

CHAPTER 7

A week after Julian's Bethlehem experience, he was summoned to Herod. He found the ruler on a couch, emaciated, pale, and irritable. A purple silk coverlet lay over his naked body.

"Come in, Legate," he said weakly. "Will you have a drink of fine wine?" He pointed to a table laden with bottles and goblets.

"Not today," Julian hedged. He tried to inject a note of concern in his voice. "How are you feeling?"

"Nothing helps me. I've gotten rid of all my physicians. I think they'd like to kill me with their foul mixtures. What I want to know is how we missed capturing the little impostor in Bethlehem. I was told you returned only at my command."

"Yes, but a woman, not a newborn infant, occupied my time. I have a harlot friend there whom I visit frequently. I avoid such indiscretions here in Jerusalem for your sake." Julian bowed slightly, face lowered to avoid telegraphing his lie.

Herod's eyes gleamed. "My spies have been remiss. If she's worth traveling that far to service, you must bring her here sometime when I'm feeling better."

"Of course, sire. But I'm leaving for Sepphoris now, so you'll have to wait. Remember, you asked me to report on the projected flax harvest this year in Galilee."

"Ah, yes." Herod closed his eyes for a few moments. Julian waited for him to continue. "After I sent you off with those three crazy astrologers, I spent the night on the palace roof, looking for that cursed star. There wasn't any star with a comet's tail. Just ordinary blinking stars. Did you see it at any time?"

Julian shook his head. "You know shepherds have nothing to do but spread rumors. They are all too eager to have their legends fulfilled."

"Let me tell you what I did that night. I summoned my high priest and scribes to reveal to me where the Messiah would be born. They all pleaded ignorance. My soldiers, sent with you to Bethlehem, found only one baby boy in a miserable stable. His parents had nothing. I've lost my belief in prophecy. When my present orders are carried out, there'll be no male baby left to challenge my reign."

Julian's eyes widened. What kind of a plot had Herod hatched?

"Last week, I sent invitations to mothers of boys under the age of two years to bring them to the temple today. It's important that they show off their sons to their powerful ruler, don't you think?"

Julian had no idea what he was insinuating, so he answered, "A fine idea, sire."

"I'm sending you to Masada, before Sepphoris, with a message to General Leander. If you wish, stay a few days in my palace-villa on the mountain top. You'll enjoy the beautiful women there, most of them Romans. I've taught them all their bedroom skills." He laughed. "This miserable dysentery keeps me from enjoying those pleasures, but, you will see I have created other amusements for myself."

A servant came to the open door and waited to be acknowledged.

"Yes, yes," Herod said impatiently, "out with it."

"Quartus has completed his mission at the temple, and wishes to report to you on it."

Herod swung his bare feet to the tiled floor with a wild-eyed expression and said, "Send him in. Julian will now see how a sick man can conduct important business from his bed."

A brute of a man entered the room. He wore full war gear, with sword in its scabbard and metal breastplate. Julian was repelled by his evil, overbearing look.

Quartus said with a triumphant smile, "We killed every little bastard that came, sire. And their mothers, too, as you had instructed. They thought you would reward them with denarii for having borne a boy child. If that young king was among 'em, we got him for sure."

Herod clapped his hands with satisfaction. "He would be among them. The fake would be one of them!"

Quartus continued, "In many cases, we were able to kill both mother and child with one mighty thrust of our sword. We had cleared everyone else out of the Court of Gentiles and locked the entrances. You should have seen the blood squirt from their little bellies! There's a gory mess to clean up, sire, What shall we do with the bodies?"

In his excitement, Herod had dropped his drapery and stood like a naked vulture. "Burn them on the sacrificial altar, of course! And use plenty of incense everywhere for a few days. You have done well, Quartus, and your men will be rewarded."

Quartus nodded and left.

Julian stood paralyzed by what he had just heard. He began gasping for air and retched over and over again. Finally, the vomit flew across the marble floor. Holding his hand over his mouth, he fled down the ornate stairs, his ears ringing with Herod's raucous laughter.

An aide of the procurator waited at the exit doors and handed him his orders for General Leander at the Masada fortress. Julian debated whether he should disobey them and leave directly for Sepphoris. News of this massacre of the infants would travel faster than the wind. He must learn if any mother and son from Sepphoris had accepted Herod's vile invitation. He had to see Anna as quickly as possible. She might think that Mary and Jesus had been caught in the fiendish trap. She and Cleophas had left Bethlehem without knowing if the holy family had made their escape.

He had no choice. He must deliver Herod's message to Masada. The wily king always kept close watch on him. This was no time to incur Herod's wrath. He wouldn't tarry at the mountain villa, but hurry as fast as possible to Galilee.

*   *   *

When Julian rode up the hill to Anna's home, he saw great hostility in the faces of the passersby. Some ran to neighbors', as if he brought the plague.

One man yelled at him, "Killer of women and infants!"

Then he realized that Herod's infamy had reached Sepphoris. Every Roman would be held responsible for the insane massacre, since Herod was the slave of Rome.

Julian rode his horse inside the courtyard today and closed the gate. His strong rap on the door brought no response. He walked around the place and called loudly, but no one answered. He was about to return to his horse and go into the market place. Perhaps Cleophas was at his sandal shop. Before he could leave, an angry group of men burst into the yard and rushed to him. They carried clubs and yelled, "You tools of Herod must die like the infants did!"

Julian was so stunned by the mob that he stood uncertainly before them. As they came to him, they stopped, each waiting for the other to attack him. Before he could speak, Cleophas came running from behind them.

"Stop, everyone!" he cried. "This Roman helped the holy family flee from Bethlehem."

"You know that for certain? The family is safe? Where?"

Cleophas, of course, didn't know if they had escaped Herod's soldiers. He hesitated, trying to figure a way to prove they were wrong.

Julian yelled at them, "Mary and Jesus were not among the massacred people at the temple. They are free from danger in a secret place far from here."

"Why should we believe you, a legate who takes Herod's orders?"

Cleophas stepped in front of Julian, turning his back to the mob. "Is that the truth, Julian?'

Julian whispered, "I put them on the road to Gaza, while I led the soldiers to believe they had fled to Galilee. They must be in Egypt by now, or I would have heard of their arrest."

The leader of the hostile group shoved Cleophas aside. "A woman neighbor of ours went to Jerusalem with her year-old baby boy, on the invitation of Herod. She thought she would be rewarded by him. She was slaughtered like a goat. You were in Jerusalem at the time. What did you do to stop the carnage?'

Another man jumped forward, yelling, "One dead Roman for all those murdered mothers and children isn't enough! But we'll settle for that today!" He raised his club and went for Julian.

Cleophas leapt to intervene. The terrible blow hit him on the head. He dropped to the ground, blood gushing from his scalp. Julian reached for his sword in the scabbard. When the men saw it, they turned and fled to their homes.

Julian gathered Cleophas in his arms and carried him into the house. A trail of blood marked their passage. He called for Judith or Barnaby, but the servants had not yet come back. He placed Cleophas on a couch and went in search of a cloth to stem the flow of blood. He brought back a towel and pressed it tightly against the wound. It was then that Anna arrived.

When she saw her husband, pale and limp, she rushed to him and felt for a pulse. She shook her head. Then she saw the mantle of death close around him.

Julian returned with water in a basin and cloths. "That insane mob killed him," he said. "He was trying to protect me, Anna."

"They had to take their outrage on someone. I left Cleophas to take some herbs to a sick woman—else I'd have been here. Perhaps I could have persuaded them of your innocence." She ran her hand over Cleophas' bleeding face. "I'm too late to revive him. The soul has escaped his body." She buried her face in her hands, and her body shook with grief.

Judith returned from the market, and on learning of the tragedy, became the strong anchor for everyone. First, she closed Cleophas' eyes, then turned to Julian, saying, "Carry him into the second room on the left, where I can wash and prepare his body. I'll send Barnaby for the gravediggers. I know where he wants to be buried, and there'll be time for the ceremony before dark."

Then she put her arms around Anna. "You know how he adored you. He had led a full life, with honor. Not many men were as lucky as he was. Now he has gone to the bosom of Abraham."

Anna felt paralyzed. Kind and loving Cleophas deserved a better death than dying at the hands of hot-tempered rabble-rousers. She was angry at God for having ruthlessly stripped her of a loving husband just when she lost Mary and Jesus to an uncertain life in Egypt. How would they be able to survive in a foreign land? Cleophas knew how to allay her fears about them.

Julian returned and sat down beside her. He took one of her cold hands in his, saying, "May I speak to you of Mary and her family?"

This roused Anna, and she said, "Oh, yes. You are certain they weren't caught in Herod's monstrous net?"

"They got safely away. If Herod had trapped the family on their flight to Gaza, he would have had no excuse for killing all the other boy babies."

"You're right, of course." She began to weep again.

"What can I do now to help, dearest heart?"

She did not look at him but said, "Cleophas would want to have three flute players and three voluntary mourners to accompany him to his grave. Someone can help you at the synagogue."

"I won't ever forget he gave his life to save mine. I'll be back shortly."

Barnaby quickly spread the news to the townspeople. Since a dead person had to be buried within eight hours, friends and the curious began coming almost at once. There were a few arguments about who was to carry Cleophas in his shroud to the burial site. None of the guilty neighbors appeared for this chore.

Judith had dressed him in his best suit and anointed his body with nard. In his hands, Anna placed his Essene writings. Then Barnaby and Judith quickly sewed up the shroud.

Julian returned and insisted on helping carry the body to a small clearing a hundred cubits from their home. It was a beautiful spot, surrounded by flowering bushes. Cleophas had chosen it recently when Anna and he had gone for a walk. There would be no vault cut into the hill-side, such as his brother, Joachim, had. The grave was flush to the ground, according to Essene custom.

While the flutes wailed and the hired mourners per-formed noisily, Anna prayed in a whisper. "Oh Lord of mercy, hear my plea for Cleophas, a good and loving hus-band, and send the leader of the angels, Michael, and the loving messenger, Gabriel, to march with me now in my agony. I entrust him forever to your divine care."

She opened her eyes and saw Julian directing the oth-ers. She knew what he must be thinking: "Why don't you people cremate the dead the way we Romans do?"

He came to her as soon as the body was covered in the ground. "Will you place some sort of monument here— a cut stone with his name on it?"

"No, no. He would want only a plain, whitewashed marker. Will you join us at the house? Judith has pre-pared a meal for the mourners."

Julian laughed bitterly. "No Jew breaks bread with a pagan. You have enough pain for today. I deeply admire you Essenes and am deeply touched by Cleophas' sacri-fice."

She flashed him a grateful look. "Today, Mary and Jo-seph could have brought me comfort. And you, who have been a rock of strength during this horror, sail off to Rome when I need you very much." She paused and then continued as if talking to herself. "I've sent a courier to Cleophas' brother, Salamo, in Shiloh. He will come soon. Once again, I must put on sackcloth. Actually I'll be in mourning until the death of Herod."

"What do you mean?"

"Until that monster is dead, Mary and Joseph and my beloved Jesus can't return here."

"That may be years away, although Herod is a dying man. News of his death will not reach their hiding place for a long time. You must rebuild your life as you did following the death of Joachim. Within six months, your faith allows you to remarry. Then I will come to you with my plea. I stayed in Palestine only because of you. The Delphic oracle told me you would have three husbands. I will be the third."

"We are both long past the romantic yearnings of youth. I am a grandmother of fifty-two years. Once, I hated and feared you. Now, your friendship is one of my most treasured possessions. Will you write me from Rome?

He ignored the obvious answer, saying with deep seriousness, "I'm a few years older than you, but I still have the fervor of a young man. I intend to take you to Greece, where there is such beauty of art and literature. Your own people have never recognized how good and talented you are. Herod has robbed you of both a daughter and grandson, but you are not the only victim of his madness. You Jews are a difficult people—full of incomprehensible prejudices, masters of intrigue. There's only death in the future of Palestine. I want you with me in Rome."

Anna tried to lighten the conversation. "Are there really seven hills there?"

He nodded. "You'd love it. It's a city of temples. Caesar Augustus found it built of brick but made it into one of marble. I have a house there, waiting for you. It's a different world from here, Anna." He paused, then a smile spread across his face. "The main event of each day in

Rome is a trip to the baths. Bathing to us is as necessary as breathing. So, every morning, think of me in Rome—having a bath!"

Anna smiled wanly. "You are an incorrigible foreigner. I admit I need your friendship. I shudder to think that Jesus and Mary would have had a sword thrust through them had it not been for you. I'm eternally grateful."

"I don't want gratitude. I want your love. It's outrageous to speak of it at a time like this, but I may not see you for months. You may marry again. You have held my heart captive most of my life. I admit I'm no celibate, but if you would marry me, I would be faithful—I swear by Almighty Jupiter."

Anna shook her head sadly. "I am not free like you. The laws of my people are inflexible." She held out her two hands to him. "Cleophas was the kindest man in the world, an ideal husband for whom I had the greatest affection. I will never get over his cruel death."

Julian kissed her fingers and said, "You can perform miracles. Healing this tragic loss won't be impossible for you."

"Dear Julian, while you are being royally entertained by Caesar Augustus, I'll be gathering herbs to treat the sick. We come from different worlds. I am of the earth." There was great pain in her voice.

"No, no Anna. You are of the sky—always beyond the reach of my arms."

She closed her eyes to stop the burning tears, and whispered, "Come back to Galilee, Julian. Come back soon."

Julian did not answer. But before she could prevent it, he kissed her passionately on the lips. Then he strode off, shocked to realize he was trembling.

Chapter 8

Salamo did not come immediately to Sepphoris following Cleophas' death. It was two weeks before the temperamental and artistic brother put in his appearance. He made no apology to Anna, but, to make amends, presented her with an exquisite mirror of polished metal—one of his own unique creations.

This rare gift and his devoted attention to her dispelled her original annoyance with him. He was almost a stranger to her, but she had heard that his boyish charm and ready flattery endeared him to women of all ages in Shiloh. Cleophas claimed he was equally popular with men, due to his delightful way of telling racy stories.

Anna recalled their past meeting. It was when his wife had died, and she and Cleophas left their infant daughter with Judith in Sepphoris. The child's death during their brief absence was directly connected in Anna's mind with Salamo. She wondered, did she subconsciously re-sent him for this reason?

Today, looking at his compelling brown eyes that matched his unruly mass of hair, his ready smile and expressive, artistic hands, Anna guessed he was accustomed to having his way. He was five years younger than she, and Cleophas called him impulsive and egotistical. They were not close brothers. Yet his talented creations of bowls and vases were prized throughout Palestine.

The first thing Anna did was take him to visit Cleophas' grave. Then, they rested on the grassy hillside and talked of her unusual life. She had not heard from Mary and Joseph, so the uncertainty over their whereabouts with Jesus weighed constantly on her mind.

Finally, Salamo said, "It's a shame for a lovely woman like you to have lost two husbands. Your next marriage must be to a much younger man."

Anna frowned. "My next marriage? I won't marry again. I shall spend my days in healing work and spiritual growth."

"Nonsense! You are too fascinating to deny another man your companionship." He took one of her hands and held it tightly.

Anna thought him too lavish with his compliments, too intimate in his attitude toward her. When she tried to pull her hand from his, Salamo kissed it warmly before letting it go.

He became serious . . . "Are you aware that Galilee is overrun now with legionaries? Herod is close to insanity. His mind is warped by the constant plotting of his sons and the deceit of his unscrupulous wives. The moment he dies, chaos will result. That's why I came here to protect you. A wealthy widow can be easily victimized."

He was so sure of himself, Anna thought. "Do you plan on remaining in Sepphoris?" Her voice was intentionally flat.

"You'll need someone to manage your affairs. I know you get a substantial income from your flocks. You own that Nazareth home which you keep for Mary, and you've gotten other properties from my two brothers." He smiled and stretched out full length on the ground. "I like it here."

She answered sharply, "I need no caretaker! I adjusted to widowhood once before."

"It's different this time, Anna. You weren't prepared for Cleophas' death. You dare not be alone in the violent times ahead."

Anna was dumbfounded by his determination to take over her life. She needed time to figure out how to cope with his audacity.

He sat up and continued unabashed with his plans. "I will open a shop similar to that of Cleophas' in the market place. I have many fine art pieces and beautifully crafted jewelry. I know your servants use a separate building, which I'll take over as my workshop. Judith and Barnaby can move into your large house."

He rose and pulled her to her feet. As they walked toward the house, he slipped his arm around her waist. "Didn't you know that Cleophas asked me to take care of you if anything happened to him?"

She shook her head and withdrew from his arm.

"He should have told you. Now, be a darling, and give me a chance to help you. You're still in shock, I can see. When the violence breaks out, you'll be glad I'm here."

"What I need, Salamo, is time to readjust my life. I don't need you. I really don't want you. Please don't put pressure on me."

Salamo kept silent until they entered the house and were seated in the living area. He took a new tack. "You look so sad, Anna, darling. What you need now is more excitement in your life. I suspect there's a secret side to you—one quite daring." He laughed softly. "I didn't sit around mourning after my wife's death. I joined a resistance group. No, not the radical Sicariis. My men work on new projects to help our people gain independence."

"That sounds dangerous," Anna said with alarm. "Don't get me involved in your endeavors." She wished he had never come here.

Salamo continued as if she had agreed. "That little house of yours will be great for my conspirators to meet in regularly."

"I don't like it at all! I don't want strange men coming into my yard to plan a revolt! Go home, and work out your noble plans there."

"Darling, darling. We have to know how we can work most effectively when Herod dies. Then the country will burst into flames."

"I don't want you here. Rome's military might will destroy all opposition in no time. You have no weapons to match their swords."

Salamo put on a pious air that disgusted her. "We are people of God. They are abominable heathens, murderers, parricides, and sodomites." He jumped up and flailed the air. "We'll find a way."

Anna was stunned. "You are too hotheaded. We need moderate leaders. How would Galilee survive if Rome didn't buy our flax and olives?"

Salamo looked aghast at her. "So you are resigned to continued Roman occupation?"

"Yes, until the Messiah can start his active ministry."

"What nonsense! You think we should wait until your grandson is grown? He may not even be alive! When I was in Jerusalem recently, thousands of people had gathered on the Mount of Olives to revolt against Herod. Resistance is gaining momentum in every province." His anger subsided, and he began to plead. "Please, Anna, don't be selfish. Let my men come here quietly to make our plans. The Romans must not suspect our intentions."

"What intentions?" Anna was visibly angry.

"To put an end to the Herodian dynasty. They aren't true Jews, Anna. They're Idumeans, not descendants from Abraham. Herod's sons will be as vile as their father. They'll continue to bleed us white to maintain their lavish, dissolute lives! Have you ever seen Herod's palace in Jericho?"

She shook her head.

"It's an enormous, vaulted structure of Hellenistic style. There are rooms at numerous levels, colonnaded courts, loggias, and several swimming pools. Think what it would look like all in flames!"

Anna was shocked. She jumped up and walked into the courtyard. Salamo followed her. Flushed with anger, she asked him, "What good would destroying a palace do for our people?"

Salamo laughed and changed like a chameleon. "It was just a fanciful idea, Anna. Don't take me seriously. I can dream can't I? Tomorrow you must show me your accounts. I'll be keeping your books for you. You mustn't get in trouble with the Roman data gatherer!"

Anna sat down on a bench to figure out how to cope with this relative. He was playing a game with her, she knew, but why? She was desperately lonely, and he did everything with such good humor, it might be comforting to have him there. He said a revolt was about to hit Galilee. She would need a man for protection.

He came to her and dropped at her feet. "All you need to do is meditate and pray and continue your good deeds. I'm here to take care of you." He took her hands again and kissed them. Then he held them hard against his cheek.

Anna wished her sister, Esmeria, would come and ad-

vise her what to do with Salamo. But she was seriously ill
and unable to travel. Anna admitted she was desperately
lonely. Why hadn't Julian written to her? Salamo worked
so fast. Before she could come to a firm decision, he had
cleared the two servants from the small house and
moved his belongings into it. It was all done with such
speed and adventurous attitude that she felt foolish protesting.

When her mourning period was over, Anna realized
with a sense of shock that her life was no longer her own.
Salamo supervised her every move, charming her, waiting on her like an eager lover, cajoling her into agreeing
with his decisions. He flattered her beyond expectation,
and kissed her whenever she approved of his actions.
She was sure she was being lured into a trap. Yet, she
found herself yielding more and more often to his requests.

Weekly, his confederates came there to engage in
lively discussions. She could hear their intense arguments far into the night. They were radicals, no doubt
about that, yet Salamo never mentioned these meetings
and continued to ingratiate himself with her.

What bothered her most was that he took to wearing
Cleophas' clothes, which she had intended to give away.
Then he sweet-talked Judith into cooking lamb and
other meats for him, even though he knew Anna ate no
flesh. She tried to be fair about this. He was no Essene
and so could not be expected to follow her beliefs. Yet, it
was pleasant to share meals with this delightful compan-
ion. He went shopping with her, and, on the Sabbath, he
read to her the wonderful words of the old prophets. The
neighbors frequently asked why they hadn't married.

She knew why she didn't surrender totally to him. She
was waiting to hear from Julian. He had promised to return in six months, but a year and a half had passed

with no word from him.

One day she asked Judith, "Has any message come for me from Rome since Salamo arrived?'

"Yes, there have been at least two letters—one just a couple of days ago."

"Did you see them?"

"No, Salamo took them and tucked them into his girdle before hurrying to his room."

Anna flushed. Was he stealing Julian's letters to her?

The next evening, she decided to ask Salamo about them. She said, "I've been expecting a letter from Rome. You may not know that Herod's estranged daughter, Salina, lives there. Have you seen such a letter?'

Salamo's face was an innocent mask. "I know nothing of a letter to you, Anna darling. I have received several from my copper supplier."

She was stymied. She waited until he went into town to his shop and then searched the room. She found no letters, but there were many sketches of Herod's palace and grounds in Jericho. Salamo had not drawn them, so Anna dismissed their significance from her mind.

Salamo occupied more and more of her attention. One evening, he took her out into the garden and after she sat down, he dropped to the ground at her feet.

He asked with that innocence she had come to recognize as the prelude of something special, "Do you ever wish you had another child?"

"Of course. I long desperately for Mary and Jesus, yet I've had no word from them these many years."

"Anna, I've restrained myself from telling you how deeply I love you. Will you marry me so you can have that child you want?"

"You think it possible at my age?'

"It would be fun finding out, wouldn't it?" he asked with a roguish grin.

She hedged, "I must wait a little longer." She thought of Julian. Had he fallen in love with a Roman woman and had no intention of coming back to her? "I admit I've grown dependent on you. Yes, I care about you very much. And I would love to bear another child. Firstborn Mary was with me only three years; Mary Cleophas lived less than two years."

"I can't wait any longer, Anna. You are my constant passion. Tomorrow I'll go to Jerusalem on business. When I return, we will be married." He was so confident of himself. He sprang to his feet and lifted her into his arms. Then he kissed her hair, her cheeks, her nose, teasing her to raise her lips to him. When she did, she decided to wait no longer for Julian's return.

Two days after Salamo left, sensational news rocked Palestine. Herod the Great was dead! His legacy, however, brought no cheers from his subjects. The Roman colonies were split up among three sons, each born of a different mother.

Herod Antipas was named tetrarch of rebellious Galilee and the region east of the Jordan, known as Perea. He was a wicked, licentious man who secretly dreamed of ruling as great a realm as his father. Archelaus, more cruel even than Herod the Great, became ethnarch of Judea, Samaria, and Idumea—areas where most of the people lived. Finally, to Philip, a learned man who spoke only Greek and lived like a Greek, went the poor area in the north and east of the Sea of Galilee. This was the domain of the brigands.

During Salamo's absence, Anna stayed indoors, not daring to leave the premises. The age-old dream of liberation from the Romans sprang up everywhere. A man named Judas the Gaulonite placed a crown on his head in Galilee, encouraging various factions to revolt. The people became increasingly volcanic. Then, the news

came that Herod's mansion in Jericho has been burned
to the ground and his stable of prized horses stolen.
Anna remembered the sketches in Salamo's room and
his weekly meetings with radicals. The political fury he
had promised was here.

When Salamo returned to Sepphoris, he was unusually talkative. Between bits of cheese and bread, he related to Anna the events that had taken place in Jerusalem.

"I got there just after Herod's funeral and joined the
crowds in the Court of the temple. We heard the new
ethnarch, Archelaus, make his first address. He asked the
people, 'How can I please you?' Their answer was to be
expected: 'Cut taxes, and punish Herod's cruel advisers.'"

"Did he consider this?" Anna asked.

Salamo shook his head. "He became furious and refused to hear any more pleas. The crowd got angry and
rioted. A former slave of Herod incited many to set fire
to his palace."

"Were there people killed?"

"More than 3,000 died in the court. That fired my men
to seek revenge. We went to Jericho and . . . "

"Sacked the palace," Anna finished his sentence.
"What became of the magnificent horses Herod kept
there?"

"I have one of them outside. There was nothing to be
gained by destroying them. Everyone there took one and
rode off."

"You had planned this for a long time, hadn't you?'

Salamo saw she disapproved, so he justified his act by
saying, "The refusal of Archelaus to listen fired us into
action."

Anna sighed, saying, "Revenge is never pretty. There's
a fanatical side to you, Salamo, that worries me."

"You don't approve of our avenging all those deaths by
burning down Herod's extravagant villa?"

"There will always be other palaces for you to burn—
Masada, Caesarea, Herodium. When will it end?'

They walked out into the garden and continued to ar-
gue. Anna asked him then, "Who has the courage to tell
Augustus to come to his senses and get rid of the
Herodian dynasty in Palestine?"

Salamo answered in a triumphant voice, "I will!" He
paused for a moment, then added, "I will organize a group
to sail to Rome and demand an audience with Caesar."

Anna was stunned. She bit her lip, angry at herself for
baiting him. "I don't want to lose you. It would be a dangerous mission." She took his hand and pulled him down
on a bench beside her.

He took advantage of her now, saying, "We must get
married tomorrow!"

Anna hesitated. "Won't things have quieted down in a
month?"

"I can't wait that long, my love. My men and I must
sail within the month. Now is the time to bring our plea
to Rome. You've kept me in torment long enough. You
must bear me a son. I hope he will one day be able to say,
'It was my father who faced Caesar Augustus and brought
about an end to the Herods.'"

Salamo was so intense and persuasive, Anna con-
sented to the marriage. Her life became suddenly romantic and full of surprises. Salamo didn't disappoint
her. He was a passionate lover, far more ardent and demanding than either of his brothers. Her longing for
Julian faded under Salamo's ardor. He also was intent on
proving he was a better husband than his brothers. Anna
convinced him he was, so he became happier and less
frustrated. He kept delaying his voyage to Rome, waiting
to be assured that Anna had conceived. When she did,
he promptly gathered up his five most articulate men
and told them to pack for the voyage.

He explained to Anna, "Forgive me for leaving you now, but Archelaus announced he will raise taxes at harvest time. The farmers can't take it. Revolt is spreading. I can't stay here, creating beautiful jewelry, while people have no bread and are forced into slavery. Someone has to be bold enough to face Augustus Caesar with the truth." He waited for her approval.

Anna put her hands over her face for a moment. A deadly fear came over her, and she didn't want Salamo to see it. "I am proud of you, and will pray daily for your success. I shall be lonely."

"It's for my unborn child I'm doing this. My mission can't wait."

Anna sensed he had more to tell her. He carried a burden she didn't understand. "Let us walk and enjoy our last twilight together," she said.

He took courage from the dim light to relieve his thoughts. "Anna, my brothers thought an artist's works do little to help people who are crushed with the might of Caesar. This voyage to Rome is a chance to prove I can do more. Joachim called me an amusing storyteller and a womanizer. He was an unrelenting Pharisee. And Cleophas, a cold-bath-a-day Essene, never thought I was devout enough."

"You don't have to prove anything to me, Salamo. I'm grateful for the happiness you've brought me and for the child I carry." She realized then that his carefree attitude and amusing stories were a cover for his deep inferiority. He didn't think he was the equal of his brothers. He had married her to prove he was.

She continued, "Everyone in Sepphoris is so proud of what you're about to undertake. If anyone can influence Augustus, you can. Will you bring him one of your exquisite copper bowls?"

Salamo's frowning face broke into a smile. "I hadn't

thought of that. What a good idea!"

The next morning, Salamo and his company of men departed for Caesarea, riding the horses rescued in the torching of the palace in Jericho. They hoped to board a waiting Venetian ship, which would take them across the Mediterranean to Rome. It would be a hazardous journey, whether in a passenger ship, equipped with a single square sail, or a cargo vessel that put in at every island for trading purposes. The fall storms had begun, and a severe one could hold a ship prisoner in port for a couple of weeks. Salamo had no idea how long the journey would take.

Anna had frequent nightmares worrying what might happen to him. As her child grew within her, she wondered if it would be as beautiful and bright as Mary. Or would her third child be as fragile as Mary Cleophas?

Her sister, Esmeria, warned her that births so late in life often produced deformed children. "Prepare for an idiot!" she said. Anna flinched, and her temper flared. "God gave me this child to replace the other two. She will be perfect, I know!

* * *

The disaster that Salamo had foreseen struck Sepphoris shortly after his departure. Judas, the Gaulonite rebel, gathered a rough army of brigands and took over Sepphoris during the absence of Herod Antipas. They torched the royal palace and began stoning and beheading those who resisted them.

Herod called on Varus, Governor of Syria, to rescue his domain. Under his son's command, he sent first Thracian archers and Galatian infantry to ring the town and prevent movement in or out. Only the rich Pharisees and scribes, who paid huge sums of money, were allowed to escape.

These foreign soldiers were undisciplined. Ordered to take all rebels prisoner for sale as slaves, they became more and more murderous. The brigands put up so much opposition that Varus ordered the town burned to the ground. First, the markets were destroyed, then the soldiers moved into the residential districts to burn everything they could.

Barnaby, Anna's loyal old servant, barely escaped with his life when he ventured into the outskirts of Sepphoris. He told Anna, "We have no way to defend ourselves. Once the town is in ashes, the bandits will come into the hills to set up camp."

"Hide in the brush, Barnaby. Judith, stay here with me. There must be a way to save our lives."

Anna walked to the edge of the hill where she had a good view of the flaming city. People ran, screaming, out of burning houses. Children were struck to the ground by enraged soldiers. Women were grabbed and carried off to be raped. Crowds of men were put in chains and dragged away. Terrified donkeys and camels ran wildly, in their attempt to escape the holocaust. Before burning the taverns, soldiers stole skins full of wine and drank greedily as they staggered among the dead and injured.

Judith clung to Anna, crying, "There's no place for us to be safe!"

Anna stood as if frozen, reaching out, out into the ethers for a solution.

She spoke as if to herself, repeating the words of the forty-sixth psalm, which she had memorized as a select virgin in the temple. "Be still, and know that I am God: I will be exalted among the heathen, I will be exalted in the earth."

Then she turned to Judith. "These men are souls sent forth into life by the heavenly father. Let us prepare food for them. Bake bread quickly, boil eggs, and I will mix a refreshing drink for the hungry men."

Judith looked at her in disbelief. "They will kill us!

Anna spoke quietly. "The God of Jacob is our refuge. Show no fear. We are centered in God's universe. He will not desert us."

Anna's hands trembled as she filled a jug with red wine diluted with water and flavored with honey. Julian liked this beverage and called it *posca*, she recalled. There was a table in the front court and, on it, Anna set metal goblets and the large wine container.

While Judith quickly baked flat loaves of bread on the embers in the fireplace, Anna cut up cheese and spread out platters of dried fruits, olives, and the hard-boiled eggs.

She told Judith, "These men are bandits, totally lawless, yet we must treat them like others of our faith. We have only a few hours to prepare for them. There is no place for all of us to hide. Barnaby is an old, crippled man now. He would be killed at once, so it is up to us to persuade them we are alone and to let the house stand."

Judith was astounded. "We will be raped and then killed," she said.

"Stay out of sight in the house. I will greet them alone."

Another hour dragged by before she saw a group of nine men desert the smoking, crushed town and point toward her home set high on the hill. She waited by the table for them, speaking before any one of them could.

"I know you are all exhausted, so I prepared food and drink for you. Please sit down here and serve yourself." She was surprised she was able to keep her voice steady. "Here is red wine. I knew you'd be thirsty."

The unexpectedness of her gesture confused the dirty, unshaven molesters. "Where is your husband?" the leader demanded.

"He has gone to Rome to plead for your rights with

Caesar. Upon his return, I will tell him how well-behaved you men were in the midst of the carnage below."

The astonished men looked at each other and grinned, then hurried to the freshly baked bread, cheese, and fruit. They soon emptied the jug of diluted wine as Judith came out of the house with a pan of honey cakes. Her face had a terrified look.

"Why don't you give us some meat?" the leader asked roughly.

"I'm an Essene, and it is against our belief, you know, to eat flesh."

The other men guffawed at that, but the leader stopped their laughter. "That's all right," he said, weakening.

Anna again took the initiative, saying, "Whenever you are hungry again, you will know we will give you food here. There's no house left in the town below." Anna sensed that they had planned on burning down her house as they had all the others. She could see that the leader was befuddled by her unexpected hospitality and fearlessness.

"Line up, men!" he ordered his dirty followers. Then he said to Anna, as if he had to account to her for his actions, "This city has been plundered, and our men have all the slaves they can control. We want to go to Nazareth before the day's over and torch it, too." He forced an unpleasant laugh.

Anna pointed to the smoking town below. "Who are those new soldiers? Aren't those your shackled prisoners they've taken?'

The brigand's face showed fear. "Syrians! The Romans have called in Varus' best troops. We're beaten here." He turned to his ragged men. "Let's head for Nazareth!"

Seizing what food they could handle, the group disappeared among the trees. Anna was worried about Barnaby.

He was a frail old man now and moved slowly. She waited a half hour, then set out to find him by calling his name as she went. He soon answered her as he emerged from a small cave in the hillside.

"Are you both unharmed?" he asked fearfully.

When Anna nodded and smiled, he came to her, and she embraced him warmly. He continued, "I prayed every moment for your and Judith's protection. I feel ashamed for having deserted you."

"No, no. The order had gone out to kill all men—young or old. Seeing you with us would have meant more danger for us."

"Then you think my prayers saved you?' His expression was so full of hope that Anna nodded vigorously.

"Barnaby, you had great influence with God. He heard your prayers because you are a truly good man. Come, Judith will serve you a delicious meal in celebration of our lives."

Anna retired to her bedroom, in a near state of collapse. She managed to whisper, "Great God of all, you directed me to do the right thing. For this, I owe you our lives."

CHAPTER 9

Julian forced his way through the heavy morning crowds on the meandering streets of Rome. He was headed for the palace of Augustus, his patron and friend, who had personally paid for his years of expensive treatment in an Athens sanitarium. Typhus and malaria had kept Julian between life and death ever since his departure from Galilee.

Julian adored Augustus. It was incredible that the sickly adolescent, nephew and adopted son of Julius Caesar, had become the giant of the most powerful empire in the world. They had shared many youthful outings when the future ruler was known as Octavianus. Even in those days, he was a physical weakling and walked with a pronounced limp, due to rheumatism. Julian recalled that, in winter, the future ruler wore beneath his woolen toga an undershirt and four tunics. In summer, he dared not expose himself to the sun. Julian wondered if his needs had changed much with age. Augustus had ruled for nearly thirty years. Yet, he clung to old friends and his soldiers, lavishing them with money and gifts. Always, he shunned the luxuries of the nobility and lived a pious life.

Julian saw that Rome had changed during the last five years. At the Forum, the marketplace was now ringed with numerous small temples to the gods, all copies of Greek masterpieces. He stopped from time to time to admire the colonnades, the numerous statues, and the great edifices lining the Sacred Way. This led him to the temples of Jupiter and Saturn on the Capitoline Hill. Today, these countless gods seemed ridiculous. Hadn't Anna said there was only one God for all people? When he lay in the sanitarium with raging fever and agonizing pain, he was tempted to cry out to Anna's God of Love for help, but never did. Was Roman worship a pagan act as she claimed? It saddened him that she had not replied to his many letters from Greece. He had been too sure of himself.

It was late morning, and the crowds had gathered in the Forum to listen to the orators. A fortune-teller tried to persuade him to enter her booth, but he was fearful of her forecast and went on to a bathhouse for a hot bath and an olive oil rub.

Proceeding to the palace, he passed its formal gardens and several bathing pools before entering a covered portico. Beyond was the atrium where a fountain, surrounded by flowering shrubs, created a delightful symphony.

Entering a great hall, where marble columns supported the vaulted roof, Julian was approached by one of the dozen armed sentries for identification. With a snap of a finger, a slave was called to conduct Julian up a winding staircase to another slave, who took him across marble floors and past walls inlaid with sumptuous mosaic. Here, arch, vault, and dome competed with each other for admiration. Finally, Julian was asked to be seated in a small vestibule while the servant consulted with his master.

Immediately, he returned to conduct Julian into a high-ceilinged room supported by lofty marble columns and decorated with famous works of art. Near a window, Augustus reclined on a couch, nearly hidden by a gold-embroidered coverlet.

Julian approached him reservedly, but the emperor called at once to him. "Dear Julian! How reprehensible of you to try to die in Greece! How are you now?' He raised himself to a sitting position and took both of Julian's hands in his. "Sit down beside me."

"Thanks to your generosity, I've had the best of care and am now recovered," Julian said.

"Good!" the ruler replied, throwing off the coverlet and looking at his visitor with great affection.

Julian noticed that Augustus' sandy hair had grayed and his skin was paler than Julian had remembered, yet beneath the merging eyebrows were clear and penetrating eyes.

"You'll retire now in Rome, won't you?" Augustus asked.

"No, I spent so many years in the provinces, I want to go back to Galilee."

"You love someone there?"

Julian nodded.

"You'll get a handsome retirement from me, but you're too old now to marry." Augustus wound a woolen scarf about his neck, saying apologetically, "I have to fight constantly for my health. Some days, I think of starving myself to death and get it over with."

"Why such ridiculous thoughts from the second Romulus?"

"I have lived too many lives and died too many deaths since I avenged Caesar's murder. Life is changing rapidly. The once-strong fiber of my empire has begun to rot. The people crave luxury instead of simplicity. The senators come rarely to meetings. Sexual license has replaced honored marriages. Our language is dying under the influx of Greek words. Our statues are being created by Hellenistic artists." Augustus stood up and began to pace the floor.

"The Empire is still great, sire. You are worrying unnecessarily." Julian was hard-pressed to know how to handle all the emperor's dire statements.

"I tell you, Julian, the empire is showing cracks in its armor. None of the young men want to enter the army. I have to count on Varus of Syria with four of my legions, to do the fighting for us in cantankerous Palestine. Will you stay with me now and advise me during the absence of Tiberius? I sent him to put down some of the rebellions in the colonies. Perhaps you don't know that I have made him my adoptive son and co-regent."

Julian tried to cover his dismay at this development. To him, Tiberius was cruel and totally dominated by his mother, Livia.

He said, "I cannot stay in Rome. I promised someone years ago that I would return."

"I'm disappointed. But, this morning, you will be at my side when citizens are allowed an audience to present petitions. I have been told there's a group here from Galilee. I'll want your advice on how to deal with them. These men are from Sepphoris or Nazareth, where there's so much revolt now."

A feeling of dismay hit Julian, but he replied, "I'll make suggestions if I can."

"Well, you know more about these inscrutable Jews than anyone here. Come, we will go now to the small theater where I will hear the citizens' pleas."

The first man brought before him complained about the thieves entering homes at night; the second man asked for street lights for the unlit, uneven sidewalks; a third man demanded recompense for having broken a leg when thrown from one of the emperor's horses. After telling them he would consider carefully their requests, he motioned for the group from Galilee to approach him.

"Will your spokesman come forward with your petition?'

The leader was a handsome, dark-haired man, who gingerly held forth a document.

Augustus admonished him, "Don't hand me your petition as if you were giving meat to a tiger. Introduce yourself."

"I am Salamo, an artist from Sepphoris. I have brought you one of my copper creations as a symbol of my allegiance."

Augustus whispered to Julian, "Do you know this man?'

"No, but ask him if he's married and to whom. That might help me identify him."

"Are you married and have a family?" Augustus asked.

"I recently married for the second time, and my wife expects a child this year. I plead for a reduction in our exorbitant taxes."

Julian spoke then. "Your wife's name?"

"Anna bat Stolan."

Julian's mouth opened in shock. He was stunned to learn Anna had remarried during his long illness. Oh, Jupiter, you have betrayed me!

"May I question this man further, sire?'

Augustus nodded.

"How long have you been married to this woman?"

"Three months. She was married to my older brother,

Cleophas, but he was accidentally killed."

Julian gripped the back of the throne chair so hard his hand cramped. This was the remaining brother whom he had never met. Oh, Anna, why didn't you wait for my return? Why didn't you answer my letters? He stood in despair, so Augustus then spoke to Salamo. "I will consult with my experts on Galilee tonight regarding taxation in your area. If it is unjust, I will order them reduced."

"The people were about to revolt when I left Sepphoris. They must have relief. I cannot sell my art objects when there is little money for food due to your demands in sesterces. I am an artist of renown in Palestine. Look for yourself at the gift I bring you."

Augustus examined the lovely bowl. He turned to one of his guards. "Fill this bowl with denarii and let him fill his pockets. You have come a long way, and you have a hazardous return journey at this time of the year. May the gods go with you."

After the petitioners left, Augustus studied Julian for several moments. Then he said, "You were disturbed by this man. What did he say to upset you?"

"It's a long story, sire. Like you, I now wish I were dead."

Caesar's penetrating mind sensed what had happened. "No, no, my friend. Tomorrow I will give a banquet in your honor. You will forget your disappointment when you see the beautiful women who will attend."

"I want to leave for the docks tomorrow. I must sail for Caesarea as soon as possible. I must learn what happened in Sepphoris."

"You will sail when I tell you and not before. I have much to discuss with you regarding conditions in Palestine. I need your advice on how to handle that explosive area of the Empire."

Julian bit his lip and bowed deeply. He owed this man his life. "Forgive my impetuous speech. Your wishes will always come first."

Augustus nodded and said amiably, "In a few months, I will consider your departure. The winter season has begun, and the Mediterranean Sea can be rough and dangerous for our ships. I want you to stay in Rome until you are totally recovered again."

Julian nodded, but kept his eyes lowered.

Augustus broke the strain by saying with enthusiasm, "Next week I will take you to the home of my friend and adviser, Silvanus. He has promised to roast a wild boar, and there will be women of the nobility there, some of whom will attract you, I know. Perhaps two young poets will also be there. They often come to read parts of Virgil's *Aeneid*. You'll like them and will forget your problems in this sparkling company."

"In the spring, sire, I must return to Galilee. I once had good friends there. Perhaps none are left." His voice broke on the last sentence.

"What do you want to do this afternoon, Julian?" Augustus asked. "I can make several suggestions if you wish."

"No, not today. I have a friend in the outskirts whom I want to visit."

Augustus walked to the door with him, his arm placed affectionately about his shoulders. "Come early tomorrow. Remember our Roman dinners begin in the middle of the afternoon."

Julian knew that Salina had moved into the home of Senator Titus Vincens when she fled from Palestine and Herod the Great. He hoped she was still living there, since he had to learn more about Anna. Why had Venus been so cruel as to strike him down in Greece, so he couldn't return to her? There was a tie between them that three marriages couldn't break. At times he hated her for not waiting for him or answering his letters. Yet he couldn't forget her gentle nature, her regal beauty and that strange power she manifested. He was in torment not understanding why she married again.

His route took him past flowering gardens, stately marble columns, and rows of statues leading to the Senator's mansion. But there was no beauty in anything today. He had never felt more depressed.

A slave greeted him at the door and conducted him across the polished floor of the large entrance hall. They skirted a deep basin in the center of the room. It was set directly below an opening in the roof for catching rain water in the winter. They continued to a private wing of the house past a group of laughing children who were playing, with knuckle bones.

Finally they reached a small waiting room off this court. He spent the next quarter of an hour staring at the hunting scenes and floral designs on the high walls.

Finally Salina entered. She had changed into an attractive, mature woman with an aura of supreme confidence. Julian rose and smiled broadly. She spoke first.

"I'm delighted to see you again, Julian. Did you just come from Palestine?"

"No, no. From Greece. Illness has kept me in a sanitarium these past few years."

"I'm sorry. You are well now, I hope?" She indicated a chair and they both sat down.

"Yes, and you?" he asked.

"I'm very happy. The Senator has adopted me, so I'm treated like one of his children."

"I'm pleased," Julian replied. "You have no intentions of marrying, Salina?"

"I may, depending on circumstances. I have made many friends in Rome. No one knows I'm the daughter of Herod. She paused, then asked, "Where are you staying?"

"With Augustus. We were devoted childhood friends. He could never partake of sports due to a rheumatic infection. I used to spend my leisure time with him. He's a modest and magnanimous man."

Salina then asked the question that was on both their minds. "What's the news about Anna?"

Julian shook his head sadly. "I came to ask you that. I've heard nothing from her since her husband, Cleophas, was killed. I was shocked to learn by chance that she has remarried. This time to the third brother—named Salamo."

"Who told you that?"

"I attended the customary meeting Augustus holds each morning for petitioners. Among them was a group from Galilee, begging for a reduction in taxes. Salamo claimed that Herod Antipas has raised them enormously and the province is revolting."

Julian rose and began pacing the floor. He continued, "I've written to Anna every month since I've been well enough. Why hasn't she answered? I was so sure she'd wait for me after the death of Cleophas." He ran his hand through his heavy head of graying hair.

Seeing his distraught look, Salina consoled him, "It's obvious she never received your letters. I know she loved you. Shall I write to her and explain your concern?'

Julian's voice was strained. "She's lost to me now. I'll remain in Rome for the winter. The climate here is much better for me than Galilee. Perhaps one day I'll return there. Not now. It would be too painful."

Salina asked, "Has her daughter, Mary, and family returned yet from Egypt?'

"I have no way of knowing that. They dared not come back so long as Herod the Great was in power."

"Anna probably is alone now. That's sad."

Julian spoke angrily. "She's expecting a child by this—this Salamo, so she won't be alone for long!"

Salina clapped her hands with joy. "A child at her age? That's a miracle! How I wish I could go to her right away! But there are few ships leaving for Caesarea now due to the stormy seas. I hope her husband reaches home before the baby is born."

There was a long silence before Julian cleared his throat to ask, "Do you worship the one God Anna talked so much about?'

"Yes, Remember, my ancestors were Idumeans forced to convert to Judaism long ago. There are many Jews living in Rome now. We are free to worship as we please."

Julian sat down again. He spoke in a perplexed tone, "I wonder what the truth is. Every time an emperor dies, he is made a god. Must I worship thousands and thousands of divinities?"

Salina skillfully changed the subject. "The latter part of this winter month, there'll be a festival to honor Saturn. Stay in Rome for that, Julian."

"I remember it well. The rich people exchanged apples, figs, and nuts; the poor got corn and oil." He paused, and a smile of remembrance lit up his face. "As a child, I always got a new tunic and shoes. Our slaves had the day free."

"Spend the festival with me, Julian," Salina proposed eagerly.

"No promises yet. Remember, I'm a guest of Augustus." He stood up to leave. "It's getting dark. Thank you for seeing me."

Salina followed him to the outer courtyard. "You Romans go to bed so early and get up before dawn. I'll never get used to it." She extended her hand to him in farewell. "I'll write to Anna at once and keep you informed."

Julian was puzzled by Salina's warm reception. He wondered for a moment if she was eager for a liaison with him now that Anna had remarried. He laughed out loud. He might consider it. Their marriage, so long ago, was never consummated.

* * *

When Julian reached the palace, a slave greeted him with a request to eat with the emperor. Augustus' wife, Scribonia, had just celebrated a charity dinner for orphans and had retired early.

Augustus was in an expansive mood. "It is a joy to have you here, Julian," he said. "My only pleasures come from my loyal subjects. The legionaries are my family. Women, you may have guessed, are no longer of interest to me."

Julian argues, "If your 200,000 soldiers are your family, then why aren't they camped in Italy?"

"For a good reason," Augustus said with a soft laugh. "Our culture and beauty here must not be destroyed by battles." He tossed aside the coverlet on his knees and stood up with difficulty. "Give me your arm, Julian. I want to show you where I sleep."

The ruler took him to a small room containing only a couch, table, and chair. The walls were bare of decoration.

He said, "My wife's bedroom is populated with many statues. I prefer simplicity. Ill health has forced me to come to terms with nature. And you?'

Julian assisted him to his bed and sat down in the solitary chair. "I survived in Greece due to the sulfur baths and cold fomentations you recommended. So, perhaps I too, better understand nature's laws now."

Augustus developed a coughing fit, and, when it had subsided, he said, "Call me Octavianus when we are alone. It recalls our deep friendship when I was a crippled youth. Only you forewent the games and wrestling matches to remain at my side. I've often wondered why."

"I saw a penetrating and resourceful mind like no one else's. You insisted on making me an audience of one for your addresses. One day, you'd pretend to preside over the senate; the next, you judged an important trial or spoke at a ceremonial banquet. I learned a lot from you."

"What do you suggest I do to reduce the agitation in Palestine? It grows worse every year."

"Put an end to the Herodian dynasty. Then make Palestine a part of Syria. Radicals and agitators in every province have kept alive the Jews' age-old dream of liberation."

"You drive a hard bargain, old friend. I may not live long enough for such an ambitious project. You know my lifelong motto: *Festina lente.* Make haste slowly. Yet, I'll consider your suggestion. The only ambitious Herod is the King of Judea. He takes after his scheming father." He pulled the covers over himself, saying, "Sleep well, and ask the gods to advise me."

CHAPTER 10

During the next two weeks, Julian spent his time going to several baths in the city, playing dice with his emperor, and visiting the Circus Maximus to bet on the chariot races. He discovered that he no longer enjoyed the gladiatorial fights or the killing of wild animals in the amphitheater. At first, the mock battles on artificial ponds were amusing, but he soon tired of them, too. His greatest joy came from reading aloud to Augustus from the works of Virgil and Horace and visiting the libraries.

When Julian experienced attacks of weakness from his former malaria, he visited the hot springs in the outskirts of Rome. They were operated by Greeks, who expressed surprise that he had survived malaria. It was held to be a fatal disease.

Finally, Silvanus, legal adviser to the emperor, sent Augustus the promised invitation to a wild boar dinner. Julian was to be included, and Silvanus promised to provide a woman partner for him. She turned out to be his ex-wife, Salina. She came with her adoptive parents, Senator Titus and wife, Allegra.

Everyone gathered in the atrium with Augustus and his wife, Scribonia. He was eager to tell them of his latest achievement.

"I've just instituted regular sea service to India," he said with pride. "One hundred and twenty of our ships will now carry corn and fruit there and bring back needed spices. Also, I sent one of our ships a week ago to the Palestinian port, Caesarea. It bears my envoy, Valerian, whom I've commissioned to learn why those colonies have become so rebellious. Galilee appears to be the worst."

Before anyone could offer a comment, he turned to Julian, saying, "I purposely sent Valerian on the same ship as that complaining group of Galileans. You remember, they requested a remission of the new taxes raised by their governor, Herod Antipas."

At this moment, a slave came to conduct the guests into the *trilinium* for the feast. In the center of this dining area was a large wooden table, surrounded on three sides by couches for reclining while eating. Silvanus and his wife took their places on the right-hand side, as was the custom for the host. Across from them were seated Augustus and Titus, with their wives. Julian and Salina were directed to the sofa on the remaining side.

Servants promptly took the sandals from everyone's feet—a custom that helped keep the silk cushions clean. Then, since all food would be eaten with the fingers, a silver basin of warm water for washing hands was passed around the table.

As soon as the honey-sweetened wine was set before them, Augustus raised his goblet in a toast: "To the friends of the Empire—past and present! And may the

Augustan Age last for at least 500 years!"

"To the empire! To the empire!" everyone chorused.

Immediately, the roasted boar was brought in and placed in the center of the table. Julian led the applause for it. One slave remained to slice the meat and see to it that each guest had a mound of it on his silver plate. Then, everyone reached for the black olives and colorful winter vegetables surrounding the boar meat.

The conversation grew animated as the heady wine played its role. Julian, reclining on the soft cushions next to Salina, felt her move close to him. This puzzled him, but he did not embarrass her by moving away.

She whispered, "There are still three servings to go, Julian, so we'd better forego more of the roast."

Next came the fish course—oysters and crayfish served with a light sauce—then blackbirds roasted whole with their feathers on. Julian found himself unable to munch on these delicate morsels, but Salina ate two of them with obvious relish.

Again, the basin of warm water was passed around the table so that clean hands would be ready for dessert. It was an elaborate array of pastries, nuts and dried fruits.

When everyone could eat no more, Silvanus took his guests back to the atrium. There, long benches had been placed for the performance of a male pantomimist. He was a talented actor, playing many roles by changing masks. A woman's chorus recited the plot, and the evening ended with enthusiastic applause.

Before anyone could rise, a slave approached Augustus with a parchment roll. The ruler's face registered shock as he read its message. Everyone stopped talking and waited for him to speak.

He said solemnly, "I have terrible news. The ship on which my envoy, Valerian, sailed for Palestine last week, caught fire on the third day out. The weather was beastly and the ship sank with no survivors. I am devastated."

There was a long silence in the room. Then Augustus turned to Julian. "Those Jewish petitioners from Galilee took the same ship. I feel badly about that, too. Perhaps you will know how to notify their unfortunate families. Their spokesman, I recall, gave his name as Salamo."

Julian nodded grimly, then whispered to Salina, "He was Anna's husband—younger than she, a talented artist. I dread sending her the terrible news, especially since she carries his child."

Tears sprang into Salina's eyes. "She's a widow for the third time. I'll go to her as soon as the winter storms are past. Will you be going with me?"

He shook his head and answered with bitterness, "She'll enter her long mourning period again. There's nothing I can do but notify her of the tragedy and tell her to inform the other families."

Julian's mind raced. At least now there were no more brothers to convince her of a levirate marriage. Yet, since she had not answered his many letters from Greece, his case would be hopeless. When spring came, he would return to Delphi and consult, once more, Apollo's oracle. Only if its priestess assured him of Anna's love would he return to Sepphoris.

Salina watched him closely. "If you wish, I'll tell Anna that I've been with you and that you look very well after those miserable years of fever. Shall I give her your love?'

Julian spoke angrily. "No, no!"

"You underestimate her. A woman who can bear a child at her age must have a lot of love left to give someone."

"Yes, another Jew!" He led her across the atrium to an alcove. She sat down, taking his hand and pulling him down on the marble bench beside her.

She asked, "You find me more attractive now?"

Julian was surprised by the question, but answered truthfully, "Yes, yes. You're a lovely woman. I never thought differently."

"Then forget your lifelong dream of marrying that saintly Galilean. You'll always be a Roman, worshipping Mars and Jupiter.'

"And Venus and Vesta," he added with a smirk. "Can't you see I've changed? During my long illness, there was a transformation in me. How, I can't say. But it began actually eight years ago. My thinking and my attitudes became different after I hid Anna's grandson under my cloak and slipped him past your father's sentries in Bethlehem. Herod, in his jealous rage at the report that a new king had been born, would have run a sword through him. Or drowned him in his swimming pool. His name, I believe, was Jesus or Joshua." He was silent for several moments before continuing. "Even now, in recalling the incident, I experience a feeling of joy. I often awaken at night, dreaming that I still hold that blue-eyed, red-haired infant in my arms. I'm galloping past the guards heading south on the road to Hebron."

"That was a dangerous escape, Julian. No wonder you recall it often." Salina stood up and offered him her hand in farewell. "The senator and his wife are leaving," she said.

Julian joined Augustus and Scribonia, waiting for four guards to come with lanterns to light their way back to the palace. Two of the attendants preceded them, and two followed.

Augustus took Julian's arm, whispering, "I saw you were upset about the Galileans' drowning. The gods willed their deaths, the same as that of Valerian. Since you didn't know those men, why are you concerned?'

Julian replied in a strained voice. "That disaster may have altered my future. Ever since you sent me to Palestine, I've been on a relentless search for happiness. The death of one of those Galileans could mean a new life for me."

Augustus looked at him quizzically. "You obviously pursue an old love. Perhaps Salina and you will get together again. She seemed especially attentive to you tonight."

Julian shook his head and smiled wanly. "I've lived too long abroad. Palestine draws me like a magnet. Due to my continual absence overseas, I have few friends here. And all of my relatives have died or moved away. I really have only you, Octavianus."

Augustus appeared pleased at the use of that name. "Your long illness has made you less of a fighter. I can understand that. You know that you may select a piece of land, either here or in Palestine, for your retirement. But until you leave us, we'll pamper you like one of our family at the palace. Our new ships can now make the journey to Caesarea in twenty-five days, so it's not so far away."

Before Julian could reply, Scribonia joined them. "You are like a brother to me, Julian. When you are here, Augustus is cheerful and uncomplaining. You are the best medicine for him, so please stay in Rome as long as possible."

Julian thanked them both warmly. They had reached the palace atrium, so said goodnight and parted. Once in his bedroom, Julian paced the floor. Would Anna welcome his return to her? His hands trembled as he struggled to imagine meeting her. She had become his relentless obsession. The older he got, the more he had to be near her. She was so gentle and eager to help, yet so remote. What baffled him was a deep sadness in her beautiful topaz eyes.

He sat down on his bed and slipped off his sandals.

Then he turned and fell on his knees. He recalled vividly the time when Anna had taught him to pray to his guardian angel. He had promised her he'd do so every day, but he never did. The idea was ridiculous: Romans prayed to countless gods, not angels.

Yet, it was important now to recall the words she had taught him so long ago. Suddenly, they came to him from the depths of his memory. Anna was speaking them. He repeated them now, aloud: "I have a guardian angel assigned to me by divine decree. Through this angel's love, I commune with the heart of God."

He began to sob uncontrollably. It was as if a great burden had lifted from his heart. He wanted to laugh with joy, but he prevented himself from doing so. Growing sober, he warned himself, "There was some kind of magic in those words. I must tell no one of them. I must never repeat them."

CHAPTER 11

Anna held a parchment roll in her trembling hands, not daring to open it. Salamo had told her he would not write to her. She turned the roll over and saw the seal of Augustus on it. Oh God, was Salamo in prison? He was a radical and could have angered the Emperor with his plea. This letter might change her life.

Salina had arrived on the same ship as the message from Rome. She had not yet had a chance to tell Anna of her husband's death.

Anna began releasing the roll and saw that it was written in Greek. It couldn't have come from Salamo. She spread it wide and saw the bold signature, "Julian Flavius Maxim."

As she read it, her face showed increasing shock and grief. Through flowing tears, she said, "He's dead. Salamo's dead."

Salina came to her and pulled her down on a couch.

"Read it to me, Anna."

Anna took a deep breath and spoke softly, "This is to inform you, on behalf of Augustus Caesar, that your husband, Salamo of Galilee and the town of Sepphoris, was drowned en route to Caesarea. The ship on which he and his companions sailed exploded and burned in a storm when only a few days out of port. All aboard perished in the sea. I have no further details of the tragedy. I offer my deepest sympathy to you and the families of the other members of his party. Regretfully, Julian Flavius Maxim."

Anna reread his carefully written Greek words. It was for Salamo that she felt heartbreaking sympathy. He had never seen his infant daughter, Mary. "Oh, Holy God, why do you take one husband after another from me? Why do I live on and on?"

She was about to lay the letter down, when a small slip of paper fell into her lap. It, too, was written in Julian's careful hand. "I leave now on a personal mission to Delphi, Greece. The gods have not yet revealed to me my future. Do you know what lies ahead for me?" She crushed the paper in her hand.

"He could have written me these past five years. We were friends, and he saw me through some of my most difficult times."

Salina frowned. "I don't understand what you're saying, Anna. Julian was at death's door from malaria and then typhus for all those years. He has just now recovered. He told me in Rome that he wrote you monthly, with the departure of each ship, yet never had a reply from you. You are certain you never received any of his letters?'

Anna shook her head, stunned and puzzled by the information. "Someone wanted to direct the course of my life—that's obvious. She paused, deep in thought, then covered her face with her hands and sat motionless for several minutes.

Salina said gently, "Perhaps Julian's letters never left. Someone there could have taken them—as a prank, perhaps."

"They left Greece. They arrived in Palestine. This I firmly believe. Who are my enemies? Who would want to interfere with my life? One lost letter, I can understand. Two lost letters are always possible. But no more. I'm bewildered. I'm angry."

Anna rose and paced the floor. Salina hurried to the kitchen and made a pot of a relaxing tea. By the time she returned, Anna had full control of herself and sipped the honey-sweetened brew gratefully.

"You were in love with Julian, weren't you?" Salina asked.

Anna was taken aback by the question, but replied evenly, "We had a special kind of friendship. I grew to trust him. You remember how he came to my rescue when Ezra, the Essene, was killed before me."

Salina said, "I remember, Anna. After that incident, I, too, began to like Julian. He has changed tremendously. He's more gentle and caring. He has no woman in Rome, I know. Women find him difficult to approach. He is devoted to Augustus and seems content with his life. I would consider remarrying him now."

Anna sensed that she was probing. She didn't understand herself, so could not explain her ambivalent feelings. A wave of jealousy came over her at the thought of Julian marrying anyone. She fought it determinedly, saying, "Julian rescued Jesus from Herod's sword. I am permanently indebted to him."

Once again, custom demanded that Anna put on sackcloth. The rain and winter-cold days kept her indoors, so she devoted her time to her growing infant. Mary Salamo was a dark-haired charmer who inherited her father's stunning good looks. Anna had loved this ebullient younger husband in a far different way from her deep passion for Joachim or her satisfying relationship with the Essene, Cleophas. To her, love came in many colors and manifested itself on different levels. Each was good, and she regretted none of her marriages.

Now that Salamo was gone, she tried to analyze his intense need to dominate her. Could it be he felt inferior to his older brothers? They didn't understand his artistic interests, and he certainly couldn't talk about sheep and goats with enthusiasm or debate the merits of the leathers Cleophas used for fine shoes.

Then a devastating thought came to her as she rocked her baby to sleep: Salamo married her, not from love, but to prove to himself that he could win their former wife. That's why he took charge of her life as if she were a helpless woman.

The next question she asked herself was, "Why did I marry him, since I had had two good marriages?" The answer was undeniable: In the continued absence of Mary and Jesus, she wanted a child of her own more than anything else in the world. Salamo made that dream possible. She loved him for that, and she had no regrets, even if she didn't understand his secretive nature.

Yet, there was an emptiness always in her heart—a deep hunger, a void that came from no contact with Julian. Angry thoughts filled her mind. "This pagan is a thorn in my emotions. For nearly four decades, he has appeared and disappeared with regularity—always claiming his love for me. It's a game of pursuit he plays. He wants the thrill of the hunt. We are lifetime combatants—I try to turn him to a belief in one God; he stubbornly clings to thousands of gods. We are light years apart. Yet I long to see him again, to feel my heart leap when he turns that penetrating, long look at me. No, I hope he never returns here!"

The spring days came and fluctuated between chilly and roasting temperatures. The hot, dry, east wind brought haze over the landscape and turned the mountain grasses brown. Thunderstorms appeared out of nowhere, followed by cold rain. Then the *sharav* that had killed her second-born infant returned for another cycle of scorching heat and chilling rain. Finally, the summer month of Tamuz arrived one morning, and with it, Anna felt a heightened tempo to living. Something good was going to happen.

Leaving Judith to care for the growing Mary, Anna walked down the hill to the shattered town. There was no market place in Sepphoris now, but a dozen square, mud-brick houses had been hastily built amid the devastation. There were no more radicals left here. All had been killed or crucified by the Syrian army. For the time being, she must make the hour-and-a-half walk to Nazareth for necessities.

She missed Salina, who had returned to Rome. Her only other visitors had been Esmeria and her daughter, Elisabeth's, family. Seeing their remarkable John, who was only six months older than Jesus, brought intense pain to Anna. Where was her grandchild? She had seen him only in Bethlehem as an infant, yet thought of him daily and with great longing.

She retraced her steps to her home, trying to forget the horrors that had destroyed the once-lovely capital of Galilee. As she was about to enter the house, she noticed three people climbing the hill toward her. A bearded man held the hand of a young boy, and a barefoot woman in tattered clothes followed them. Her head-covering was so close around her face that Anna couldn't recognize anyone she knew. This was obviously a poor family come to beg for food.

Then she heard the woman cry, "Emi! Emi!" The

woman burst into tears of joy, running toward them. They all laughed and wept at the same time as Anna embraced Mary and Joseph. Then she turned to the waiting child. She was stunned by the beauty of this eight-year-old. His eyes were sapphire jewels, and his hair was a curly tumble of deep gold. Anna took him in her arms, unable to speak.

When she finally released him, he spoke first. "At last I meet you. I've talked with you many times in my dreams. You are such a good listener!"

"Every day, I tell you how much I love you, Jesus. Blessed God, I thank Thee for bringing you all back to me."

Anna hurried them into the house, asking one question after another. Joseph was quiet. He had noticeably aged. His face was as dark as a Bedouin's. His clothes were nearly in shreds, and his feet were raw and bleeding.

Judith immediately brought everyone a pan of water for washing hands and feet. Anna came with olive oil and towels.

She said, "After you have eaten, you will all bathe and sleep. There'll be clean clothes laid out for everyone. How far did you travel today?"

Joseph answered wearily, "Almost nine hours. All I want to do is go to sleep."

"Not before I show you my surprise," Anna said in a laughing voice. She left the room to return with the infant Mary Salamo. She explained to the surprised family, "I married Joachim's youngest brother, Salamo. This was his great gift to me before he was lost at sea."

Mary held out her arms to take the infant. "You named her also Mary?"

"Somehow the name helped keep you alive. She is my third Mary. Later I'll catch you up on my life."

Jesus came quickly to Anna. "May I hold her?' he asked. "I want to bless her with long life."

Everyone looked with surprise at each other. Anna spoke quickly, "Yes, hold her and bless her, Jesus." Then he did a strange thing. He made the sign of the cross over her. Anna wondered if he already knew what his destiny was.

As the travelers ate hungrily of the barley soup and freshly baked bread, Anna assured them that her Nazareth house was still vacant and waiting for them. Tomorrow, they would load the donkeys with household goods and food and move the family to Anna's former home.

"We are penniless, Anna." Joseph said. "I must try to find work right away."

"Don't worry," Anna replied. "I have a fine income and will provide for your family. You must take time to recover from your long journey. Everything I own is intended for your welfare. I know you have had years of misery, so I intend to make up for them."

Joseph was so overcome with emotion, he could not reply. Mary's eyes filled with tears. Jesus came to Anna and held one of her hands between both of his. Nothing else in the world could equal the joy she felt in being able to provide this family with their physical needs.

"You must all lie down and rest," she directed them, seeing Joseph's head bobbing and his eyes closing.

Jesus spoke quickly, "I'm not tired, now that I've come home. I want to stay with grandmama."

Neither parent admonished him, so he remained with Anna, inspecting everything in the house. Then he asked, "May I go into the yard and look at the animals in the pen? Also, I see there's a small house at the back. May I look in there, too?"

"Of course. Everything is new to you, so enjoy exploring."

Anna had closed the house where Salamo held his meetings with his revolutionary friends. She had touched nothing upon learning of her husband's death. It was too painful to be reminded of his many hours spent in this house. When Jesus did not return within a half hour, she went looking for him. The door stood open, so she watched him inspecting everything in the place. He examined the hand-hewn benches and table, the reed mats on the floor, the candelabrum of original design. He poked and probed in the rolls of bedding as if he were ferreting out a treasure. Then, unaware of Anna in the doorway, his eyes traveled about the room, looking high at the walls. He jumped onto a bench, got down and located a stick. Then he climbed back near a different place and probed with the stick near a mud brick at the ceiling-join. He tried to pull the brick out but couldn't. Then he leapt down and noticed Anna watching him.

"I need a ladder," he said. "Where can I get one?"

"Just outside, Jesus. What are you searching for?"

"I don't know. There's something hidden up there. I sensed it the moment I entered." He ran and brought in the small ladder.

"It must be here," he said poking about. Then he succeeded in removing a short mud brick. Behind it was a packet of parchment papers.

"Who could have put them there?" Anna asked, stunned by the find.

"Someone who didn't want you to see them." He unwrapped the package, exposing several letters.

"Can you read Greek, Grandmama?" He handed her the letters.

"Yes, my sister Sobe taught me Greek a long time ago."

Anna looked at the letters in astonishment. They were from Julian—tender, loving messages written with great difficulty during his long illness. There was only one per-

son who could have hidden them there—Salamo. It saddened her to learn he had trusted her so little. He had
really never grown up; yet the act of going to Rome to
speak with Augustus Caesar was a dramatic gesture to
prove his worth. During their short marriage, he had frequently lied to her—little lies that meant nothing, actually. Out of fear of losing her, he had intercepted her
letters and hidden them where they would never be
found. But he hadn't counted on a child with special
powers to ferret out deceit.

Jesus interrupted her thoughts. "What do the letters
say?"

"They speak only of love, my child. They are personal,
so I cannot read them to you. You met the man who
wrote them, although you won't remember it. He saved
your life when Herod's guards sought to kill you. He
risked his own in escaping with you from Bethlehem."

"He was a very brave Jew. Does he live in Galilee?"

"Brave, yes. But a Roman then in the employ of Herod
the Great."

Jesus looked at her with surprise. He thought a moment, then said, "One day I will go to Rome and meet
him, and thank him."

"If we are lucky, he may come to Galilee. But not for
some time, Jesus. Maybe not in my lifetime. You have
years of study and growth ahead of you in preparing for
your destined life work. Much can happen in that time."

"I'm happy to have found the letters for you, but I
won't mention them to anyone. Mother would scold me
for poking around in someone else's place. I'll put the
mud brick back so no one will ever know it had been a
hiding place."

"Perhaps someday, I'll let you read the letters after I've
taught you a little Greek. You'll be attending the synagogue every morning in Nazareth to learn Hebrew and

more of the holy Torah. I'll leave you now to your adventures."

Anna took the letters to her room and reread them several times. They were filled with love and concern for her, in spite of Julian's own misery. "If you were here, I know you could heal me quickly," he wrote. "Now that you have neither husband nor child, can you come to me? I will make all arrangements for you." What must he think of my not answering him?

All of Julian's letters were written, believing she would not marry anyone else. Salamo, immature in so many ways, had been fearful of her friendship for a pagan, so he stole the letters. Had he truly loved her, or was the marriage his way of proving to everyone he was his brothers' equal? Impulsive and self-centered, he had to dominate her to reassure himself constantly of his worth.

"Oh, Salamo. You gave me a beautiful baby. That was more than enough."

Anna heard Jesus come into the house, so she hurried to him.

"Don't you want a nap?" she asked, studying his tanned, quiet face. His deep-set, piercing eyes held a great power in them, but when he directed them to her, they became soft and childlike. She thought he was the most interesting, dynamic child she had ever seen. He answered her in a soft voice.

"No nap. I get my strength from the ethers. You know who I am, don't you?"

Anna nodded, her eyes brimming with tears.

He continued in a serious tone. "I'm curious. Did you love each of your three husbands?"

The question came as a shock to Anna, but she answered truthfully, "Yes, but each one in a different way. My love is a fountain that never stops flowing."

"I like that expression. Emi tells me that you can heal people. But I can do something else." He paraded before Anna.

"What's that?"

"I can look into the mists of the future."

"What do you see there?"

"Millions of people worshipping you because you heal the crippled—even bring the dead back to life." He came to Anna and put his arms around her waist, burying his face in the folds of her robe.

Anna laughed. "I've never had such flattery before!"

"I mean it. Long after you die, some who pray earnestly to you will be made well, and hundreds of houses of worship will be named after you."

"That's a giant forecast, Jesus!"

"Time will tell!" Jesus laughed and ran out the door and across the yard. Anna followed him and watched as he climbed a tall tree with the alacrity of a cat.

"I can see Jerusalem from here!" he called out.

Joining in the game, Anna cried, "How's the weather there?"

"Hot. And I smell the horrible reek of burning animal flesh and the nauseating smell of incense. Jerusalem will be my undoing. It's in Galilee I intend to perfect myself and do my preaching."

He climbed back down and came to Anna. She hugged him to her, saying, "You'll become an Essene, I can see that."

Mary, refreshed from her nap, came to the door and called to them. "Let's begin packing so we can move to Nazareth tomorrow."

Anna looked at her firstborn, incredibly radiant after her rest. She had put on one of Anna's loosely flowing muslin robes, and her auburn hair matched the color of the embroidered flowers in the garment.

"Mary, my darling, I have never seen anyone as beautiful as you." Anna turned and called to Jesus, "Are you coming in?"

He was examining the flowers on a bush and did not answer.

Mary explained, "He needs to be alone."

"There is a fragrance of roses about him," Anna said with a puzzled look.

"Yes, Mother. It has always been so—even when we lived like wild birds, never knowing where our next meal would come from, or when Herod's long arm would reach out and snatch us."

"At least you'll have him with you for a few more years." Anna saw a flash of pain cross her daughter's face.

"No, he has already slipped from me. He's now on his great mission. I cannot change what has been preordained. But I hope to bear other children in the years ahead."

"That will bring me great joy. But nothing can make me happier than I am now, having you home again."

* * *

Serene summers gave way to irritable winters, and the youngsters grew strong and happy in an atmosphere of devotion. Jesus eagerly waited becoming thirteen and celebrating his bar mitzvah.

He often visited his grandmother when schooling was done, but shocked her one day by saying, "I've been talking to the caravan drivers. One day I'll join a caravan traveling to the Orient. I want to learn about the lands where the three magi live. I must know how yellow, brown, and black people there think. Do they really differ from us Jews?"

"You mustn't leave Palestine yet. Think how much pain and worry you'd cause your parents and me."

"The religions of Tibet and Persia and China may have great merit. I must study them."

Anna sighed and pulled him onto a couch next to her. "How long will you be gone?"

"Perhaps five years. It's a vast realm to cover, and I'm a slow walker." He laughed joyously.

Anna could see he acted independently of his family. "Then you intend to be not just the Messiah of the Jews, but the savior of the whole world?"

Jesus nodded and took one of Anna's hands in his. "Great dreams, I know. I will leave soon after my bar mitzvah. You'll be the first to learn I'm gone. I can't bear parting with my family." His voice broke and he fought back tears. "If you find bread and cheese missing from your cupboard, tell my mother and Joseph."

Anna was silent for a few moments, then said, "See that jar on the kitchen shelf? There will be coins in a bag in it for your journey. You must take them else I'll be frantic with worry. Promise?"

Jesus nodded. "Thank you, dearest of grandmothers. You can master fears for me with love. Tell my blessed mother that her pain will vanish in the healing love of God. Say to her," he hesitated and bit his lip to keep it from trembling, "Say that she is the flame of my soul, and my eternal love for her will lessen her pain." He left her then, to run like a child about her yard, and soon departed for home.

Anna sat, as if paralyzed, for a long time. His words were etched on her heart, yet, as time passed, she heard him speak no more about joining a caravan. It had been a childish dream of adventure.

*   *   *

On the first Sabbath after Jesus' thirteenth birthday, the religious ceremony of bar mitzvah took place in the new synagogue in Nazareth. After Jesus read from the scroll of the Torah, proud Joseph stepped forward to recite the words of moral severance from the youth: "Blessed be He who releases me from the responsibility of this child." Jesus smiled warmly in response.

That afternoon, Mary held a gathering for him so that he could deliver his first discourse. He had prepared his speech well and began, "We Jews are biologically a mixed people, so remember that all men come from the same source and are shaped by God out of the material. Therefore, we must love all mankind."

He paused a few moments before continuing. "The Divine Presence rests on each of us. Whether one is a stranger or native born in Palestine, there is but one Law for all. Have we forgotten that we, too, were once strangers in the land of Egypt? We dare not discriminate against the Gentiles and Samaritans here."

Joseph was so elated by his performance, he told him, "Your mother and I will take you to Jerusalem for the Passover festivities. We'll see the beauties of the holy temple again."

Jesus answered, "They are of no interest to me. I want to talk with the priests and the rabbis."

"I keep forgetting your childhood is past." Joseph turned to Mary and shrugged his shoulders.

She said, "He is now responsible for his own actions. We must let him be free."

Joseph nodded, saying, "It's not easy for me to see such independence."

Ten days passed before the holy family returned to Anna. They appeared jubilant about an experience within the temple grounds.

Proud Joseph related, "Jesus disappeared from us while we were looking at lovely Persian ornaments in a booth, and for three days we had no idea where he was.

We started for home, thinking he was somewhere in the group of pilgrims headed north, but finally were forced to return to the city to look for him."

Mary continued in an excited voice, "We found him having an animated discussion with two rabbis. One said to us, 'This young man is truly remarkable. He speaks the wisdom of the ages.' The other rabbi said, 'We could learn much from your son.'"

Jesus stood, slightly embarrassed by their enthusiasm, but when Anna turned to him with a quizzical look, he remarked, "I proved something to myself in talking with those learned men. I'm convinced now that when I'm eighteen, I can begin my life's work."

Mary spoke in a serious tone, "Don't rush it, dear heart. Your life will be one of great joy and tragic sorrow. Enjoy these maturing years in Galilee."

"There's so little time, Emi," he replied sadly and left them to stroll in the yard alone.

Anna remarked, "Jesus and you are like one entity. He will never say 'good-bye' to you, Mary. He will leave suddenly and under God's guidance. We can only pray that his years of wanderings will be few."

Chapter 12

Shortly after Augustus Caesar learned that his envoy, Valerian, had been killed in the explosion of the Palestine-bound ship, more devastating news reached him.

He had ordered Varus, Governor of Syria and servant of Rome, to send a large army to subdue the rioting in the colonies. Varus decided his son should take troops into western Galilee to drive out the revolutionaries. They were undisciplined hirelings who plundered the royal palace in Sepphoris, slaughtered the men, and sold the women and children into slavery. Finally, they set fire to the town before continuing on their rampage of other villages in the province.

An enraged Augustus called Julian to his study. He said, "The Empire can't endure when we count on unreliable hirelings like Varus' Nabateans to do our work. Have I been wrong in keeping my legionaries on this side of the Mediterranean?"

Julian sat down across from his Emperor, debating if he should speak his mind.

"Come, come!" Augustus said irritably. "You've spent most of your adult life in Palestine, so should be able to advise me."

"Sire, I put the blame on that greedy Herodian dynasty. Herod Antipas of Galilee caused this revolt by increasing once again the burdensome taxes. Remember, the temple in Jerusalem also demands more and more from its followers, so the peasants are being crushed from both Rome and the Judean priesthood."

Augustus was silent for a few moments, then said with a laugh, "You've lived too long among them. You are only half Roman now and the other half—dare I say it? Jew."

"I speak the truth as I see it." Julian hesitated, then said, "I came to say 'good-bye'. I'm leaving at once for the Apollo oracle at Delphi."

"You have problems? Isn't your retirement allowance enough for your needs? Shall I increase it?"

"No, no. I must find out if I should settle down in Rome for the rest of my life or return to devastated Galilee."

Augustus stood up and placed his arm around Julian's shoulders. "So a foreign woman draws you there. From the reports I've received, you may regret such folly."

"I hope the oracle will advise me if she still lives."

"You can always come back to Rome. In either case, I will grant you a large plot of ground on which to spend your life. I have a long memory. You were the only friend of my frail early youth. I remember how we played mental games when the others our age wrestled or shot at the mark with bows and slings. Now I have the power to grant you anything you wish—almost anything."

"Dear Octavianus," Julian replied with a laugh as he used Augustus' youthful name, "I'd like to borrow a horse to take me to the port."

"Granted. And a servant to return the animal to my stable, of course."

They walked about the garden, each reluctant to separate. Then a messenger hurried across the grass to the emperor, with a papyrus roll. Looking at the seal, Augustus said, "It's from Herod Antipas." He opened the roll and after hurriedly scanning its beginning, he read aloud, "I barely escaped with my life during the destruction of Sepphoris by Varus' mad hirelings. My new capital will be built on the western shore of the Sea of Galilee. I will name it Tiberias, and the lake's name will be changed immediately to "The Sea of Tiberias." I have plans to put a gold roof on the palace and build a stadium that can seat ten thousand.

"As for Sepphoris, I intend to rebuild it later, but will give it a new name in your honor—Autocratoris (Emperor).

Julian shook his head with amazement. "Like his father, Herod Antipas has grandiose plans for spending the blood money he has extracted from the people. Since he's pro-Roman, will he run Galilee the way you'd like?"

Augustus shook his head. "I don't think so. I've learned he's working with a new aristocratic sect to further his ambitions. The leaders are Pharisees who call themselves 'The Herodians.' It's a curious development, don't you think?"

"It's dangerous, but you should be able to control him. Now I must say farewell."

"May the gods shower you with every favor until I see you again, Julian." The two men embraced and Julian headed for the royal stables.

*   *   *

It took a month for Julian's ship to cross the Ionian Sea to the coast of central Greece. After a day's ride inland on a rented horse, he reached the sacred precinct of Apollo. It was located on a series of artificial terraces on the lower slopes of Mount Parnassus. Leaving his animal at a nearby stable, he walked slowly along the winding Sacred Way that led to the great temple.

It was an awesome rectangular structure, built in Ionic style. Great caryatids on high pedestals took the place of columns to support the identical porches on either end. Seeing a large crowd waiting to enter, Julian took time to admire the votive monuments and statues bordering the path. Here, too, were the treasuries—those houses built by famous people or cities. In them were stored votive offerings and priceless articles.

A priest, seeing Julian, came toward him asking, "You wish to speak to the oracle?"

"If Apollo will permit it," he answered humbly.

"It is late in the day, but I will see if the high priestess will consider your plea. Follow me."

As the pair reached a side door, the priest stopped. "First you must remove your *calceus*." He pointed to Julian's four-banded sandals.

Julian waited nervously. He had put on his best wool toga for the occasion and pinned on it the golden emblem of an eagle encircled with a laurel wreath, testifying that he was an official from Augustus Caesar. Yet the thought of talking with a god, and above all, with the multifaceted Apollo, was unnerving.

In a few minutes, the priest returned, indicated Julian was to enter, and led him to a spacious room. He closed the door, leaving Julian uncertain what he should do. In the dead silence of the room, he was nearly overcome by a heady incense that came from elegant black and red vases set along the walls.

In the center, rose a great pedestal decorated with a running frieze that depicted giants and Heracles in mortal combat. This, Julian knew, was the magic tripod on which the high priestess would sit as she communicated with Apollo. Julian continued to study his surroundings. Placed around the room were several bronze statues of warriors and a few wooden female statues with marble heads, feet, and hands. A long, elaborately carved bench followed the back wall, but Julian was reluctant to sit down without an invitation. He stood awkwardly, waiting for something to happen.

Then the air became electric, yet he could see no one. A slight rustle of garments called his attention to a side door. It was the priestess entering. She glided past him, a dramatic woman with dark hair flowing over her shoulders. When she inclined her head slightly to acknowledge his presence, he looked into penetrating, deep blue eyes that caused gooseflesh to rise on his skin. She mounted the steps of the tripod and sat down in a gold-cushioned chair on the top.

Julian stepped forward, then prostrated himself before her.

She spoke in a warm but authoritative voice. "Welcome to the temple of Apollo, God of Prophecy. I see you are Roman. What can the God of Light do for you?"

Julian's voice cracked with nervousness, but he managed to say, "Gracious priestess, I must learn what the future holds for me. Where shall I spend my remaining years?"

The priestess turned her face up as if listening to the words of Apollo above her. After a suspenseful wait, she turned to Julian, saying, "Your destiny lies in the land of the Hebrews."

He opened his mouth to ask the most important question: Was Anna still alive? Unable to endure a negative reply, he kept silent,. Then the priestess asked a curious question: "Have you no children?"

"No."

"Never become so old that you can't hear the voices of youth. It is from the mouth of a young one that wisdom will come to you."

Julian's spirits dropped. He had no association with children. The oracle was being devious. He waited for several minutes, not daring to speak.

Finally the priestess said in a soft voice, "Apollo is now silent, but look for a sacred oak tree outside of the south wall. Sit under the tree for a time. If the leaves rustle, your future will be a happy one and Apollo will bless you." She descended the steps and floated by him.

Julian made his way out, bitterly disappointed. Then he remembered the oak tree. He located it and sat beneath it with little confidence of results. The leaves dangled motionless in the still air. He stretched himself out over its bulging roots, yet nothing happened. He shoved aside his thoughts of the leaves and thought of Anna. Had she been killed or forced into slavery like the other women in Sepphoris? He couldn't bear living if she had died in ignominy. He had no family left in Rome. He had spent so many years in Palestine that it was home to him. There was great strength in the people of that area. Rome was beginning to weaken and like a tottering old man, walked now with uncertain steps.

In despair, Julian rose to leave. He stopped as a brisk gust of wind moved across him. Then the leaves danced on the branches, and their rustling was like distant music of the spheres. He spoke aloud to the tree, "Thank you, Apollo, for blessing me! I will leave for Palestine at once."

CHAPTER 13

After a month's sea journey, Julian disembarked at Caesarea, a port he had helped Herod the Great build. It was humming with activity. Wheat, oil, salt pork, and dried fruit were piled on the docks, waiting for export.

He saw a small ship about to depart and called to its owner, "What's your cargo?"

"Balm from Jericho, going to Rome."

Julian knew it was being sold for the price of gold, and bloody disputes arose over the ownership of just one bush. The scent trade produced the wealthiest merchants anywhere.

Caesarea, now the capital of Palestine, had been built on solid foundations that ran over two hundred feet into the sea. Gigantic stone blocks protected it, and extensive warehouses stretched along the port.

While waiting for a merchant to find him a fine horse, Julian strolled about the pagan city. The streets were profusely decorated with statues, since the city was three-quarters Greek. He passed many small Jewish workshops and exchanged his Greek drachmas and Roman denarii for Israelite shekels.

When he returned for his horse, he was pleased to find it was a stunning Arabian stallion. "Get out of town," the owner advised. "The Jews and Greeks have started to riot. It's not easy for the Jews to be subjects of a foreign power in their own homeland. For your own safety, join the caravan down the street. They're going to Nazareth to join the Silk Road to the Far East."

Julian took his advice and found himself with an amazing company. There were Babylonian merchants, elegant in satin brocade with gold rings in their noses; black men from the Sahara; escaped slaves; peddlers; copper-skinned Abyssinians; shepherds; mercenaries looking for hire; Arabian horse traders; and messengers carrying letters for Herod Agrippa, King of Judea. No one appeared to notice the well-dressed Roman in such a remarkable group of travelers.

One thing they had in common—each carried a staff for protection and a dried gourd with a stone in it to get water from wells or streams.

Called the "Royal Road," it was well-constructed near the city. There, it was sixteen feet wide, made of paving slabs, and providing pull-out places so carts could pass each other. But, to Julian's dismay, slabs soon gave way to tamped earth. A succession of deep wadis caused many carts to overturn, temporarily blocking all progress.

When the sun dropped low, Julian rode ahead of the caravan to get a room in one of the bustling inns along the heavily traveled route. Most of the men camped in the open air, since the weather was pleasant.

It took two and a half days for them to reach Nazareth, and, on the final morning, Julian put on a fine linen tunic, shaved, and even scented his hair. This could be the most important day of his life.

He rode toward Sepphoris with growing apprehension, dreading to see the once-lovely capital in total devastation. To shorten his agony, he urged his stallion faster and faster. Was Anna's house still there? Was she still alive?

His spirits soared as he turned a bend in the road and caught sight of her home. He galloped into the yard, jumped from his mount, and ran to the front door. He rapped loudly, but a couple of minutes elapsed before it opened. Then he faced a stunning young boy who appeared to be about thirteen years old. Penetrating blue eyes looked quizzically at him. The sensitive face was framed by long-curled, auburn side-locks.

Julian asked, "Does Anna, widow of Salamo, live here?"

"She has gone to a neighbor but should return shortly." The voice was pleasing and melodious.

"I'm a friend of years past. My name is Julian. I've come from Greece just to see her."

"Please come in and wait for her." The boy motioned to a chair, saying, "That's the most comfortable one."

"And who are you?" Julian asked as he sat down.

"Jesus, son of Mary and Joseph, grandson of Anna."

"I'm most happy to see you again, Jesus. I saw you once as a baby." Julian laughed and made no explanation of his words.

"You have undoubtedly traveled far. Would you like a drink of water?"

"Yes, thank you, Jesus."

When Jesus returned with a filled goblet, he remarked, "You say you just came from Greece. They are pagans, and you must be, too."

"You Jews call us that. One god or thousands of gods—does it really matter?"

Jesus moved a stool close to Julian and sat down. "Since you must have come from Caesarea, did you see a merchant caravan on the way here?"

"Yes, it has arrived and will leave tomorrow morning for Baghdad and Bactra and other places in the East."

"I must join it. I'll have to go home as soon as my grandmother arrives. You see, I stayed to take care of her infant. Her servant, Judith, is in Jerusalem."

"What makes you want to go to these unknown places? You are so young."

Jesus looked far away. "I must learn the religion, the customs, and the languages of India, Nepal, and Tibet. The East is a repository of ancient wisdom. Before I begin my life's mission, I must learn how to heal, how to perform exorcisms, and how to purify men's hearts so they will stop killing each other. I want to travel the great Silk Road and speak to the people along its route. I want everyone to know of God's glory."

"Why not stay in Palestine?"

"No, no." Jesus grew thoughtful. "He who would be master, must first be servant. I have so much to learn. You see, I did not come into being only for the Jews."

"You mean you came for us Romans, too?" Julian was amused.

"Yes, and one day far into the future, it will be you Romans who will revere my teachings most."

"You speak in riddles, Jesus. Don't you hate me?"

"How can I do that? You are in me, and I am in you."

Julian shook his head, then asked, "What can the men of the East teach you that Rome and Palestine can't?"

Jesus stood up and began walking back and forth before him. "I must learn self-mastery and how to control the elemental forces. I must learn the art of bilocation and alchemy. I must be able to change water into wine and multiply one loaf of bread into hundreds." He paused, but Julian could think of nothing to say. Then he added, with a serious frown, "The hardest thing to learn will be to change uncertain souls like yours, to release the imprisoned splendor that exists in everyone."

Julian was stunned, but he managed, "How does one do that?"

"Through love, only through love. I intend to redeem many sons of men one day. There must be holy men in the East who will teach me some of life's mysteries. Perhaps by studying their ancient philosophies, my understanding of all races will grow."

This youngster was amazing! Julian had the courage to ask, "Could you learn to love a Roman like me?"

"Of course. If you will believe in my one God, I will love you forever, here and hereafter, with all my heart."

"Have the rabbis in the synagogue taught you all this?"

"Not all. Some lessons come to me from angelic emissaries. Do you know anything about angels?"

"A little. Your grandmother taught me to pray to my guardian angel long ago. I admit I have rarely done so." Julian looked down at the floor in despair.

Jesus asked, "Why do you appear so depressed?"

"I wonder if Anna still cares for me." His voice broke.

"Is that so important to you?"

"My happiness depends on it."

"You love her?"

"I adore her."

"She carries a sadness about her that can't be explained just by the death of her husband. Perhaps you are responsible."

"What can I do to make her happy?" His pleading eyes moved Jesus to respond at once.

"Accept our one God. Cast aside the thousands of deities who have no real power over your life. If you will believe in our Lord, he will make your way perfect and give you eternal life."

"Could I then be always with Anna?"

Jesus nodded, then rose and came to Julian. "Take my hands in yours. Feel the exchange of heat between them. Love is like that. We give, and it comes back immediately. The more love one gives others, the more one has for himself. Look at me. Could you love me?"

Julian was surprised by the question, but answered readily, "Yes, that would be easy."

"Could you love one with leprosy, or a Herod obsessed with power and hatred?"

"No. That would be impossible."

"Until you can do that, you have only begun to know the meaning of love. Yet, it is possible to learn to do that. Look with love on all fellow beings. It won't hurt you a bit. And then you will, one day, walk like the Roman gods you now worship."

Julian found himself agreeing with the wisdom of this young man. In his features he saw much of Anna, and he found himself feeling love toward him—a stranger. Or was he a stranger? This was the infant he had buried beneath his cloak and carried past the sentinels sent by Herod to kill him in Bethlehem. Now the boy, come of age, wanted to be *his* savior. It was bewildering.

Before he could respond to Jesus' last remarks, Anna arrived. She entered the room with that swinging walk that delighted him. She stopped abruptly when she saw him. Her lips trembled as she spoke, "Julian? Is it really you?"

He held out his arms to her, and she rushed into them, sobbing.

Jesus said loudly, "I must leave now, Grandmama."

Julian released her, and she kissed Jesus several times. Then the youth turned to Julian, and the two exchanged a long look. Julian smiled broadly and held out both hands to him. "You've won, young man. I accept the God of Israel."

"Did you hear that, grandmama? He is my first convert!"

Jesus laughed with joy, ran to the kitchen, and gathered up the bag of coins and food always ready for him. Then he left by the kitchen door, fighting back a flood of tears.

It was several minutes before Julian released his hold on Anna. Then he kissed her softly and tenderly, over and over again.

"You are aware, Anna, that your grandson went to join a caravan in Nazareth?"

She nodded and a wave of pain crossed her face. "Neither his mother nor I have been able to talk him out of this venture. He says God has willed it. It is to God he listens for advice." Then she bowed her head in prayer. "May the Lord God protect him and bring him peace in all the lonely places he must walk." She pulled Julian to a couch beside her. "I have said good-bye to him a hundred times, thinking each was the last."

"The merchant caravan in Nazareth today is a fine one. You can rely on the driver taking good care of Jesus."

Anna held tightly to his hands. "You are changed, Julian. You look wonderful. What has happened?"

"I accepted the one God of my beloved Anna," he whispered with lips close to hers.

"Oh, Julian, dear Julian, my life is now fulfilled."